THE
SHIELD
OF
MARATHON

A HEROIC TALE SET AT THE BEGINNING OF
THE PELOPONNESIAN WAR

RORY HEADREN

Typeset in Sabon

Typesetting and publishing by UK Book Publishing
www.ukbookpublishing.com

Cover design: Kobir Miah
kobir-miah@live.co.uk

ISBN: 978-1-912183-12-8

THE
SHIELD
OF
MARATHON

PROLOGUE

THERE WAS A SHORTAGE of oar blades in the busy shipyards of Athens, also terebinth pitch, flax and hemp; a major setback for a powerful city-state which in recent years had become the greatest sea power in the known world. In normal times, these deficits would have been quickly rectified, but war was looming on the borders of Attica, and old alliances were shifting and changing.

Because of the warlike intentions of the Spartans, one-hundred and fifty miles to the west, and a greater need for command of the seas in order to keep control of their disgruntled far-flung allies in the Delian League, Pericles, the elected leader of Athens, had ordered an immediate upgrading of their fleet, and at the numerous shipsheds down at Zea and the other harbours on the Piraeus peninsula, skilled shipwrights strived to oblige. Awaiting delivery of timbers and pitch from Macedonia, however, many ships lay idle. The price of the cargo had risen, terms and conditions having been applied by Perdiccas, King of Macedonia - always a tricky negotiator.

In retaliation against Athens, which was supporting his brother Philip's challenge for the crown, the king was stirring up trouble between Athens and her allies, one of which was Potidaea, a vital port on the Chalcidice peninsula. Although a province of Corinth, Potidaea belonged to the Delian League and paid tribute to Athens, but a battle of wills ensued when this colony was persuaded to withdraw her tribute - drawing in the superpowers of Athens, Corinth and Sparta.

CAUGHT UP IN THIS crisis was the small city-state of Plataea.

THE SHIELD

AS TIMELESS AS HOMER'S tale of ill-fated Troy, Plataea's inspirational story of loyalty and valour would be told and retold throughout the ages as an account of the ultimate achievement for all Hellenes - honour and glory.

To walk the streets of this small city was to be in the company of ghosts whose deathly shades returned to the place where they'd fared in life. These were the dead of Marathon and of Artemisium, who fought Darius, King of Persia - and of the final Great Battle eleven years later against his son, Xerxes, King of Kings, fought on the plain of Plataea within sight of their city-fortress.

At Marathon, only tiny Plataea answered the call to all Hellenes for reinforcements, sending her entire army to fight side by side with Athens and her allies, thus for all time sharing the glory of that miraculous day when their greatly outnumbered forces defeated a mighty Persian army. At Plataea, in the temple built in memory of the city's stand against the 'barbarians', all those who'd made their lasting sacrifice at Marathon were forever remembered in a roll of honour, carved into a plinth of finest Pentelic marble, upon which stood the glorious statue of the immortal Athena - created by the master sculptor and architect, Phidias of Athens.

Foremost on this list of martyrs was the name of Agristones, saviour of the Athenian general Miltiades; hero of Marathon. Using his shield to protect Miltiades from Persian swords beating down on him, Agristones' body was cut to pieces, but Miltiades lived to win the battle, save Athens and the valued freedoms of Hellas.

This same hoplon of battle-scarred bronze, the remnants of which still survived beneath its heavy adornment of gold plates and precious stones, was housed in the Temple of Athena; an idolised and sacred relic, venerated not only by Plataeans, but by all Hellenes.

PART ONE
THE CITY

ONE

THE SUN HAD NOT yet risen when Theomenes, second son of Eubalos, Plataea's Chief Magistrate, silently moved through the corridors of his father's villa near Hysiae. His father would still be sleeping, and when he passed the half-opened doorway to his brother's quarters, he could hear him snoring loudly. Having just completed his two years of military training, Alexeis was recovering from the unrestrained celebrations shared with fellow comrades the day before. Alexeis the warrior, Theomenes thought bitterly. Just turned twenty and already offered a junior command in the Plataean garrison. He was in a sour mood. His father had given him an errand he thought any slave could accomplish. The door to his father's study opened suddenly, and in the light of the oil lamps he saw Orchas, his father's ancient estate manager, struggling out with the farm accounts. As expected, the old man totally ignored him as he shuffled by with his bundles of papyrus rolls. As far back as Theomenes could remember, his father's personal slave had shown little respect for him; mocking him when he thought he could get away with it. Even the servants think I am incapable, thought the boy, angrily.

On reaching the stables he ordered Mydon to bridle up Cyclops, and to get himself another mule ready, while he climbed up to the roof rafters to choose two bronze daggers from the small arsenal he kept hidden there. Mydon shuddered, remembering Theomenes' threat that he would be sold to work in the brutal silver mines at Lavrion, if either the Magistrate or Alexeis ever got knowledge of the secret cache.

Mydon couldn't remember any other life than the one he shared with his young master. They'd grown up together. He believed he was sixteen, the same age as Theomenes, and he shared every aspect of his life, which included the beatings they both received whenever the headstrong youth got himself into trouble.

'Put sheepskins on the mules, Mydon!' Theomenes shouted down. 'We don't want sore arses!'

They pushed their weapons into their boots, put on woollen cloaks, and with a wide-brimmed petasos apiece, led their animals out into the half-light of the early spring morning.

A pale sun was just kissing the ridge of Mount Cithaeron as they rode towards the city. Already there was traffic on the road. Heavier than usual because of the forthcoming events. They allowed the mules to travel at their own pace, the malevolent remaining eye of Cyclops shining like the pale blue light of Sirius. The big white mule was not an obliging animal and some thought he had an evil disposition, but there was a bond between Theomenes and his mule. Both behaved as though the world had shortchanged them. They were a rebellious pair.

When they reached the crossroads at Hysiae, they halted at the garlanded marble shrine to the golden haired Demeter, giver of food to humankind, and allowed their mules to drink in the nearby river. Here, a road went north through Boeotia to the city of Thebes and south through the pass of The Three Heads, climbing steeply over the mountain into Attica and its capital, Athens. Everywhere humanity travels, news is brought from afar. Here, Theomenes hoped to learn the latest from the far flung borders of his quarrelsome, scattered nation. They mingled with the pilgrims and fellow travellers, and after leaving a donation in a large copper vessel already filled with similar coins, accepted the offered cups of refreshing water from the attendants at the sacred well, all the while listening for anything of interest.

Tensions were still fraught between the superpowers, Athens and Sparta, and trust seemed in short supply. News from the north spoke of the continuing expensive siege at Potidaea, causing unlooked for shortages in Athens. Potidaea, even though a colony of Corinth, paid tribute to Athens and her port was vital for the import of grain and timber, but factions averse to Athens were encouraging the Potidaeans to revolt. Gossip abounded that people in the capital were becoming increasingly unhappy with the decisions of their once revered leader, Pericles. The persistence in building long defensive walls connecting the port of Piraeus with the city of Athens was thought to show a lack of trust, according to the Spartans, who built no defensive walls in their own land, relying on the strength of their warriors to protect them, and as they watched the rival power of Athens increase, so did their fears increase for their own future. Nothing new, Theomenes thought, until he heard Thebes mentioned and then his ears strained to listen. A party of assorted traders on their way south, travelling together for company and safety, spoke of seeing Theban soldiers close to the Asopus, and of hearing rumours of more than usual raids on outlying farms in Plataean territory.

'Theban scum!' muttered Theomenes to Mydon. 'If they're stirring up trouble, they'll wish they hadn't. They'd be well advised to stay on their own side of the river.'

He went to join in the conversation and probed the travellers for more information, but details seemed vague. Such talk was rife these days but put down to mere scare tactics on the part of the Thebans. 'They're not fools,' said one man. 'They won't venture south of the Asopus and risk punishment from Athens!'

They carried on westwards towards their destination, and on reaching the bridge leading to the Gargaphian Gate, the main entrance into Plataea, got caught up in the slow-moving column of tradespeople and farmers bringing donkeys and ox-drawn carts laden with produce for the approaching festival. On top of one of the twin towers, Theomenes recognised the stern features of Diokles, commander of the garrison. Standing next to him was Stephanos, his tall second-in-command, and rumoured to be Diokles' future son-in-law. Before long, it will be Alexeis looking down on me, he thought sourly. Theomenes tried pushing Cyclops through the crowd that was now pressing about the bridge. 'This is madness, master Theo!' shouted Mydon. 'We should have used the eastern gate!' Ahead of him he heard loud voices calling for people to make way, as out through the gate rode a group of horsemen, equipped for hunting. Theomenes pulled roughly on the bridle but got little response and looked around anxiously for a place of safety. He was too late. The riders were approaching him at speed as the sharp, hissing crack of leather whips parted the crowd. He was given no chance to avoid their coming and in a heartbeat they were upon him.

Their leader was a bare-headed, golden-haired Adonis, on a powerful white stallion which he handled with great skill. Over his broad shoulders he wore a vermillion cloak embellished with the silver threaded emblem of their city, The Marathon Shield, and white leather elaborately spurred boots directed his snorting steed, 'Aithon'. His god-like visage was immediately recognised and eager cries of, 'Phalinus! Phalinus!' rose up from the throng. Resembling a mythical hero from Homer's poems, he bore down on Theomenes, giving no indication of having seen the youth.

3

At his back followed five impatient riders mounted on equally highly bred steeds, together with their hunting hounds, barking excitedly. On the leatherbound wrist of one of the riders, Plataea's general, Eupompides, flapped a magnificent hawk. They all carried lightweight bows and javelins for the hunt, and they bore down on Theomenes as though he were the quarry.

In panic, knots of people blocking the bridge scrambled to avoid the slashing whips and flying hooves. Theomenes let out a curse as Cyclops, in terror, bucked and kicked, nearly throwing him to the ground, as the horsemen on the mule's blind side, came sweeping by. A graphic vision flashed through his mind of his mangled body trampled to a pulp, then he felt a whip strike stingingly into his flesh, drawing blood from his cheek. He cried out in pain and rage. Recovering fast he dragged on the reins, and kicked Cyclops through the gap left in the wake of the last departing hunters. His eyes glinted in triumph when he saw the company had slowed due to the packed crowd ahead, and with perilous momentum he careered into the imperious noble who had cut him so maliciously. Theomenes recklessly made a grab for the man's leg and in return received a kick from a vicious spur, giving him another painful slashing across his thigh. A menacing hush descended on the crowd nearest the action as if sensing some dreadful event was about to unfold.

Theomenes burned with anger, and his fingers felt for the blade concealed in his boot. Then he saw the rider in the vermillion cloak, unhurriedly move his powerful animal towards him, and he hesitated immediately. The man's penetrating green eyes regarded the youth with calm curiosity. General Phalinus, Plataea's chosen son; descendant of Agristones, the hero of Marathon, and newly appointed Guardian of the Marathon Shield, since the recent death of his noble father, Andreas. 'Who is this boy?' he asked, looking around at his comrades for an answer.

'He is Theomenes, lord,' the nobleman Naucleides responded, grasping roughly at Theomenes' tunic. 'Second son of Eubalos of Hysiae. His brother Alexeis will be joining the garrison soon - but this boy is a scorpion!' he snarled. The contempt in his tone was not lost on Theomenes and he glared back at him, unflinchingly.

The slightest of smiles moved the corners of the Guardian's mouth as he regarded Theomenes with renewed interest. 'I am well acquainted with your father, and your brother,' he said calmly. 'Is my associate correct? Are you a scorpion?'

'Lord, I sting when I'm stung!' Theomenes replied, with as much courage as he could muster. 'I was struck without just cause.'

Nauclides moved closer and looked down on Theomenes with an ill-concealed desire to do him harm. The highly strung horse under Eupompides, with its rolling eyes and grinding teeth, was making the one-eyed mule nervous and he was near to bolting.

'Come, boy,' said Phalinus, suddenly impatient. 'For your respected father's sake, give me your hand in friendship and we'll say no more about it.'

Theomenes managed to control Cyclops enough to regain composure and didn't move; his brow, darkly knit in stubbornness. 'When I have an apology I will gladly do so,' he said obstinately.

Exclamations of anger arose from the nobles and Phalinus silenced them with a raised hand.

'The boy presses you too far, lord!' hissed Nauclides, as he lifted his whip to strike again. 'He needs a lesson in good manners and a good thrashing!'

'We'll leave that for Eubalos to decide,' said Phalinus, looking sympathetically at the boy's torn cheek. 'Apologies cost nothing. Here, Theomenes. You have mine. Take my hand and we'll end the matter,' he offered again.

Theomenes felt the eyes of the watching, expectant crowd willing him to do so. He wiped his palm on his tunic and reached to grasp the hand of Phalinus. His hypnotic, intelligent eyes looked directly at Theomenes, radiating a sense of mutual understanding, and with the morning sun illuminating the hair of Plataea's favourite son like a golden cloud, for a moment Theomenes was transfixed and he completely forgot about the pain of his wounds.

The huntsmen rode off at speed, kicking up dust, the falcon flying high above them. When Mydon was finally brave enough to approach, he found his master staring thoughtfully after them until they were out of sight.

TWO

AS THE DUST SETTLED, and the chatter about what had unfolded, calmed down, Theomenes and Mydon refocused on getting into the upper city. 'Why are we going into the city, master Theo?' asked Mydon, a little nervously. 'Your father instructed us to go to the estate of Anatolios. It's another four miles to Leuctra.'

'I have someone to see, Mydon. My father does not need to know of this diversion,' replied Theomenes, testily. Mydon was used to getting his master out of trouble but glancing at Theomenes' bleeding gashes, he thought, how do we get out of a beating this time? Mydon was sent off with the mules and an obol to wait at a near-by tavern.

'Make sure your wine is well watered, Mydon. I need you sober,' remarked Theomenes. 'And give Cyclops a handful of grain. He behaved well today.'

Amara was seated near an upstairs window, in a position where she could watch the street but, for the sake of propriety, not be seen from below. Her concerned thoughts were for her husband, Imbros. She worried that she had kept him in this city for too long, all because of her love for Plataea. She suspected that his own city of Athens was never far from his mind, and she was certain he missed the stimulus only the famed capital could provide. Also, filling her thoughts was the fact that she had not, as yet, borne him a child, but that misery she would endure, privately. When she saw Theomenes hurrying towards the house, she called for Ianthe, her housemaid, to open the door to him immediately, and went downstairs to greet the friend she had known since childhood. 'I came immediately I received your message,' gushed Theomenes, on entering. 'Is anything wrong?'

Amara held up her slim hands in alarm. 'What trouble have you been in this time, Theo?' she gasped. 'You're covered in blood! A bowl of water, quickly, Ianthe,' she ordered, pressingly, 'and bring some honey for his wounds.' Turning concernedly to her friend, she added sweetly, 'Imbros has spare tunics, Theo. You can borrow one of his.'

As he was giving her a quick recount of what had happened at the gate, Amara gently touched a tear in his tunic and Theomenes took a quick intake of breath. Being this close was so unexpected, and the heady aroma of rose oil from her elaborately braided hair affected him so much, he had the urge to kiss her. Her linen dress of the palest apple-green, was as fine as silk, accentuating her beautiful figure perfectly, and the bright gold of her pretty ear-rings could not compare with the dancing flecks he saw in her concerned, dark eyes. He felt his skin burning up and it was not from his wounds. He hoped that his admiration for her did not show! He was relieved when the maid called for him to choose a fresh tunic, but his blushing returned immediately on seeing Amara's perfumed garments hanging in the closet she shared with her husband.

Amara was waiting for him in a very spacious room, according to Plataean standards. Several leather upholstered couches embellished with gold tassels were set against the walls of a richly decorated sitting-room. Egyptian matting, recently scattered with crushed scented flowers, covered the floor and exquisite statues in marble and bronze, the work of Imbros, stood grandly between each of the couches. Amara poured out a cup of wine and handed it to Theomenes.

Looking at him seriously, she said, 'I need to talk to you about my husband.' Lulled by her sweet voice, he vaguely heard her say, 'patronage'.

'Patronage, for Imbros?' he asked, puzzled.

'I want Imbros to be happy with his decision to live in Plataea,' she told him anxiously. 'I think he only stays here because of me.'

'But your husband has many patrons - Admetus...?' suggested Theomenes.

'Admetus does appreciate Imbros's work as do other prominent Plataeans,' replied Amara, 'but you know my husband. To be accepted here he underrates his work. I know he is a good sculptor, perhaps even a unique one, but he needs someone of influence to promote him. In Athens he could be a great man. Plataea doesn't know how fortunate it is to have such a fine artist.'

'I think you are being overanxious,' said Theomenes, glancing around a room which would not look out of place at his father's villa, 'but how do you think I can help?' he asked, amazed.

'Speak with your father, Theo,' she pleaded. 'He has influence.'

'My father!' laughed Theomenes, harshly. 'You would do better to catch the ear of my brother. My father listens to little of what I have to say. As far as he is concerned, I am a lost cause.'

Amara looked at him kindly, and said, 'I know you think that Theo, but believe me, your father loves you more than you realise.'

She reached forward, taking Theomenes' hand in hers and looking at him with her gentle eyes, asked, 'For me, will you ask him to talk to his brother, your uncle - in Athens. He could do so much to promote my husband's work.'

'I will talk to him. I promise,' he replied, avoiding her gaze. 'You have my word.' Some promise, he thought immediately. My father wouldn't listen to me, if I were bleeding in a gutter.

The touch of Amara's cool fingers on his arm inflamed him again and he badly wanted to encompass her beauty in an embrace that was hardly chaste. How much he yearned to kiss those parted lips and for a mad moment, he almost did. Instead, hiding his thoughts under a muttered farewell, and feeling decidedly foolish as well as ashamed for insulting his friend, Theomenes almost collided with a stool as he fled from the room.

THREE

THE WORLD OF IMBROS was filled with gods and goddesses, heroes and heroines and the most sublime representations of the human form. Their stone and marble busts peered down from crowded, powdery shelves. Olympians in burnished bronze watched over him and rows of terracotta figures stood in mute witness to his concentrated labours. In his bustling, dusty workshop in an alley off Icarus Street, Imbros was concentrating on his latest creations. One, a clay statuette of the god Zeus, about two feet tall, was nearing completion. From a mold of this effigy would be cast a finely sculpted bronze figurine which would travel with him to Athens, together with other fine pieces he had created. The forthcoming Great Dionysia would be a good opportunity to display his skills, according to his wife.

The other bronze artwork of the goddess Athena, patron of the arts and bestower of wisdom, but also goddess of war, the last of which Imbros chose to overlook, was completed and he was very satisfied with the result. She was to be presented as a gift during the forthcoming spring festival to stand in the home of a man highly honoured by the City Elders, Admetus, the scholar and historian. Imbros found himself regarding this particular piece many times during the day, and he knew why. By his exacting standards, it was the nearest likeness to his beautiful wife, Amara, he had ever achieved.

An Athenian by birth and parentage, Imbros now lived in Plataea, a small city just over the border into Boeotia, but for many years a staunch ally of Athens. So valued was Plataea's loyalty, the little fortress was allowed to share sacred rites and ceremonies, normally exclusive to Athens. When just a young boy, he had been taken to see the first temple statue by the great artist and sculptor, Phidias of Athens - the golden statue of Athena in Plataea. It was from that moment the awestruck Imbros decided he wanted to be a sculptor, and later he fulfilled his dream to become an apprentice to the master. The goddess brought much needed coinage to the tiny city-state. Multitudes in need of help or in thanksgiving had stood at her feet over the years, and the city continued to prosper. It was said that Phidias had been so inspired by his beautiful creation, that he went on to construct the colossal bronze of Athena on the acropolis in Athens, so tall she could be seen out at sea. Imbros had not yet seen the master's latest marvel, the great seated statue of Zeus on Mount Olympus. One glimpse, it was said, could move a man's soul.

Satisfied, Imbros set aside his modelling tools and called for Georgios, the eldest son of Seleukos, Amara's uncle. At just fifteen he was proving to be a promising apprentice. He was keen to learn and would be watching closely as the skilled craftsmen moved the god through the various processes of waxing, mold firing and bronze casting. Polishing and finishing would be done by his bondservant, Sophos, an old man with many years experience, having worked in the same studio in Athens where Imbros had served his apprenticeship. The final adornment of gold and silver, embellished with precious stones, would be designed by Imbros, in his distinctive style. It had been a good decision to bring Sophos to Plataea. He was now passing on his skills to two sturdy young brothers rescued from a dubious future in the local stone quarries, enabling Imbros to fulfill his ambition to create beautiful bronze statues as his mentor Phidias had taught him.

He was feeling more confident lately. His adopted city had given him some wealth, although not enough to satisfy his wife, and also a little status, with welcome commissions increasing apace. His thoughts did sometimes return to his home city of Athens and the renown he may have achieved there, but he had learned to appreciate his life in Plataea - for his wife's sake. One day soon he would build a larger studio where he could take on more challenging commissions, and perhaps his skill as a sculptor would become known in enlightened, flourishing Athens. Day-dreaming, his thoughts were of his comfortable, untroubled home behind its high walls, where that morning he'd sat with his wife Amara sharing their early morning meal, in the private sanctuary of their inner courtyard. Unusual for a man of his standing, he preferred to spend as much home time in his wife's company, and until they'd been blessed with children, their household would run according to their shared desires.

Amara was Plataean and he had fallen in love with her at first sight. Her beauty was evident to all who had eyes to see, not just to Imbros with his discerning admiration as an artist, and he was all too well aware of the second glances his wife often received. The soft darts of Eros struck them simultaneously and within a few months of her sixteenth birthday, they had married. Three years later, they were still very much in love.

'I think your latest creation will be most beautiful, Imbros,' she had said to him that morning, as she looked across the table at the wooden panels covered with charcoal sketches of various parts of her anatomy. 'Your mentor would be proud!' He had been making last minute alterations to a proposed statue of Aphrodite, while studying the graceful curve of his wife's neck, and he chuckled to himself as he recalled the mischievous smile she had tried to hide.

'And why wouldn't she be beautiful, when you are my muse,' he'd replied, laughing. 'You are the original!'

'Yes, but I will age, Imbros, and grow fat. Aphrodite's body will never grow old,' she'd responded, pouting at him, seductively.

He'd walked around the table and gently caressed her shoulders and the adorable, shapely symmetry he strove repeatedly to emulate. He'd murmured into her neck, 'You know my sweet, whatever I do I could never reproduce your exquisite contours, and I can't make love to a lump of metal!' The sigh she had made as he moved his hands down her body, stirred him still.

FOUR

THE JOURNEY TO THE great estate of Anatolios of Leuctra, the best horse trainer and breeder in Boeotia, was mercifully uneventful and they made good time. Anatolios and Theomenes' father were old friends, Eubalos having a passion for horses bordering on obsession. Separated from several other enclosures, where Theomenes observed with admiration a variety of horses of the highest quality, was the birthday gift from Eubalos to his first born. The dark as night Thessalian stallion, high-stepped around it's enclosure, head and tail held high as though for appraisal, then snorting and stamping it charged suddenly at the rail, startling the mules.

'Why bring the mules, Theo?' asked Anatolios. 'It would be quicker to ride him back. He goes like the wind!'

'My father does not trust me to deliver the beast unmarked,' replied Theomenes, resentfully. 'Not one mark of whip or spur must be seen on its flesh or else I will be the one to feel the whip.'

'It looks as though you already have, lad!' smiled Anatolios, kindly, as he looked at Theomenes' flesh wounds.

'That is another business entirely,' said Theomenes, his fingers moving suddenly to touch his cheek. Having known the sullen youth since his birth, the noble Anatolios took the hint and questioned him no further.

Secured between the two strong mules, the stallion gradually settled down to a steady pace and by afternoon, they were back at the stables near Hysiae, to be greeted by an excited Eubalos and his head groom. The Magistrate ran his hands over the dusty limbs of the animal, all the while pointing out its attributes and beauty, checking for any grazes.

As it was led away to its new stable to be fed and watered, Eubalos called out to his groom.

'Make sure he is well turned out for this evening's presentation, and I want his mane and tail braided in the colours of Alexeis!' Turning to face Theomenes, he slowly scrutinised the still livid gashes on his young son's body. 'Is there anything you need to tell me, Theo?' he asked, wary of the answer.

'Nothing, sir!' replied Theomenes, with conviction and he added quickly, 'It was an accident, that's all. No dishonour has befallen our family name, father.'

'Does my son speak the truth, Mydon?' asked Eubalos, watching him intently.

'Every word is true my lord,' answered Mydon, bowing low, half expecting blows.

Instead, Eubalos shook his head, wearily. 'My old friend Admetus is here already. I must go and welcome him. Be ready to greet our guests arriving this evening, Theo, and try not to be an embarrassment on your brother's special day!' he added sharply. At that moment, looking at Theomenes' grieved expression, Mydon had little desire to change places with his young master.

FIVE

FOR THE SECOND WEEK OF Anthesterion it was unusually hot. Labourers out in the fields wore straw hats to protect themselves from the sun, and even the odd donkey, trotting in front of a cart, was seen wearing a tattered petasos. Behind the walls of the city, the narrow shaded alleys provided some relief and the baked, lime-washed and brightly painted houses stood with shutters closed to keep their interiors cool.

Corinna, wife of Demetrius the shoemaker, was delighted with the abundance of sweet-scented flowers on her rose and myrtle bushes, and she visualised how well they would decorate her house for the festival. The long swings already hanging down from the trees throughout the city, would also be prettily garlanded for the enjoyment of the young people at the festival, her own beautiful dark-eyed daughter, Phoebe, being one of them. 'I believe this is a good omen,' she asserted to Eudora, her long-serving housekeeper. 'Last year we had such a good crop of almonds, do you remember? I think this year will be even better. We must give thanks to Demeter, our benefactress, for this blessing!' and the two women walked in good humour, to decorate the city's shrine dedicated to the goddess.

In every quarter of the city, courtyards and plazas were fragrant with the aroma of acacia blossom and the mountain slopes were ablaze with myriad flowers of every hue. Above Mount Cithaeron, there was not a cloud in the sky.

In the Theatre of the Shades, a small marble amphitheatre carved into the lower slopes of Mount Cithaeron, the actors were making use of the modest facilities to rehearse for their special performance in Athens in a few weeks' time, but before 'the big one', the Great Dionysia, nearly forty miles to the south, they'd broken their journey at Plataea to take part in the local spring festival of Anthesteria. They laughingly agreed that behaving badly for the entertainment of the festival goers would require no rehearsal whatsoever and to increase their prospects of having a good time, some effort was being put into becoming acquainted with the locals. One of the troupe, Clytes by name, sheltered from the warm spring sun under the shady parasol of a solitary stone pine, his head aching from the excesses of the previous night. He tried to concentrate and watched his fellow actors, Leon and Panthas, closely, because at that moment he could not remember his cue. The dual sins of too much wine and a generously proportioned, insatiable woman, whose name he also could not remember, had made him drowsy.

He was wondering why he, an Eleusinian, had come to Plataea in the first place. They'd had numerous more inspiring venues to choose from. He thought the people insular and unsophisticated, but his contempt had lapsed temporarily the night before. What was her name, he puzzled? The wife of whatshisname? Big in olives but nothing else, she had told him. I can remember that, he thought smiling, and he stretched out his long legs like a contented cat.

From the back of the stage, members of the troupe rolled out the ekkyklema and the jarring of the iron wheels made Clytes flinch. On the platform were placed two daybeds and the additional furnishings necessary for the next scene. His cue went unheeded and he cursed softly as Panthas beckoned him urgently to the stage. 'One more lousy week and we shall be on our way to Athens,' he muttered to one of the stage-hands as he stumbled down the steps. The festival of flowers and wine would start in two days' time and take place over three days - if he survived that long.

SIX

GLAUCUS FROM THESSALY, SOMETIMES called 'Flamebeard' because of his red hair, but more usually, just 'Helmsman', earned from many years at sea, still had the Oeroe river to cross before he reached the fortress city. He had travelled a long way from the house of his widowed sister at Larissa, the capital of his home state, first by ship to Delium on the coast of Boeotia and then overland towards his original destination, Thespiae at the foot of Mt. Helicon. As head of the family he was performing his duty in delivering a dowry to his sister's future son-in-law, a successful but dull ceramics importer by the name of Pamphilus.

During a purchasing trip to the horse plains of Thessaly, in the company of his aged father, Pamphilus had been surprisingly impressed by the robust dancing performed at a local festival. In particular, he was smitten by the fifteen-year-old girl with the strong, lithe body and child-bearing hips. He was the last of his line, recently widowed and childless, and pressure was being put upon him by his father to find a suitable new wife, so after negotiating a favourable dowry with her guardian, a no-nonsense but obviously caring uncle, father and son had returned to Thespiae to give the family the welcome news.

When Glaucus started out he had custody of two family slaves, that rare creature, a willing mule, and a generous pouch of silver. Now, since being attacked by a band of thieving low-life, while he'd stopped to give his companions a rest, he had none of these things and the good prospects of securing a favourable marriage for his niece were also lost. His dagger was taken from him, but lying against a tree and unnoticed by the robbers, was his long-handled axe. He'd unstrapped it from the mule in order to hack down some wood for a fire and making a grab for this fearsome double-headed weapon, the fiery Thessalian fought like a Spartan in the futile defence of his slaves and pack-animal. He quickly dispatched one of the thieves and at least two others would bear indelible scars, before they made off hurriedly with their loot, heading in the direction of Thebes, not bothering to take with them their dead comrade.

He decided there was no point in carrying on to Thespiae to deliver only bad news. No point in returning to Larissa, to face a distraught sister and a tearful niece. The Athenian fleet was still blockading Potidaea, holding the suffering city under siege, so he decided his best course of action would be to travel down to Piraeus in the hope of getting a quick commission on a cargo ship. Perhaps a long voyage. He yearned to be back at sea again. He would send messengers to his sister and to Pamphilos, the suitor of his niece, with the promise that the dowry would be paid, somehow.

Bruised from the attack and weary with walking he decided to break his journey and with some of the hidden coin he still had stitched into his cloak, make an offering to Athena at Plataea to ask her for vengeance. Perhaps Plataea's golden goddess would be sympathetic to his heroic efforts on the road, and on hearing the distant horn blasts, he quickened his step to get behind the gates before they closed for the night. At the gatehouse, he was asked to relinquish any weapons and reluctantly he unstrapped the buckled belt across his back and handed in his axe, a fine Thracian implement of some age and beautifully engraved. Although it had been washed in the waters of the Oeroe, the tassels attached to the shaft still held some remains of blood, but the guard asked no questions.

Driven by hunger and an almighty thirst, his first port of call was not the temple, but a tavern.

Its interior was only a little less crowded than the congested street and a heady miasma of aromas immediately assailed his senses. A mingling of stale wine, sweating bodies, various cheap meats being cooked and, as he passed to the rear of the room, the stomach wrenching taint of urine coming from the latrines, out back. When his eyes refocused, he could just see through the smokey gloom of the oil lamps, exacerbated by the low-ceiling, that all the benches were occupied, but he finally found a solitary seat in a dim corner near the kitchen. At his elbow a group of young men were so engaged in a loud and belligerent argument that they barely glanced at him. Glaucus called for wine, but immediately thought perhaps he should move or leave this establishment altogether. These youngsters were getting very drunk and there could be trouble. They had obviously recently completed their military training and Glaucus noticed the badge of 'The Marathon Shield', the city's emblem, on their leather tunics. From their loud quarrel, however, it was apparent that more than one of these newly qualified soldiers had strong Theban sympathies, and they were drawing menacing attention from others in the room.

Each of the soldiers was taking turns in jumping on the benches, shouting out toasts to their comrades. 'To Epiktetos - 'Hawk-Eye'! May his arrows always find their target!' Loud cheers erupted from the group. 'To Iairos - 'Strong-Arm'! His javelins are carried on the wings of Nike!' Cups were banged loudly on the table.

'To Alexeis!' shouted a young soldier by the name of Simonedes.

'Alex left for Hysiae yesterday, you wanker,' interrupted a sneering Timotheos. 'He is celebrating his birthday today, remember? No doubt with other Athenian toadies. You should listen to my father!' he declared, belligerently, and glaring around the room, he pointed indiscriminately at the increasingly offended customers.

'It's time we stopped being arse-kissers to Athens,' he carried on shouting. 'Celebrating their festivals? Huh! We have our own Boeotian heritage.'

From around the room, there were angry murmurings of disapproval and the tavern owner, getting concerned about how quickly talk like this could lead to violence, ineffectually flapped his arms about, trying to quieten the group.

'You've had too much to drink, Timotheos, as we all have,' said his friend Artemon, anxious that he might say too much. 'You are talking wildly,' and he bundled him to a seat, whispering urgently into his ear.

Simonedes, a longtime friend of Alexeis, was a little worse for wear, but even in his fuddled state, he realised that Timotheos was being detrimental to his friend.

'Well, if Alexeis was here,' he announced loudly, balancing unsteadily on a stool, 'he would put you right about the Thebans, Timotheos. If you don't study your history, the same mistakes will be repeated. That is what Alexeis would tell you,' he mumbled, as crashing over the table, he knocked the wine into the lap of the helmsman.

Glaucus had had a bad day and it wasn't getting any better. Suddenly, he rose up to his full height, dabbing furiously at his wine soaked clothing.

'You think you're fucking soldiers? My arse!' he yelled. 'Eunuchs in the harems of Persia would make better soldiers!' Pounding the boards with his huge fists, he glowered at them. 'Spawn of the Victors of Marathon?' he roared again. 'Ha! You sound as though you're still sucking at your mothers' tits!'

The room went suddenly quiet. Clytes the actor, sitting near the entrance with some newly acquired companions, witnessed the growing disturbance and smiled with amusement at the stranger's slight to the manhood of the ill-disciplined young soldiers. Gradually, he moved himself to the edge of the bench to facilitate a quick exit, but then heard a loud shout as the arrogant young man going by the name of Timotheos, suddenly produced a knife. 'No weapons!' yelled the tavern owner, desperately. But the red-haired giant had swiftly grabbed the man's wrist and squeezed it so hard, the dagger dropped to the floor. Their arguing having ceased, the soldiers turned their attentions to silencing the loud-mouthed stranger and moved in to grab him. Then the room erupted.

With an agility that surprised everyone, the big man with the red hair, gripping the edge of the table boards with bear-like hands, upturned them, sending jugs of wine and water in all directions. A second soldier aimed a blow at Glaucus. It connected so fully with his granite chin that Clytes, from across the room, heard knuckles crack. It seemed to have as much effect as a fly landing on a rock. Helpless in his agony, the attacker became a standing target for the red-haired giant, and swearing a plethora of oaths, Glaucus directed a well-aimed kick to the man's unprotected crotch. There was now pandemonium in the room as flying fists as well as wine cups connected with flesh and bone and Clytes, like it or not, had become part of the melee. The fiery giant was obviously a stranger here, like himself, and he didn't like the odds stacked against him. The actor landed a hefty punch into the belly of one soldier who was trying to grapple with the redhead and as his comrade came to his aid, swinging wildly, he ran straight into the actor's fist and caught it right between the eyes. When he saw the flash of a blade, he dodged the wicked point and grabbing the man's arm, twisted it behind his back. Then, bringing clasped hands down on his attacker's neck, felled him as though with a log.

As men were rushing for the door and comrade helped comrade to his feet, Clytes paused to take a breath, only to be confronted by the blood splattered, big man himself. In his fury, he didn't recognise Clytes as an ally and before Clytes could pass on this information, Glaucus sprang at him with a yell of triumph. Clytes let him come on and then quickly stepping aside, and before the big man could change direction, put all his weight behind a two-handed punch which momentarily stopped the Thessalian in his tracks. Much to the actor's surprise, the giant stumbled backwards against a wall, before shaking his head for a moment, then like a rampant bull, he charged. With the lightness of an athlete, Clytes leapt backwards to seat himself on the edge of a table and thrusting his legs forward, hit Glaucus full in the chest. He staggered, and Clytes jumping down, crouching like a wrestler, threw the colossus from the hip. His mouth half-open in disbelief, arms and legs splayed, Flamebeard, winded, hit the earth floor.

As Clytes was about to move in, shouts were heard from the street. He heard two words. 'Guards! Justices!' then hands were pulling them apart and dragging them toward the door. 'Run!' they were told, as the remaining occupants sped off. One of them, a local barber, had in his possession a bronze dagger. He had seen it fall when the fracas broke out and he'd made a grab for it. No-one seemed to notice, but now he panicked. When he ran out the door, he threw it away.

For a few seconds the helmsman and the actor stared absurdly at each other. Running down the street towards them were several armed soldiers and an officer. Clytes, the first on his feet, ran off in the opposite direction. Glaucus, finding himself alone, ignored the calls to stay where he was, and charged after him. Darting quickly down a side alley, into almost total darkness, Clytes was startled to find the way blocked. The narrow street ended at a high stone wall. Without hesitation, using finger and toe holds, he climbed nimbly to sit astride the impediment. Pausing to look back he was dismayed to see the giant had followed him and he could hear the soldiers were not far behind. He knew there was no way the fugitive could climb the wall unaided, but he didn't want to sit around to be arrested himself. He'd had enough dealings with the law and did not want to forfeit his present privileges, granted by his status as an actor. 'Not my responsibility!' he mumbled, guiltily, as he readied himself to jump. Then, on hearing urgent shouts, he groaned, 'Oh shit!' and repositioning himself on the wall, shouted to his pursuer to hurry up, as he braced himself for the challenge. Reaching down to grasp him by the hand, he dragged the leviathan, painfully and not without difficulty, to safety. By the time the soldiers reached the wall, the two men were gone.

Glaucus followed behind Clytes dutifully, through the cluttered back-yard of a wheelwright's workshop, over another wall, then a maze of alleys and back streets, passing a stinking tanner's yard, not knowing where he was being led, but somehow he trusted this lanky landsman. When they were sure of no sounds of pursuit, they finally stopped for breath on the corner of a street of brothels and more taverns, and a wide street leading to the upper city. For the first time, they took stock of each other. Suddenly, Glaucus chuckled heartily and then the chuckle became a laugh, as he pointed a finger at Clytes' face. Clytes gingerly touched his forehead and winced. He felt a large swelling, half-closing his right eye, and when he took his hand away he saw it was covered in blood. His head was thumping as though being hit with several small hammers and he glared back, unbelievably, at the laughing big man. Then, he too started to laugh and both men fell against each other, helplessly slapping each other on the back. Clytes realized he liked this 'larger than life' stranger, and he hadn't enjoyed himself so much in a long time.

'Come, friend,' Glaucus said at last. 'Let us find somewhere to share a bowl. I've a tongue as rough as a hog's back! Oh, and I'd better tell you now, friend, I'm short on funds.'

'Oh, you have something more useful than silver,' answered the actor.

'And, by all the Gods, what is more useful than coin?' roared Glaucus.

'Hands like a bear and a kick like a mule!' laughed Clytes, amicably.

'Whoever you are, you're pretty adept yourself,' replied the helmsman with feeling, rubbing his bruised chin.

Following the agile actor once more, he found himself being led to a coarse but lively brothel where cheaply perfumed, soft companionship was openly on offer. Clytes approached one of the women; a scantily clad, ample prostitute who was known to him and she entwined her soft arms, invitingly, around the actor's neck.

'This one will give comfort to your bruises!' laughed Clytes, pulling the generously proportioned Sappha towards Flamebeard.

'She will suit me well', chuckled Glaucus, admiringly. 'Not for me, the small breasted women, the Athenians love so much!'

'Sappha, bring us some food and wine, my cherub,' said Clytes with a grin. Then slapping the helmsman enthusiastically on the back, he leapt up the stairs to find the luscious Tanagran known as Anthousa.

At the taverna, Stephanos, the captain of the guard, was carefully examining a bronze dagger found near the entrance. The tavern owner, wanting to avoid a flogging for allowing weapons to be used within the city limits, tried to allay blame. He liked the big redhead. He liked the way he had taught those young men a lesson, but he knew the owner of the blade with the carving of the goddess Harmonia on the handle and did not want trouble. When questioned, he mentioned seeing a big, red-haired stranger handling the knife.

'He was not from around here, captain. He looked as though he had travelled some distance and he had Thessalian coinage on him.'

'We'll find him!' responded Stephanos, grimly, as he looked around the room, strewn with broken furniture and shattered pots. When the soldiers left, the tavern keeper remarked to his cook, 'If he has any sense, he will high-tail it out of here at first light. I liked him, but what else could I do? I don't want any trouble with the family of Naucleides!'

That night, Anthousa was awakened by a loud bellowing coming from the street. Looking down from the window she watched as an unwilling Glaucus was being dragged off by three soldiers. He was shouting loud enough to wake the dead, but not Clytes. Prostrate, from a surfeit of drinking and love-making, but also due to a large swelling on his temple, he would not wake for some time. The Tanagran, used to such disturbances, let him sleep on and gently eased her perfumed body back into their warm bed.

SEVEN

GLAUCUS HAD AMUSED HIMSELF all morning by throwing stones at the rats. With his legs chained to the wall, he was getting a little anxious that he might run out of missiles, so when the summons arrived to attend court, it came as a welcome relief. Still in chains, he was pushed onto a cart and driven through the noisy city to the courtroom. Everywhere, from shrines and temples to the most humble of dwellings, flower garlands adorned the labyrinth of streets and squares, and traders stalls and amusement booths were being set up in every available space. A group of bare skinned children ran beside the cart, shouting up at him. With his flaming red hair and beard, they thought he was part of the entertainment. Keeping his shackles hidden, Glaucus pulled silly faces back at them making the children scream with laughter. He thought of the delectable Sappha and how they had planned to celebrate the spring festival together - in between clients - it would be a busy few days for her. It seemed like a long time ago.

There was one junior magistrate present at the courthouse together with

Stephanos, the captain of the guard who had been on duty the previous evening, and two of his soldiers. Also, Clytes. The two men nodded to each other and Flamebeard's fears receded a little on seeing the affable actor, leaning nonchalantly against a stone column. He was his only defence witness and not a particularly presentable one, with his bruised eye and a swollen gash on his forehead. He'd done his best to conceal his injuries, Glaucus noticed with amusement, by wearing a floppy cap pulled to one side. Glaucus eyed the judge with open contempt. The rats were friendlier, he thought, scornfully. The man was tight-lipped and obviously in ill-humour and he drummed his fingers irritably on the document in front of him.

'Your name is Glaucus - from Thessaly?' the magistrate asked, after several uneasy moments of silence.

'It is! I am!' boomed Flamebeard, as he dragged himself closer towards the table, deliberately making the chains clank across the floor.

'Hold him!' shouted the Inquisitor to the startled officer, and Glaucus was roughly dragged to a pillar by the soldiers and securely shackled. Returning to his seat and recovering composure, the magistrate asked the captain, agitatedly, 'What do we know of this man?'

'Apart from the offence he is charged with, we have learned very little, your honour,' replied Stephanos.

Beckoning Clytes forward, the judge asked him, 'Can you give us any information about this individual? He is a companion of yours I believe. I have had your identity checked so I know you were asked to come to our city to entertain us during the festival. Your intentions are not a concern to me. But this is!' and he produced a bronze dagger and placed it on the table. 'How long have you known this man, who is here before us?'

Clytes was, by now, confused. When he heard the news that Glaucus had been dragged from Sappha's bed in the middle of the night, he assumed it was because of the ruckus and the tavern owner wanted recompense. The production of the dagger was unexpected and he knew it could go badly for the Thessalian.

'How long have you known this man?' repeated the judge, sharply.

'Since yesterday,' replied Clytes and he directed an apologetic look towards Glaucus, who was glowering angrily from the hard marble floor.

Glaucus heard a sigh of resignation from the magistrate who had turned his searching gaze towards him.

21

'It is a most serious offence to use a weapon within the precincts of the city,' he told the chained man. 'It is a flogging offence at best. You say you are from Thessaly but your dagger bears a Theban emblem!'

'What dagger?' asked Glaucus, incredulously. 'I lost my dagger on the road to Thespiae, as well as other things. I was outnumbered in an assault, otherwise I would not be here in your piss pot of a city!'

'My captain has witnesses who will swear that you were the bearer of this knife,' replied the magistrate. 'Before I pass judgement, do you have anything to say in your defence?'

'You are mad!' shouted Glaucus, struggling in his chains. 'I swear, by all the Gods on Mount Olympus, I'm not spying for Thebes!'

'Maybe a flogging, or worse will loosen your tongue! Take him away,' said the magistrate. 'Keep him chained until the festival is over, captain. Then use whatever means necessary to get the truth out of him.'

EIGHT

A COOL BREEZE CAME down from the mountain, stirring the branches of the trees on the edge of the amphitheatre, and wafted through the sanctuary of Dionysus. It made the oil lamps flicker in their wall niches.

Eubalos, standing next to his old friend, the historian Admetus, pulled his cloak closer and shivered. They were part of the assemblage of local dignitaries, gathered with the citizens of Plataea, to watch the initiation ceremony of the forthcoming Spring festival of Anthesteria. A time of joy when men, women and children, slaves included, could enjoy the ancient rituals and customs, but also of sadness when the dead were remembered, their souls briefly welcomed into the world of the living.

A respectful silence spread throughout the spectators as they watched down the long avenue of blazing torches at the advance of the priests and their attendants, and thin trumpets played plaintively as the sacrificial goat, dressed with ribbons, was led into the precinct. One of the torch bearers was Theomenes and he stood grimly still as the procession passed by him. He had been a torch bearer the previous year and the ceremony had seemed interminable, but this year, Phalinus would be making a speech. He hoped he would hear clearly from his place in the line.

Far from the glow of the torches, in the shadows of the amphitheatre, sat Corinna, together with her daughter, Phoebe, and her slave housekeeper, Eudora. Her husband, Demetrius, was somewhere in the crowd at the temple, wearing his finest blue-green chiton, but they searched in vain to see him in the multi-hued assemblage. They were not alone in the theatre. There were several people they recognised from the town, together with their families and also a large number of their slaves. From the darkness they watched the brilliant spectacle of the nobles in their rainbow of colours. Corinna thought the commanding figure of general Eupompides, looked particularly magnificent. Silently, they all waited eagerly for their Shield Guardian to appear.

As they approached the altar, the temple elders were each presented with a floral wreath entwined with ivy, sacred to Dionysus, offered by the young temple boys. A garland was also placed around the neck of the young male goat. To Theomenes, the ensuing prayers and singing seemed to take an age, and he felt sympathy for his father and the old historian still standing in the now chilly evening air. As the priests and acolytes took their places on the dais, the High Priest of the temple stepped forward and with arms raised, called out clearly to the God of Wine, to invoke his presence at his temple home. His voice rose higher and higher, and respecting the shared beliefs in his congregation, intoned ancient liturgies both Ionian and Boeotian, passed down from the beginnings of their race.

At the sound of pipes and flutes, and dithyrambs being sung, all eyes turned to watch the coming of the deity in the form of the actor Clytes, riding in a wagon drawn by a lusty mule. His fellow actors, Leon and Panthas, dressed as satyrs with their long ears and tails, did not disappoint with their exaggerated genitalia, as they danced and sang their way down the lighted avenue. Clytes, in his heavy black beard and wig, sat theatrically still, for all the world as though he was the Wine God. He thought it was a part most suited to him. For the people in the crowds, this was the moment that signalled the beginning of the festivities and their spirits lifted immediately on watching the activities of the actors, acrobats and musicians. Clytes and his troupe put on a good show and Eubalos and many others murmured their appreciation, looking forward to seeing more of them during the days ahead.

With a garlanded 'Dionysus' seated on his high throne, in a place of honour on the dais, it was time for Phalinus to approach the altar. There was expectation from everyone present that this would be a special occasion, as it was Phalinus's first Anthesteria as Shield Guardian. On mounting the steps, he stood for a moment, thoughtful, dignified, his long simple white tunic fluttering in the breeze as he looked around graciously at his fellow Plataeans. The High Priest stepped forward, and indicating to the golden-haired Phalinus to lower his head, he placed upon it a gilded circlet in the form of interwoven ivy leaves. Then a young altar boy nervously approached, and fitted a large gold armlet to the Guardian's powerful upper arm. It was in the likeness of the three headed serpent on the monumental column at Delphi, dedicated to Apollo after the historic, victorious battle of Plataea, and in the fluctuating light of the oil lamps, so fine was the engraving, the serpents looked as though they were alive.

As Phalinus took his place to speak before the large assembly, a light wind stirred his graceful robes, making them billow and ripple. As he raised his arms to speak, a gasp of amazement arose from the crowd. He looked as though he was floating. He looked like a god.

'Plataeans! Friends of Plataea! Citizens!'

His voice rang out clear and strong so that all around could hear. To the young Theomenes, the voice of the Shield Guardian sounded deeper and held more authority than he remembered it from the previous day at the gate, and the feeling of affinity which affected him then, now turned to one of regard.

'I welcome you all to this year's Anthesteria, in solidarity and remembrance. This year my own son, Akylas, now three years of age, will drink his first wine, starting his journey to becoming a man; a citizen of our esteemed city. He will be taught the ancient ways of our festivals, demonstrating our respect for the gods, who know all. He will learn of the skills and mastery handed down to us from our ancestors, by which we survive and prosper. Their shades will visit us again soon and my son will remember the welcome we will give them. Plataeans!'

Theomenes and several others were startled and looked at Phalinus, anxiously. 'Plataeans, let us also not forget the sacrifices made to defend this privileged way of life. Some of our older citizens know first-hand just how fragile our freedom and the prosperity that comes with it, really is. I know there are amongst us, those who question our allegiance with

Athens and the democratic liberties we all enjoy, preferring instead the old ways of rule by strength or inheritance, not merit; offered by Thebes. Do not be fooled, dear friends. Our way of life has been hard won by brave, far-seeing souls. It may now fall to our generation to make those same hard decisions, for talk of war is on the lips of many men. In three days' time, after our festival, we shall meet to discuss our thoughts and decide on our future course of action - in the democratic manner.

Until then, citizens - the new wine has been opened! I wish us all a joyful and reflective celebration!'

The unperturbed goat was led to the altar and held firmly with cords by two of the younger priests, while the prayers of the High Priest rang out in praise of the deity. From a silver phiale, Phalinus poured a libation of the new wine over the goat's head; then as the animal bowed in reverence to the wine god, with a swift movement he cleanly cut the animal's throat. Wine and blood mingled together and flowed into the earth in thanksgiving to Dionysus, their god and benefactor.

NINE

'I'M LOOKING FOR THE prisoner, Glaucus? From Thessaly? Big man! Red hair!' shouted up Clytes to the guard pacing the wall at the east gate. 'Is he here?'

'Oh, he's here alright,' replied the sentry. 'Can't you hear his bellowing? You'd think it was a bull we had chained up! Show yourself, citizen. Walk into the light so I can see your face.' At sight of the actor, still in his guise as Dionysus, the soldier fell back. 'What the.....? Are you taking the piss?'

'I am the actor and musician, Clytes of Eleusis, come to entertain you during your festival,' announced Clytes, flamboyantly lifting up his wig. 'My friend of short acquaintance is, I believe, in custody in your gate house.'

'Are you drunk?' shouted down the guard.

'I may have been when I started my search, but I have walked the length and breadth of the plateau to find this place, therefore I am probably not - anymore,' replied Clytes, burping loudly.

'Go to the left tower door,' indicated the soldier, 'and knock there. If you try anything, you will end up chained to your fat friend!'

Clytes could hear Glaucus, before he saw him. He was arguing with one of the soldiers on duty at the gatehouse and Thessalian expletives were bouncing off the walls. The warder shook his head, wearily. 'He's lucky we can't understand him, and it's a sacred holiday or else we'd shut him up - permanently!' When the helmsman set eyes on the tall actor, he stared in amazement. Clytes pulled down his beard and grinned.

'My friend, am I glad to see you!' cried Glaucus and then he roared with laughter. 'I knew you were jealous of my fine beard,' he said, stroking his red bush. 'What a sight you are! And what have you got there?'

'This skin is for you,' said Clytes, 'fresh from the mixing of the new wine. I've left another with the warder,' said Clytes, winking.

'Let's get to it, my friend. I have a thirst that would drain the Hellespont!' Both beards were soon soaked in wine and to the relief of the guards, there was calm at the gatehouse.

TEN

FOR MORE THAN A week now, Marissa had been aware of a rather handsome, intermittent visitor to her father's house, and although she had questioned the servants as to who and what he was, she had been unable to find out anything, except for his name - Nicander. Her father kept this stranger apart from the rest of the household and only his closest acquaintances appeared to enjoy the newcomer's company. Something else she noticed was the deference given to him. Marissa, cousin to Amara, but of a totally different character, was intrigued to the point of angry frustration. Interrogating her mother only brought forth, 'He is a merchant of some renown and your father wishes to trade with him. That is all you need to know, Marissa, so please stop asking.'

Marissa, at the age of twenty, was a year older than her cousin, but still unmarried. This was not from a want of suitors approaching her father, Limaois, or that she was not interested in men, but being intelligent and strong willed she resented becoming the property of any man she married. The interest she had in this Nicander, surprised her. All she waited for was another glimpse of him, but that evening she waited in vain and spent a restless night longing for morning. The attractions of the festival had so far failed to excite her, but at day-break she sent her housemaid to her cousin's house, with a message, asking; 'If you are attending any events today, can I accompany you?' If Nicander didn't come to her, then she would somehow find him.

To Marissa, the city had never looked more beautiful as she and Amara, accompanied by their chaperones, made their way to the agora to meet Imbros. The cousins in their fine clothes drew admiring glances as they walked serenely through the crowds, delicate veils covering their mouths, fluttering gently in the warm breeze. They sighed together at sight of the garlanded swings, remembering back to when they were younger, and how their mothers had made such a fuss of dressing them up, spending far too much on hairdressings and fine fabrics. The girls, realising much later, it was to attract future suitors. They passed through streets packed with stalls, the various cries of the vendors merging into a single cacophony. Small children, wearing their flower garlands, screamed and laughed at the mime artists and jugglers. Amara smiled sadly, as she thought of her own unfruitful state. She bent down to press an obol into the palm of a poor beggar, sat with his staff and bag in the doorway of a workshop, closed for the holiday. She was scolded by Ianthe for doing so, but at that moment, not understanding why, she had felt empathy with the man in his rags.

By the fountain, talking to friends, they found Imbros. He greeted the two women with effusive compliments which made them both giggle, as it was so unlike Imbros to be so publicly demonstrative.

'We have just come from Naucleides' house and I can tell you that his hospitality is second to none!' he enthused, his face a little flushed.

'Have you forgotten about the presentation to Admetus, Imbros?' asked Amara, concerned. 'Marissa wishes to go, so she will accompany me. We will see you at the house of Callias, in a little while,' she added, pointedly.

The women with their entourage of servants, swept out of the agora, smiling behind their veils at the merrymaking seen all around them. Actors, under the unruly guidance of Clytes, were travelling around the city entertaining the crowds, and were now in the agora. Clytes, ever appreciative of a beautiful form, danced his way over to the two young women.

'The goddesses Hera and Aphrodite have come down from Olympus to enjoy our festivities!' he announced, flamboyantly. Playing a tune on his lyre, he continued to follow them. 'You are the most beautiful flowers of the Anthesteria! Clytes, is at your service - day or night!'

'That's far enough,' said Galenos, manservant to Marissa, pushing the actor away, gently. 'Try your tricks elsewhere.'

'The wine must be good this year!' laughed Marissa. 'I'm looking forward to trying some, myself.'

As they left the marketplace to make the ascent to the villa quarter, a high-spirited family group passed them. It was Phalinus, taking his young son, Akylas, to the temple of Dionysus. Akylas, now three years of age, had taken his first small cup of watered wine, as was the custom at the spring festival and his father, carrying him securely on his shoulders, proudly showed the Plataeans their future Shield Guardian. The small golden haired Akylas, naked except for the garland of wild flowers in his hair, waved excitedly at everyone, the wine making him feel wonderfully giddy and silly.

Marissa had been hopeful of seeing Nicander somewhere in the city and consequently she was wearing her most clinging blue linen peplos, embroidered with silver threads. Her thick dark hair was fashioned in the latest style, held in place with ornate combs and covered in a fine Koan silk scarf of sky blue. Many appreciative comments were directed at her - she was unmarried, a distinctive good-looker, and would be given a substantial dowry by her desperate father, but over her drawn veil, the eyes of Marissa sought only one man.

Admetus was delighted with the presentation by his peers, of the statuette of Athena, in acknowledgement of his exhaustive and continuing, some thought boring work of late on the history of Plataea. When he ran his hands over the gilded form, he blushed and looking around the room, caught sight of the sculptor, steadying himself against the wall.

'I have always admired your choice of consort, Imbros, and it pleases me greatly to accept this most beautiful creation of yours. I feel I know your wife's form as well as you do! She will bring me much pleasure in my old age and will stand in a place of prominence in my villa!' There was laughter from around the room. 'I will not bore you with a long speech, my dear friends,' he went on, and there was some good natured clapping from the assemblage. 'As an historian of our beloved city, my chronicles have, as many point out to me, been lacking in drama of late. Apart from the heroic achievements of our Olympic athletes, of course!' and he joined in the applause and cheers from the room. 'But I do not wish for drama. Our capricious gods are forever listening. Eris has already thrown the 'apple of discord' and we must pray that our leaders are wise enough to avoid her provocation.'

He was interrupted somewhat abruptly by Callias, who carried with him a cup of wine. 'My dear Admetus,' said his host, effusively. 'I congratulate you on your stamina, not only for your exhaustive writings, but your reputation for oratory is well known to all. What can you tell us about this wine?'

'Cleverly done', said one man to his companion. 'I thought he might talk all night.' Wine began to flow and so did the crude jokes. Someone gently pushed the doors closed.

Marissa, from the open doorway of the gymnaeceum where the women were gathered, had seen her father enter the andron to join the other dignitaries, but he came alone. Hopeful that Nicander was in the room but out of sight when the doors closed on her view, she decided to wait, albeit impatiently, until the presentation was over. She wondered what was happening to her. She felt foolish and very young. Due to the generosity of their hostess Euphemia, the wife of Callias, they were made to feel welcome and the women present enjoyed a delightful evening of music and poetry, with good food and plenty of excellent wine to savour. They could hear the celebrations in the andron progressing from convivial to uproarious and Amara, feeling she could wait for her husband no longer, and concerned that their servants would soon be too inebriated to get them home, urged Marissa to leave with her. Marissa was in an animated state. She was actually enjoying the evening, and being a talented player of the challenging kithara, took her part in the musical entertainment, the soulful sound of the kithara blending perfectly with her sweet voice. It took some persuasion by Amara to get her to leave the party - and finally give up all thought of seeing her Nicander.

The night air was cold as they left the house of Callias, and cloaks were borrowed to cover the women's flimsy clothing. Lighted torches led their way as the party goers hurried through the streets, still busy with revellers. Passing a garden, Marissa suddenly stopped on seeing the decorated swings, and cried out to her cousin, 'Oh look, Amara! We must try them. Do you remember how high we would go? Come, Galenos, you can push us!' To Amara's dismay, her cousin was soon high in the air, her bare legs flying freely, as though she was a young girl. Suddenly, the garden was brightly illuminated as more torches were carried down the street and groups of high-spirited citizens passed by. 'Amara?'

As soon as she heard her name, Amara knew who called her. 'Oh, Imbros, I can't get Marissa to go home. Can you do something?'

'I want *him* to push me!' shouted Marissa, soaring above the garden.

'Who me?' responded Imbros, nervously.

'I think she means me,' replied the tall man standing next to him.

'I hear you have been asking questions about me,' Nicander said to Marissa, as he helped her gently down from the swing. 'But I wonder if you will like the answers.'

Eleven

WITH THE COMING OF night, the advance guard of three-hundred heavily armed hoplites with their generals, marched south from The City of the Seven Gates towards the Asopus river and the plain of Plataea, the glow from the torches illuminating the club of Heracles on their distinctive oval shields. Colourful plumes swung from their captains' helmets, and the bright tips of the spears carried by the soldiers moved like a long column of flames as they were urged onwards by their flute players. In their boots of leather, the troops marched surely and purposefully over the uneven terrain on their way to making history and achieving immortality.

Lykaon, known as The Wolf of Thebes, glanced back at the faint lights of his diminishing city. He smiled with sly amusement as he remembered his farewell of the predatory Larachne, wife of his uncle Pythangelus. His black hair, worn long in Spartan fashion, was tied back with a green ribbon, chosen by her.

'The Plataeans must suffer for the contempt they have shown for Thebes!' she had told him fiercely as she pushed his naked body roughly from hers, her dark Persian eyes flashing. 'I wish I could be there to see their downfall!'

He'd reassured her. 'You will see what's left of their precious city soon enough, my love. Their idolised shield will be brought to Thebes, or my own shield will be my funeral bier! The jewels prised from that false icon will soon be yours,' he'd promised her boastfully, and she'd rolled on top of him, clawing savagely at his bare flesh with her long, painted nails. He'd responded by biting her hard, dark nipples as they brushed against his cheek, and she'd cried out in her passion, 'my bad, bad wolf'!' He gave a harsh laugh at the memory.

Ahead of him marched his unsuspecting uncle, Pythangelus, general and Boetarch of Thebes, the prominent crest on his bronze helmet swaying in the night air. His strongly held belief that a sustainable negotiation with Plataea could be achieved, and should at first be sought, was not what the vengeful Lykaon and others had in mind. The young man was filled with resentment at Thebes flaunting, pretentious neighbour, but particular jealousy was targeted at Phalinus, Shield Guardian.

'He's been elevated to the heights of a minor deity by a worshipping, sycophantic populace!' he'd screamed earlier at Mihrab, his Asian bodyguard. 'I don't want anyone to bring him down but me!' he said, threateningly.

It was on the heights of Mount Olympus, on the open palaestra, the sports field at Olympia, that Lykaon got his first close look at the man with the sun in his hair, who was to become the focus of his jealous spite. Although it had been over five long years, the deep sense of envy had never left him and during that time his feelings had grown into an unnatural hatred, an almost pathological desire to do the Plataean harm. Perhaps it was the man's supreme handsomeness that was the cause of his instant resentment. For, with his honed, perfect physique he was unquestionably, male beauty personified. The green-eyed, wheat-haired Phalinus. Winner and champion of innumerable athletic events and admired near and far for his feats in both arms and sporting challenges. But greater than all this, was his having been raised to almost godlike status as Guardian of the Marathon Shield at the Plataean Temple of Athena.

Remembering back, Lykaon's hand tightly gripped the pommel of his sword. The humiliation rankled still. At the age of eighteen, it was to have been his first competition with the adults in the six laps horse race, and his father had paid a small fortune in acquiring and training a suitable animal. Lykaon knew he hadn't put in enough training himself, leaving it to others to get the horse fit, and so to even his chances he'd bribed a rival to pull up his horse during the race. Unfortunately, he'd tried to bribe others too, and as Phalinus was also in the race, word soon reached his ears. Pelonus, Lykaon's father, as owner of his son's entry, had to contribute an enormous amount of coinage to the Olympic Committee in recompense and Lykaon, as well as the rider who'd accepted his bribe, were banned from competing in the next Olympiad or in any of the annual games in the intervening years.

As it turned out, this young untamed wolf was not in Hellas during those years. Before he'd reached the age of nineteen, he'd gone on to commit more serious misdemeanors, and was eventually sentenced to ten years in exile, forcing the tolerant father to accompany his wayward son to the shores of Asia Minor.

There was another event at that Olympiad which also remained vividly in the mind of Lykaon. A moment when Lykaon saw a weakness in Phalinus, the knowledge of which had sustained him and fuelled his future plans for The Shield Guardian. It was a boxing bout with the vicious himantes; gloves constructed from thick leather strips which were bound about the hands and wrists, leaving the fingers free. An unprotected face could be reduced to a bloody pulp in a few seconds. Matched pairs had not only to be tough, they had to be agile also, for the skill came not only in landing blows but also in successfully avoiding them. A gymnast as well as a boxer, Phalinus proved able on both counts. Fighting naked, their bodies oiled to display their muscled forms to the spectators, with no quarter given and none looked for, the contestants fought to win, and win quickly.

The first blow was delivered by the powerful horse-tamer from Boeotia. He was fast and cunning. A feigned blow with his left hand at first surprised Phalinus, and the match might have ended then, had it not been that Phalinus, accomplishing a remarkable feat of speed and suppleness, sprang back on the balls of his feet. A well-aimed blow from the mighty right hand of his opponent, instead of blinding him, grazed across his cheek drawing a line of blood. For the briefest of moments Phalinus's green eyes flashed in astonishment, but he recovered instantly and seized his chance as the horse-tamer became momentarily unbalanced. Pummelling into him with merciless blows, he kept them coming, knowing he would not get another chance against such a skilled boxer, until his opponent fell to the ground, his nose broken and blood pouring from his mouth. It was all over in just a few moments but the onlookers were well satisfied at this display of skill. There was also much appreciation for the attention the contestants had given to developing their bronzed bodies to the peak of perfection.

Lykaon remembered clearly what happened next. Phalinus, instead of closing the business with a well-placed blow, knelt over the fallen man and raised him up. The end of the match had not been called and the horse-tamer from Boeotia could well have taken this chance to fell his opponent. But with his swollen eyes barely open, he chose not too and conceded defeat to the judges, declaring Phalinus the winner. Lykaon never forgot what he saw as the Plataean's 'Achilles' heel'. Phalinus had a virtuous streak.

Lykaon, marching at the head of his Thebans, savoured the moment when this glorified Plataean would soon be at his mercy.

The Persian, Mirhab, was well used to Lykaon's ravings. For the previous five years he'd been attached to, the then, exiled Theban's household in Sardis, Lydia, a province of the mighty Persian empire. Although not much older than Lykaon, he'd been chosen by Larachne to be a mentor and bodyguard to the young wolf; to expand his education in Persian ways, especially after the untimely death of his father Pelonus, three years earlier. At that time, Larachne was the second wife of Pelonus, having bewitched the lonely, rich widower who'd accompanied his son into exile, so far from his Boeotian homeland. There were rumours that Pelonus had been poisoned. Rumours which involved not only his beautiful wife, but also Mirhab and even the young wolf, Lykaon.

News of the impending war between Sparta and Athens coincided with word arriving from Lykaon's uncle Pythangelus, now prominent in Thebes and having enough wealth to influence the right people, that his punishment of ten years' exile had been shortened to five. Now at the age of twenty-three he returned home as soon as he could board a ship, bringing with him his ambitious step-mother - and Mirhab.

Larachne, not one to accept an empty bed or an empty purse for long, all too easily seduced the wealthy Pythangelus, her late husband's brother. Pythangelus, somehow convinced that this sultry vision would soon be pursued by many younger suitors, married her in haste.

At his uncle's elbow strode Diemporus, also a general and Thebes' second Boetarch, easy to distinguish because of his curly black hair and elaborately coiffed beard. He was also deemed weak by the more ruthless faction of the Boeotian League, led by Eurymachus; a highborn noble of Thebes. Eurymachus had schemed with Naucleides of Plataea, a man close to Phalinus, for many months and now all was in readiness. What mattered to The Wolf and the one-hundred under his own command, was getting into the city, where Lykaon had plans of his own.

Due to the poor light, and concern for horses losing their footing, the nobles went on foot with their men, but as they all knew their destination and were confident of their meticulously planned stratagem, there was little unease in the column. By the time they reached the Asopus the weather had changed for the worse, and a strong wind was now blowing from the north-east, bringing with it heavy droplets of rain. The column halted as prayers were said, calling on Zeus to fulfill the oracle, prophesying the success of their venture. All but two torch bearers were ordered to douse their flames in the dark waters as resolutely the three-hundred forded the river and in the blackness, set foot on Plataean territory. Lykaon drove his spear tip into the earth as an act of possession and smiled. There'd be no turning back.

Following in their wake, was the main army of one-thousand men; hoplites, archers and slingers, to be let into the city once the advance guard had gained possession. But their progress was slow. Darkening storm-filled skies had turned the dusty road into a ribbon of glutinous clay. On Mount Cithaeron, thin rivulets soon became raging torrents and the streams feeding the rivers Oeroe and Asopus rapidly overflowed. By the time the main column reached the Asopus, it was in full flood and impassable. Trapped on the banks, with only their shields as protection from the driving rain, the Thebans prayed again to Zeus, this time for him to command Aiolas to reign in the horse-shaped spirits now charging down from the mountains, causing chaos. Their commander, in frustration, watched the waters continue to rise, and prayed that the advance force would achieve its objective.

TWELVE

'IT'S A YOUNG MAN'S contest,' said Eubalos, wistfully to Orchas. 'Oh, how I remember winning round after round, and you would win the cakes too. I haven't forgotten. All I can do now is be a judge and enjoy watching.'

'I will enjoy more than just watching,' boasted old Orchas.

'I hope my son doesn't make a fool of himself,' confided Eubalos. 'Why has Phalinus asked Theo to be a guest at his house tonight, I wonder?'

Orchas, knowing the full account from Mydon, of Theomenes' encounter with Phalinus at the gate, didn't answer.

The two men, master and servant, walked the wet streets to the house of Phalinus, stepping out of the way of people tarring their doors to ward off bad luck. While the shades of the dead walked abroad, so could evil, and every precaution was being taken. Baskets of buckthorn were on display everywhere, the leaves bought by the fearful, to be chewed in order to purge the body of any malevolent impurities, the branches being used to cleanse the house of evil spirits. From the groups of merrymakers wandering about unsteadily, some with their Dionysian masks askew, it was evident that some parties had already started and they received several jovial invitations to join in, as they made their way to the villa area near the acropolis.

Clytes thought he stood a very good chance of winning against these Plataean rustics, especially with Glaucus locked up. He bragged to Anthousa and Sappha that he wasn't the 'wine god' only in costume! He was overwhelmed with invites to take part in the competitions, which would carry on throughout the night, but he found it harder than he'd presumed. These Plataeans could drink! He did win some of the ceremonial cakes and in all fairness decided to share them with Glaucus at the guardhouse, together with 'the ladies', if the guards were still friendly.

After the heat of the previous days, people now looked to the skies. A storm was building. Zeus the cloud-gatherer, first cloaked the moon, then sent down torrents of his life giving rain which poured off the rooftops into the streets. Kaikias, god of the north-east wind, released from his island prison, blew across the plain, driving the rain like darts into the city. The flower garlands were soon torn apart and floated down the streets. Torches were extinguished. Streets were plunged into darkness.

On the mountain, wolves howled.

By the time they reached the jail-house they were drenched, and the trio were relieved to reach shelter. Clytes called out to the guards, and held up the skins of wine as an inducement for them to be admitted without the usual inquisition. The guards had changed since his previous visit, and they were not in a festive mood.

'What do you want here?' shouted the soldier, Timotheos, angrily, illuminated by the brazier on top of the tower.

'We have come to celebrate the festival with the prisoner, and we bring wine and cake for the watch!' shouted Clytes, hopefully.

'Be gone from here, actor!' shouted Artemon, who was also on the watchtower. 'There will be no admittance tonight!' Clytes proceeded to argue but was rewarded with a stone being thrown and the three friends had to admit defeat.

'My oratory skills must be dulled by the wine. Well, you can't win them all,' said Clytes, trying to make light of things. As they made to leave, he glanced up at the tower. Something odd was going on.

THIRTEEN

'THE ORACLES HOLD GOOD, sire,' spoke Mirhab, quietly. From the cover of the pines and thick underbrush on the lower mountain slopes, the three-hundred looked down, grim faced, on the unsuspecting city. Bonfires could be seen smouldering, doused by the rain and torches were hurriedly carried through the streets by the late night revelers.

'It's ours for the taking!' replied Lykaon, fiercely. 'Now, it all depends on Naucleides.'

Behind them in the woods, shields collided, the metallic ring resonating alarmingly. He would have dealt sharply with the offenders at any other time but he was impatient to get down off the mountain. The weather was worsening. Wolves could be heard not far off; and the men were eager for action. All eyes were on the east gate of the city, where a signal was expected, indicating that all was in readiness. This was a precarious part of a well organised plan. If Naucleides' treachery had been discovered, it could be a trap.

Lykaon thought back to the auspicious oracle and smiled, grimly. This was his destiny. It was foretold by the great Zeus, the father of all the gods - and the scheming Larachne, the adulterous wife of his uncle. It was her shrewd reasoning that the more distance put between his consultation with the all-knowing gods and enemy ears - and those of her weak husband - the better. So, due to his own arrogance and also because he valued the advice of the ambitious, seductive Larachne, the mysteries of Apollo shown to the prophetess at Delphi were dismissed; in favour of a future envisaged by Zeus, revealed to three old women living near an ancient oak tree at Dodona. Subsequently, the previous autumn; bearing offerings for the dual deities at the sanctuary; fine Persian silk provided by his co-conspirator for the goddess Dione, and a splendid bronze dagger of his own for the god Zeus, he had set out on an arduous journey north; to a land of mountains, rolling thunder and bitter cold winds.

The words of the oracle were burned into his memory.

Thebes will rule all Boeotia under Sparta. Zeus is displeased with prideful Plataea. The temple built to honour his daughter, Athena, now honours Agristones and 'The Shield'. He awaits the man of courage who will restore his daughter's house.

Lykaon had no doubt he was that man. He amended the prophecy only slightly and deleted two words - 'under Sparta'. Now it was perfect!

During the ensuing months, he had done all he could to ensure the omens ran true by placing spies in Plataea to note the movements of the garrison, and the guard changes on the city gates. Eurymachus had done much to persuade some of the nobles to remember their Boeotian ancestry, and had promised them positions of power in return for their leadership in these uncertain times. Phalinus especially, was watched discreetly, his movements regularly noted by Theban sympathisers.

A hand gripped Lykaon's shoulder, tightly. It was Mirhab, his second-in-command.

'The tower beacon! It's the first signal, captain. They have secured the gate!' he exclaimed, eagerly. Word was passed back through the trees to the anxiously waiting men and their captains quickly issued commands for cloaks to cover all shields and to expect orders to advance. The honour of leading the advance guard had been awarded by Pythangelus to his nephew and it was Lykaon's company of one-hundred that led the way down the slippery mountain slopes towards the city walls.

FOURTEEN

CLYTES STAMPED OUT THE torch he was carrying and the trio were immediately plunged into near darkness. The only light now came from a tower beacon where the Eleusinian thought he'd seen something happening. Signalling? Treading through the mud, he pulled the women brusquely towards shelter, under the awning of a barn which stood within viewing distance of the East Gate. 'What's going on?' muttered Anthousa, testily. Her short sodden hair was like a black cap and droplets of rain fell from her nose. 'Why all the drama? Glaucus will miss a skinful of wine - so what?'

'I know those two soldiers,' muttered Clytes almost to himself, his mind racing. 'Glaucus and I recently had a difference of opinion with them. I want to stay around for a while - make sure the 'big man' isn't in trouble.'

'We're all going to drown if we don't get out of this rain,' said Sappha, miserably. 'You can visit him later,' she suggested, eager to leave the dismal place.

Before Clytes could reply, a sudden activity at the gatehouse made him signal to the girls to be quiet. Emerging from the guardroom came several figures and from the rushlights they carried, the Eleusinian could see they were equipped for combat. The three watchers stared in bewilderment as the bar to the gate was lifted and soldiers dragged open the wide gates. Almost immediately, marching purposefully through the opening into the light of the torches, came a relentless column of heavily armed hoplites. Beneath their open helmets, determination and self-confidence was written on every visage. The soldiers paused as they entered the environs of the walled plateau as though waiting for orders, and Clytes watched intently as a second brazier was lit. After some moments, more of their numbers then poured through the gates, led by their richly armoured commanders, before the entire column advanced quickly on its way towards the centre. Despite the poor light, Clytes was able to identify their insignia.

'Who are they?' Sappha asked, fearfully.

'Thebans!' Clytes, whispered. 'Your neighbours. They're trying to cover their shields but I noticed the club of Heracles.'

'But what are they doing here?' she asked, unable to make sense of what she was seeing.

'Well, they've not come for the celebrations. Look at their strength of arms. Plataea is being invaded!' Clytes told her. 'You must warn the city! Get to anyone you know in authority.'

The two women looked bewildered. 'Our clients are not from that class, darling,' replied Anthousa, apologetically.

'Well someone in the garrison?' suggested Clytes, urgently. 'Surely they're not all celibate!'

The two girls replied as one. 'Diokles!' they responded. 'What are you going to do?' asked Anthousa, worried.

'I'm going to wait here,' he replied, 'and try and get an idea of their numbers. And I've got to find out what's happened to Glaucus.'

Anthousa hesitated. 'Go!' Clytes, urged. 'Keep to the back-streets and don't get caught!'

The rain was as relentless as the invading force, and the route across the plateau quickly became churned to ankle deep mud by the soldiers' boots. Finally, he watched the column vanishing into the driving rain and the gateway stood open and empty. Under cover of the storm, he darted towards the gatehouse and hid beneath the steps leading to the tower, watching for any movement. His prayers were answered in the form of Timotheos, descending from the look-out. Clytes grabbed him by the neck and wrenching the dagger from the soldier's belt, pressed the blade against his throat.

'Keep out of this play-actor!' Timotheos spat, contemptuously. 'Get back to your whores!'

He tried to break free only for Clytes to squeeze the harder. Half-choked, the son of Naucleides was dragged under the steps and stripped of his weapons. Clytes listened for any sounds of activity. Most of the welcoming guard had left with the invasion force, but there could be others.

When he picked up the sword, his face darkened. It was like shaking hands with an old friend. One he'd tried hard to forget. Memories flooded back of fear and pain and were quickly pushed away. 'Get up!' he snarled. 'Now - open the jail, and the prisoner had better be alive or you'll be sorry!'

Glaucus was not alone. Shackled with him and only barely conscious was Alexeis, together with an enraged Stephanos, and two others. One was the jailor from the previous night. The other was Simonedes, a soldier of the watch. 'Release them!' Clytes ordered.

'What in Hades is going on?' boomed Glaucus, after releasing more than a few joyful exclamations at seeing Clytes. 'These Plataeans are not very hospitable, my friend!'

Clytes hauled him upright and he immediately started stamping his feet and rubbing his legs furiously. 'Chain him!' said Clytes, pushing Timotheos to the floor.

Simonedes, a friend of Alexeis, shook his comrade gently and managed to get him to stand. 'They overpowered us,' Simonedes explained. 'Timotheos struck Alexeis - hard!' he added, angrily, and he kicked the son of Naucleides viciously in the ribs. 'Alex saved your skin many a time, during training. You piece of shit!' he shouted at him.

After allowing them all a swig of the wine brought by Clytes, Stephanos cried, 'All of you who are able, follow me! We have work to do!' They headed for the two towers, flanking the gate - three men to each tower.

Cautiously they mounted the steps. The wind was much stronger on the top and the noise covered their approach. Artemon was clearly seen in the glow of the flaring brazier. Wrapped in his cloak, the rain streaming from his helmet, he was staring intently towards the river, looking for any signs of approaching torchlights which would signify the arrival of the main Theban force.

'Put down your weapons, Artemon!' shouted Alexeis, who was supported by Simonedes. 'We have Timotheos.' The look that passed through the soldier's eyes was not lost on Clytes.

Ah, more than mere comrades, then, he smiled to himself. From the second tower, there came sounds of action and across the bridge uniting the towers, came Glaucus and Stephanos together with the jailor, dragging two Theban hoplites.

'Now, talk!' yelled Stephanos to the chained prisoners, taking the place of Glaucus on the floor of the jailhouse. They needed little persuasion, and from the boastful information given, it was as Clytes had feared. This was just the advance guard. The main army was on its way. They set about closing the gate and to make it difficult for anyone to reopen it, Stephanos jammed a spear head into the bolt, then broke off the shaft.

'You must get to Phalinus!' said Stephanos urgently to a pale Alexeis, still weak from the blow. 'He will know what to do,' he added, positively. It was decided that Glaucus and Clytes should accompany him.

'A good walk in the rain will kill or cure!' boomed Glaucus, and with the young man supported between them, they followed the muddy trail left by the invading column, fearful of what they would find. Stephanos, Simonedes and the jailor, stayed behind to guard the gate and to ensure it remained closed.

FIFTEEN

THE VILLA OF PHALINUS reflected the openness of life enjoyed during the Anthesteria. Throughout the day groups of people had come and gone, citizens and slaves, women and children. During the three days of the festival no doors would be closed. Theomenes had never been to the villa before and could not help his feeling of pride when his shocked father told him of the special invitation. Also invited were Orchas and Mydon because on this day, slaves also took part in the contests, as equal competitors with their masters.

The custom was according to the myth of King Pandion of Athens, and the unexpected arrival at his house of his friend Orestes, who had recently murdered his own mother. Because the king did not want to turn away his friend, but also not contaminate his other guests with his crime, he devised a way of the symposium continuing but without offence. So, unlike the usual situation, where conversation was considered obligatory and everyone shared wine from the same krater, he made everyone drink at independent tables, drink from separate cups and also in silence. In compensation for the lack of discourse, he made it a competition. Whoever downed his cup first, won a round. Whoever won the most rounds, was presented with a filled wine-skin.

Theomenes did not try to win any of the rounds. He was forever conscious of his father, the judge at the competition, and it would be all too easy for him to break the rules of silence. Also on his mind was his brother Alexeis, who was on watch at the East Gate, in the wind and the rain - his first night on duty as a new member of the city garrison. Much as he felt honoured to be a guest that night with so many nobles, he would have preferred to be in his brother's place.

The rounds continued due to the extravagant generosity of Naucleides who had, at his own expense, presented several jars of excellent Thasian wine to the symposium, very little of which, Theomenes noticed, he drank himself. The rules of silence were hard to keep and many were beginning to drop out. Heads nodded forward and some fell asleep, including Orchas.

Phalinus and Eupompides were of only a few left in the competition when a commotion in the outer room made Phalinus suddenly jump to his feet. Before he could reach the door, it burst open. It was Diokles. Rainwater ran from his helmet and military cloak. He gripped a sword and his eyes were filled with urgency. 'Armed Thebans, my lord! They are in the city!'

Eubalos looked at his son. His haunted eyes conveyed one word - Alexeis.

Before anyone could make a rush for the door, Naucleides motioned for everyone to stay where they were. He was joined by some of the men in the room and they surrounded Phalinus. 'What is going on?' demanded Eupompides, his eyes blazing in fury. 'Do you know anything, Naucleides? Speak!'

'You no longer give orders here!' glared Naucleides. 'We have taken over Plataea on behalf of the Boeotian League,' he announced, haughtily. 'Athens no longer holds authority here. Thebes is our capital. Plataea is under our control, but there will be no bloodshed if everyone stays calm and does as they are told. Do not resist. It will only result in unnecessary killings. The men of the town are too drunk to fight. The people will understand where their allegiance lies. They are Boeotians. It is their natural heritage.'

Diokles was relieved of his spear and short sword by two men from Naucleides' household, then shoved into the room to join the other adherents of The Shield Guardian. Theomenes had to support his father who was overcome with shock. From another room, where several other slaves, male and female, had been enjoying a similar evening, there was shouting, as into the symposium they came, herded like animals - Mydon among them -being beaten unnecessarily by followers of Naucleides. He immediately tried to get to his young master, but felt the slash of a cane across his back, forcing him to huddle with the other slaves in a corner of the room.

'You will come with us to the agora, Phalinus,' Naucleides asserted, no longer giving the noble his title. 'You can see with your own eyes that any resistance is futile. 'Talk to the people as I have indicated. Your family is safe - for the moment!' he added, threateningly. 'The rest of you will remain here until you are sent for,' he said, looking directly at Eubalos.

Trying to maintain calm, Phalinus did as was commanded. He was marched to the marketplace, under armed guard, uncertain of what awaited him there. As he passed through the streets, he saw inebriated citizens, totally unaware of the events unfolding around them.

What fools we've been, he thought, passionately. His heart beat faster on seeing the force of arms occupying his city. The agora was ablaze with torches spluttering in the driving rain, the look of cruel determination on the faces of the Theban soldiers, sending shock waves through his scrambled thoughts. His first priority, he realised, was to gain time. Time, in order to fully assess the situation. Time to get a runner sent to Athens with the dire news, and await reinforcements. Time for people to sober up!

SIXTEEN

PHALINUS WAS TAKEN STRAIGHT to the bouleuterion, now heavily guarded by enemy troops, standing grimly in the continuing downpour. Inside the Assembly Hall, there was chaotic activity with groups of Plataeans talking urgently with one another. On seeing Phalinus, they rushed towards him, calling out his name in relief. Admetus came forward and took his hand. 'Treachery, Phalinus! We have been betrayed by our own people!' The Shield Guardian went calmly from one group to another trying to bring reassurance, as more people were dragged or pushed into the chamber. Eubalos and his son Theomenes were brought in and immediately sought the comfort of friends already there, questioning anyone with information as to any news of Alexeis.

The citizens were split in their opinions as to just how dire was their situation. A fair proportion thought nothing would happen. Athens would come to their aid. Others brought up the 'oath' sworn by the Spartans, fifty years previously when Pausanias, the Spartan general, in gratitude for Plataea's heroic stand against Xerxes the mighty King of Persia, made all the allies swear to protect the city for evermore against unjust aggression or enslavement.

'We are on holy ground!' declared the historian, Admetus. 'The Spartans will never break the oath!' Several voices in the crowded chamber shouted eagerly in agreement.

'But these aren't Spartans!' shouted a fearful voice from within the crowd.

Keas, the silver merchant, motioned to be heard, his ample belly quivering with the exertion. He was concerned about the wealth held in the shrine and temple treasuries beyond the city walls. The importer Timasion seemed only concerned for his shipment of animal hides due to arrive shortly at the port of Kreusis. Other merchants were vociferous about their stockpiles of goods, all distribution stalled.

Phalinus looked at them as a father would look at his children. It is the shock, he thought, sadly. This is not the time to be worrying about trade agreements. His main concern was to keep everyone calm until he could get more information as to the size of the Theban force; assess the number of Plataeans that had turned their allegiance to Thebes, and to determine whether Naucleides could be trusted - when he said there would be no bloodshed.

A shout from the main entrance silenced everyone. Hoplites, with weapons drawn, roughly pushed the frightened people aside, opening up an avenue through the room towards the dais. In their wake came two richly armoured nobles, Pythangelus and Diemporus, Boetarchs of Thebes. They were followed by Eurymachus, a Theban noble of great influence and co-conspirator of the treacherous Plataean, Naucleides. Behind them came several citizens recognised by the crowd, and cries of, 'Shame!' and 'Traitor!', were heard from every quarter. Limaois, father of the feisty Marissa, was one of the traitors. Callias, host of the presentation to Admetus, another.

A herald announced Pythangelus and he strode onto the dais, calling for calm. 'Plataeans! Fellow Boeotians!' he announced, vigorously. 'We represent the Boeotian League and we are here to free you from your enslavement and the tyranny of grasping Athens! The increasing dominance of Athens must be stopped, and we welcome you back into the League as brothers and fellow adversaries of these unwelcome intruders in our land. Ill-winds are coming which will blow across our neighbouring plains, and we must stand together in remembrance of our common ancestry in order to withstand the onslaught. If you agree to our terms, I give you my word that no harm will come to you.'

'I don't believe that,' murmured Admetus to Eubalos. 'They will want to put their own oligarchs in our place. And since when were we brothers?'

As if he had overheard the old historian, Naucleides angrily pushed his way through the crowd. 'This is not what was promised to us by Eurymachus!' he shouted at the Boetarchs. 'Why do you think we in Plataea helped you to bring about this successful outcome? Not to live in fear for our own lives! We demand that our enemies be eliminated, as was agreed!'

There was uproar in the chamber and more soldiers were quickly ordered in; roughly crowding the people to the rear of the chamber. Phalinus had to be restrained by several Plataeans as he tried to reach Naucleides. 'That man is mine!' he swore vehemently, in a sudden burst of anger.

'The choice is yours!' boomed Diemporus, now on the dais. 'Join us and there will be no violence!' The Boetarchs were well aware that the main body of their army, one-thousand strong, had not yet reached the city. Their small advance-guard could well be vulnerable to a counter-attack. Keeping the populace in ignorance of this fact was imperative until reinforcements arrived.

With palpable fear of reprisals if they didn't agree, and hopeful of the promise of no violence against them if they did, the frightened and confused citizens voted reluctantly to accept the Theban terms.

Eubalos, Chief Magistrate and respected Elder of Plataea, was instructed to speak to the people crowding into the agora, anxious for news. Accompanied by the two Theban Boetarchs and Eurymachus, he looked suddenly old and frail. For a brief moment, Zeus illuminated the city, as lightning flashed and crackled over the mountain tops and thunder rolled across the plain.

'Be calm!' called out Eubalos, and he looked up at the skies as though speaking to the god himself, then down at the waiting populace. 'Do not be afraid. Your council has negotiated with our Theban neighbours and we have been promised that no harm will come to us.' There were shouts of anger from the crowd, that violence had already been perpetrated, but when Eurymachus menacingly placed his hand on the shoulder of Eubalos, there was a sudden hush.

'Please return to your homes,' said Eubalos, worried that trouble could erupt at any moment. 'We are in no danger,' he added, glancing nervously at Pythangelus.

Under a curfew which only the Thebans knew they had not the numbers to enforce, the people were ordered back to their homes. Phalinus and other possible trouble-makers were accompanied by an armed guard, and placed under house-arrest.

SEVENTEEN

A STORM WAS RAGING OVER southern Boeotia, flooding the plains and swelling the rivers. While time permitted, Clytes, Glaucus and Alexeis were urgently spreading the word to those not under guard, the Theban force being insufficient to monitor the entire city.

Imbros was shaken and confused as he left the Bouleuterian, his nerves on edge as he skirted the pandemonium of the torch-lit marketplace on his way back to Amara. A gasp parted his lips when he glimpsed a figure in the darkness. Hiding in the shadows was Clytes, his head and face covered by his wet cloak. Only his piercing eyes revealed the tension he was feeling. Clytes grabbed Imbros by his tunic, forcing him against the wall.

'What faction are you!' he snarled. 'Athens or Thebes?'

Uncertain as to how he should reply, Imbros asked, 'Tell me who you are, first!'

The actor, feeling he had nothing to lose, told him he was a travelling player from Eleusis.

Relieved, Imbros replied, 'We are neighbours. I am Athenian born. I've seen you - in the agora - you were talking to my wife! At any other time, I'd beat your head in!'

'Ha!' said Clytes. 'Better save your fists for the Thebans!'

'We have surrendered, haven't you heard?' Imbros told him, his voice filled with anger and shame.

'Can you get me to someone in authority - now?' urged Clytes, and remembering the name the women had dreamily spoken of, he said, 'Phalinus?'

'He is under house-arrest,' replied Imbros. 'What does an actor want with Phalinus? You'd better tell me what's going on.'

At the house of Theanatus, a renowned visionary and friend of Plataea's general, Eupompides, Alexeis was being gripped by the shoulders.

'Are you sure that's what you saw?' asked Theanatus, his eyes staring, trying to visualise what he was being told.

'I was there!' protested Alexeis. 'I heard what Timotheos and Artemon said. They were boasting that it was only a matter of time before the main army reached the city. Only a few hundred came through the gates, and Glaucus, Clytes and I followed them to the agora. No other soldiers arrived. The main army has been held up at the Asopus! You are my last hope. Everyone else is under armed-guard. Theanatus, you of all people should know what to do!' he urged.

The young seer paced the room. 'Eupompides, Phalinus, Diokles!' he exclaimed. 'Our men of strength are under house-arrest and impossible to reach! Alexeis, if I hadn't at the last moment accepted an invitation to the house of a good friend, I would be with them! My friend's guests had travelled a long way and were in need of my services, otherwise I also would have been at the house of Phalinus for the contests. Obviously, that is what Naucleides expected. We don't have much time,' he said, urgently. 'We have to spread the word quickly.'

Later, at the house of Imbros, in the dim light of a single oil-lamp, men were gathered together to listen to the messenger recently arrived from the hastily devised headquarters of the soothsayer.

'Theanatus thinks they will be at their weakest just before dawn,' he told them, earnestly. 'But timing will be crucial. Any later and they will see their way around the city. It has to be while it is still dark. The signal will be one long blast on a horn. Are we all in agreement?'

'We aren't the subjects of Athens or Thebes!' spoke up young Theomenes, passionately. 'We can fight our own fights!'

Eubalos looked on sadly. 'You have no experience of war, Theo. I'm not saying I disagree with you, but I am afraid of the consequences if we do this. I am an old man and my time is running out. I fear for your generation, Theo.'

Georgios, a young relative of Amara, was as eager as Theomenes for a fight. 'We make our own decisions in Plataea! We're an independent city-state and Thebes has no authority over us. We can defeat them!' All the men, citizens and slaves, with the exception of Eubalos, moved to the centre of the room, eagerly grasping each other's hands, their eyes bright with determination.

'Let us give up prayers to our protectress,' said Eubalos, quietly. Imbros led them to stand before his beautiful but much smaller copy of the imposing Athena statue - now guarding The Marathon Shield in her locked temple. 'We need her to give guidance to Theanatus on his proposed strategy,' he added, with conviction. 'The gods demand sacrifices when men try to emulate them!'

As they left the room, Eubalos grasped Theomenes by his arm. 'Find Alexeis!' he pleaded. Theomenes turned to Georgios. 'Are you with me?' he asked, thrilled beyond belief that his father entrusted him with this responsibility. The too young and too eager Georgios, replied, 'I am, Theo!'

Wherever houses were crowded together, nimble messengers, some of them children, leapt from rooftop to rooftop, spreading news of the planned revolt. Through open windows, messages were thrown and under cover of darkness and the lashing rain, brave souls crept down the alleyways distributing whatever weapons could be found. A terrible fear of being under the cruel yoke of the Thebans, galvanised the Plataeans into taking action. They were aware that the main force of the Theban army could arrive at their gates at any moment and speed was of the essence.

Night was their ally. Torches and lamps were extinguished. They would rely on their own intimate knowledge of the streets and landmarks. Under cover of the noise of the storm, barricades in the form of carts and wagons were dragged to block strategic arteries of the city, and people passed secretly from one part of town to another by breaking through the clay brick walls of their houses. The family of Loukios the dyer, watched with mixed emotions as their much admired fresco of a ferocious lion being attacked by a pack of wolves, was fast reduced to rubble. A scene which Loukios boasted he had actually witnessed on their own mountain of Cithaeron, while out hunting.

In the crowded downtown quarter of taverns and whorehouses, Glaucus had been busy spreading the word with the help of Sappha and Anthousa. The men and women, slaves included, of this poor area, were as enraged at the invasion as the more affluent Plataeans and were just waiting for the signal to use the weapons they had hastily gathered together, which included several heavy cooking pots.

A small scene of normality witnessed by Anthousa was of Glaucus, happy at their reunion, presenting a delighted Sappha with a pretty comb which, despite the urgency of their situation, she instantly fixed into her cropped dark hair.

EIGHTEEN

THEANATUS GAVE THE ORDER and the soldier, taking a deep breath, blew the signal. Around them men of the lower city, freemen and slaves, called on their respective gods, adding prayers for their mothers and loved ones. 'No lights and no noise,' he murmured as his instructions were passed on down the darkened alley, where more Plataeans were gathering. 'You all know where to go. May Athena be guiding us this night!' Emerging from the narrow alleyway, the men diverged and through the unlit streets, two wet streams of men moved silently towards the agora. People poured out of their houses to join them, women included, bringing whatever weapons they could lay their hands on.

In the agora, the Thebans had been startled by the sudden, mournful sound of the horn, and Lykaon shouted exultantly to Mirhab. 'It's our main force! They've arrived!'

Before he could say more, loud shouting could be heard from all sides of the marketplace, and charging at them from the plateau came hundreds of Plataeans, screaming and yelling, weapons raised. The Thebans, although cold and wet from their night in the rain, were well trained professionals and immediately formed a circle, grounding their spears into the earth to form a defensive barricade of brutal spikes; their shields held ready to fend off their assailants. Within their tight formation, they were impregnable and easily repulsed the attacking force. At first the Plataeans found it impossible to break it, with several of their number falling under a hail of javelins. Time and again they charged with their spears, pushing the

Thebans tighter together, but they were unable to get close enough to use their swords, until from the rooftops, missiles of tiles and bricks began to rain down on the invaders. The women and slaves of the town, Anthousa and Sappha included, were stripping the roofs of anything that could be dismantled, and with terrifying screams, hurled down their projectiles relentlessly onto the heads of the Thebans. Unable to protect themselves from above and below, they finally broke ranks. In disarray they fled the agora, seeking cover in the surrounding streets. In the darkness, they realised too late that many alleyways were blocked, and being unable to form an effective defence, many found themselves trapped and at the mercy of the enraged Plataeans. Bombarded yet again, from windows and rooftops above them, the Thebans became disorientated and those who weren't killed or captured, fled in all directions. The city was fighting for its life.

Theanatus, accompanied by scores of Plataeans, headed towards the upper-city to rescue Phalinus and the others. The Theban guards were watchful - they had heard the trumpet blast but had no way of knowing the reason for it.

'It's all over!' shouted Theanatus. 'You are outnumbered! Die if you wish or put down your weapons and surrender to us, now!'

Seeing how many Plataeans surrounded them, and hearing their shouts of anger, they reluctantly capitulated. Other men were similarly freed from the upper-city and together with Eupompides, Phalinus and Diokles they sped towards the agora. Weapons taken from the Theban prisoners were quickly distributed among the men, who'd previously only carried slingshots or tools.

Lykaon having evaded his pursuers, and being furnished with a plan of the city by Theban sympathisers, knew exactly where to go. He shouted to Mirhab and the dozen or so of his men who hadn't fled already, to follow him.

'Get them to the temple!' he ordered Mirhab. 'We're going for The Shield, while we have time!'

Because of the festival, they found the temple locked and the usual attendants absent, but a large dog, disturbed from its chained sleep, immediately leapt up, barking ferociously - teeth bared. A loud cursing came from one of his men, then a gargled scream as the dog bit into his ankle. The soldier savagely dispatched the animal, then kicked it to one side.

'Break it open!' Lykaon ordered, angrily.

The only objects heavy enough for battering-rams were two tall tripods of heavy bronze, ornately decorated with owls, a symbol of Athena, standing each side of the temple entrance. His men unceremoniously heaved them from their place of honour, and after several attempts, zealously smashed through the bolts of the great wooden doors. Inside, the temple was aglow with the ever-burning oil lamps, illuminating the magnificent statue of the Goddess Athena. The young female lamp attendants were cowering behind her and screamed for mercy when the grim-faced soldiers burst through the doors. They soon realised the intruders had no interest in them, and inching their way towards the open doors, fled into the night. Behind them they heard the crashing sounds of their temple being mercilessly stripped of her treasures.

Theomenes, accompanied by Georgios and Mydon broke away from Imbros and the other men of the artisan quarter and headed in the direction of the East Gate, seeing all about them their fellow Plataeans in scenes from their worst imaginings. Groups of women, wailing as they carried away their dead loved ones, blood and mud splattered. Bodies of Thebans, their armour stripped from them, left to bleed in the red rivulets now spreading throughout the city. Theomenes hesitated on seeing the drenched, bloodied body of a comely slave, her short hair decorated by a pretty comb. Whoever bought that trinket will miss her, he thought. Fighting back his feeling of nausea, he knelt down and swiftly covered her mangled body as best he could with her scanty garments. Screams and shouts could be heard all around them and through the streets, packs of barking dogs ran wild, crazed by the smell of blood.

The three young men also felt the blood lust and took off in baying pursuit when they saw a Theban soldier, running disorientated, towards the altar of Zeus. Before they could reach him, he crashed forward, struck through the neck with an arrow. Stunned, they stopped running and looked all around, warily. From behind the altar came Epiktetos, 'Hawk-Eye' to those who knew his skills with the bow.

'You could have let us have him!' cried out Theomenes, angrily.

'I've saved your lives, children!' called out the archer. 'All three of you together were no match for a cornered hoplite. If you're looking for action, I would advise you to join forces with men of experience!'

'You could join us?' Theomenes suggested, with fake bravado. 'We're going to find out if Alexeis is alright. He was on duty at the East Gate earlier.'

Epiktetos jumped down from the plinth to join them. 'Alexeis is fine, Theo. He was involved in some action at the watch but he has recovered. I saw him earlier with that giant of a man. The one with the flaming red hair. The redhead was swinging a double-headed axe! Never seen anything like it, Theo! What a sight he looked. I saw him take a Theban's head clean off with one stroke. Quite a few surrendered after that!'

Theomenes was both relieved and sorry to hear the news of his brother, and he and Mydon exchanged looks of some disappointment. They'd both imagined a similar scene, with a grateful Alexeis rescued by his younger brother, and now they felt deflated. They were suddenly eager for some action - any action.

Shouting from the opposite side of the marketplace, made them startle and they watched as a flight of young women ran wailing across the agora. They couldn't hear what they were shouting, but suddenly a group of armed men were seen running in the direction of the Athenian Temple.

'I think they're ours!' exclaimed Epiktetos, quickly fitting a fresh arrow to his bow, and the four set off after them.

Within the temple, into the soldiers spread cloaks, were thrown gold and silver platters, candleholders and any precious statuettes that could be broken from their plinths. Mirhab, the Persian, callously kicked over the marble statue of Arimnestos, Plataea's distinguished general at the Battles of Marathon and Plataea, then he climbed up to the alcove where the embellished relic was housed, and was almost blinded by the blazing light reflected in the gold and precious stones. It took four strong men to catch it in a spread out cloak, as Mirhab toppled it from its home, so heavy was the ornamentation.

'Head back to the eastern gate we came in by!' Lykaon ordered his men. 'And don't stop for anyone!'

He stood over The Shield, and quickly controlled a feeling of awe as he looked at the famous relic.

'It's just an ordinary hoplon, covered with gold!' he barked, as his men held back from lifting it. He spat on it to emphasise his contempt.

At that moment a roar of rage was heard and all eyes looked towards the portico. Phalinus and several armed men were charging through the open doorway. They had arrived from bitter hand-to-hand fighting in the streets, and blood lust made them wild-eyed and terrifying. The looters quickly dropped their heavy bundles and prepared to meet their attackers. Around the feet of the enormous statue, under the gaze of the goddess, unblinking and seemingly unconcerned, began a desperate struggle for survival.

NINETEEN

PHALINUS SAW HIS OPPORTUNITY and quickly brought down his first adversary before the Theban hoplite could lift his shield. A quick thrust through his exposed neck, cut a main artery and blood gushed across the marble floor. Badly done, thought Phalinus angrily, as, struggling to keep from sliding, he turned to punch another soldier hard in the face with his shield, before smashing the heavy handle of his sword into his skull. The crashing sounds of metal on metal resounded around the temple as the Thebans fought ferociously to escape with their stolen acquisitions. Lykaon jumped onto the plinth of the great statue and, protected by Athena's immense shield, ornamented with the fearful image of Medusa, was able to cause harm to whoever approached him. 'Come down, you coward!' shouted Diokles who was below him but unable to touch him. The sound of excited young voices coming from the main entrance, made him glance back momentarily, and he immediately felt the cut of Lykaon's heavy blade. Dropping his shield, he grabbed his useless left arm, a hanging flap of skin exposing bloody muscle and bone. An arrow flew past the veteran soldier, and struck the throat of a Theban poised to strike him down.

Theomenes and his friends, Georgios and Epiktetos, together with Mydon, could hear the commotion as they rushed up the temple steps, but were not prepared for what they saw or what they could smell. Blood was everywhere, making the marble beneath their feet slippery. Georgios nearly gagged. Mixed with the sweat and the fear, it was something the youth had never experienced. Epiktetos was the first to gain control and quickly dispatched a soldier next to Diokles, then grabbing a sword that had been dropped, leapt forward, hacking wildly at a shield held defensively by one of the Thebans. Georgios, with a blade given to him by his father, followed his lead, yet before he could even raise it, he fell forward, a great gash opening up his back. He said the word, 'Mother!' and was still. Theomenes and Mydon rushed to him, but his life was gone. They pulled his limp body out through the entrance, in a state of shock.

Lykaon could see that his plan to take the precious relic was about to fail. It was too heavy. He shouted to Mirhab to hack off the jewels. The rubies, emeralds and sapphires were promised to Larachne. The Wolf of Thebes jumped down from the statue and entered the fray. In full hoplite armour, unlike most of the Plataeans, he ferociously taunted his opponents, and they kept well back from this manic swordsman.

Phalinus, witnessing this desecration of The Marathon Shield by a Persian, fought his way through to Mirhab, roaring at the outrage. Theomenes hearing this, picked up his sword and rushed to his aid, with Mydon bearing his shield, pushing in after him. Time seemed to stand still for the young Theo as he fought side by side with his idol, slashing wildly, hoping to make contact, with Mydon desperately trying to protect him. The image of the club of Heracles suddenly blocked out his view and the blow from the shield knocked Theomenes off his feet. He was on his back in the mire with trampling feet all around him. Over him stood a sweating Theban soldier, his sword raised. Mydon, using the shield he carried to strike at the attacker, tried to force the hoplite away, but he had little effect. Theomenes thrust his feet forward kicking hard at the soldier's legs and the blade missed his chest but struck deeply into his groin. Phalinus, seeing the boy go down, turned his shield to deflect a second deadly blow from the Theban's sword. It was a noble act, but a fatal error. With no time to fasten his cuirass, the movement caused a gap to open up between his front and back armour plates. Lykaon seized his chance. Thrusting his sword deep into Phalinus' side, he twisted it cruelly, grinning triumphantly. He knew it was a mortal wound. The blade had pierced his heart.

When Phalinus fell, the Plataeans ceased their fighting and rushed to him, the Thebans momentarily forgotten. Those still able, fled from the temple, Lykaon shouting at them to follow him. Mirhab, the powerful Persian who had cut down young Georgios, ran out into the night still carrying his looted gold.

Their blood mingling as it flowed across the temple floor, Theo lay transfixed, staring into the dead eyes of his hero.

TWENTY

AMARA AND HER HOUSEMAID Ianthe, had taken refuge on the upper floor of the villa, and locked themselves into the bedroom furthest from the street. The men of the household had joined the revolt, even portly Cosmas the cook, and he had never handled a weapon in his life due to his nearsightedness. When they heard shouting coming from below them, they were terrified, but it was only Cosmas returning with news that Imbros was safe and bearing his strict instructions that on no account were they to leave the house. No sooner had he left the women, when they heard more commotion, this time it was raised voices. 'Mistress!' called out Cosmas in alarm. 'It is your cousin, Marissa!' Amara quickly unlocked the door and rushed down the stairs, Ianthe not far behind her. 'He pushed past me!' said the stout cook, glaring at the man with Marissa. 'It's alright, Cosmas,' said Amara, trying hard not to be alarmed by what she saw.

The pair standing before her were almost unrecognisable. Gone was the confidence, the haughtiness. Nicander looked like a noble animal, cornered, ready to strike. Marissa, obviously in love, looked desperate.

'We had nowhere else to go, cousin,' said Marissa, pleadingly. 'My father has been arrested. We had to run for our lives! You have to believe me, Amara. I knew nothing of this!' Amara felt only compassion for her kinswoman, and tears filled her eyes.

'Oh Marissa, how could your father have been so devious! So foolish! You are, of course, welcome in my house. You will stay with us, cousin.'

Marissa looked at Nicander and then back at Amara. 'I cannot stay, my dear,' she replied, taking Amara's hands. 'Nicander has to get out of the city before Eupompides finds him, and I will leave with him.'

'Who are you?' asked Amara, staring at Nicander, surprised at her boldness. Nicander, despite his wet and bedraggled state, assumed some of the nobility she had noticed when he stood next to her stocky, and not so tall husband, the night of the swings.

'I am Nicander of Sparta, first cousin of our exiled King Pleistoanax,' he stated, unflinchingly. 'My presence in your city was to act as envoy, a secret negotiator from King Archidamus - after the Thebans had successfully welcomed you back into the League. The offers I bring from Sparta are no longer relevant.'

Amara's mind was reeling. What if Imbros had been here? Nicander could have killed him, or he could have killed Nicander! 'You cannot remain here,' she said, frightened that Imbros could return at any time. 'You must leave the city before daybreak.'

'All the gates are locked and guarded, Amara,' said Marissa, desperately. 'We have tried!'

Cosmas, who had been quietly listening and shrewdly understanding the predicament his mistress was in, asked if he could make a suggestion. 'Do, Cosmas! What is it?' asked Amara, hopefully. Cosmas had been born into a poor farming family who lived near Hysiae and he and his sister were sold into slavery when they were both quite young, when his father died of a fever and their mother was unable to feed them. His first placement, he told them, was at a slaughterhouse near the East Gate, but what he told them next made them look at him with hope in their eyes. Near the twin towers, he told them there was a smaller gate; a not easy to find, postern gate. 'It will be locked and bolted, but I doubt if it will be guarded,' he suggested.

Nicander was instantly alert and eager to find this gate. 'I have to leave now! Get me anything that could break through the bolt!' Amara and Cosmas hurried off to the woodpile and Amara chose an old but large axe, which she thought Imbros would not miss. When she returned, it was apparent from the look in Marissa's eyes, that this was the last time she expected to see her cousin.

TWENTY-ONE

FEARFUL OF REPERCUSSIONS, BECAUSE of her father's involvement in the revolt, Nicander was unwilling to leave Marissa with her cousin, and was now fully committed to getting them both to Sparta. Adrenalin was pumping through him, and after so many years of military training under harsh Spartan principles, every fibre in his body was contributing to one purpose - survival. Under cover of pitch-black side streets they edged their way forward, halting momentarily when the light of carried torches passed across their place of hiding, when Nicander would cover them both in his wet cloak. All over the city, illuminated by bonfires and brandished rushlights, Marissa witnessed scenes of horror. When she saw a Theban soldier hanging by the neck, his noose a garlanded swing, she thought of another swing with sweeter memories and almost screamed. Nicander, knowing why Marissa was so affected, despite his hardened demeanor, held her close. They saw the Theban Boetarchs, Pythangelus and Diemporus, tied together with ropes, being shoved into a cart. A naked body was already slumped there. It looked like the Theban conspirator, Eurymachus, but Nicander couldn't be sure. It's not Lykaon, he thought to himself, knowing from his covert visits to Thebes for meetings with the Boetarchs, that the young man wore his hair long, like himself.

The local knowledge of Marissa enabled them to dodge and weave their way across the plateau without being caught; towards the district of warehouses, corrals and slaughterhouses mentioned by the cook, Cosmas. All they had to do now was find the postern gate without being seen, but as they looked along the wall towards the East Gate, they could see lights, and in the glare, fighting men. Nicander recognised one of them instantly, by his horse-tail hair whipping the air. Lykaon and his fellow Thebans were trying to break through the gate but were outnumbered and having a hard time of it.

Marissa suddenly shouted. 'It's here!' She came running up some steps which plunged into darkness behind her. With her wild straggled hair and burning eyes she resembled one of the Keres, the female spirits of the dead, rising from the grave. Plataea would pay a heavy price for not placating the souls of the dead, on this night of the Anthesteria, according to the ancient custom. The citizens had forgotten them. They had other matters on their minds.

Nicander, knowing he would stand a better chance of survival with some hardened soldiers as support, called out imperatively to Lykaon. 'Lykaon! To me! There is a way out!' The Theban broke away from the fighting and ran wildly towards Nicander. His energies were almost exhausted, but his will to survive was undiminished. Nicander noticed he was covered in blood and he looked deranged. With Marissa holding the axe, Nicander and Lykaon felt their way in the darkness towards the bolt and once found, the two men took turns to hack at the iron until they broke through.

Lykaon ran back up the steps, shouting to his men and the large number of fellow Theban hoplites who had made their way to the East Gate, to follow him, but they were being attacked ferociously by the Plataeans. Two of them, Stephanos and Simonedes, who had been freed with Glaucus earlier, brought down the powerful Persian, Mirhab. He seemed intent on keeping hold of his looted treasure and almost died because of it. The warrior seemed invincible. Finally, leaving his bundle behind, he managed to get away from them, running up the steps to the top of the wall and throwing himself off into nothingness. Others followed him over the top, in their desperate attempt to escape, some only to be killed by the fall.

Clytes, who had returned earlier that night, to help man the gates and give support to the Plataeans he had left there, had brought with him several of his tavern companions, as well as numerous others from that district. Their weight of numbers was their only strength, for the weapons they carried were more useful in a workshop. Suddenly, something made Clytes freeze. He heard a loud yelling and a name being called which made his blood run cold. Running towards the source, he saw a Theban hoplite, his long hair tied like a horse's tail, hanging down his back. As he watched, intensely curious, the Theban removed his helmet and quickly wiped his arm across his brow. Clytes's heart pounded. The hair was longer, but after five years the strong, dark features were still the same. 'Lykaon! At last!' he breathed. 'He's back!'

He ran towards him, yelling; brandishing a sword given to him by Alexeis, from the garrison stores. The Theban turned to face his tall lean adversary, then cursing as recognition dawned, sped down the steps and out through the postern gate into the darkness. Not stopping to see how many had escaped with them, Nicander, Marissa and Lykaon hurried from the walls of the city towards the Asopus river and the safety of Thebes.

Attacked on all sides by desperate Thebans trying to get down the steps, Clytes cursed angrily as his sworn enemy escaped him. Simonedes and Stephanos rushed to his aid and with the help of others, forced the soldiers back the way they had come. Chased in all directions as they frantically sought another exit, they were eventually cornered and forced to surrender. With the help of Zeus and his thunderbolts, the city had been saved.

Eupompides immediately sent a herald to Athens to keep them informed of the current situation. Also with the herald, went a private letter to Pericles, informing him of the tragic death of Phalinus, Shield Guardian.

TWENTY-TWO

WHEN CLYTES RETURNED, LIMPING to his lodgings, Anthousa was startled at the change in the actor's demeanor. The wounds he'd received while defending the East Gate, had been treated, although blood still seeped through the bandages. His whole body was shaking as though he had a fever and all offers of solace were refused or ignored. She had seen how he handled himself during the attack and nothing had fazed him, but something, other than the wounds, had obviously happened because this was a different Clytes. Agitated, he asked where Glaucus was, and when told he was eating at a nearby tavern, he went to find him.

Since the capture of the Theban advance force, Glaucus and Clytes were being repaid for their heroic efforts by not having to pay for any of their food or wine. In fact, people were in competition with each other to invite one or both of them to their homes as guests. Already outside of a generous breakfast of pancakes, cooked for him at the household of Corinna, the shoemaker's wife, Glaucus thought it would be rude to refuse the platter of greasy pork sausages offered by the tavern keeper. The very same man who'd been responsible for him being arrested and put in chains, and now couldn't do enough for him.

When Clytes sat down, gingerly, wincing with pain, Flamebeard was just mopping up the grease with some barley bread and offered him some. 'Lovely bread, Clytes. Fresh from Hysiae this morning. Best I've tasted!

You look as though you should be lying down, my friend,' he said with genuine concern, when he saw the ashen look on the actor's face.

Clytes picked up some bread, while glancing at the big redhead in wonder; at the bruises and gashes covering his face and arms. 'Does anything quell your appetite? I would really like to know?' he asked, good-humouredly.

Glaucus bellowed, 'I've not always been this filled out, my friend!' he said, grimacing at the memories. The redhead looked fatherly at the actor, and shaking his head at the sight of his wounds, judged Clytes just wanted to listen, so he talked on. 'We had a small farm once, my old man and I. We worked our balls off trying to make a living. All we got out of it was backache and heartache. As you know, my country breeds the best of horses, but we were no good with horses. I think it was my red hair. Seemed to spook them. It was wolves that killed the old man, in the end.' He stretched out his thick, muscled legs, rubbing them appreciatively.

Apart from a couple of hungry stray dogs, eager for scraps, and a few people rushing by with more serious matters on hand than socialising, there was little to disturb them and both men, as different in looks as two people could be, sat with their backs against the wall, both agreeing that what had happened in Plataea was just a foretaste of what could happen, if negotiations between the two friends, Pericles, the political leader of Athens and Archidamus, King of Sparta, were not successful.

'How did you end up a sailor, then?' asked Clytes, willing Glaucus to keep talking.

'Well, I was so damned eager to leave that hovel and near starvation,' rambled on Glaucus, 'I walked to the Pagasaean Gulf and got myself on the first ship that would take me. A small merchant ship heading for Lesbos. I was fifteen. Never saw my mother again. I've seen things that nearly made my eyes pop out, my lanky friend. I know every port from Sicily to The Black Sea and beyond. I fared very well at times, I can tell you, and I did my bit to support my sister. She had a handsome dowry when she married. She's on her own again now though, a widow, with a peach of a daughter. Those thieving rogues!' he shouted, angrily, remembering his stolen possessions. 'If I could only lay my hands on them!'

'Did you ever really hate anyone, Helmsman?' asked Clytes, leaning back against the wall and taking a very large gulp of wine.

'Well it wouldn't be pretty if I found the murdering wretch who killed Sappha, if that's what you mean,' said Glaucus, looking strangely at Clytes. 'What's up my friend? You seem on edge, and I don't think it's your scratches.'

'The other night, during the fighting at the East Gate, I saw someone. At least I think it was him,' replied Clytes, tensely. 'It was dark. He escaped with some of the Thebans before I could be sure.'

Glaucus put down his cup. 'Who did you think it was?' he asked, anxiously, seeing the face of his companion grow paler. 'Did he do this?' he said, pointing at the bandages.

'No, Helmsman, this has nothing to do with him. I'm referring to the bastard who destroyed my family,' Clytes answered. 'My sister, my brother and my father. My mother had died some years previously, thank the gods! Do you want to hear this?' he asked Glaucus, hopefully.

'Now, you've got me intrigued, actor - go on.'

Clytes, after a heavy sigh, continued. 'We lived in Eleusis. My sister Eupheme and I used to be attendants at the Sanctuary of Demeter. It was there I first realized I had a particular talent for the theatrical.'

'Ah, the Land of the Laughless Stone!' interrupted Glaucus. 'I married a girl from there!'

'You're married?' asked Clytes, in surprise.

'Don't sound so shocked,' replied the redhead. 'I was married. She divorced me. I know what you're thinking, you handsome bastard. How could such a scarred crag of a face as mine, attract a wife? Well I didn't always look like this. When I was younger, I could have rivalled you. Anyway, this is not about me - tell me what happened?'

'The man I speak of, Lykaon, came from Thebes with his family and friends to Eleusis for the festival,' continued Clytes, seemingly relieved to be telling the tale. 'He was wild. A bad lot. Aged about eighteen, then. My brother Ariston was so impressed by the whole glamorous family, that he became friendly with them, showing them around, making them welcome in the town. But they acted as though they owned the place, demanding the best of everything. Ariston just got too close.' Clytes stopped talking and sat staring blankly, unable to proceed.

A group of armed soldiers suddenly blocked the door of the inn, glanced around the room, one raising a hand in greeting, then moved on.

'Go on,' said the Thessalian, encouragingly.

'Lykaon became interested in my sister,' explained Clytes.' She was only fourteen and performed at The Well of the Fair Dances at the temple, during the ceremonies. The interest was not reciprocated. She was an individual, my sister, a promising poetess. Foolishly my brother started playing dice with Lykaon and his friends, and was losing more than he could afford. He thought they were cheating, but was unable to prove it.' At this point in the story, Clytes paused, then continued, talking animatedly. 'One night, they demanded he immediately pay what he owed them, but he couldn't. So Lykaon took his payment. With the help of the scum with him, he raped my sister, and killed my brother when he tried to protect her.'

'By all the gods!' gasped Glaucus. 'And during the festival. He is black-hearted, indeed! Where's your sister now?' he asked, with concern.

'She drowned herself, Glaucus,' said Clytes, quietly. He made another grab for the wine. 'My brother was just seventeen,' he continued with effort, his face hardening. 'My father died before his time, with the shock of it all. I was nearing the end of my military training and was allowed time off to attend the trial. The monster's father, Pelonus, said his son's actions were totally out of character and tried to blame the drinking of the special potion, the kykeon at The Sacred Mysteries for altering his state of mind. Ha! That went down well with the judges! He was sentenced to ten years in exile, but I knew his family would bribe the right people to get the term reduced. I've been watching for his return since that day!'

'Well, well, actor!' said Glaucus. 'And here was I thinking you only had wine and women on your mind! But how did an actor learn to fight like a demon? I've seen you in action. You didn't learn that overnight.'

'Like you, Glaucus I've spent time at sea - but under no flag,' replied the actor, defensively.

'Zeus!' swore the helmsman. 'By the look on your face, you don't mean fishing. Piracy! That's a brutal life, friend.'

'I was left with family debts to repay,' said Clytes, by way of explanation. 'You were in no danger, 'big man',' said Clytes, suddenly looking a lot older than his twenty-five years. 'It was some time ago and in Cretan waters - out of Athens' reach.'

'So, what are you going to do now?' asked Glaucus, regarding

Clytes anew.

'As soon as I'm able to walk, I'm going to Thebes, find him and kill him!' replied, Clytes, grimly.

'I guessed that's what you were going to say!' said Glaucus, thinking that the life of his new found companion was not likely to continue for much longer.

'And, what will you do now, Helmsman?' asked Clytes, a little sadly, realising their lives would soon be taking separate roads.

'I suppose I'll travel on down to Athens soon, as I'd planned. They'll be building up their fleet I expect and in need of crews. I doubt if our paths will meet again, friend, after this week,' said Glaucus, with some emotion. 'May the gods protect you in your endeavour, Clytes. If you insist on following it through.'

'If it takes me the rest of my life, I'll get him!' he promised. 'Now, where's your best wine?' he shouted to the tavern keeper. 'We have many toasts to drink!'

TWENTY-THREE

BY THE TIME DAWN had spread across the plain, and sunlight cruelly exposed the carnage and destruction which had occurred in just a few hours on one spring night, the attempted Theban takeover of Plataea was over, but deep mourning had begun.

Hatred towards the Theban prisoners was palpable and Eupompides desperately tried to keep a clear head in order to maintain control of events. By mid-morning, after the failed assault the previous night, the main force from Thebes had crossed the swollen Asopus and was now at Plataea's gates, demanding the return of their soldiers. They had received news of their defeat from the escape party, which they'd met on the road, and as Eupompides had expected, they had on the march taken many prisoners from the countryside, in revenge. They were now to be used as part of the bargaining process.

An intense period of negotiations followed, with bitter longstanding recriminations on both sides. Concerned for the safety of their fellow Plataeans who were still in the fields, the city council promised to return the prisoners, if the Thebans allowed their captives to go free, and if the army returned to their own land without causing any injury. The terms were accepted. The army retreated and the Plataeans were brought from their farms to the safety of their city fortress. The Plataeans then killed their prisoners. 'We did not say they would be returned alive!' said Eupompides, grimly. They numbered one-hundred and eighty of the original force of three-hundred, the rest having been killed during the revolt, or had escaped back to Thebes. Naucleides and his son Timotheos, Marissa's father Limaois, the wine importer Callias, and other traitorous Plataeans who had not managed to escape, were also put to the sword.

When a messenger returned from Athens, he brought instructions from the council not to harm the prisoners, until it had been decided what should be done with them. The response from the Plataeans was: 'Too late! Justice has been done!'

In the agora, following a trumpeter's signal, a herald read out at regular intervals, the personal message received from Pericles, offering his heartfelt condolences on the death of Phalinus. Men wept and women wailed openly and felt no shame. The Thebans had paid a heavy price for their audacious attack, but the price paid by the Plataeans was greater. Phalinus was dead. It was as though the lamp which lit their world had been extinguished.

TWENTY-FOUR

FUNERALS WERE FREQUENT. THERE were so many, the usual lengthy formalities were excused. Glaucus, enraged about what had happened to Sappha, was being comforted by Clytes and Anthousa. 'Why did she have to come looking for me?' he asked Anthousa, for the second time. 'Some lowlife killed her because she was wearing my gift. I'm sure of it! By wearing it, she drew attention to herself. Why did she have to wear it that night? It was only a cheap thing.' No-one knew where Sappha had been born. She never knew herself. But in the poor community where she plied her trade, she was precious, and Glaucus and Clytes as strangers in the city, were touched at the numbers who attended her simple funeral.

For the funeral of Phalinus, the mourners numbered in their thousands, as they came from far and near to see The Shield Guardian, one last time.

Lying in state, the shining Shield of Marathon as a pillow for his golden head, he looked as though he were only resting, so relaxed were his features. His wife, Akaterina, and other female relatives had dressed him in his full military armour with his sword at his side and his shield covering his chest. His distinctive helmet had been handed to his three-year-old son, Akylas, and his mother had lifted him up so he could place it to rest on his father's shield.

Looking through tears at her deceased husband, Akaterina, supported by her family screamed out her grief as she beat her fists on her breasts, her eyes crazed with despair. Resembling flapping ravens, Phalinus' female relatives, all dressed in black, demonstrated their genuine grief also, in tearing at their hair and crying out their lamentations. Little Akylas stood at the back, dwarfed by his great-uncles, Androdamos and Ektor, and other male members of his family. He was trying to be strong, as his mother had instructed him, but distressed at witnessing her great loss, silent sobs shook his small body.

Before dawn, the procession to the tomb of his ancestors began, accompanied by the entire population as they paid their final respects to Plataea's noble son, who had sacrificed his life for another, just as his famous ancestor had done on the battlefield of Marathon. Usually the funeral of such an illustrious personage would be attended by musicians and singers, but such was the great sense of loss, the only sounds following Phalinus to his grave, were of weeping.

TWENTY-FIVE

IT WAS A SORRY group that arrived at The City of the Seven Gates, the morning after the Plataean revolt, and the Theban populace, already informed of the disaster by a herald, did not receive them warmly. When word arrived later that their soldiers had been returned dead, they immediately blamed Larachne and Lykaon for the calamitous outcome, the object of their main condemnation, Eurymachus, having been executed along with the rest of the prisoners, was beyond punishment. Many thought that their Boetarchs' plan had been overridden by the more aggressive faction of the Boeotian League. Larachne, the outsider, with no husband to defend her, was particularly castigated.

'I am to be banished!' she screamed at Lykaon, on their first and last meeting, after his ignominious return. 'You promised me Plataea! And where are my jewels?' she yelled at him, while furiously pacing the floor.

'I killed their Shield Guardian!' he protested. 'Their precious golden boy is no more!'

'Don't you understand, you idiot, that the people blame us for the executions. If you hadn't been so obsessed with killing Phalinus, the Plataeans might have negotiated! You are not wanted in Thebes any more than I am, but don't think you are coming back to Sardis with me. I am leaving and I am taking Mirhab with me. What you do is of no interest to me. And, my token, which I see you still wear in your hair, I will have that back!' Before he could stop her, Larachne rushed at him with a knife, and Lykaon watched in horror as the green ribbon, still attached to his lustrous, black horse-tail, fell heavily to the floor.

'You bitch!' he shouted, and went to grab her, only to have his arms forced behind him by the powerful Mirhab. By falling into a water-filled ditch, the Persian had miraculously survived his leap from Plataea's city walls, but without his stolen gold, he was once again considering his best options. As usual, they would be with Larachne. Besides, if all the Athenian allies fight like the Plataeans, he thought, then it's back to Lydia for Mirhab.

Since they'd been children, surviving in the grimy back streets of a Cilician town, Mirhab had been at Larachne's side, and he had remained loyal. Not because of any affection he held for her. Larachne did not inspire affection. He stayed because it suited him. Only he knew the murky story of her colourful and nefarious past. He knew for a fact, that she was not descended from Assyrian nobility, as she proclaimed, but was in fact the daughter of a poor feltmaker from Tarsus. Determined to escape her humble beginnings, she quickly learned how to please men, and had gradually clawed her way up the slippery and sometimes bloody social ladder, by using her beauty and cunning to lucrative effect. Until another opportunity presented itself, the revenues from her estate at Sardis would have to sustain her - and him.

Nicander, leaning over the bed, gently shook Marissa. He was unsure as to how she would react, waking up to this new life which had been forced upon her. On the road, during their flight from Plataea, she'd nearly collapsed on hearing the boasting from Lykaon that he'd slain The Shield Guardian, and had even talked of wanting to go back. Back to what? That little fortress will be crushed if there is a war, Nicander thought grimly. Knowing how determinedly his fellow Spartans were building up their army, he wanted to get Marissa to his homeland as soon as possible, while the roads and seas were still open.

When their travel arrangements were finally organised, and with horses acquired for the journey, they found themselves with a larger armed guard than expected. Lykaon, being banished from Thebes, with his new second-in-command, Hippodamus, and thirty mounted followers, together with their slave attendants, were to travel with them - financed by Lykaon's new inheritance from the estate of his late uncle Pythangelus.

TWENTY-SIX

BY THE FAILED ATTACK on their city, the Plataeans had been given a wake-up call. In the course of almost fifty years of comparative peace, their city had become prosperous. It boasted many fine buildings, and the homes of the citizens provided every comfort, but regrettably they had failed to maintain their fortifications. Following years of neglect, Eupompides ordered an immediate start on strengthening and rebuilding the city walls, and surrounding ditches would be deepened to make their city a fortress once again.

Diokles, his throbbing left arm supported in a leather sling, was determined to get his city prepared for war. As a mercenary some years previously he had fought with the Spartans in putting down a helot revolt and he had experienced first-hand what a disciplined Spartan phalanx could do. The so-called Athenian alliance was forever in disagreement and revolt, and although it was a mightier adversary than the aggrieved helot slaves of Sparta - it could not afford to take the Spartan intentions lightly. More than anyone else in Plataea, Diokles understood that their recent success against the Thebans had been narrowly won.

The city was in shock and demoralised but now needed to be concentrating on its future survival. He sent out his captains to scour the city and beyond in search of able-bodied auxiliaries. Like mother hens rounding up their chicks, from craftsmen, merchants, shopkeepers and farmworkers, who had completed some military training, he managed to swell the ranks - the calm and encouraging words of his officers masking their true fears.

Standing on the platform of one of the twin towers commanding the Gargaphian Gate, Diokles gazed north over the plain. Looking across to a stretch of meadowland between two streams, he could see where archery and javelin practice was being carried out, the strident shouts of instruction could just be heard above the activity directly below him. From this vantage point he could keep watch on the progress being made on deepening and widening the defence ditches. He made a silent prayer to Athena that all would be done in time. He loved his resilient little city, and would do his utmost to save her.

In spite of every threat, advice and bribe, Plataea was committed to stand with Athens. Other states were still making up their minds.

For several days they waited and watched for messengers, expecting news that the Spartans had marched into Attica. People dwelling in the outlying villages and farms began to hasten towards protection within the city walls, and a steady movement of the displaced with their precious livestock and possessions began to swell the confines of the plateau.

Gallopers in search of enemy activity found the countryside empty of any patrols save for their own. They scouted east and west along the banks of the Asopus, their natural boundary with Thebes, encountering no trouble, but saw evidence of abandoned farms being raided and robbers making the roads unsafe.

To alleviate the overcrowding, Diokles ordered lines of tents to be set up across the plateau to house the small but growing army of conscripts, under the command of officers from the regular garrison. One of them, Alexeis, son of Eubalos, had slept little since the Theban attack. This was his first command and he took his duties seriously. Diokles had placed his trust in him and like Diokles, he would defend Plataea with his life. News that his younger brother, Theo, was ill with a fever, was also on his mind. The wound received in the fight at the temple was deep but not thought life threatening, his attacker having missed the main artery. His father, Eubalos, thought the illness was brought on by grief over the death of Phalinus.

When a messenger did arrive he came not with news of Sparta, but with instructions from Athens. Pericles was sending a contingent of Athenian hoplites to help defend their city and all women and children, the elderly and the infirm, were to be evacuated to the capital. Livestock was to be taken to the island of Euboea. Preparations were to be started immediately.

TWENTY-SEVEN

WHEN THE ATHENIANS ARRIVED at Plataea, it was not a time of rejoicing. Some of the men in their ranks had been chosen because they had old family links with the city or at least with southern Boeotia, but this was no homecoming. They found chaos and confusion, with many citizens refusing to leave their properties and possessions, for an unknown future in a city many of them had never seen.

Heralds read out announcements in the marketplace at regular intervals, reinstating what could be taken with them and what would have to be left behind. The craftsmen of the city were particularly disheartened. Some of their workshops had taken a lifetime to establish and shutting down their furnaces came hard. When the shrines and temples were emptied of their wealth and statuary, crowds gathered, wondering if they would ever set foot in their sacred places again and fervent, emotional ceremonies were carried out by lamenting priests throughout the city, while time allowed.

At the Temple of Athena, a heated debate ensued between Eupompides, Stephanos and Diokles on the one hand and Admetus, Eubalos and Keas the silver merchant, on the other.

'The Shield remains where it is!' said Eupompides, indignantly. 'So long as Plataea stands, the city's talisman stays!'

Keas, lifted his hands in supplication. 'It must go to Athens, Eupompides!' he pleaded. 'It is far too valuable in worth as well as sentiment, to be put at risk.'

Eubalos and Admetus agreed with Keas. 'The Thebans could come back for it. Have you thought of that?' added Eubalos. 'And it is not just a symbol of freedom for us Plataeans. Every Hellene is inspired by the story of The Marathon Shield. It does not just belong to us. Over the years, people from across Hellas have added to its worth. The jewels alone are worth a fortune!'

'If The Shield goes, the heart of the city goes,' said Stephanos. 'We have lost enough. Phalinus gave up his life saving it. Take the other treasures, but leave us this. Its sentiments are what we are all fighting for!'

'Well, if it does stay, Athens may be inclined to send more help,' remarked Keas, looking at his colleagues for reassurance.

'We have to organise the removal of the libraries and the official records,' said Admetus, his voice quaking with emotion. 'We will put it to the Council that The Shield stays in Plataea. May the gods protect you all!'

Eubalos, in a cart pulled by Cyclops, sat with Theomenes' head resting on his lap as he tried to cushion his son from the jolts caused by the ruts in the road. Mydon sat beside him, with a sponge and water, trying to keep his master's fever at bay. All the praying by Eubalos for his son to live was being equalled by the fevered, silent prayers of Theomenes, to die. They were part of the long, unhappy column of Plataeans, making their way to the safety of Athens' walls. In a carriage close behind, was Admetus, clutching his bronze statue of Athena, by Imbros, and surrounded by papyri rolls. He was thinking back to the evening of his presentation when he suggested that people thought his history of Plataea had been boring of late. I warned them that the gods would be listening, he thought, and sighed. He had spent his last evening with Imbros and Amara, together with her worried parents who were distraught at Amara's decision to remain in the city to care for her husband, now a fully integrated member of the garrison. The cook, Cosmas, being unsuitable for any military service, would be joining the parents' new household in Athens, but Ianthe would remain in Plataea, being one of the women chosen to cook for members of the garrison.

Athens had sent a force of eighty hoplites, under the leadership of a young and proud captain by the name of Lecadonis, to swell the military and help guard their city, and it was Athenian cavalry riding up and down the moving column, protecting the worldly wealth of the evacuees from real threats by robbers.

Diokles, despite his injured arm, was determined to play his part and was keen to change his 'soft' new recruits into a fighting force. He shook his head often, at what had become of the men of the city in their years of peace, despite the Olympian olive wreaths won by some. At his usual watch at the Gargaphian Gate, he was witnessing a scene, which was anything but usual. Apart from the soldiers and the women who would look after them, his city was being abandoned and he had just said a sorrowful farewell to his wife and children. His daughter, Micca, searched tearfully for Stephanos, her hopes of being his wife someday, now shattered. Diokles' son, being too young to serve with him, was a particularly hard parting, and he had struggled to give them all some reassurance.

'Athens has her walls and her ships. You will be protected there. You'll starve if you stay. It is not safe to farm the fields. We will be together again soon,' he'd tried to reassure them, with as much confidence as he could muster.

He strained to see them in the mass of people and wagons, slowly moving out through the gates, starting their long journey to Athens, but then his vision blurred as, blinking back rare tears, he could look no more. His last sight was that of golden haired Akylas, sat perched on his father's white stallion, the vermillion cloak with the shining symbol of The Marathon Shield, enveloping his tiny frame.

PART TWO
THE WAR

TWENTY-EIGHT

THE HEAT CAME EARLY that year, when the forces of Sparta began to assemble outside the long walls of the Dorian city of Megara; to hold the isthmus against a possible attack from Attica.

By the time commander Skopas had arrived, the dusty city burned with glowing luminescence beneath a gradually warming sun, making the waters of the gulf an incandescent turquoise blue. It was from here on this narrow strip of land between the Gulfs of Corinth and Saronica, on a fertile plain spilling over with vineyards, olive groves and black goats, that mighty Sparta intended to launch her first assault into Attica.

It was often said that the art of comedy originated in Megara, but Skopas saw little evidence of such a boast, except for their manufacture of the ugly, ill-fitting labourers garment, the exomis, for which their city was dubiously famous. What he did accept was the shrewdness and guile of the Megarians. They were past masters of playing the double game, depending on Athens for succour when it suited them while also negotiating, both politically and economically with Sparta and her allies. Had they not, on occasion, taken up arms against both powers?

Her present membership of the Spartan Confederacy was a prime example of the said style of Megara's wheeling and dealing. She saw in Athens' recent dilemmas, an opportunity to overthrow Pericles' recent economically crippling decree, barring Megara from using any ports in Attica. A harsh reaction from Pericles, they thought, just because a few of their people had broken a sacred vow and cultivated some of the Sacred Meadow land of Demeter, on lands bordering Megaris and Attica. Needless to say, she was trusted by neither side, but Megara had little choice in being two-faced, situated as she was, between Sparta, Corinth and Athens - the mightiest city-states in all Hellas.

In the cool privacy of his own pavilion, Skopas had finished with the young Thracian. She said her name was Epyaxa and she had pleased him well. Procured by Thales, his aide-de-camp, from Megara's principle brothel, she had been more than generous with her skills and he had twice shot his seed. Now, having sent her back to a waiting Thales, he washed carefully and with the help of a young slave, fastened on a leather cuirass over his soft linen tunic, and went out to inspect the camp.

The whole strength of his command so far amounted to barely a thousand men, though Sparta's allies were trickling in at the many rendezvous points. He was assured by the Spartan Council that now winter was passed, many more would be joining them, but his king, Archidamus, still chose to deal in unrealities, as if by having the boldness to invade Attica head-on, some unseen and dreadful retribution might rebound upon him.

It had been many months since a decision had been agreed to march against Athens, but with the politicians still arguing, Skopas and his men sat idly beside the Gulf. In his impatience, he had put forward counter-strategies to the Council of Elders, which had been ignored; his proposals as to how he would conduct the war, falling on deaf ears. His suggestion of a seaborne night attack on the harbour of Piraeus was laughed out of the Chamber, being thought impossible to execute. And his proposal to penetrate Attica as far as the lands of Lavrion, cutting off their silver supply, was also thought too ambitious. But then he was an ambitious man and an even more impatient one, and not typical of his race, the Spartans on the whole being religious people and cautious about entering into hostilities.

Skopas sniffed his disdain. Someday, he thought, in this approaching fracas there would be those who'd wished the Council had listened to him more attentively. He doubted also that Pericles was willing to fight a large land battle anytime soon. There had been explicit instructions given to the Athenian military and all civilians to retreat behind her great walls; to leave the land empty and barren for the invader. The gathering of their enemies at the gulf for all to see, gave Athens plenty of warning about an imminent invasion, and properties were being dismantled and crops destroyed by the Athenians' own hands. Very soon, Skopas thought, there would be nobody to fight and nothing to loot.

TWENTY-NINE

SKOPAS DRILLED THE MEN hard in preparation, as they waited by the sea, making use of the nearby low hills for running in full armour. Any wild game they startled, of boar or deer, made good javelin practice and added necessary variety to their short rations. Because of import restrictions being imposed by Athens, their Megarian hosts were struggling to supply sufficient food for the growing army encamped on their soil, but the soldiers, in units of fifteen, were well used to watching each other's backs. They had lived and trained together all through their military service, many since they were children of seven years of age and were used to doing whatever was necessary to fill the belly of every comrade in their tight group.

On the plain, there was regular practice with teams pitted against each other, their bronze shields used as battering rams in an attempt to force the opposing team backwards across a line, defined by markers behind them. With strident shouts and insults coming from their captains, the strong-willed warriors pushed forward until their well-developed muscles bulged, and sweat poured from under their heavy cuirasses. Mingled with determined screams and curses from the men, it looked very impressive to the newly arrived party from Thebes, and any one of them watching, who'd not seen Spartan warriors in action before, was awe inspired as time and again the harsh drill was repeated, leaving many men with painful injuries, which were suffered without complaint. 'If this is how they treat their own, what will they do to the enemy!' remarked one of Lykaon's men.

The band of thirty Boeotians led by The Wolf of Thebes, was warmly welcomed by Skopas and he recognised immediately in Lykaon, a man of his own mind. This Boeotian seemed as eager as he was to begin the war, and in their joint frustration, the soldiers would be drilled mercilessly.

Nicander and Marissa had gone immediately to general Skopas's tent and were awaiting him there. The clash of shield on shield and the war cries of the Spartans being drilled so harshly made Marissa apprehensive, knowing that these very soldiers could be involved in an attack on her own forsaken city before long, and she clung to Nicander for reassurance.

Skopas, when entering his tent, flung back the curtain dramatically, bearing the demeanor of a man in full command of his situation. Having been informed by Thales that Nicander, cousin of exiled King Pleistoanax had arrived, and was in his tent waiting to talk to him, had momentarily made his mind race with uncertainties. Surmising from a brief conversation with the Theban, Lykaon, however, that his command was not in question, he hurried to receive his guest. Seeing him in the arms of Marissa, his lips curled in a knowing smile, which was not missed by Nicander.

'My dear Skopas. I am pleased to see you!' said Nicander, gently releasing Marissa and coming forward to greet him. 'Before we talk, can you provide a tent for myself and find suitable lodgings for my lady? We are both in need of rest and refreshment.'

'Of course, of course!' replied the general, giving a questioning glance at Marissa.

'Afterwards, we will discuss the current situation, before I travel on to Corinth tomorrow,' continued Nicander, pacing the tent; dust falling from his travelling cloak. 'I need to know the numbers you have here now; how many you expect to arrive, and from where?' he continued, as though dictating a letter, not looking at Skopas. 'I'm aware of the food shortages, having met with the oligarchs earlier today. They are grateful for our help, naturally, but are concerned as to how long the army will remain here. They are most eager for us to make a move on Athens soon, and break this crippling embargo. I will be reporting all this to Archidamus as soon as I reach Sparta, and I will ask for further shipments to be sent from our own reserves.'

Looking at Marissa, fiddling with the broken strap on one of her sandals, her long limbs reclining awkwardly on a folding camp chair, he realised how tired she must be, when she glanced up at him with languid eyes, and he made a sign to her that they would be leaving soon.

'Let me have your report and any letters you wish me to carry home, Skopas,' he said hurriedly, 'and a note of anything you wish me to report to the king.'

Skopas, wondering who the striking woman was, who'd arrived with Nicander, couldn't stop glancing at her. High-class courtesan, most likely, he thought to himself. But she's not wearing much make-up. I wonder what she charges for............?

'General, can you do these things?' asked Nicander sharply, catching Skopas looking lasciviously at Marissa.

'Of course! Of course!' the general repeated.

'I hope you bear good news regarding Plataea?' asked Skopas, deferentially, when Nicander returned later that evening to share a meal of fresh caught fish, olives and herb bread.

'I do not, Skopas, as it happens,' replied Nicander, pouring some wine.

'The Thebans totally misjudged the situation at Plataea, and I'm afraid they do not hold the fortress as they'd expected. They lost a tenth of their army in the attack, including their Boetarchs. One of them, Pythangelus, was the uncle of Lykaon, the Boeotian who travelled here with me.'

'This Lykaon seems a keen commander and just the kind we need on our side!' remarked Skopas, picking a fish bone from his teeth.

'He is hot-headed and ambitious and it is because of him and his followers that they lost so many of their army!' said Nicander, in exasperation. 'He acts first and thinks later.'

'Well, perhaps we Spartans think too much?' suggested Skopas.

'Use him,' said Nicander, purposefully. 'He seems to have no fears, but don't trust him. He is only interested in self-aggrandisement, and he is still rankled over the humiliation at Plataea. Don't say I didn't warn you!'

'Oh, I will find a use for him, and I am obliged to you for the information,' answered Skopas, thoughtfully.

Later, as Nicander stood up to leave, Skopas cleared his throat, and Nicander looked at him questioningly. 'Yes?' he asked.

'What do you want me to do about the woman?' asked Skopas.

Nicander looked at the ground, silent for a moment, then replied sharply. 'The lady will be coming with me!'

Skopas raised his hands and backed away from Nicander. 'Of course. My apologies!' he spluttered. 'I understand. Why drink water when you can have wine, eh! Very nice! If she is your woman, then, of course, of course!'

'Tread carefully, Skopas!' responded Nicander with displeasure, then raising the tent flap, made a swift exit before he struck the man for his impudence.

The following morning, they set off on their ride west towards Corinth, taking with them other Spartans returning home, together with several helot slaves in attendance. The last sight they saw of the camp was of a man being dragged to be flogged, watched by Skopas and Lykaon, astride their horses. The culprit was a Theban. He had a sign around his neck with one word on it, 'thief'.

'Unless we get more supplies to Megara, there will be many more floggings!' remarked Nicander to one of his Spartan companions.

'Stealing food is to be expected with rations so short. Just don't get caught!' replied the soldier, grimly. 'I bear such scars myself.'

THIRTY

'COME, COME, BROTHER!' URGED Hypatos, as he beckoned frantically to his servants to help the exhausted travellers through the gate. 'My house is your house, for as long as you need it!'

When the party of desolate refugees, drawn in a cart by a one-eyed mule, finally arrived in Athens, they were given a warm welcome at the city villa of Hypatos; a wealthy landowner. His brother Eubalos tried hard to conceal the emotional and physical exhaustion which had slowly weakened him since the Theban attack. Theo was still not responding to him and on the journey to the capital, had lost so much weight, he now feared for his life. 'I received your message about poor Theo,' fussed Hypatos, 'and I have a room prepared for him. Plenty of light, and airy too. My women will soon get him well. Don't worry, Eubi!'

On hearing his childhood name, Eubalos finally did break. 'My horses, brother! The army has commandeered my beautiful horses!'

In an effort to calm him, Hypatos said, soothingly, 'You will be well compensated, Eubi, they are fine horses.'

'Compensated!' groaned Eubalos. 'I don't want their money. My life's work, Hypatos! Their pedigrees are second to none. Sensitive, noble creatures that have felt neither whip nor spur.'

Hypatos put his arm around his brother's shoulders and led him to the care of his wife and servants. 'You are stressed, brother, and suffering from exhaustion. Let Atheni and her household attend to you and Theo.' Then talking quietly, so as not to distress the others, he said in a hushed voice. 'All our lives will be changed by this war, brother, not just those of your horses. We must all be prepared to endure sacrifices.'

Since the attack on Plataea by the Thebans and the killing of the prisoners, it was accepted in Athens that war with Sparta was now only a matter of time. Pericles believed that Athens was impregnable behind the city's defences, and with her Long Walls guarding access to her harbours at Piraeus, where her mighty fleet was moored, precious grain would continue to flow in from the Black Sea. With income from their silver mines, and also wealth accumulated from dues of the Delian League, the people would not starve, even if the harvests were destroyed. His orders to abandon all surrounding villages and homesteads were not well received by all country dwellers, however, and there was much grumbling as they left their farms, to squeeze into the crowded conditions in the metropolis.

Corinna and her daughter, Phoebe, together with their family slave were caught up in this massive displacement, and like hundreds of others, needed somewhere to stay. They knew no-one in the capital. Consequently, with many of their neighbours from Plataea, who also had no family or friends to take them in, they were given temporary accommodation in a large, unfinished temple dedicated to Hephaestos, god of blacksmiths, fire and volcanoes, situated near the agora. On top of a hill crowded with the noisy and dirty, fire belching workshops of the metal workers, the Plataeans thought, miserably, that their new home resembled Hades. The homeless Plataeans were totally disorientated by the crowds and the noise, and the enormous scale of their surroundings. They had never seen anything larger than their own temples, which were modest in comparison to the grand edifices in Athens. The more mature members of the group of refugees said they felt like outlanders in what they'd thought of as their capital, and confided that they could never call this seething melting pot of humanity, 'home'.

With all normal formalities suddenly halted, it was Phoebe who at first approached their new situation with courage in her heart, and in the company of Eudora as chaperone and others from her home-town, was eager to explore the famed city she had never expected to see in her lifetime. It took only one trip to the agora for her excitement to turn to embarrassment. The poorest slaves of Athens, she soon realized, seemed better dressed than anyone in her party, who were looked upon with what Phoebe could only describe as casual disdain by the city-dwellers.

'They stare at us as though we were going to steal from them!' she cried later, to her mother, Corinna. 'Don't they know my father and others are risking their lives to remain loyal to Athens?'

Corinna, worn down with worry due to their reduced circumstances, concerned for her husband, Demetrius, now part of the garrison forty miles away in Plataea, wearily told her daughter to go and help Eudora to prepare their meal. With only hanging drapes to give some small amount of privacy between families, the shoe-maker's wife, wondering why the gods had brought this dreadful plight upon them, went to lie down on the meagre blankets which formed her bed. Outside the temple, like the poorest of beggars, the people of Plataea were thanking the Athenians who were coming with food and blankets - and offers of work.

Watched over night and day by the women of the household, Theomenes suddenly sat upright in his bed one morning, and cried out, 'Father!' His haunted eyes were wide open; his fevered ramblings impossible to decipher, as he stared at a blank wall. Once again his thin frame was gently laid down, and his burning skin cooled with chamomile water. Hypatos, hearing the shouts, went to seek Eubalos, but then thought better of it. He would let him sleep on. He'd quickly come to realise that it was not just his young nephew who needed care. His elder brother, Eubalos, was becoming a concern to him, also. He seemed withdrawn and troubled beyond comfort. At first, Hypatos thought it was just exhaustion, but soon he had his suspicions that it may not be a physical malady at all.

The previous evening, Eubalos had been emphatic about discussing his financial affairs with Hypatos, who was the executor of his will. In these changing times, he'd said he wanted to be sure that his business affairs were being handled in the best possible way. But, when Eubalos wanted to add an appendix to his will, stipulating that in the event of his passing, Orchas and other specifically chosen slaves were to be made free men, Hypatos had looked anxiously at his brother. 'Eubi, you and Orchas will be grumbling at each other for years to come and become an embarrassment to your grand-children,' he'd joked, trying to turn their conversation to happier thoughts.

When his wife came quietly into his library, he looked in shock at her tearful face. 'Oh no!' he exclaimed, rising quickly from his chair, thinking his nephew had taken a turn for the worse.

'My dear, it's not Theo,' she tried to tell him through her sobs. 'It's your brother! He has gone from us!'

'His heart was broken, and I didn't understand,' said Hypatos, sorrowfully, as he looked at the pale figure of his brother, curled up as though from pain, on the bed. 'He lived through the best of times,' he said, sadly. 'I actually think I'm relieved that he will not suffer the terrible times which must surely come.'

Bending over the bed, Hypatos touched the cold hands of Eubalos, and spoke directly to him as though he could be heard. 'I will take care of your boys, brother. I will make all the necessary arrangements for Alex and Theo to receive their due inheritance, as we discussed. I will make young Theo my heir. I'll treat him as though he were my own, Eubi,' he said, speaking softly. 'Orchas shall be given his freedom as you instructed, and I promise he will not starve. May your sweet soul reach the Elysian Fields soon, brother. We will give sacrifices to the gods for it to be so.'

Turning to his wife, he said, quietly, 'Orchas is due to arrive from Hysiae any time now - after he's overseen the last of the horses transferred to the cavalry. I don't know how I'm going to break the news to him - or to poor Theo!'

THIRTY-ONE

THEOMENES LAY SHAKING WITH fear at the thought of those terrible eyes. As he lay in his own sweat on a bed in an unfamiliar room, the blackness gradually replaced by the half-light, his confused senses told him, yet again, that it had all been just a dream - a nightmare!

Since the untimely death of the Lord Phalinus and the bloody affair in the temple, details of the dream changed, but it never varied in its horror.

In a mist, he holds the decapitated and grinning head of that vile creature, Medusa the Gorgon. She who had once been the love of Poseidon, God of the Sea, in the far-off days of her youth and beauty. But because of her constant vanity, she stirred the wrath of the beautiful goddess Athena who changed her fairness into that of a monster, and now one look from her hideous face, with writhing snakes where once was her golden hair, could turn men to stone.

In this recent dream, he is sitting at his father's table with his elder brother Alexeis and the historian, Admetus. There is also an unknown girl. A beautiful girl. He wants to learn her name. Upon the table, are set jugs of sweet wine and bowls of grapes and Egyptian figs. It is the briefest of interludes and soon fades. Then, he is attending a wedding feast where everyone is garlanded with garish, exotic flowers. Somewhere in the room music is playing softly.

The familiar faces vanish and only the girl remains. Somehow, he knows that this beautiful creature can be his if only he can win her love. But then she bares herself unashamedly to him, throwing her discarded garments brazenly at his feet. The girl's firm erect nipples are dark stained with the thick juices of crushed grapes. He reaches forward eagerly to grasp them. Her fingers move along his inner thigh as she gropes for his member. As he reaches out for her, the dream changes again to a recurring theme.

Armed men burst into the Feast Hall and proceed to hurl well aimed javelins in his direction, and the clash of weapons drown out the music of lyre and horn. Drawing his sword, he rushes headlong into the fight only to slip to his knees in a widening pool of blood.

Medusa's head is once again in his hands. Keeping his eyes tightly shut he displays aloft the fearful countenance to the faces of his attackers, as a hundred warriors are transformed into a phalanx of motionless, mute shapes.

He looks upon his handiwork in triumph, but in doing so he has forgotten Medusa. The head of the Gorgon has twisted in his grip so that he comes eye to eye with the nightmare of her malevolent gaze. Then comes the terror-instilled scream. It seems to erupt from some hidden place, galvanising him into a state of half-consciousness. The scream is his. Then, silence.

The first rays of the sun fill the room, as a dawn rooster crows him back from the fog of the other world. A dark and winding river passes in a gentle flow across his semi-awakening. The stream meanders across an arid plain. It was as if he were, like Icarus, surveying the earth from a great height. It is only when his eyes refocus that he realises he is looking up at a crack in the plastered ceiling.

What did it all signify? His terminus? For when he'd looked into the red-orbed eyes of the death-dealing she-devil, it wasn't Medusa he saw, but a terrified, wide-eyed image of himself.

Then the mist engulfed him again.

THIRTY-TWO

ORCHAS, NOT USUALLY AN emotional man, wept openly on being informed of the death of his old master, Eubalos. The last memory of him at his estate at Hysiae, was not a happy one, when arrangements were being made for the transfer of the horses to the Athenian cavalry. Eubalos had been civil to the officers sent from the capital, but only Orchas noticed how his master had aged during the proceedings. The news that the slave had been given his freedom did not lighten his mind but made him feel even more bereft. Everything he had known and trusted, since being taken into the Eubalos household, was no more. His first act on becoming a freed man, was to hand over to Hypatos a heavy bag of gold and silver, the inadequate recompense agreed by Eubalos for his precious horses. All but three. The black stallion belonging to Alexeis, which was now with him at Plataea, and two matching greys, which Orchas and the head groom had brought with them to the stables of Hypatos; Eubalos's own horse, 'Astor' and the stallion's daughter, 'Selene' - a fine horse Eubalos had personally chosen for Theomenes' future use.

The news also grieved Orchas, that Theomenes was still not fully aware of his surroundings, and he was shocked to see how thin the lad had become, despite the constant care of his aunt. He sought out Mydon who was living in the slave quarters nearest the stables, where he was taking care of Cyclops. Mydon knew that when Theomenes finally awoke and asked, 'Where is he?' he would most likely be talking about the mule and not his father, and Mydon wanted to be sure that Cyclops would be there, hale and hearty, to greet him.

Orchas was in time to pay his last respects to his old master and friend, before the cremation the following morning. It would proceed without either of the sons and heirs being present, but many exiled Plataeans attended the lying-in-state of their late Chief Magistrate and in the continuous line of grieving mourners were Corinna and her daughter, Phoebe. Theomenes was still in his own dark dreams and Alexeis was too far away to be summoned in time. All the funeral arrangements were organised by Hypatos and his wife and no expense was spared in the sending of Eubalos's soul to the Underworld.

Drawn by Astor and Selene, the body of Eubalos in a richly decorated carriage, was followed by a large grieving procession through the streets of Athens early dawn, accompanied by torchbearers and flute players, out through a city gate to a prepared funeral pyre of dry faggots and aromatic cedar. Surrounding the pyre, the mourners, including Admetus the historian, shouted out their last farewells to Eubalos, as Hypatos, his nearest male relative, threw a lighted branch onto the oil-soaked wood, sending fierce flames up into the heavens.

As soon as the ashes were cool enough, they were gathered up and placed in an ornate urn and carried back to the house of Hypatos. The feasting and drinking went on throughout the night and it was during these commemorations, that Theomenes, in his room at the top of the house, suddenly opened his eyes and asked the startled slave girl keeping watch at his bedside, for water.

The death of his father affected Theo more than he ever thought possible, especially since he wasn't with him at his end. He'd always respected Eubalos, but until now he never realised just how much he'd really loved him. He started reflecting on times when he had been taken by Eubalos on hunting trips into the mountains, many times when Alexeis was away doing his military training, and he'd had his father's sole attention. He always felt as though his father was comparing him unfavourably to his elder brother, so the trips usually ended in arguments. He would give anything to have those times back again, and behave differently.

His uncle and aunt were his family now. His aunt, Atheni, a compassionate lady with a lively personality, was like a mother to him, which at times he found a little overpowering. Eubalos had told him that his mother, Helena, like the beauty who'd brought about the siege of Troy in the ancient tales, was unmatched in all of Boeotia, for her loveliness. She had died before he was three years of age. He'd never asked for more details, and now it was too late. One day, when the times were safer, he would go back with Alexeis to their estate in Hysiae, and place their father's ashes next to those of his beautiful wife, in their family tomb. Until then, his father's remains would spend time with his ancestors, in their lavish mausoleum at the Keramikos cemetery near the Dipylon Gate.

'Do you think you're strong enough to go to the stables?' asked Atheni, a week after Theo had come out of his illness. 'I'm more than ready, aunt,' replied the eager young man, looking much improved after a week of good food. 'I hope he remembers me.'

On nearing the stables, Theo could not stop himself from calling out the animal's name. At the sudden sound of his master's voice, Cyclops brayed and whinnied in return, loud enough to make their heads hurt, while his bulk tried to break through the stable door. 'My goodness, Theo, he knows it's you,' said Atheni. 'Do be careful. You're not strong enough to handle him yet.'

Without stopping to listen, Theo climbed over the wooden fencing separating Cyclops from the horses, and began hugging the great white head, rubbing his neck and ears. Cyclops pushed his big head into Theo so hard that Mydon had to climb over also and step between them. 'He'll have you crushed and you'll be back in bed!' he said, concerned, as he managed to pull the mule back a little.

'How have you got on?' Theo asked Mydon, still fussing Cyclops.

'He's a bit of a handful, but we seem to have reached an understanding,' replied Mydon, giving the animal an exasperated look.

'If you make a friend of Cyclops, it's for life,' said Theo, looking at his mule, as he would a staunch ally.

'I don't understand what you see in the brute,' spoke Atheni, dismissively. 'He's only an ass,' and she winked mischievously at Orchas, standing beside her.

'I had just the same problem with my father,' replied Theo, with slight irritation. 'I remember the trouble I had in keeping my father from putting him to slaughter, just because he had one eye and was difficult to handle.'

'How did you acquire him, then?' asked his aunt, pretending she'd never heard the story before.

'It was on a hunting trip on the mountain of Cithaeron, about five years ago,' began Theo. 'We all three were there, Orchas, Mydon and myself so they can vouch for what I say. Father and Alexeis were there too. We'd had no luck and were heading back down the mountain, when we heard such a loud braying. A screaming almost. The hairs on my head stood on end! I can't remember who decided we should find out what was happening, but anyway, we followed the sound and we saw a big white mule being attacked by the largest boar any of us had ever seen. But we'd heard of him. He was known to all around as 'The Impaler', a killer of many farmers' livestock.

The mule was in a bad way, and the boar seemed to be getting the best of it. Kept attacking the mule on the same side. Its white hide was covered in blood. It was my father who noticed that the mule only had one eye. Alexeis wanted to kill the mule as well as the boar. The mule was of no use, he said.

His well-aimed arrow struck The Impaler straight through the head, and I'm not sure why, but I begged father to spare the mule. Maybe I said it just to go against my brother. I'm not sure. Anyway, father said he would spare the mule, but only if I took care of it myself. Not Orchas or Mydon or anyone else. Just me. For five years I fought father and Alexeis, to keep Cyclops from the slaughterhouse.'

Orchas interrupted the story by making a loud cough. 'Did I tell anything wrong, Orchas?' asked Theomenes, a little bewildered.

'Your father thought by caring for him it would give you a sense of responsibility,' said Orchas. Something he thought was sadly lacking in you. And it worked - somewhat. You never burdened anyone else with his care in all that time.'

'So, father would not have had Cyclops killed, whatever I did?' asked Theomenes, incredulously.

'Let's just say, it suited his purpose to let you think so.'

Theomenes reflected for a moment, past events taking on new meanings, and he realised with sudden clarity that the old man spoke the truth.

'When you are fully fit,' said Orchas, 'I will introduce you to 'Selene'. She is your father's last gift to you. Let's hope Cyclops won't be too jealous.'

THIRTY-THREE

LOOKING AT NICANDER'S BACK as they rode in single file between the cart tracks along yet another dusty road towards Corinth, Marissa suddenly realised that she was not afraid anymore. I'm where I have always wanted to be, she thought, surprised. She made a silent prayer to the goddess Athena, to help her to be brave in whatever future the gods had mapped out for her, and especially to instill in her the courage to stand by the man to whom she had chosen to give her love. She felt shocked at the emotions she was feeling, after all that had happened, but as she looked at the red cloaked figure ahead of her, his long black hair blown by the warm wind, she had never felt so alive. No matter what dangers I have to face, she thought, vehemently, I'm not going to live my life hidden away in the women's quarters. No matter what Nicander thinks! Remembering back to Megara and the incident in the tent, when Skopas had found her clinging to Nicander like a child, brought blushes to her cheeks. That Marissa belongs in the past, she swore to herself.

She became aware that they were approaching the rich city of Corinth, long before being told of it by Ortronus, one of the Spartan slaves accompanying Nicander from the camp of Skopas, back to his homeland. The young Plataean, who until recently had been no further than her own city's environs, was astonished at the crowds moving with them along the road, and their group had to move aside because of the constant stream of carts and heavy wagons travelling in both directions. From high on her horse, she could see far out into the gulf; at the comings and goings of a multitude of ships of all sizes, the sunlight catching the rhythmic movements of their banks of oars. In the port of Lechaeum, there were so many ships, she thought that a man could walk across the waters of the harbour without wetting his feet. And even on land, she saw ships being drawn on wheeled transports along a marble wagon-way which traversed the narrow isthmus. Where are all these people going, she thought questioningly, until Ortronus informed her that cargoes arriving at Lechaeum on the northern coast were being transported the short distance overland to the port of Cenchreae on its southern shore - and vice versa - to avoid the treacherous sea currents around the cape, Kavomaleas.

'Round Kavomaleas and forget about home!' he told her, so dramatically, she smiled involuntarily.

More crowds continued to push them along, until they saw the city itself and the immense citadel of the Acro-Corinthus blocking out the sky. On top of this magnificent rock, which dominated the entrance to the Peloponnese, sat the famed Temple of Aphrodite, known by every sailor in the known world because of the tale that one-thousand temple prostitutes were available there, their services paying for the upkeep of the sacred temple dedicated to love and eternal youth. Whether the numbers were exaggerated or not, the story was believed and the sailors and their money poured into Corinth. On a hill, dominating the city itself stood the shining Temple of Apollo, with its marble covered limestone columns carved out of single blocks of stone. Marissa, looking around at the great number of temples and monuments, had never seen such grandeur. Everywhere, there were signs of wealth and luxury, and she imagined that Athens must be like this.

Having sent one of the helot slaves ahead days previously to notify him of their arrival, Nicander hoped they were expected at the house of Propodas, one of Corinth's richest oligarchs, and he led his party directly to the villa. Before entering the gates, he jumped from his horse, and led it to a stone channel of free-flowing water, beckoning the others to do the same. Helping Marissa from her horse, she almost fell into his arms with weariness, but tried to hide the fact that her legs could hardly hold her up. He took her to a bubbling fountain fed by one of the many underground springs in Corinth, and here they splashed their faces in the welcome coolness, ridding themselves of the layers of dust which covered them.

Seeing Marissa look down at her garments with disgust, Nicander said sympathetically, 'You will find everything you need in Corinth, my dear. Your head will be turned by what you see here, but choose wisely. In my own country of Sparta it is frowned upon to look too ornate,' and he glanced deliberately in the direction of a group of women passing by, looking more like butterflies than respectable women, or so Marissa thought as she watched them glide by, holding their dainty parasols against the sun's glare.

'I have a lot to learn, Nicander,' replied Marissa defiantly, 'but I can assure you, my head won't be turned by unnecessary frivolities!'

'Wait until you see the hot baths in the house of Propodas, before you say that!' he said laughing.

'Marissa,' he confided quickly. 'My time here is going to be taken up in meetings with Propodas and the Council. I may not have another chance to speak to you before tomorrow. Please trust me in what I am about to say. Do not become too close to Ortronus, or any of the other helots. They are not to be trusted and must be kept at arm's length.'

'Oh, Nicander!' said Marissa, shocked, 'I'm sure Ortronus didn't mean ....'

'No exceptions, Marissa!' replied Nicander, sternly. 'Believe me when I tell you that our lives could depend on how you behave towards the helot slaves. We will be in my homeland soon, and it will be expected of you to act accordingly.'

Marissa's thoughts suddenly returned to Plataea and to her own household slaves. Where are they now, she wondered, fearfully? All their lives had been torn apart through no fault of their own and feeling the injustice, she rounded on Nicander, fiercely.

'No danger will come to you by any action of mine, Nicander! I've made my choice to be with you. Are you regretting your choice?' she asked him, her eyes flashing.

'From the moment I saw you flying through the air on that child's swing, you had me hooked like a fish,' replied Nicander, amused.

'And now, Nicander?' she asked him, firmly.

'You have me in your net, dear girl. There's no place I'd rather be,' he said, his dark eyes shining.

'I'm never going to let you go, Nicander!' Marissa told him, passionately. 'Wherever you go, I go!'

'A net I can cope with Marissa, but not a cage!' he answered, taken aback at her assertiveness, but wiping a wet strand of hair from her fresh washed face, still dripping with water, he softened and said, 'We'll see, my own jealous Hera! We'll see.'

He was nearing the end of his diplomatic mission on behalf of his Spartan King, Archidamus, but this particular meeting would require all his skills of tact and persuasion. He'd had dealings with Propodas in the past and knew him to be one of the faction calling for mighty Corinth to withdraw from the Peloponnesian League. With Sparta still in the process of building up her navy, she relied on the superior triremes of neighbouring Corinth for protection, and for transporting troops in wartime. The threat to withdraw her support at this particular time, with war imminent with Athens, had to be taken very seriously indeed.

THIRTY-FOUR

NICANDER, MAKING USE OF the luxurious facilities afforded by the house of Propodas, groomed himself as though preparing for battle, which he thought he was, if he was to influence the debate with Propodas and the other oligarchs. He doubted if many houses in Corinth had their own private hot baths, the city dwellers making use of the outdoor public baths fed by hot springs in the area. His long black hair, washed and groomed and treated with scented oil until it shone like glass, was pulled back from his strong features, in neat braids. With no adornment on his toned body, he was dressed in a simple knee length Doric chiton of linen, and new sandals which Marissa had suggested he buy for the occasion.

Nicander knew his meeting with Propodas would not go well. As a warrior, from a noble Spartan family, he was frankly embarrassed at being unable to give a satisfactory defence of his homeland's continued procrastination to attack Athens. It had been many months since the Spartan Council had promised the Corinthians they would attack Athenian territory, if she continued to threaten Potidaea, but still there was no move from Archidamus.

'Where is your promised help for Potidaea?' Propodas shouted, his face flushed with anger. 'By staying within your homeland, risking nought, you have allowed Athens to get the upper hand! The Athenian fleet has some of our own people trapped within the city! When will your king understand that by being so cautious, he is allowing Pericles to drive our alliance apart? If Archidamus does not make an attack on Attica soon, our Council has already decided to break with Sparta and form an alliance with ....' He did not finish.

'I understand your frustration, Propodas, but I do not think a hinted alliance with Athens is a genuine threat. Athens has been no friend to Corinth, of late.' He searched for a mitigating explanation. 'We have an old king in Archidamus, and while my kinsman King Pleistoanax is in exile, we have his son, who is too young to have any influence,' continued Nicander. 'I am on my way back to Sparta and my report will, I am sure, make Archidamus aware of the dangers of holding back any longer. Let me speak with your Council tomorrow, and I will convince them that to remain in the Peloponnesian Alliance is in the best interests of both our states.'

With his calm demeanor and noble bearing, the tall Spartan succeeded in taking the heat out of the discussion, and Propodas agreed to let him talk to the Council. The rest of the afternoon was taken up by talks with other leaders of the city in the hope of getting some of them on his side before the Council meeting, so as he had expected, he did not see Marissa all day.

In the evening, he attended a sumptuous gathering of Corinth's most powerful men. Propodas allowed his hunting dogs to join the symposium, and their long bodies lay outstretched under the couches. It was a convivial evening, the men resting on cushions, while musicians played woodwind and stringed instruments for their entertainment, and as the ornate wine kraters were filled and refilled, flaunting female dancers performed and conversed with the guests. All tensions, for the moment forgotten,

Nicander, after a large krater had been emptied for the fourth time, and as delightful perfumed courtesans were brought into the andron for the men's pleasure; made his apologies to his host for leaving early, blaming the long journey from Megara.

He wanted Marissa, not a perfumed substitute.

THIRTY-FIVE

FOR ALL HIS DIPLOMACY and tact, and keeping his temper in check during some very bruising exchanges with the Council, Nicander felt he was making little progress in placating the Corinthians. They had not mellowed since the heated debates of the previous year at the Spartan Assembly, when the Corinthians praised Athens for her dynamism and energy and bemoaned the fact that their Spartan neighbours were so reluctant to leave their homeland to assist their allies, that said allies were either left to the mercy of their enemies or forced to seek other alliances for protection.

Nicander stood his ground, describing how in Megaris, with Skopas as commander, a thousand troops were at that moment protecting the isthmus from any invading force from Attica.

'Ha!' said one of the councillors. 'We know of your general Skopas! He lingers overlong at our Temple to Aphrodite on his travels to and from Sparta!'

'He is a fearless general,' responded Nicander, somewhat offended, 'and the soldiers under his command are being well prepared.'

'But, where is the army, Nicander?' spoke Propodas, exasperated. 'A thousand men is not enough to convince us you mean to attack. The Peloponnesian League, in this very city, agreed last year that Athens had broken the peace treaty by attacking Potidea. The longer you wait, the stronger Athens is becoming!'

'I have recently come from Plataea,' said the Spartan seriously, 'and as you probably now know, the Thebans failed dismally in their attempt to take the city. They lost over a tenth of their army in an attack which was audacious, yes; but unsuccessful. I can tell you that since the time of the Congress last year, Archidamus has been securing the finances required to withstand a war with Attica. We do not want to repeat the mistake of Thebes, and attack before we are certain of success. When Archidamus hears my report, I can assure you, he will understand that the time is at hand. If Sparta, your longtime friend and ally, has not taken a major force into Attica by the time the grain is growing high on their plains, I swear by any god you name, that I will deliver myself up to you, as a hostage, to do with as you will. That is how certain I am that Archidamus will act.'

'We have heard Spartan promises before!' shouted one of the councillors.

'You haven't heard mine before!' answered Nicander, firmly.

Having done all he could to placate both the Megarians and the Corinthians as he'd been instructed by his Spartan Council, Nicander set off back to his homeland. He was in no doubt that Archidamus must make some gesture to satisfy their allies, or else he would witness the break-up of the mighty Peloponnesian League, and this is the advice he would be giving to his king.

On the long journey south, he would have plenty of time to educate Marissa about what to expect on their arrival in his own country, and the way of life she would experience in Sparta.

THIRTY-SIX

IN A TINY ROOM, loaned to him at no charge by Alexandros the carpenter, Clytes the Voice-Ringer woke, face up on a crumpled bed.

He'd not slept well. Partly because of his injuries, but mainly because his mind was in turmoil. Anthousa stirred sleepily next to him. Warmly wrapped in a blanket, and only half-awake, she stretched out her arm across his bare chest. Drawing back the coverlet, he traced a finger between her breasts, then down her belly to the dark tangled bush between her soft thighs. She stirred again to brush aside his wandering hand in mute protest. He looked at her, as she sank back into honeyed slumber, and smiled. His member was erect. The only part of me still in full working order, he mused. Then, rolling gently on top of Anthousa, he transported them both to a rhythmic, quiet ecstasy.

'Insatiable,' she murmured, before covering herself against the chill and, so as not to disturb her again, Clytes gently eased his legs from the bed. Pale sunlight streamed through a small, unshuttered window, and becoming aware of the murmur of the city coming to life, Clytes, shivering, went to look down on the street below.

It was just over two weeks since the Theban attack, when he had been forced to pick up a sword and return to a world of killing. Since coming face to face with the man he believed had wronged his family, stomach churning thoughts now filled his mind, and he wasn't sure how to deal with them.

War seemed inevitable. Thebes would not forget the humiliation of their crushing defeat at Plataea and the execution of her soldiers. Also, Plataea would not forgive the invasion of her city during a religious festival, and the violation of the sacred oath.

He carefully stepped over the sword and scabbard on the floor, presented to him by Diokles and a grateful garrison, in recognition of his bravery. It had been taken from Pythangelus, uncle of the man he was seeking, and in other circumstances, Lykaon would have received this expensively embellished weapon as part of his inheritance. The fact that it now belonged to him, Clytes the Eleusinian, gave him a tangible connection with his arch-enemy and he would take great care of it, until he was able to plunge it into the Theban's dark heart.

A half-filled jug of good Thasian wine, purloined from the house of the traitor, Naucleides, still sat on the floor, and he took a long drink. It would aid him in his resolve to go through with his plan.

Lykaon! The name he'd heard someone shouting above the chaos of that dreadful night during the festival of Anthesteria. It had to be him! The bastard he had been waiting five long years to find. He stood looking at Anthousa for a moment longer, remembering how she and Sappha had shown great courage. The night Phalinus and many others gave up their lives. But, for the grim-faced Eleusinian, only one name mattered to him now. He swore by Zeus and all the Gods on Olympus, that his family would be avenged.

Washing, then dressing hurriedly, he decidedly scooped up the blade and scabbard, fastening the leather belt about him. His fingers folded over the gold pommel, and he smiled grimly, remembering that only a few weeks before, his new found friend Glaucus had been arrested for supposedly carrying a knife. How things had changed. Now, most men went armed.

THIRTY-SEVEN

CLYTES QUIT PLATAEA AT daybreak under threatening rain clouds that hid the peak of Mount Cithaeron and, because the early morning air was chilled, he'd wrapped himself in a heavy woollen cloak donated by a grateful Plataean. Under his cloak, besides the prized weapon, he carried a bundle containing a change of clothing, his theatrical accoutrements and food for the journey, provided by a tearful Anthousa. As he approached the sentries, they were just unbolting the oaken Gates of Gargaphia. They instantly recognised the actor because of the part he had played in the saving of their city. The reluctant hero was now a familiar face.

'By all the gods, have you tired so soon of our city's hospitality, Clytes?' called out Epiktetos, brightly, on seeing the actor was dressed for travel.

'Only a comedian such as yourself could be so damn cheerful this early in the morning, Hawk-Eye!' Clytes responded, affably.

'I've been told you're on a quest, Clytes,' called out Simonedes, who was also manning the gates. 'I trust you know what you're doing. Why don't you stay? We could do with men like you in the garrison.'

'There's someone I have to find, Simonedes, and I've stayed too long as it is,' the actor replied, determinedly. 'I doubt if we'll meet again - so I wish you both well. May Athena watch over you and guide you,' he declared, loudly, acknowledging the sentries and the men arriving to begin work on the ditches. 'I've discovered you have a city worth defending!' he called out to the men.

Simonedes approached the actor, offered his hand and gripped the Eleusinian's firmly. 'I pray you find who you're looking for,' he told him, with sincerity.

Clytes, nodding, gave a final wave, then turned away and left the city that had surprisingly brought Lykaon back into his life. For a while Simonedes watched him go, his eyes blinking against the drizzle.

'Whatever quest he is on, it has sent him half-mad,' said the archer Epiktetos, coming to stand beside him. 'I never saw such a change in a man.'

'That may be,' agreed Simonedes, 'but there's not one of us can say he hasn't been changed by what's happened here.' He spoke in a low voice, almost to himself, thinking of the dead of a few weeks ago. Of his elderly parents making their way to the safety of Athens. The massing of the

Spartan army on the Isthmus.............

The road Clytes took would lead him to Thebes. After that, only the weight of the sword hanging from the belt beneath his warm cloak was all the reassurance he needed. The spring rain fell lightly on his cheeks as he struck out northwards, and despite the hindrance of one troublesome leg wound still not properly healed, he settled into a steady pace. Soon Plataea, where a weeping Anthousa lay in a tiny room, was lost to his sight in the mist.

He left the open trackway, heading for the less conspicuous cover of woodland and orchards, walking through a landscape broken by small streams and hills; deliberately skirting the settlements and farmsteads, to avoid any distractions. Once, he caught sight of a lone wolf, probably drawn down from the hills by the sounds of animals on the move, for the land through which he travelled was being evacuated, and confused calls from humans and beasts alike could be heard everywhere. The inhabitants of the villages and settlements were going to the metropolis; their livestock, hunting dogs and some family pets, were being rounded up and taken some miles to the east - to the island of Euboea. Clytes found it difficult to imagine that this thriving, prosperous land would soon become a place for robbers, cut-throats and Theban patrols.

'You can't do it on your own!' Glaucus had argued at their last meeting, just days previously. 'If you won't let me accompany you, then why don't you come with me to Athens?' he urged. 'You'd be there for the Great Dionysia. Haven't you been rehearsing for it for months? Remember the saying about sticking one's head in the lion's mouth? You don't stand a chance, Clytes!' he insisted. 'We don't know how many escaped back to Thebes. Somebody could recognise you, friend!'

'I'm after a wolf, not a lion!' Clytes said, smiling. 'You worry too much, Glaucus. This is something I must do alone.' The Eleusinian could not be so ungracious as to point out to his companion that, with his unnatural bulk, coupled with the flaming hair and beard, the helmsman would stand out like a glowing beacon.

'Well, try not to talk too much,' Glaucus had added, a mite petulantly. 'That cultured Eleusinian accent of yours could give you away.'

It had all sounded so simple then, but now, as he approached the Asopus and looked onto Theban territory, he began to realise the perils involved in the task he'd set himself. Still under the shelter of the trees, he paused and took out the bread and goat cheese that Anthousa had packed for him. The Asopus was now a mere gurgling stream, and Clytes mused that had such been the case on the night of the assault, Plataea may have been lost. Had the main Theban force not been delayed by the unnatural strength of the flood that night, it might have been a different story.

Looking around to make sure he was not being observed, he began to make himself ready.

THIRTY-EIGHT

GONE WAS THE BRONZED smooth skin topped by glossy dark curls. No more, the lithe movements of a young man in his prime. To anyone passing by, here was a wizened old man, his legs like two bows, bent with age. His hair and beard, long and grizzled, and matted with dirt. His filthy rags, torn and stained. He drew piteous glances from people who, looking at his grimy legs, saw marks where he had either been beaten or attacked by dogs, and they hurried by, thanking the gods it was not one of them.

Clytes had managed to reach The City of the Seven Gates without being questioned. In fact, so good was his impersonation, he was avoided. Leaning on a stick which he had roughly fashioned from a fallen branch, he shuffled along, glancing neither right nor left, mixing with Boeotian travellers merging at the crossroads, before heading into the city.

Clytes glanced furtively up at the citadel and the impregnable Kadmeia Palace, wondering how he could gain access through these fortifications, for surely, this is where Lykaon would be.

He wasn't the only beggar in the city he noticed, and when he approached the doorway of one the houses which formed part of the overspill from the city proper, he was pelted with stones by a poor creature already staking his claim there. 'Get away!' snarled the man, angrily. 'Find somewhere else!'

Clytes, shuffled over to him, warily. 'I won't bother you,' he mumbled in a weak voice while coughing, consumptively. 'But can you tell me how I can get inside the citadel?'

The beggar stared at him for a moment, wondering what this old man was asking. 'Be wary, old fellow. The city is in mourning for her dead and times are not good in Thebes for the likes of us. The blessings of Zeus Xenios are not appreciated. We are more likely to get a beating than a welcome. Now move along before you attract trouble!'

'One thing, only,' croaked Clytes, with a harsh cough. 'Can you give me any news of Lykaon, The Wolf of Thebes?'

The beggar looked at him in alarm. 'Go away, old man, before I thrash you! That name is not to be mentioned in this city!'

'Are you telling me he's not here?' gasped Clytes.

'He has been banished. Haven't you heard? Who are you?' asked the beggar, nervous, yet at the same time, curious.

'I need to find him!' replied Clytes, urgently.

'Well, you'll have a long walk,' replied the beggar, suddenly relieved that he might be able to get rid of this persistent and unwanted companion. 'He left last week with his followers. Thirty of Thebes best warriors. They've gone to join the Spartan army!'

The beggar was certain his eyes did not deceive him. The old man seemed to grow in stature and his eyes blazed with an unnatural light. Suddenly he appeared stronger, taller...............

'Zeus Xenios!' the elder cried out, believing he was in the presence of the disguised God of Gods. 'Kurios! Lord! Here! Take my place!' he pleaded, believing the god had descended to test the townspeople on the welcome they offered to strangers. 'I'll find another!' and he hurried off, leaving his meagre belongings behind him, eager to spread the word. In a short time, the god Zeus was reported to be abroad in the city. Clytes grew in the telling of the tale. He was soon twelve feet high, and his eyes were not brown, but red and blazing fire. Many people, still shocked by their grief, believed the story that the God of Gods had visited them, but others were more skeptical. Surely the all-seeing Zeus would know where to find Lykaon the Wolf, so who was this stranger who sought him?

THIRTY-NINE

THE THEBANS WERE DISTURBED by the story spreading about the city, that a magical being able to change shape and height, was in their midst, but by the time a search party had been organised, Clytes was on his way south, avoiding the main road, heading as fast as he could towards Athens.

As he'd neared the Boeotian capital, he had seen for himself the Theban hoplites in full training. Their thick-set bodies, naked to show their superior power and strength. A thousand and more of these meat-filled country boys, preparing to join forces with the Spartan army, where Clytes guessed they would eventually meet up with Lykaon and his band of followers. If an attack was to be made into Attica the most likely route would be via the Eleusinian Plain and his own home town of Eleusis, where his life had abruptly changed to become one ruled by vengeance and hate. Oh, what sweet justice, to kill him in Eleusis, he thought, his eyes filled with hatred. Eager to get as far from Thebes as possible before night-fall, he was back across the Asopus by the time the sun was setting over the Gulf of Corinth to the west.

Just when he had decided to roll up in his cloak, to sleep until daybreak, he saw a light in the window of a small dwelling and went towards it, cautiously. Although now in Plataean territory, Thebans could already have moved into the abandoned farmsteads which were closest to their border, but before he could approach any further, a great hound with hackles raised and teeth bared, rushed at him barking and growling, fiercely. 'Shit!' he exclaimed, as he tried to protect himself, by running toward the nearest tree. A voice was heard and the brute suddenly fell silent and loped back towards its owner. Clytes could make out the figure of a wiry youth, bearing a rough bow and arrow, ready for firing.

'Throw down your weapons and remove your clothes!' the boy shouted, 'or I will set the dog on you!' Clytes, thinking he did not want any more leg wounds, did as he was asked, then approached the archer, with his arms raised.

After inspecting his bag of theatrical paraphernalia, the youth allowed Clytes to approach the house. 'I didn't think any Plataeans were still here,' Clytes said, calmly, trying not to frighten the lad. 'You're a bit close to the border. Aren't you afraid of being attacked?' The lad handed him back his clothes. 'Here, put them back on!' he insisted.

Ducking his head, Clytes entered the modest room, lit by a glowing fire in the centre. Around the fire sat an old woman and two small children, who looked up at him, fearfully. 'He's not Theban!' spoke the youth, reassuringly to his grandmother. 'Look!' and he showed the bag of props to the surprised children.

'Is this all of you?' asked Clytes, concerned.

'My father went to prune the vines with our slave, four days ago,' said the boy, glancing worriedly at his grandmother. 'Our goats and mule have also gone. She won't let me go look for them,' he said, his voice breaking.'

'They could be waiting for you, Angelos!' the old woman, wailed. 'There is only you left, to protect us.'

'Why haven't you moved into the fortress?' asked Clytes. 'Don't you realise, war is coming? This is no time to be trimming your vines. It will be Thebans who'll benefit from the crop. Tomorrow, I will look for your father, Angelos, but if your herd has gone, then you must make ready to move to Plataea and from there, most likely to Athens.'

Clytes was later awakened by the sound of the dog's sharp barking. It was early morning and light was just filtering through the shutters. Angelos rushed immediately to the window, peering nervously through the gaps.

'Horsemen! Two!' he gasped. There was a howl, then silence.

'Smoke!' shrieked the old woman. 'They're going to set fire to us! Oh Zeus! Oh Demeter! Help us!'

As Clytes looked at their only exit, flames were already eating into the wood. In desperation, he emptied the piss pots, water skins and a jug of stale beer onto the blaze, tossing earth from the floor at the fire, in an attempt to protect the vulnerable occupants. He grabbed his sword and handed his knife to Angelos. 'Keep beside me!' he said to the youth, looking reassuringly into his eyes. The door was broken in and two armed men burst into the room. The old woman screamed, and clasping the two children to her, sank to the floor in shock.

Clytes, sword in hand, immediately attacked one of the soldiers. Clad in full armour, his bronze breastplate giving him more protection than the linen chiton worn by Clytes, the Theban fought back ferociously, forcing Clytes to manoeuver around the still hot embers of the central hearth. Angelos stood braced ready for the second soldier to attack him. Instead, the soldier bent over the boy's grandmother, and grabbing the children by their arms, he started dragging them towards the door. The old woman threw herself on the children in an effort to protect them and the soldier, thrusting his weapon into her, felled her to the ground. The blade went through her frail body so easily, it also pierced the body of her grand-daughter, who was trapped beneath her, and the child was killed instantly. In revulsion and grief, Angelos ran at the murderer, screaming, but the soldier held his blade to the neck of the crying small boy in his grasp, telling him, 'Back off!' and looking at Clytes, he yelled, 'Both of you!'

Clytes lowered his weapon, fearing for the child, and the two Thebans backed out of the house with the boy held in front of them, as hostage. Moments later, they were on their horses and the sounds of galloping hooves faded into the distance.

Angelos, cradling his grandmother, strived to hear her dying words. 'Never forget you are a Plataean, Angelos,' she whispered, then with renewed strength, told him firmly, 'Never forget The Shield!' before her life was taken from her.

They never found Angelos's father or the slave. Clytes believed they'd been taken into captivity by the Thebans, as well as their livestock. With the help of Clytes, the youth buried his grandmother and baby sister, and then set fire to what was left of his homestead, together with the vineyards. No murdering Theban would ever benefit from them.

'Can I go with you, Clytes?' Angelos asked the actor, pleadingly. 'I'm good with the bow and arrow. I never miss when hunting hares,' he boasted, proudly.

'Well, that's good to hear, lad, because your targets will be larger than hares from now on,' said Clytes, grimly. 'How old are you, Angelos?' he asked, now in a quandary as how best to help this boy.

'I'm thirteen but very strong, although I don't look it,' he said, hopefully.

'Tall for your age and wiry,' remarked Clytes. 'I was the same, at your age.'

Now, in the company of a reluctant guardian, the boy hurried from the only place he'd ever known, as they set off towards the protection of the low wooded slopes of Mount Cithaeron, and the route which led to Athens.

From their vantage point in the hills, they watched the continuing forced migration of the herds from the lands of the Plataeans. Word was spreading about the impending war, and there were scenes not witnessed here since the Persians had attacked them, many years ago. Horses, sheep, goats and cattle, were on the move, together with mule and ox-drawn wagons piled high with crates of geese, various kinds of poultry and food stuffs. Running hither and thither, were the hunting hounds and pet dogs. A frightened donkey could be seen bucking and kicking, its loud braying clearly heard. There seemed to be no order, only chaos.

Clytes remarked to the boy at his side, 'I've been thinking, Angelos. Maybe, you should travel with them. You'll be safer on Euboea, and there will be many who could do with the help of a strong lad like you.'

'But what about you, Clytes?' answered Angelos, nervously. 'If you are going to Athens, I would rather stay with you.'

'I have plans, Angelos,' said Clytes, trying to avoid the boy's eyes. 'It would not be safe for you to stay with me.'

The boy tried to hide his fear, when he said, 'Well, I could at least try and find a position.'

'That's a good lad!' said Clytes, endeavouring to appear unconcerned. 'Let's go see who is travelling. You may know some of them.'

They had no luck with the first groups they encountered. Clytes wasn't going to let the lad be exploited. But when he saw a herd of exceptional horses being driven towards them, he was interested in finding out who owned them. From one of the riders herding the horses, he found out they belonged to Anatolios of Leuctra, and that he was taking his prize stock out of the clutches of the Thebans or the Spartans or even the Athenians, for that matter.

'What kind of master is he?' asked Clytes, curiously.

'Are you looking for work?' asked the rider.

'I'm not, but this boy is,' replied Clytes, beckoning the youth over.

'Well, I am the owner of these horses,' stated Anatolios, as he looked the boy over. I could make use of a willing lad, too young to be taken by the army. The Thebans are already taking every good horse in the territory to increase their cavalry, but I have ships waiting at the port of Oropus to take my best lineage horses on the sea crossing to Eretreia. You can join us in getting my horses safely to the island,' he said to young Angelos, 'and also for their care afterwards. Unless the Athenian cavalry find us of course and commandeer them, but we will play a cunning cat and mouse game before I let that happen!' he said, sternly. 'We are moving on now. Are you going to join us then, or not?' he asked, looking kindly at the boy.

Angelos looked quickly at Clytes, then threw his arms around his waist, gripping him tightly. 'I'm going with them, Clytes!' he said, bravely.

'A good decision,' he replied, trying hard to conceal his emotions. He lifted the boy up, to sit behind Anatolios on the broad back of his restless stallion, and Clytes watched as they rode away after the fast moving herd, the humble bow of Angelos, bouncing on the boy's slender back.

'Now that was hard!' muttered Clytes, to himself. He was surprised at how attached he had become to the boy, who had looked just as he had at thirteen. But it was for the best, he tried to convince himself, and he focused his thoughts on his own cold future. A future in which there was no place for responsibilities.

FORTY

THE MORNING AFTER TAKING his farewell of Clytes, Glaucus immediately left Plataea for the south, in the company of the actor's travelling companions in the theatrical troupe, Leon and Panthas. On the journey the pair recounted to the helmsman how they'd tried to persuade the popular entertainer to come with them, but without success, and they left in the forlorn hope of finding a suitable replacement for the Eleusinian when they arrived in Athens. They were not looking forward to explaining to the young playwright, Baras of Athens, and Terches, his extravagant older lover and sponsor, that his comedy, 'The House of Wrongdoings', was now missing its most charismatic actor. Clytes had a way of working a crowd like no other, and he would not be easy to replace at such short notice. The Great Dionysia would be attracting all the famous and talented of the entertainment world from every quarter of the empire, and there would be fierce competition for the acclaim of the discerning Athenian citizens. Clytes had left them with an unexpected vacuum, and Leon and Panthas discussed and fretted about it, all the way to Athens.

The roads as they reached the capital were crowded, not only with people attending the festival and those bringing wares to sell to festival goers, but also groups of concerned families worried about what had happened at Plataea. They were arriving at the capital with drawn wagons and handcarts, containing all their possessions, and not all of them had relatives or friends to take them in.

Seeing the chaos unfolding, Glaucus didn't linger. He needed work, and without Clytes to delay him with his company, the delights of the festival held no allure for him. As soon as he was suitably fortified with food and wine, he parted from his anxious companions and made for the ports on the Piraeus where he expected to find cheap lodgings. Fortunately for the helmsman, he was known thereabouts; because the overcrowding he had encountered in the city was just the same, if not worse, at the ports. He had never, in all his years of coming to the Piraeus, seen so much activity.

'Bless me Poseidon, if it's not Flamebeard!' shouted the inn-keeper, when Glaucus entered his heaving, rowdy establishment. Lumbering towards the man, pushing others aside, Glaucus gripped him firmly by the hand.

'Borus! You old dog!' roared Glaucus. 'Am I glad to see you, old friend! I'm in need of a bed, until I find a commission. Anything, just so long as it isn't the floor.'

The inn-keeper lifted his hands in apology. 'Glaucus, for you, I will need two beds! It just can't be done, big man. I can have a bed made up for you on the floor of a storeroom. It has no window, but you can have the use of it, and that's only because you are a friend. You can try elsewhere, but it will be the same story wherever you go.'

Glaucus could see for himself that the inn-keeper was speaking the truth, when he walked towards the harbour mouth later in the day. The town of Piraeus, with its wide, grid planned streets, was normally teeming with the hustle and bustle expected at such a prestigious port, but now there were added groups of people huddled together in doorways, and on any piece of spare ground where they could put up a temporary shelter. When stopping to ask some of them who they were, he found they had travelled from a variety of vulnerable places along the coastline, some from towns without the protection of walls, or homesteads without enough manpower to put up a defence. They were all placing their trust in the protection offered by the Long Walls, which stretched from Piraeus to Athens, and the strength of the mighty Athenian navy. This is where they would be safer, if the Spartans were to attack.

As usually happened with Glaucus, children soon gathered about him and like a whale surrounded by suckerfish, he moved about the town and harbours, followed by a shoal of chattering waifs. Everywhere he asked questions, gleaning information and gathering gossip, anything which would help him in his choice of vessel. Even a helmsman's salary would not be sufficient to replace the stolen dowry of his niece. Although he knew that Corinth was offering more than Athens for capable crew members, he had no hesitation in staying loyal to Athens, and he hoped that his reputation, earned over many years, would convince an Athenian captain to hire him. His wealth had been forcibly taken from him, and it was only by plunder and a share of potential war booty that could now replace it. He was in need of a venture which was likely to entail some danger, and a captain bold enough to take a risk.

The innumerable shipsheds, at Zea, Kantharos and Munychia, the three harbours of the Piraeus, were in full use, evident from the din coming from the long thin buildings. Glaucus, throughout the day would walk around them all, watching with great interest the triremes; the sleek, fast warships of the Athenian navy, in their various stages of maintenance and refitting. Speaking with just a few of the many hundreds of shipwrights gainfully employed, he was informed that one-hundred vessels were being made ready for an expedition around the Peloponnese. This news interested him greatly, but the complaints he heard, that shortages of various materials were holding up the refitments, made Glaucus wary that inferior materials may be used for expediency. The shortage of suitable oar blade timbers from Macedonia was causing particular consternation.

He did not believe that the naval commissioners, appointed by the Athenian Council, would cut corners because of the urgency, but if he was to take the helm of one of these ships, he wanted to be sure that only the best materials were being used. The rest of the day was spent in checking this out. The keel had to be of oak, hard enough to withstand being dragged ashore, the inner hull to be of the lightest fir, to ensure a fast ship. Most important for Glaucus, was the quality of the hypozomata, the hemp cables which under precise tension held the timbers of the ship watertight and strong enough to withstand sudden changes in course or weather. They could improve a decent ship or weaken an otherwise good ship, and so important was the secret of making this rope, that anyone found exporting one from Athens would be sentenced to death. He had memories of one of the dual hypozomata breaking during a storm when he was an oarsman aboard a Corcyran ship rounding Kavomaleas in the Peloponnese. He could hear the ship's timbers crying out, and the vessel barely made it to the island of Kythira, where one of the two spares was also found to be inferior. Since that narrow escape he had always made a point of checking such details.

In his wanderings, he picked up several other seamen who were also seeking employment as deckhands or rowers and with their joint experiences they all had opinions as to what constituted a good ship. A 'lucky ship' was mentioned fairly often and many stories were swapped amongst the seamen about the strange and extraordinary happenings on sea voyages, when the intervention of the gods turned disaster into salvation. 'Yes, a lucky ship is what I want!' a thick-necked oarsman by the name of Bion, said emphatically.

To attract a rich captain; one who would be fair and generous in sharing out the spoils, and also the best rowers; men who would be proud to pull hard for their ship, the vessel needed to look good as well as be of best quality. Glaucus, satisfied that no obvious shortcuts were being made on quality, now searched for a fearsome design which would put terror into the enemy. The small group of sailors, now accompanying Glaucus and the children in his quest, were told of a particular marine artist working in the eastern harbour of Munychia and they were all keen to view his work. Climbing the hill which looked down on the eastern seaboard of the Piraeus peninsula, they watched from the Theatre of Dionysus, the deceivingly peaceful scene of sparkling azure blue sea below. Dotted with ships under sail or oars, the harbour of Munychia resembled a round, filled wine krater below them.

As they approached the slipways stretching out from the shipsheds, a trireme was just being launched, and shouts from the lines of sweating shipwrights, holding fast onto the restraining ropes, warned the group to keep well back.

The burnished bronze sheathed ram emerged from the opening, accompanied by the pungent smell of hot timbers and curling smoke, as the vessel slid on the wooden rollers. An enormous sea nymph propelled towards the water's edge. Screams were heard as the children who were still with Glaucus, were seen crying and fleeing in all directions. On the prow, carved and brightly painted, was the image of the sea-goddess, Thetis, with her hair of fiery flames. Her face was of a fearsome, snarling lioness with blazing eyes, and she was riding fishtailed sea-horses, their teeth bared in rage. At the stern was a mighty sea serpent with a coiled body and bulging eyes; its head and protruding tongue thrusting towards the rear of the ship. First, twisting upwards to the sky, its forked tail then coiled downward towards the deck, providing a dramatic cover over the seat for the helmsman. As the vessel hit the water, it stalled momentarily, then, to the shouts and cheers of the shipwrights, it bounced up on top of the spray; a sea creature rejoicing in its natural element.

Bion was laughing heartily at the children's frightened crying, but he could not stop his own heart from pounding, and he did not laugh at all on seeing one of the young oarsmen in the group, on the ground, kneeling in prayer.

'What is the name of this ship?' shouted Glaucus, to the shipwrights.

'She is named 'Thetis' after the shape changing sea nymph, called out one of the sweating workers, mopping his brow.

'Has a captain been chosen, yet?' ventured Glaucus. The workman walked to the edge of the slipway and looking at the seamen, smiled knowingly. 'The lots have been drawn and the trierarch of this ship is Iandros, son of Paramanos!' he shouted back.

'That name means nothing to me,' said Glaucus, looking at the others for answers.

'Paramanos!' moaned some of the seamen, together. 'So? Tell me?' asked Glaucus, impatiently.

'The family are 'new money' and they seem to have no scruples as to what or who they buy!' said Bion, dismissively. 'More money than sense, if you ask me! Iandros has no experience of commanding a ship, Glaucus. His father will have paid for this year's upkeep of the Thetis purely to show off his new wealth.'

'Who was responsible for the design of the Thetis?' asked Flamebeard of the shipwright, watching with interest, from the slipway.

'That was the son's idea. He worked with the artist over several weeks until the design was to his liking,' replied the man. 'She is frightening, don't you think?'

Glaucus turned to the men who were with him and said, with emphasis, 'If the rest of her checks out, I will be registering my interest in this paragon. She is magnificent!'

'But what about the captain?' Bion enquired. 'He is untried.'

Glaucus shook his large head, tutting at the oarsman. 'Anyone who is audacious enough to emblazon his ship like that is no fool. He knows it will attract interest. It has mine already. If he is untried, then I'm not, and I can handle a crew.'

If this is his first command, thought Glaucus to himself, and his family are considered upstarts, then that could be to my advantage. I doubt he will attract an Athenian helmsman with my experience.

'I'm interested,' said Glaucus, determinedly.

'Me too then!' replied Bion, excitedly, and pointing at the Thessalian, he said, 'I've never seen such hair as yours before, Helmsman! Can I rub it for luck?' Glaucus gave out a booming laugh and replied, 'If you wish, oarsman!' and still chuckling, he lowered his head.

The workers at the slipway, taking a break from their labours, watched in bemusement as an enormous redhead had his mop of fiery hair enthusiastically rubbed by a group of burly seamen.

FORTY-ONE

WHEN CLYTES THE ELEUSINIAN finally arrived in Athens, entering through the immense northern Dipylon Gate; the most impressive of many gates into the metropolis, his first instinct was to have a hot bath. After days of travelling he felt dirty and unkempt, and being suddenly thrust into the great city after his solitary journey, he felt conspicuous by his condition. He made do, by stopping at a fountain just inside the gate; splashing water over his head and face, and removing the country dust from his feet, before immediately setting off along the Dromos which would lead him straight to the agora. He needed to find Leon and Panthas as quickly as possible, in the hope that he had not already been replaced in the play.

As Clytes walked the wide concourse crowded with people, he could see and hear immediately that the city was in full preparation for the Great Dionysia. Everywhere he could hear lilting voices ringing through the air, as poetry, both tragic and sweet, was being performed for the passing masses. Acrobats and musicians, dancers with their tinkling bells and tambourines, all the usual multicultural sideshows to tempt the populace to part with their silver. Everywhere, there were stalls piled high with all the variety of foodstuffs expected at such a great festival. In normal circumstances he would be one of the performers, recounting epic tales of the heroic deeds of gods and men. Woe betide any thespian who veered from the accepted texts. He noticed Socrates, of course. The eager philosopher was pushing his way through the crowds like a mad pelican, his bulging eyes seeking out new people to accost with his interminable questions. Clytes was tempted to stop and talk with several acquaintances whom he identified among the performers. By his long, loping stride, some instantly recognised him.

'Clytes! Good to see you!' shouted a middle-aged man standing on a wooden box, who abruptly halted his melodramatic narration to the crowd, to beckon to Clytes. 'You look like crap! What have you been up to?'

Weary, dirty and hungry, Clytes shouted back, 'I can't stop, Demardes, I have to find Leon and Panthas. I need to find out if they have a bed for me tonight!'

'Are those two cats still squabbling?' laughed Demardes, trying to shush his impatient audience with a wave of the hand. 'If you've no luck, you'll find me at 'The Red House'. I know Rhoda isn't cheap, especially now with so many people here, but she keeps a clean house. And no vermin. Do you remember her dog, Bat, the mad ratter? She still has him!' Demardes' audience began to boo and hiss, so he signalled to Clytes that he had to continue. When he started his narration again, Clytes chuckled to hear groans of, 'You've already said that bit!'

He thought he knew just where to find them. In fact, it was vital that he should, for he had to face Terches, to explain his absence from the rehearsals of the play, scheduled to be performed during the festival, and he would need back-up from Leon and Panthas. Their names were a bit of a joke of course. Anything less harmful or menacing than these outward-seeming clowns would be hard to imagine. Leon, no matter what he ate, remained as lean as a starving cat, whereas Panthas had the comfortable roundness of a well fed one. He knew they would both stand by him, if they could. It all depended on whether the playwright, Baras, had hired a replacement.

Although totally different in character the three had taken an instant liking for one another and for Clytes' part, they amused the Eleusinian greatly. His companions played their parts as women on stage superbly, and thought Clytes, only the gods on Olympus knew to what extent was acting. Having been employed by the city fathers as entertainers during the Plataean Anthesteria and now in Athens to be giving a first performance of a comedy by an up and coming young playwright called Baras, their little touring company had been kept busy.

Terches, an acquaintance of Pericles and also of the acclaimed playwright, Euripides, was one of the most ambitious and prosperous men in Athens. He needed to be if he was going to continue sponsoring his young lover's theatrical productions. Unfortunately, young Baras had not impressed the present archon with his proposed ideas for this year's City Dionysia, so his plays would not be performed in the contest, as would Euripides'. Terches had been persuaded to take on the funding of just one play - a comedy - 'The House of Wrongdoings', and this would be performed on a temporary stage, in the agora with three actors and a small chorus of twelve; six men and six boys. The playwright was not at all happy about the small number in the chorus, but Terches had promised him more funding, if the play went down well. A lot rested on the main actor, and as Clytes weaved his way through the throng, he hoped he would still have the starring roles.

At last he reached his goal; dwarfed and unnoticeable among the numerous shrines and grand marble edifices surrounding the agora. In anticipation, he approached the small wooden hut situated at the side of a modest timber constructed stage, littered with props and rolls of painted cloth backdrops, suitable for the forthcoming production. From the sounds emitting from the hut, he knew he had found his fellow actors.

'I'm telling you, that colour will never work. You're losing the whole effect, Panthas!'

'And since when did you become the great exponent of fashion, Leon?' Panthas spat back.

'It's a comedy not a bloody tragedy. That colour is too drab,' moaned Leon.

'Well, tie me down and flay me!' Panthas cried out, his feelings hurt. 'I do know the difference!'

The two players were sitting opposite each other, across a wooden trestle which was almost hidden by a vast array of theatrical costumes and grotesque character masks. A painted rural scene with cattle and goats, humorously adorned with face masks and beards, was draped on the back wall of the hut, giving the illusion it was much larger than it really was.

It was in the middle of their squabbling, that Clytes quietly made his entrance. Leon and Panthas at first stared at their unexpected visitor, suspiciously.

'Good day to you both,' the Eleusinian said, making room for his long frame and almost pushing Leon off the bench as he gratefully sat down, helping himself greedily to their bread and wine. 'Have you nothing to say?' he mumbled with his mouth full. 'Have you forgotten your friend so quickly?'

Panthas, the first to recover, leapt up and gyrated around the small area. 'Didn't I tell you, Leon? Didn't I tell you?' he cried, pointing at a grinning Clytes. 'Don't write the fellow off, I said. He'll be back!'

'By all the gods, Clytes, you look like you've been sleeping in shit,' Leon exclaimed. 'You'll need to clean up before we meet with Terches. I must warn you, he went demented when you didn't arrive with the rest of us. Baras did find a replacement for you, but don't worry, he's hopeless. He's terrified of heights! I expect they'll be relieved that you have arrived. We had to tell him all about Lykaon, and the reason you went to Thebes, Clytes. What happened, by the way? Did you find the swine?' Leon suddenly stopped babbling and looked at Clytes with concern. 'You have come back for the play, haven't you?' he asked in alarm.

Clytes had gone pale and his eyes had become bright and menacing. 'No, I didn't find him, Leon,' he replied bitterly. 'But I will! And, yes, I am back for the play.'

'How is your wound, Clytes?' asked Panthas, gently.

'It's healed sufficiently, Panthas. Don't worry about the act! Changing the subject, he enquired, 'Any news of Glaucus? Is he here in Athens?'

'No, he didn't stay,' answered Leon. 'As soon as we arrived from Plataea, he headed off to the Piraeus in search of a ship. On the journey here though, he told us the full story behind your troubles with the Theban. We understand why you did what you did, Clytes.'

'That moving mountain has a big mouth,' said Clytes, smiling. 'It will get him into trouble one of these days.'

'Not like you, eh Clytes! You don't look for trouble,' chuckled Leon. He received a gentle cuff on the head in response and the three men warmly clasped hands, glad to be in each other's company once more.

'I hope you brought your penis with you, Clytes,' said Panthas, seriously. 'We haven't been able to find another one quite so impressive. The festival players have claimed all of them. To order a new one costs a small fortune!'

Clytes laughed. 'I had to leave that one with Anthousa, sad to say. It was a good one, nice balance. It will be a fond remembrance of me!' he said, smiling at the sudden thought of her ....

From head to toe, Anthousa steadily and gently rubbed the perfumed oil over his body. The oil being tinted, she was trying not to miss any parts. 'I'm enjoying this very much, luscious, but I have to get ready for the parade!' he groaned, grasping her by the wrist. 'I won't have need of that contraption if you carry on!' and he pointed at the huge wooden phallus with its leather harness, lying on the bed. 'Will I see you later?' she asked him, hopefully. 'Try and keep me away!' he answered, smacking her on the buttocks, and she giggled like an innocent girl.

.... 'Don't concern yourself, Panthas,' said Clytes, emerging from his reverie. 'You can leave that detail to me.'

They weren't listening. They had returned to their squabbling. 'Let me put the colour on the backs of your legs next time, Panthas,' said Leon, with exasperation. 'You always seem to miss a bit!'

'Oh, fuck you, Leon! Who sees the backs of your legs anyway!' replied Panthas, his voice rising to a screech.

They stopped their arguing and both turned to look at Clytes. His head was thrust back against the wall of the hut, and he was laughing fit to burst.

FORTY-TWO

THE TRIO SENT A SLAVE to the house of Terches with a deferential letter, asking for an urgent meeting with the choregos and the playwright of 'The House of Wrongdoings', and they were hurrying to comply with the response recently received, which was not a very polite one. Terches' house was built into the side of The Hill of the Nymphs, not far from The Pnyx slopes, where, all too soon, the dramas and comedies of the City Dionysia would be performed. This was one of the most overcrowded areas of the city, where many houses were combined with small workshops; cobblers, stone carvers, pottery throwers - not an area they expected to find their lavish sponsor, Terches.

The slave bringing the message, took them directly to an unassuming door without even the ubiquitous lion-head door knocker, they noticed. Hanging from an aperture in the door, was a knotted rope and the slave pulled on it vigorously, making a perfectly cast bronze bell ring melodiously on the other side. Almost immediately the door was opened by a beautiful youth, wearing nothing more than a tiny loincloth and a pair of sandals which slapped on the stone floor as he walked ahead of Clytes, Leon and Panthas, across a shaded, tree-filled courtyard with a central well.

A door opened and two small dogs rushed, yapping towards them. 'Bobo! Nike!' a high voice called, to no avail and a fat, large breasted eunuch waved breezily, then returned to the kitchen. The dogs, still yapping at their feet, were scooped up by the young slave, unconcerned for his tender skin, and carried towards the house.

'Follow me,' he said, turning to the trio and they were led through an arched doorway, flanked on either side by exquisite statues of the gods, Apollo and Eros. They were of such graceful beauty, with manly shoulders, broad chests, flat bellies and finely tapered limbs; in yielding natural poses of relaxation and unashamed nakedness. The house, the trio gradually observed, was an indulgent shrine to the relationship between Terches and his younger lover, the aspiring playwright, Baras, and they couldn't help but notice that the theme of several wall frescoes was of male partners, mainly middle-aged men with beautiful youths, in provocative poses.

They were taken along a corridor, passing a well-stocked library, the shelves piled high with papyrus scrolls. A large desk was laid out with all the fine writing accoutrements required by their learned owner. Standing on the corner of the desk was a bronze statue of a boy playing with two small dogs, similar to the ones being carried nonchalantly before them.

Their tour ended in the andron, the main seating area, where the slave carefully set down the dogs. They immediately leapt up onto the sofas where Terches and Baras were stretched out, relaxing, and began licking their faces. 'Oh, you naughty boys! Get down!' wailed Baras, laughing. 'Take them back to the kitchens for now, Agathangelos. Ask cook to give them a treat of some sort. We are busy right now.'

'Bring back some wine and whatever food the cook can provide at short notice,' said Terches. 'Nothing too elaborate,' he remarked, looking at his guests, and frowning.

'Come with me, Clytes,' Terches ordered, suddenly rising from the couch. 'I want to talk to you alone,' and he ushered an apprehensive Clytes into the library, closing the door firmly behind them. Leon and Panthas watched them leave with nervous glances passing between them as Baras, surprised that Terches had left the room without explaining anything to him, rose to follow him, but then thought better of it and sat down again. If Terches was going to admonish Clytes in any way, for letting him down, then he would have liked to be party to it, as there was much he also wanted to say to the actor. Leon and Panthas took the opportunity to concentrate their efforts in persuading Baras that all was well with his play, now the star performer had returned, and their joint enthusiasm finally made Baras relax a little. Last minute details and changes were mutually discussed, while eyes and ears strained towards the library door.

When Clytes and Terches returned, they gave nothing away as to what had transpired between them, but the pair seemed on good terms, and when the wine and food arrived, it was shared amicably.

It was not until the trio had left the house and were walking back to their lodgings that Leon finally asked, 'Well?' And Panthas, repeated, 'Yes, well, what did he say? Are you back in the play or not?'

'Oh, that! Yes, of course!' Clytes answered, his face expressionless.

'Well, Baras wasn't so sure he would forgive you!' exclaimed Panthas, petulantly.

'It wasn't the play Terches wanted to talk about,' said Clytes, looking strangely at them. 'My exploits in going after Lykaon and getting in and out of Thebes undetected, seemed to interest him more. To put it bluntly, our esteemed employer thinks Athens could use my talents for the war effort,' he said conspiratorially. 'He wants me to meet with Pericles!'

FORTY-THREE

THE PLAY WAS NOT a resounding success. Nor was it a complete failure. Clytes tried to reassure Baras that had it been performed at The Pnyx, with a more discerning audience, the reception would have been more sympathetic, than from the large noisy mob of individuals of obviously low social status, in the agora that day. He was quite pleased with his own personal performances and the audience seemed to laugh at the appropriate times. It was always going to be risky when the plot contained a thinly disguised mockery of Cleon, a politician bitterly opposed to Pericles, and one who purported to favour the masses. One of Clytes' characters, a loud-mouthed, uncouth butcher, always listening for gossip and intrigue of the wealthy leisure classes at the whorehouse, 'The House of Wrongdoings', was not lost on the mainly poor audience, and there were some shouts of abuse accompanied by the throwing of rotten fruit whenever the 'Cleon' character was ridiculed.

Clytes did his best to make light of those incidents by pretending to gobble up the offerings, or juggling them expertly before throwing them back at the audience, and the chorus to their credit, played along with his antics. Only once did events get a little out of hand when a group of Cleon's thugs, sent deliberately to cause disruption, became very angry and climbed onto the stage. Loud booing started up again, from those who wanted to continue watching the play, and Clytes feared it could turn into a riot, but with the help of Leon and Panthas, and some of the adult members of the chorus, they managed to fight back, and cleared the stage without anyone getting seriously hurt. The play continued, and there were no further incidents, but Clytes' face mask carried a permanent dent.

The chorus, costumed in enormous caricature noses, eyes and ears, went down very well, and their sighs and moans and exaggerated expressions of surprise or dismay, caused much laughter.

The convoluted sub-plot created by Clytes as the god Eros, flying above the audience on a tension rope, firing soft arrows at the actors and into the crowds, went down well. The 'beautiful' daughter of the butcher, played hilariously by Panthas, is hit by one of the arrows and thinks she has fallen in love with a grotesque old man, only to find out much later and after many comical incidents; to her surprise and that of the audience, he is in fact a handsome young man in disguise, trying to catch the butcher at his devious plottings.

In their ludicrously padded costumes, Leon and Panthas, as the two madams of the whorehouse, had their usual excellent reception. No-one could mix vulgarity and wit so sublimely as this pair of natural artists, and even Baras laughed out loud, hearing his own words so brilliantly performed.

In the final act, the butcher is caught in one of his own underhand traps, and the old man is revealed as the handsome Clytes, together with his enormous male appendage, an essential adornment at any Dionysian festival. The phallus, Clytes had acquired from an old actor colleague, now too infirm to perform. 'Perfect balance, Clytes,' he'd remarked, appreciatively. 'Constructed like our triremes. Oak for the balls at the base and fir for the member, for buoyancy!'

All in all, Terches and Baras were pleased with the troupe's interpretation of the play, but it was obvious to Terches that his beloved Baras would be no great threat to his friend, the renowned Euripides. They would try and put from their minds, for the moment, the rotten fruit thrown at the stage, and the fact that the play had nearly caused a riot. But they were forced to acknowledge that the rabble-rousing Cleon, who could work a crowd as well as Clytes, was gaining in popularity with the lower classes. Pericles' strategy of attrition with regard to the Spartan threat, was found wanting in some quarters, and support for Cleon's more aggressive approach was gaining ground.

At least Baras was not alone in his disappointment. Euripides came last at that year's City Dionysia; his tragic story of the wronged Medea proving too strong a subject matter for the judges. But it was the talk of Athens; as was the new play by young Baras, but for totally different reasons!

FORTY-FOUR

'CLEON'S POPULARITY WITH THE masses is growing, Pericles', spoke Terches anxiously, his face reddening with anger at the memory of the scuffles during Baras's play. 'That warmonger knows how to rouse the mob as well as our actor friend here,' he said, waving a hand in Clytes' direction. 'Cleon's views appeal to the young and they want war!' he said with emphasis. Clytes noticed that Pericles was not stirred by Terches' emotional outburst. His intelligent eyes were thoughtful but not unduly disturbed, as the elder statesman walked slowly around the walled gardens of his city villa, in the company of Terches and Clytes. Despite being in his sixth decade, Pericles was still a man of commanding presence, and showed no sign of being daunted by the pressures put upon his leadership of the great city of Athens and her growing empire.

'I have known several 'Cleons' in my lifetime,' he replied calmly, 'and where are they now, Terches? For almost forty years I have been at the forefront of Athenian politics and for thirty of them, chosen by the people to be their leader. I know our people,' he said, confidently. 'The young will always look for action. Were we not the same at their age? No, I will not rush to change my views because of bullies like Cleon. Look at our city, Terches,' and he swept his arm, as though speaking to thousands of adoring citizens. 'Like the shining tip of Athena's spear seen from afar on the Acropolis, she is a beacon of knowledge, spreading civilisation to the rest of the world. Sparta and her allies will acquiesce in time. Let them beat themselves against our walls. We can afford to wait.'

Terches sighed quietly and glanced at Clytes who was experiencing first-hand Pericles' proverbial calmness and self-control. 'There is dissent among some of our allies, Pericles, as you know,' he said pointedly. 'The Spartans and the Maccedonians are stirring up trouble against us, wherever they find an ally with a grievance. We cannot survive behind our walls for long, if the grain and trade routes do not stay open.'

'Which is why you think Clytes here can be of some assistance to us?' asked Pericles, looking directly at the puzzled actor.

'He has a talent for mimicry and disguise, Pericles, and he would be an asset in infiltrating any wavering factions in the Delian League,' said Terches, eagerly. 'He was at Plataea during the Theban attack and accounted for himself very well, I am told. He saw first-hand how important it is to have previous knowledge of traitors spreading dissention.'

'Excuse me, Terches!' exclaimed Clytes, and looking disconcertingly towards Pericles, 'but I was led to believe that I was brought here to report on what happened at Plataea and Thebes, and to discuss the capture of Lykaon of Thebes!'

'Yes - The Wolf!' interrupted Pericles. 'I have been informed of this Theban. I wish to hear everything you know of the killing of The Shield Guardian at Plataea, Clytes. Phalinus was a good friend, an exceptional man, and a fierce democrat. His death is a grievous loss to us all. As you may know, his wife and child are here in Athens, under my personal care. Let us hope they can return to their fair city before too long. I have discussed certain scenarios with Terches here, and Athens is offering you all the help you need, in hunting this maniac down. But we also require your undoubted abilities in assisting our cause.'

Terches spoke up, by way of explanation. 'Cleon is becoming too big for his boots, Clytes! If you were able to gain some useful information, which could be detrimental to his reputation, well.......'

'I am only interested in finding Lykaon,' interrupted Clytes. 'I have no interest in politics.'

This brought an astonished stare from the Athens' leader. 'You may want to avoid politics, young man,' spoke Pericles tersely, thrusting out his chin, 'but politics will not avoid you!'

'If it will help me find Lykaon, then I will consider it,' said Clytes, trying to meet the leader's bold gaze, 'but perhaps you are expecting more from me than I can deliver.'

A good part of the meeting was taken up by Clytes recounting what had transpired at Plataea, and the fact that there'd been several prominent Plataeans willing to join Thebes; although the majority had stayed loyal to Athens. 'Plucky little Plataeans!' exclaimed Pericles. 'You are probably too young to know about their contribution at Artemisium in the last great war. Never been on a ship before, many of them. No knowledge of seamanship whatsoever. Valour and zeal, that's what carried the day. Valour and zeal!' He was deeply moved on hearing the details of how Phalinus died. 'He was the first citizen of Plataea,' he said sadly. 'Men of his calibre do not come along often.'

Clytes was also asked to recount the tale of how he was able to enter Thebes, which Pericles found most intriguing. The numbers of fighting men he'd witnessed being put through their paces, the horses being brought from far and wide to strengthen their cavalry, everything he could remember was recorded by a slave sitting close by. The aristocrat was particularly attentive, during the telling of Lykaon and Larachne's banishment from the city. 'So, the 'She Wolf' abandoned her cub, eh?' said Pericles, mischievously. 'I wonder who the dark widow will attach herself to next? She doesn't keep them long though, it seems!'

Clytes warmed to Athens' leader, a little, when Pericles said how saddened he was to learn of his family tragedy. 'I understand why you hunt the Theban, Clytes,' he said with genuine feeling, 'but don't let your hatred destroy you,' he told him, advisedly. Turning to Terches, he said, 'You were right to suggest I meet with this Eleusinian. He is like a shadow. Able to move about at will, it seems! I am sure you will find a use for his talents.'

Before any more could be discussed, an aide arrived, calling the leader to urgent business elsewhere, and the meeting was suddenly brought to an end. 'Let me know what he decides, Terches,' said Pericles; and giving Clytes a rather withering look, remarked, 'No interest in politics, indeed!' and he strode from their presence, leaving slaves to escort both men from the garden.

Back in the noisy streets of the city, Clytes turned to Terches. 'What have you got me into Terches?' he asked him, incredulously.

'You want to find Lykaon, don't you?' replied Terches, haughtily. 'I'm providing you with the means.'

'I believe you're risking my life as a means to impress Pericles,' said Clytes, angrily. 'I'll decide when and where - and if!'

'You'll never find him on your own, Clytes,' said Terches, knowingly. 'Work with me. Go where you like. Wherever you think you'll find him. But, if you can gather useful information which could help Pericles, then we both win. If I rise, so will you, Clytes. Think about it!'

'You'd be a fool to turn down Terches' offer,' said Leon, when Clytes had described to his companions what had transpired at the villa of Pericles. 'With the help of the state you could achieve your objective, and you might even stay alive and prosper! How many touring actors, like yourself, get to meet the great Pericles and be taken into his confidence?'

'Make sure you push for better conditions for us poor players, Clytes,' said Panthas. 'We need our own union!'

'You are such innocents,' replied Clytes, amused. 'I'm not the sort that would prosper in the rarefied air that Pericles breathes - thank the gods! I accept who I am. If I risk my life, it certainly won't be to have the ear of Pericles or his like. What? I'd acquire more enemies than a dog has fleas. I have one enemy and that's enough. Politicians - they're all bloody bastards!'

'There goes our union!' groaned Panthas.

The comfortable boarding house temporarily provided by Terches was sadly in the past and they were now in a cramped shared room, in a district of leatherworkers, and the air was anything but rarefied. It was all they could get. The city was rapidly filling up with people from the villages around Athens. The building where the actors were staying was already seriously overcrowded.

'I didn't think this many people lived in all Hellas,' marvelled Leon. 'Well, they've likely brought all their wealth with them and they will want to be entertained, so you and I will be busy, Panthas. No more touring! You also could be exempt from military service, Clytes. Why don't you stay? The city will be in sore need of your music and poetry, with this impending war dragging on and on.'

'I have a lot to think about, dear friends, but I'll not be staying in the city - not with Cleon's bullies still wanting to break every bone in my body! Eleusis is where I have to be. Lykaon has to come past there sometime. I'll attach myself to the garrison there, and wait!'

Leon and Panthas shook their heads, and sighed.

FORTY-FIVE

MARISSA'S JOURNEY TOWARDS SPARTA held some of the most precious and unforgettable moments of her young life. After leaving Corinth, Nicander had wanted to pay a visit to his exiled cousin, the second king of Sparta, Pleistoanax. Exiled fourteen years previously for apparently accepting a bribe from Pericles of Athens to withdraw his army from the plains of Attica, he had been charged with treason by Sparta, and since then had made his home on Mount Lycaeus just over the border into Arcadia. To avoid further persecution, his house was built straddling the sacred precincts of the sanctuary to Zeus Lykaios, and here he waited, year on year, for the call back home. With stories increasing that the Spartan allies, Arcadia included, were gathering their forces, he expected the call at any time and the visit by his kinsman, Nicander, naturally raised his expectations. But yet again, in spite of the emergency, he heard with dismay that Archidamus and the current ephors had still not forgiven him.

Nicander spent some hours with his kinsman, telling Pleistoanax stories of the king's young son Pausanias, named after his famous grandfather. How he was growing into a fine strong youth in Sparta, and praying daily for the return of his father. Of the happenings at Plataea, Megara and Corinth. Of Marissa. Lastly, before leaving, he made a sacrifice at the altar of Zeus and swore that he would continue to fight for the reinstatement of his cousin to the Agiad royal house of Sparta.

The days and nights since leaving Corinth had been magical for Marissa, as their party travelled through the sheltered, fertile valleys of Arcadia, fed by cascades of clear water from the green mountain slopes. She felt as though she was under the spell of some unknown enchantress. A marvel of colour, the meadows were bright with yellow crocus, scented violets, red poppies and anemones. Everywhere on the air could be heard the somnolent music of heavy cow bells, and the tinkling melody of the tiny clappers of the goat herds, as the shepherds unhurriedly moved their stock to pasture.

They bathed in shaded pools, fed by sparkling waterfalls, and made love on banks of scented chamomile. The haunting music of faraway panpipes was carried on the breeze. Lying in the warm sun, Nicander would recount the myths of the region, the home of the god Pan and his nymphs, guardians of nature and mountain wilds. Of how Pan guarded the flocks, and day and night could be heard playing sweet music on his pipes, but should never be approached. He valued his solitude because of his ugly form and would scream so loudly, it would send a man mad with panic.

'That could be Pan we hear now!' said Marissa, alarmed. 'It could well be,' replied Nicander, in a whisper. 'We'd better be more quiet in our lovemaking!' he laughed softly, and covered her once again, with his sun-warmed body.

On their journey towards the Spartan border, Nicander called their party to a halt, and within familiar sight of the mountains of their homeland, they rested the horses and ate a light meal. It was like many other stops they'd made, but when Nicander, with concern in his eyes, bade Marissa to move away from the group to speak with him alone, a cold shiver went down her back, and she found her hands trembled. The paradise of the last few days ended sharply and cruelly for Marissa at that unknown spot, chosen purely because of its shallow stream which was suitable for watering the horses.

'And what will happen to me, while you are either with your family or on campaign?' she cried, trying hard not to burst into tears. 'Why didn't you tell me you already had a wife? Nicander, why didn't you tell me?'

'Because if I had told you, you wouldn't have come with me, Marissa, and I don't want to be without you,' he answered, trying to meet her tearful gaze.

'Oh, Nicander! What am I going to do?' she sighed heavily. 'I was preparing myself for a different way of life in your Sparta, but I am no better than your slave! I can see now, that without marriage, without a home, without the support of your family and friends, what will I have?'

'You will want for nothing, my dearest, and you will be safe!' he said, with emphasis. 'What else could I do? I couldn't leave you in Plataea. Your family will all be dead. You saw what was happening to anyone who had plotted with the Thebans! I could have taken you by force, Marissa, but I wanted you to come with me, willingly.'

'How long have you been married?'

'Four years.'

'Do you have children?'

'No, my wife has not carried a child full term.'

'Oh, now I understand! You just want me to bear your children!'

'I hadn't thought that far ahead. In fact, children could cause complications.'

'How so?'

'Spartan children are considered property of the state, and Spartans are protective of their blood-line. My family..........'

'So! My Boeotian blood is not good enough, is that it?'

'It's not Spartan,' he replied, diplomatically.

'Nicander, when I dreaded the thought of being hidden away at the back of the house, spinning wool and rearing children, I had no idea that I would never have a home! Never have children!'

'Sparta is not like Athens, my love. Women in Sparta would never stay at the back of the house, and they do not spin. They have a retinue of slaves to do such things.'

Nicander tried to take her in his arms, but she pulled away. 'Marissa, you are alive. That's all that matters. And I will care for you!'

'And what happens to me if anything happens to you, Nicander?'

She drew across her veil, as a signal to Nicander that she no longer wanted to speak to him.

Until nightfall, they rode in silence. At some point they crossed the border and the men, including Nicander, got down from their horses and intoning prayers of thanksgiving, kissed the earth of Sparta. Marissa, who had thought she would feel Nicander's excitement also at this point, felt nothing but debilitating despair. For the first time since the attack on Plataea, she felt the full loss of her family, and of her small, indomitable city. Despite her firm resolve on the road to Corinth, hot unstoppable tears flowed, hidden by her veil.

FORTY-SIX

THEY FOLLOWED THE FLOW of the Eurotas river south through the valley to Sparta, with nature's protective walls, the dark looming mountain range of Taygetos to the right of them, the great Parnon Massif on their left, until the first sight of their city came into view; the acropolis, home of Athena. But this was no Athens. Moderation in all things material was the Spartan way, and this extended to their temples and monuments. One work of art which Athens could not emulate though, was their treasured bronze statue of Athena by the gifted sculptor, Gitiades; his divinely inspired, Lady of the Bronze House. Standing either side of her altar, gazing down onto the agora were two bronze statues of Pausanias, the heroic victor at Plataea against the Persians - father of Nicander's cousin, Pleistoanax.

Riders having been sent ahead the previous day, there was a great welcoming of the travellers as they entered the environs of their capital, as though they were warriors returned from battle. Cups of fresh water from the street fountains were handed up to them, while women and children and old men gathered around the horses, eager to lead them in. Nicander had never looked so happy, thought Marissa, as he clasped hands with all who got near him, shouting out greetings to those he recognised. The stares she received from the women though, unnerved her. Such women! Strikingly beautiful, but shameless! They're almost naked, she thought, looking at the high cut slits in their garments, exposing more flesh than was respectable.

Shocked but curious, she briefly raised her head to look about her as she heard more shouting. Coming into the agora she saw a group of women arriving on horseback, seated on spirited mounts as though horse and rider were one entity. A striking woman with short hair, wearing a tunic which only just covered her thighs, called out to Nicander, and urged her horse towards him. 'Welcome home, husband!' she shouted above the clamour. Marissa felt herself grow faint and she gripped the mane of her horse for fear of falling. 'Greetings, Kora!' Nicander responded, obviously delighted to see her, and the two grasped hands as equals after a long separation.

Ortronus, the helot slave who had tended to her needs during the journey, came forward and stood beside her horse. Keeping his eyes averted, he said quietly, 'We have further to go, mistress. Three miles only. A village to the south of here, called Amyklai. My lord Nicander has arranged for you to stay with a family there.' He could not help sensing her disappointment, but inwardly he shrugged. It was none of his business.

Marissa looked across at Nicander who, still mounted, was bending down speaking to an elderly man. The ancient was clasping Nicander's foot, fearing he would move away. She waited for him to look up, but they were talking animatedly and he was totally engrossed. Feeling discarded and angry, she kicked her horse to follow after Ortronus. Another of his kind hurried over to join them and between the two slaves, Marissa's horse was guided out of the agora and down through the town.

The village of Amyklai was a prosperous one being situated on the road between the port of Githium on the Gulf of Laconia and the four villages making up the Spartan capital. Here, in the wide, gently undulating valley watered by the Euratos, lived many skilled crafts people, vendors and merchants of the perekoi class; freemen but not full citizens like the spartiates, the warrior elite who were exempt from any form of manual labour. The houses were of wooden construction, and some were substantial dwellings with carvings along their eaves and also decorating the balconies and gateways. The street to which Ortronus led Marissa, had an old gnarled olive tree growing at the entrance, and surrounding the tree was a wooden seat, where several old men were sat, some looking almost as ancient as the tree. The street was a wide one with room for carts to go up and down, and Ortronus drew Marissa's horse to one side to allow them passage, closely watched by their elderly audience. 'Where are you going?' asked one of the men, sharply. He looked younger than the others and had a menacing demeanor. Marissa was by now accustomed to people treating Ortronus harshly, and the other helots that had been in her company. The helots were the third and lowest class in Spartan society. Belonging to the subjugated race of Messenians, and owned by the state, they were made to work the land, providing the food to feed the population and also carry out all the menial unskilled tasks. The Spartans, always fearful of a revolt, because of the helot superior numbers, kept their slaves in a constant state of powerlessness and despair.

Marissa was tempted to tell the old man it was none of his business, but as she had no idea where she was being taken, she kept silent.

Ortronus bowed respectfully, and keeping his eyes averted, replied, 'The house of Erasmos the instrument maker, good sir.'

The old man stood up angrily and spat at Ortronus. 'Remove your cap, before you speak to me!' he shouted.

Ortronus obeyed instantly and looking down at the ground, he continued, sounding nervous, 'I believe he lives in the Street of the Single Olive Tree.' He was angry at himself. He had misjudged the situation, thinking because these men were elderly they were no threat. The old man still had some strength and he struck Ortronus viciously several times with his walking cane. He seemed to enjoy doing so, as he exchanged malicious smiles with his old companions.

'Get down, dog!' growled the man. 'Your shadow over me is offensive!'

To the embarrassment of Marissa, Ortronus was forced to the ground and made to crawl past the elders until his shadow fell beyond them.

'Show more respect next time!' snarled the old man, and with a bent finger pointing up the street, said, 'You will see the painted sign of a lyre.'

'You are most gracious. My thanks to you,' answered Ortronus, bowing humbly. Marissa noticed there was a gash on his arm which was bleeding, but he did not seem to be aware of it, and not wanting to embarrass him further, she didn't refer to it. As they left she could feel all their eyes watching her, suspiciously.

They soon found the house with the sign of the lyre and Marissa, disheartened and frightened by her recent experiences, was thankfully made welcome by an authoritative woman by the name of Dorias, the wife of the instrument maker. She had only been informed of Marissa's imminent arrival the day before, she explained, but she had everything ready according to the message. 'I hope you will find my home comfortable, Marissa. I will have someone prepare a hot bath for you shortly and then we shall eat.' She clapped her hands loudly, and two young women ran into the room. With their heads held low, they listened to their mistress's stringent orders and then bowing, left quickly to carry them out.

'I will take you to your room, now,' said Dorias, her demeanor brusque but not unfriendly. 'I hope I have understood our Lord Nicander's instructions correctly.' Marissa was led quickly up a wide wooden staircase to a room on the upper floor, and when the door was opened, light was flooding in from open shutters leading to a small balcony. Marissa rushed to the wooden railing and looking out, saw over the high garden wall, to beyond the village boundary to the mountains in the far distance. Delighted, she turned to thank Dorias, then noticed something on the wall. 'What is that?' she said, her heart quickening as she moved to look closer.

'Lord Nicander sent my husband specific instructions but as I have told you, they only arrived yesterday. My husband says it is one of his finest,' said Dorias, proudly.

The kithara far surpassed anything she had played in Plataea. Of polished rosewood, inlaid with tortoiseshell and ivory, it was the most beautiful instrument Marissa had ever seen. Very gently she removed it from its hanging place, smoothing her fingers along the exquisitely woven backcloth, and held the plectrum which hung from its ribbon. She was just about to use it to pluck the strings when she noticed there were letters carved on it. She looked closely.

To my soul, from Nicander

'Our men are of few words but when they speak, they speak,' said Dorias. 'You like the kithara?'

'More than I can say,' replied Marissa, quietly, her hands smoothing appreciatively over the polished wood.

'Perhaps you will play it for us this evening?' asked Dorias. My daughter Arlea and I will also play. I prefer the lyre myself.'

'It will remind me of my home, back in Plataea,' said Marissa, then her eyes clouded, remembering.

'Your home is in Sparta now,' said Dorias, not unkindly.

FORTY-SEVEN

THE SHIP, TWENTY-THIRD OF a fleet of thirty, pulled its way slowly around Cape Sounion, overlooked by the awesome temple to Poseidon towering above them. Leaving the safety of the Attic coast, it threaded its way past the western isles of the Cyclades, 'the stepping stones' of the Aegean, northwards towards the Locrian coast. The trireme was the Thetis and she moved powerfully against the swell caused by the strong north wind, as her one-hundred and seventy oarsmen, hard-earning their pay of three obols a day, rowed strenuously to the strict rhythm of the piper. Despite the cooling wind, it was hot on the rowing decks, and most oarsmen were stripped bare, with only bands of cloth around their foreheads to stop the sweat running into their eyes.

Poseidon, the unpredictable God of the Sea had, they hoped, been placated. Their commander, Cleopompus, was a respected general and a good choice, the city leaders had agreed, for this particular enterprise. His talent for guerilla tactics would come into play in the coming weeks. He'd made lavish sacrifices to the deity, and now the success or failure of this enterprise rested entirely on his shoulders. The sacrificial bull had made little protest as its life was taken at the newly built temple on the promontory, but the big-hearted stallion, a generous gift to the sea god, swam for a mile or more, trailing blood from severed veins, before finally succumbing to the blue waters and entering Poseidon's deep kingdom.

The general, onboard his flagship 'Apollonian', had precise orders. To engage with any privateers operating out of the land of Locris, destroy as many of their bases and ships as possible, and leave a watchful garrison on the uninhabited island of Atalante. The marauders had been a thorn in the Athenians' side for some time, but they were now being supported by their Theban neighbours, and the clearing of these raiders from the

Euboean Straits had become vital for the future survival of the state. The waters had to be made safe for the movement of the thousands of head of livestock now being taken to the sanctuary of the island of Euboea, due to the ongoing Spartan threat. The blatant arrogance of these pirates had to be crushed.

Because this was to be a military operation, each trireme had departed the port of Piraeus carrying a full quota of heavily armed infantry, who took up some of the places usually filled by oarsmen. All told, a formidable force of nine-hundred. Further support provided by the city for this enterprise came in the form of three-hundred lighter armed marines, six score archers and the necessary supply ships. They were aware that their shallow vessels were overloaded, but the voyage to the coast of Locria being of no great distance, coupled with the fact that they would be operating far from any large enemy naval base, they put their faith in Poseidon and their trust in Cleopompus.

Each hoplite, the finest fighting man Athens could provide, was armed with a long spear and short sword; also a bronze-covered circular wooden shield with an Argive grip for easier maneuverability and stability. Emblazoned with either a fearful or protective design, these shields provided a defensive screen, yet could also be a brutal weapon in close combat. For bodily protection they wore a bronze cuirass over the upper torso, and a skirt of thick leather strips to cover their thighs. The lower legs were covered by metal greaves. To protect the head, most wore the bronze Illyrian helmet with a nose-guard and open face, but the styles varied according to the personal choice and circumstances of the wearer. Topping some of the more elaborate helmets, were colourful crested plumes of dyed horsehair.

Glaucus, through a stroke of Olympian luck, was finally back in the place for which he'd been born. He'd been given the opportunity to be 'the helmsman' once more, instead of the wandering vagrant he'd become since the loss of his possessions. And there was more good news. The eager young trierarch, wide-eyed Iandros, seated at times behind him, but more often than not standing at his shoulder, was not the spoiled brat Glaucus had expected. He treated the Thessalian almost as an equal, giving the red headed giant the freedom to run the vessel his way. It was common knowledge that the inexperienced, twenty-year-old Iandros, with his unruly mop of flaxen hair, and a body as slim as a girl's, would not have been given command of a trireme without an enormous financial input from his father, Paramanos. To allow the young man to captain a valuable ship such as a trireme, lacking sufficient training, would be madness, and Paramanos for all his faults, was not mad.

So it was this 'filthy rich' slave trader who was responsible for Glaucus being assigned to the Thetis, providing him with an opportunity to lessen his debts. Chosen by Paramanos, who'd had the Thessalian's credentials and suitability for the post thoroughly checked out, Glaucus now possessed a pouch of silver coins tucked safely into his belt; a part-payment for giving first-hand instruction on seamanship to the new trierarch; as well as keeping the veteran crew under control. Seamen could be merciless with an inexperienced captain, and Paramanos did not want his only son to be on the receiving end of their humiliating mockery, however well-intentioned.

Glaucus had not expected to warm to the young man placed in his charge, but he discovered something about the lad that he thought admirable. His instincts had been correct when he first saw the Thetis being launched. Its young trierarch did indeed want glory, but it wasn't for the sake of fame or vanity, as he'd imagined. It was for a reason totally surprising to him. Here was the only son of one of the wealthiest men in Athens, living an unearned life of privilege in high society, and he'd confessed to Glaucus that he hated everything that his father stood for. He wanted his family name to be known for his deeds of valour, rather than for the wealth acquired from men's misery in the silver mines. Glaucus respected him for that, and willingly shared his vast knowledge with Iandros, a potential general of the future.

Now, with a firm grip on the ship's twin rudders, sensing a tense Iandros behind his broad shoulder, he steered the Thetis, following in the wake of the other vessels, in single file through the narrow Passage of Chalcis. The changing currents and water levels in these narrows, defied all men's study and knowledge of the seas. Hazardous strong tidal waves, maelstroms and currents which changed direction several times a day, were a menace for even the most seasoned sailors. Fortunately, Glaucus well understood the perils of these waters from past experience. The most dangerous time occurred when the tide of water began changing direction, and to get caught in the ensuing whirlpool meant disaster for any ship.

There was little room for manoeuvre and no room for error. A trireme at its widest point was twenty feet, and The Chalcis Passage, separating the enemy Boeotians from Athenian Euboea, was only one-hundred and twenty feet, so earnest concentration was required by each helmsman. Any misjudgment could mean capture or destruction.

Once safely through the passage, with no oars lost, Glaucus was thanked by his relieved young trierarch who, day by day, increasingly appreciated why his father had been so insistent that he hire this large redhead from Thessaly.

Only one ship was lost. An overloaded supply vessel at the end of the line got caught out by the quickly changing water levels as the tide flowed down from the north into the narrows. The vessel turned over and was swept violently away by the merciless, unforgiving current of the strait. All men were feared drowned and the loss of supplies meant replacements would have to be found somewhere in enemy territory.

Glaucus was conscious of the fact that Iandros knew nothing about the financial agreement between himself and Paramanos. His urgent need to pay back his niece's stolen dowry had dulled his pride. It was only a small advance payment, after all. The rest, which was still not enough to cover his loss, would be paid when the slave trader's son and heir arrived safely back in Athens, and until then, whenever Iandros was in his sight, he would guard the young man as though he was his own flesh and blood. The Fates had guided Glaucus to his present situation, and he was prepared to follow their thread of life, to its inevitable end.

The ships, once freed from the restrictions of the passage, spread out across the wider waters of the upper Euboean straits, in ranks of three abreast. The sounds of the rhythmic splashing of the oars, and the pipers' calls were so familiar to Glaucus at his seat on the top deck, but even after much of his life spent at sea, he never ceased to be astonished at the wonder and power of these vessels. Woe betide any craft that found itself in the path of these dreadnoughts, he mused. It was with little surprise that the way ahead was clear, as they proceeded along the coastline of Boeotia unhindered, on towards Locris.

The trireme was a devastating invention of war. The Thetis measured one-hundred and twenty feet from stem to stern. She was swifter too than any other sea-born vessel of the age, with a rowing speed of up to ten knots, which could be considerably more in short bursts or at ramming speed. The vessel was not only extremely manoeuvrable, she was deadly at close quarters. At her prow she carried a bronze-covered ram which could either breach an enemies side or slice through a rank of oars. It was a terrible weapon of destruction and, like Glaucus's axe, it sought decisions.

Built from various types of carefully selected woods; cypress, pine and fir for the interior, and oak for the outer hull and keel, these high maintenance vessels were meant for speed. They were also light enough to be carried by the crew to be beached at night, to help prevent wood rot. The Thetis, like its companions, had two masts and she carried sails of flax linen, which were carefully stowed away when not in use.

The two-hundred on board; oarsmen, deck crew and hoplites, were all freemen like Glaucus. Some foreigners could be accepted as part of the crew, but these were mainly oarsmen. It was rare for such a responsible position of helmsman to be held by a non-Athenian, and Glaucus felt great satisfaction in that.

FORTY-EIGHT

A SHOUT SUDDENLY BROKE through Glaucus's thoughts. From the deck crew's hand signals he deciphered an order from the bow officer to the rowing master to reduce speed. A command which could only have come down from Cleopompus on the flag-ship far ahead.

'Why are we stopping?' It was the voice of the young trierarch.

'We're not stopping.' replied Glaucus, but suddenly seeking reassurance, felt beneath his feet for his axe. 'The signal was to slow down.' He wondered what other instructions the rich man's son had skipped during military training.

'Why, Glaucus? What's happening?' asked Iandros, excitedly.

Glaucus, catching sight of the rowing master Cassa's amusement, scowled back at him.

From his high vantage point at the stern of the ship, Glaucus surveyed the slowly passing coastline of Locris. The fleet travelled close to the shore now, and familiar landmarks were becoming recognisable. Yet even from the Thetis, which was one of the ships farthest from their objective, it was clear to see that there was no sign of the usual activity expected at a maritime centre. The harbour was deserted. Also the entire shoreline, north and south, seemed devoid of life. There was no sign of movement on land or sea that signified the Locrians had sighted the Athenian fleet.

'Where are their ships?' It was Iandros again, a hint of jubilation rising in his voice.

'Perhaps the Locrians have run off, eh Glaucus?'

Glaucus chuckled at that. Nice one. Our foes running off so that we can simply go ashore, and take our pick of their lovely possessions. If only, he thought.

'I doubt it,' he replied, taking the opportunity of the respite to wipe the sweat from his brow. 'So does our admiral, by the looks of things. He's taking time to consider his next move, that's all.'

The order came down the line to pick up a little speed. The fleet, followed by the supply vessels cautiously approached the empty harbour, and in front of the beach, they waited expectantly. There was no resistance and it was eerily quiet. Finally, Cleopompus ordered two thirds of the fleet to be taken onto the beaches, the remaining ten ships he took further along the shore, seeking out the covert enemy.

The vessels started to discharge their army onto the sands, as the seamen, laying out the wooden rollers, began hauling the triremes onto the beach. Glaucus, picking up his axe, was one of the first from the Thetis to jump into the water. With his enormous strength, he was soon busy helping to drag the ship up onto dry land.

'Don't say it!' he shouted to Bion the oarsman as he approached him.

'Well, where is everybody, Glaucus?' he asked, incredulously.

'Here, grab this rope. Let's get her onto the damned beach,' said Glaucus, breathing hard. 'I don't think we'll have to wait long before we know the answer, Bion. Keep on your guard my friend.'

Cleopompus returned without encountering any resistance, and the other triremes were added to the wooden 'town' now forming on the strand. The smell of cooking was soon in the air and the noise of supplies being unloaded, drowned out the sound of the surf. The general quickly set about organising a small party of hoplites and archers to inspect the area, and look-outs were posted on the nearest high points. When the reconnaissance party returned, the situation became clearer to the general.

The local inhabitants had been warned by the Boeotians further down the coast of the Athenian fleet's approach, and had retreated behind the city walls of Thronium. Their ships had all been taken further up the Locrian coast and were probably heading for the far side of Euboea, looking for hidden havens.

Thronium, a short distance from where the Thetis and her sister ships had beached, did not appear to Cleopompus to be well defended. Knowing they'd had little time to bring in supplies, he immediately decided to lay siege to the town. No reinforcements arrived to rescue the besieged town, and it was not long before Cleopompus forced them to surrender. Capturing the top dignitaries, he sent them as hostages back to Athens. Iandros could not be more disappointed and frustrated at this lack of activity, but Glaucus, being well aware of the vagaries of life, kept his axe close by him and his eyes watchful. As he'd concluded, it was not long before the battle-virgin Iandros got the opportunity to draw his first blood, Cleopompus having finally encountered the Locrian army.

At Alope, up the coast from Thronium, one-thousand troops were mustered to drive the invading Athenians from their lands. They also had with them Theban cavalry together with their foot soldier support, which strongly increased their strength of arms. Athenians were not usually eager to fight land battles, but the enemy on this occasion, Cleopompus, thought beatable.

'They're not Spartans, Glaucus!' proclaimed Iandros, eager to prove himself in combat. 'They're mainly farmers and fishermen, are they not? Some of which have turned to piracy, as I understand it.'

'They're fighting on their own soil, and this always makes for a dangerous foe,' Glaucus had tried to warn him before, Iandros, looking every inch the young warrior, in his expensive unblemished armour, marched off to battle. Glaucus had become used to his duties of guardian and now felt anxious at being left behind with the Thetis, one of many on duty to watch over the beached and vulnerable fleet. All he could do now was wait.

They came with the dawn, just as the night fires along the beach were about to be renewed to provide a welcome breakfast of hot soup and bread for the men charged with guarding the fleet. The previous night, from atop the rocky scarp that served conveniently as a natural look-out point, the Athenians had gazed north towards far greater fires raging along the coast, but Cleopompus had been so confident that the enemy could be contained at Alope, a surprise attack on the ships was thought unlikely.

Strangely enough, it was the silence that woke him, silence that is, apart from the murmur of the waters and the low voices of his comrades still on their shift along the shore. Glaucus rolled out from his place on the beach beside the Thetis, unwrapping his weapon of choice as he did so. He looked to where the line of steep-sided grey rocks sheltered the ships, lying like sleeping seals along the beach. Glaucus stared ahead and tried to shake the sleep from him. Could he be the only one to notice it? There were no sentries patrolling the scarp!

A single fire arrow, arching in flight, whistled over Glaucus's head and thudded noisily into the deck of the Thetis. Before he could reach it, scores came hurtling onto the ships and their astonished crews, which were quickly followed by hundreds more. The Athenians sprang to life, careering into each other, darting hither and thither as they rushed for their weapons. But the merciless bombardment from the enemy, who had taken command of the scarp, took many of them out of action. Shrill shouts and yells now rent the air as the crewmen rushed to put out the numerous fires taking hold among the dry ship timbers. Glaucus took up his position with his comrades, and hefted the long handled axe in readiness.

Onto the beach they came, in lines of a hundred or more, numbering six, possibly seven deep. Heavy infantrymen. Professional hoplites. Glaucus swore an oath. The sailors and craftsmen of the Athenian ships would be hard-pressed in the face of such opponents. As the advancing troops came nearer Glaucus saw quite plainly the oval shaped shields on the flanks, and swore again. Boeotians! And worse than that - Thebans! The very same breed who had robbed him of his slaves, his mule and his life's savings.

The lightly armed marines and crew began to pour ragged flights of javelins, arrows and sling-shot into the oncoming lines. Such gestures were of little avail and their missiles, for the most part, glanced off the shields and armour of their attackers, like harmless hailstones.

The noise along the length of the beach became deafening as the two elements closed in a fearsome melee of flashing spears and blades, as they danced between the roar of crackling blazes taking hold on the ships. A plume-helmeted warrior with shield raised, his sword wavering hesitantly towards the helmsman's bare chest, suddenly lunged to find its target. Death found him instead. It came quickly as Glaucus, who stepping back, swung his long- handled weapon with both hands, delivering a direct blow that cleaved the Boeotian's helmet in two. Blood splashed, Glaucus met the next man who, unluckily for him, stumbled over a heavy iron cooking pot. Before he could regain his footing, the axe of Glaucus fell again.

The death-dealing weapon began to take on a life of its own as it rose and fell ferociously and frighteningly about its business. Men were writhing and falling all about him, as Flamebeard cut a bloody swath through the ranks of the enemy who now, crazed with fear before this giant, fought to keep out of his terrible reach. Just how long the Thessalian fought in this unequal match he would never recall, nor how many of the foe he had slain. Only when the familiar mournful call of an Athenian horn rose above the din around him, did he break off and kneel on the gore-soaked strand as lines of heavily armed Athenian infantry, Athena's owl emblazoned on their round shields, swept by to drive the attackers from the beach.

Glaucus, Bion and the depleted mariners protecting the Thetis and its companion vessels, owed their lives to the ever watchful Cleopompus who, although directing operations against the main body of the enemy at Alope, became aware that a large number of Locrians and their Theban allies, unable to put up a resistance, had broken off from the fight and were fleeing south. Sensing that the foe was out to destroy the Athenian vessels, the wily general urgently sent a large force in hot pursuit.

Glaucus rose from his knees as more Athenians trotted by along the beach. About him, relieved crew members began throwing sand onto the numerous fires that had taken hold while others undertook the task of separating the wounded from the dead. Any Locrian or Theban found to be still alive had their throats cut. Cassa, the rowing master, who had joshed with him only yesterday, was one of the wounded, though not seriously. Glaucus, over the weeks, had come to like Cassa. The man was a professional, like himself, and since parting from Clytes of Eleusis, he was the best drinking companion around. For a brief second his mind floated back to the actor-warrior, and unlooked for hero against the hated

Theban attackers at Plataea. A complex man indeed, Flamebeard thought. And where was he now? Shagging some beauty in Athens no doubt! As he stood, staring at the ground, his hands resting on his axe, he suddenly thought, by Apollo's balls, I do miss that bugger!

'Don't tell me you're praying for them, Helmsman?' said a now familiar voice behind him. 'I can see you've been busy!'

Glaucus swung about. Relieved, he saw Iandros, grinning broadly, his bloodied short sword still unsheathed.

'Well, it seems my prayers have been answered!' Glaucus growled at last, and he managed to resist embracing Iandros in his relief at his deliverance. Bion, cleaning up the deck of the Thetis, threw him down a coarse rag, and Glaucus concentrated on wiping the blades of his axe with it. Looking skeptically at his recently acquired pupil, he asked anxiously, 'So? How was it?' He offered him the rag but it was refused.

'My first killing, Glaucus!' he said, sheathing his weapon, and looking older than the untried young man of a few hours ago. 'They were no match for us!' he announced boldly. 'Cleopompus calculated on their lack of mettle. They ran like frightened hares, Glaucus! Added to the loot we acquired, were their shields - left behind in their flight!'

Glaucus nodded, but did not reply. Those he'd slain a short while ago would be on their way to Hades now, but such slaughter never ceased to trouble him - afterwards. His stomach ached for food and he followed his trierarch, the young man's first blood still not cleaned from his blade, towards the cooking fires. He would feel better once outside of a hot meal.

Frustrated at not being able to seek out and destroy the Locrian ships, Cleopompus continued to burn the towns along the coast, and their capital city of Opus was also put to the torch. In the bay, he left a garrison on the uninhabited island of Atalante where they were to build themselves a fortress, and with two triremes left at their disposal, they would keep control of any traffic coming to, or going from the Locrian coast. Satisfied that he had done all he could to fulfill his orders, the general returned the fleet to Athens. The reception they received from the capital was more than any of them expected. The war so far had been inconclusive, and this victory on land, however small, was welcomed by the grateful population. Paramanos greeted his son as he would a returning hero, and Glaucus received his promised payment in full.

FORTY-NINE

AFTER LISTENING TO NICANDER, and being made aware of the tensions building up in the league, Archidamus, King of mighty Sparta, still hesitated about waging war on Athens, without being satisfied that once started, the league had sufficient manpower and resources to finish it. During the preceding years of peace, he had become friends with Pericles of Athens, but both leaders, although neither wanting war, believed their demands and grievances to be valid. Part of the king's delaying tactics was, for the second time within a year, to seek the opinion of the people. Nicander's report was pored over by the five ephors; then the Council of Elders, who were, as was Archidamus, all over the age of sixty, before finally putting the decision to the Assembly, where all male citizens over the age of thirty had a voice. The king, had for some time of course, been receiving delegations from various states in the league, pleading grievances against grasping, overpowering Athens. Now that winter was over, the pressure was mounting for action. So, when the question was again asked of the Assembly as to whether they should go to war, the roar of approval was again, unmistakable. Sparta, unlike Athens, acquired its tribute from the states under its formidable protection in men, rather than ships or silver, and the call now went out to draw in that promised payment. The isthmus at Corinth was soon overwhelmed by an army of tens of thousands, with allies arriving from every state in the Peloponnesian League, each contingent with its own generals, distinctive shield devices and armour. All were ready and eager to curtail Athens' excessive policies, and of course, lay claim to her excessive wealth. Skopas, still encamped at Megara, guarding the isthmus, eagerly awaited the order to cross the border, to be in the vanguard of the invasion force. To be one of the first commanders to march into Athens. To have first choice of the plunder.

But, when Archidamus finally did make a move, it was not at the behest of Corinth or Megara. He did not take the army directly to threaten Athens, but north into the Cithaeron mountain range. In need of Boeotian cavalry to protect his ground troops, and also to give his friend Pericles more time to consider; Theban demands were given priority. Unable to regain Plataea, Thebes turned her hatred towards the small mountain town of Oenoe on the border of Boeotia and Attica. Oeneo, like Plataea had once come under the dominance of Thebes, but was now a fortress protecting the border of Attica, and under Athenian control. Unlike Plataea, however, Oenoe had been given fair warning of an impending attack and her gates and walls were manned day and night.

Trees were hacked down and used as battering rams against Oenoe's gates. Ramps were built to gain access to the ramparts. All to no avail. The city had been made impregnable, and inspired by Plataea on the opposite side of Mount Cithaeron, it held fast. For too long, Archidamus wasted time before the walls of Oenoe, according to his disgruntled army, who were severely aggrieved at the lack of anticipated looting. An invasion of wealthy Attica had been a great draw for many states in the Spartan alliance, and this constant procrastination by Archidamus was blamed for their lack of spoils.

Sparta's king was hoping, of course, that the Athenians, being aware that a vast army was on their border, and watching their precious crops turning green across their land, would capitulate and accept Spartan demands, rather than risk their inevitable destruction by the largest army the Spartan league had ever assembled. But no herald came from Pericles and so, with the arrival of summer and the grain growing high, Archidamus moved his mighty army into Attica and down onto the Eleusinian plains. Skopas, at long last received orders to move his disgruntled troops guarding the isthmus, and he and Lykaon finally crossed the border from Megaris into Attica and joined up with the main army on the gulf, encamped around the city of Eleusis.

Now! At last! thought Clytes, in eagerness. Now, Pericles will bring out the army! Watching impatiently from the walls of his city, his haunted eyes were strained for sight of the distinctive Boeotian helmets and the shields emblazoned with the Club of Heracles. Somewhere he knew, in that body of men was Lykaon, but in the mass of tightly packed troops and the swirling dust, it was impossible to distinguish one marching column from another. Tents as far as his eyes could see were pitched across the vast plain, the pennants flying from long poles, denoting the territory occupied by each state. But still no defending army marched out from Athens.

They had to watch as their crops were trampled and burned before their eyes. Their precious olive groves, hacked to pieces.Vines were ripped from their supports. Villages and farmsteads set alight. Anything of value, looted. And still no sign from the east.

Finally, Clytes and the others on watch saw dust clouds in the distance, rising from the direction of Athens. Citizens hurried to arm themselves and their small cavalry unit was made ready for action. Men from the garrison manned the main gates, ready to lift the bar, as behind it, an armed force of determined Eleusinians lined up, Clytes included, spears held ready, prepared to do battle. But all that arrived, emerging from the dust cloud was a small valiant, but useless contingent of Athenian horse. They'd come along 'The Sacred Way', the pilgrim route between Athens and Eleusis, and were stopped at a place called The Brooks. Being vastly outnumbered they were sent back with their tails down, accompanied by shouts of, 'Cowards! Why don't you come out and fight like real men!' Although too far away to hear these insults, behind the walls of Eleusis, Clytes and his comrades were thinking much the same about the Athenian army, and of themselves. Having witnessed helplessly the destruction of their family estates and livelihoods, the people were filled with great anger, frustration and shame, but against such a vast force they knew it would be suicidal to open their gates.

It became obvious to the Eleusinians that no force was coming to their aid, and fearing the lower city would be overrun, Clytes and others in the garrison helped move the families and their possessions into the inner-walled area on their acropolis, to the environs of the sanctuary of Demeter and her Mysteries - to await their fate. Clytes, being in the place of his sweetest memories, also his worst nightmares, was in torment. His obsession unabating, his destiny unfulfilled, he was more determined than ever, and yet it occurred to him that perhaps it was not Lykaon's, but his own fate to die at Eleusis, as had happened to the rest of his family. Sitting by The Well of the Fair Dances, with poignant memories coming to him of his sister's enchanting dancing, her sweet voice enthralling the initiates; with unusual piety, he prayed for salvation and guidance.

'A herald!' shouted one of the soldiers. 'A herald is coming!' Clytes hurried back down the hill, jumping two wide stone steps at a time in his eagerness to hear what was said. The horseman halted before the gates of the outer wall and holding aloft his herald's staff, he called out:

'Eleusinians! Listen to the words of King Archidamus of Sparta! He speaks on behalf of all members of the Peloponnesian League. The sanctuary of Demeter is held sacred by all the Hellenes. No attack will be made on her temple or the environs of her sanctuary by any state in the league. Anyone of our forces found entering the sacred area will suffer the death penalty. This is the promise of the magnanimous King Archidamus!'

Having delivered his message and acknowledging that it had been understood, the herald swung his horse about and galloped back towards the large expanse of tents spreading out from the walls of the city. The following day, Archidamus, with still no herald arriving from Pericles, being unable to inflict any further harm on the Eleusinians, continued moving his army eastwards, destroying all in its path - getting ever closer to Athens.

Clytes, believing the goddess Demeter had spared him in order that he may fulfill his purpose, left his city as soon as it was safe to do so. This time he did not travel alone. Four of his cousins, together with some comrades from his two years of military training, and over four-hundred young men of Eleusis, travelled with him. With farmland ruined and no employment in the city, starvation threatened. Leaving behind enough men to guard the acropolis, they said emotional farewells to their families, and followed in the wake of the Spartan army, keeping well out of sight of any patrols. They passed through what had once been the olive groves of Clytes' family farm. Only black, smouldering stumps remained. It had been taken over by the state to cover the family debts and court costs, and sold at auction to another family.

'We did try to buy back the farm,' said Adelphos, one of the four sons of Callidora, sister of Clytes' father. 'But we were outbid.'

Clytes stopped to look down the well, it's fresh spring water once such a gift to their smallholding, now polluted by manure thrown in from the deserted animal pens.

'It's of no consequence now cousin,' Clytes replied, grimly, 'but I thank my aunt and uncle for trying.'

His hand moved slowly along the stone wall of the well and he patted it gently. It looked, to Adelphos, like a gesture of final farewell. Clytes then followed the others without once looking back.

The rising dust ahead of them soon blotted out the sun, as more than sixty-thousand marching men with cavalry support and accompanying supply wagons, headed east through Attica, turning the land from green to smouldering black as they went. Having been on exasperating garrison duty at Eleusis, the eager young men now wanted to experience some action, and if their own army wouldn't come out and fight, then the only adventure would be that found on board a ship. Finding The Sacred Way lying open to them, the displaced Eleusinians would soon put some distance between themselves and the invaders.

Brothers, Arkadios and Adelphos, cousins of Clytes, would avoid Athens and go directly to the Piraeus and many others agreed with them. Not all though, were heading for the sea. His aunt Callidoras had pleaded with her sons to separate; two to go to the capital and two to go to the port. That way, she hoped she would see some of them again. Clytes, remembering the words of Terches, entrusted a message to the two cousins intent on reaching the capital. Detailing as much as he could of the strength of Archidamus's army, the route it was taking, and the accompanying allied states he recognised. The pilgrim route being too narrow, Archidamus had taken his army through the wider pass between the mountains of Parnes and Aegoleos, towards the lands of Acharnea.

'I'm not sure what you will make of Leon and Panthas, cousins,' said Clytes, smiling, 'but they will make sure the message reaches Terches. The Athenians will see from the burnings what route the army is taking, but let's hope my message will give them some prior warning. Tell them I will send more news when I can. You have their address. Just find them quickly!'

'And where are you going, Clytes?' asked Adelphos, eagerly. 'With us to Piraeus, cousin?' as he flung his arms around the shoulders of Clytes' and his brother Arkadios, his eyes alive with a sense of adventure.

'I'm going to follow the army, Adelphos,' he replied, determinedly.

'On your own?' replied Adelphos, in astonishment. 'You can't be serious?'

After listening to useless protestations, Clytes embraced his four cousins in turn, wishing them all well, and at a fork in the road, they separated. With a small group of their fellow citizens, the brothers Alastor and Audas continued along the pilgrims' route, which would lead them directly to The Sacred Gate at Athens, while the brothers, Arkadios and Adelphos and the majority of the impatient young men of Eleusis, took the road which travelled around the peninsula to the port of Piraeus.

Clytes, wrapping a cloth around his nose and mouth to keep out the billowing dust, set off alone, travelling in the wake of the Spartan host. Soon he was swallowed up in the stifling gloom, his shadowy, spectral form following resolutely in the footsteps of his nemesis, drawn on by the reverberating sound of pipes and drums.

FIFTY

YOUNG PLATAEANS WOULD OFTEN enquire of their elders, how long a mutual hostility of such great magnitude had existed, between their neighbouring Boeotian states - Thebes and Plataea. Some thought it began almost fifty years before, with the last major assault on the lands of the Hellenes by the Persians under Xerxes, when Thebes, led by a strong Median faction, decided to throw in its lot with the barbarian invader, whereas Plataea had sided with Athens and Sparta. Others argued that it had started a decade before that, at the great Battle of Marathon, when Thebes, unlike Plataea, failed to send support. But the mistrust by the Plataeans of their stronger neighbour Thebes, began long before either of these events. Despairing of ever being strong enough to control Theban subjugation and exploitation, Plataea, which was very close to the border with Attica, sought and received help from the Athenians - and for almost ninety years, had been a loyal friend and ally.

The Thebans, having long felt betrayed by their smaller neighbour, who always seemed to be on the side of the victor, had honed a virulent hatred of 'plucky little Plataea', a term often used to describe this little fortress. Even this annoying description merely added flame to the fire of their past humiliations.

Almost six months after the latest Theban attempt to subjugate them, the Plataeans were preparing for the ways of war once again, and in that short time their city had witnessed many changes. A garrison of four-hundred Plataeans and eighty Athenian hoplites, together with a hundred women left in the city to care for them, were all that remained to occupy and defend the city.

It had been decided early on, that without more reinforcements from Athens, it would be impossible to defend the entire plateau so most activity now took place on the acropolis and time had not been wasted in improving its defences. The lower quarter, once a place of lively city life, was gradually being dismantled. There would be fewer places for an enemy to hide, and also a clearer view would be opened up for the archers and javelin throwers, should the Thebans attack again. Apart from the temples and civic buildings, all useful building materials were taken to fortify their shrinking town, and wagons were in continuous use as loads of timbers, bricks and rubble were transported up the slope by the sadly depleted population.

Activity in this area had not entirely ceased. The men of the garrison drilled there daily and more than one confrontation had occurred between Lecadonis, the young but uncompromising captain of the Athenian contingent, and Plataea's general Eupompides, relating to what each of them thought was the minimum requirement of prowess and fitness. It was Lecadonis who'd argued successfully that the women should also be given the opportunity to defend themselves, and now some of them, including Amara, wife of the sculptor Imbros, took part in some form of military training. With Imbros's guarded approval, she attended the training sessions enthusiastically, and he had to admit that his wife was now fairly competent with bow and arrow.

First to be taken to the safety of the acropolis, was the coveted Marathon Shield. Reluctantly removed from its sacred home in Athena's, now emptied, temple, it was given sanctuary on the citadel's highest point, where it could be better protected. In Plataea's older sanctuary dedicated to Hera, the powerful 'Queen of Heaven'.

No-one was more aware of their dire situation than Diokles. His short stocky figure with a well-toned muscled body, a body which boasted a map of many scars, was standing in the morning sunshine next to Stephanos, who had just begun his shift on watch. They were looking keenly at a fire burning in the distance. Tall, dark Stephanos, like his immediate superior, was dressed in full uniform, covered by a long cloak; and watching the scene before him, his hand twitched to use the spear in his grip. Two men, with a close bond between them, but very different in character. Diokles the disciplinarian, proven, solid, dependable and, in happier days, the expected father-in-law of Stephanos. The younger man, impetuous and quick to anger, bore respect for authority somewhat lighter. The pair of them gazed out over the plain to where a tall column of black smoke curled lazily upward in the distance. 'Tyrenne, I suspect,' Stephanos ventured. 'I wouldn't have thought there was much left to burn there!'

It had been some time since the pair of them had ridden far from their walls. With Theban patrols constantly harassing the countryside, and marauders seeking easy pickings, the countryside beyond the city had become a dangerous place.

'That's Simonedes' farm, I believe,' said Diokles, sadly. 'Or rather, it was.'

Stephanos, frustratedly threw a rock from the rampart in the direction of the blaze, and cursed softly. 'We should be out there, killing the bastards!' he muttered, angrily.

'We've been through this a dozen times, Stephanos!' Diokles responded wearily. 'They're far stronger than us and could pick us off piecemeal. Our duty is to protect the city.' He nodded in the direction of the smoke. 'Out there we'd not stand a chance. If we begin attacking their patrols, it would surely bring the Spartans to our gates. Galling though it is, we have to wait for more Athenian support.'

Four months previously, after much delay and hesitation, the Spartan army, commanded by their king Archidamus, crossed the border into Attica and began a systematic destruction of the state. Mercifully, it bypassed Plataea.

Stephanos chuckled bitterly. 'First Thebes cosied up to the Persians. Now it's Sparta. I think they'd form an alliance with Hades, if it meant our destruction. By all the gods, how they must hate us!'

'It's a reciprocal agreement!' Diokles added, darkly. Turning away he looked down on the activity happening below him, into a now almost impregnable fortress. 'For the moment we stay here and we hold firm,' and then, almost to himself, added, 'They dare not come into our city again, not without the approval of the Spartans.'

'Ah! The Oath! Let's hope you're right,' said Stephanos, and he also turned his back on what was happening, hoping his rage would abate by doing so.

Below them men were parading, forming ranks for Eupompides' morning ritual of inspection. Lecadonis, leader of the Athenians, was striding up and down the lines of his hoplites, seeking out any slovenliness.

'How are you both getting on?' asked Diokles, nodding toward the Athenian captain.

'We aren't - much!' replied Stephanos.

'I like his attitude,' Diokles remarked.

Said Stephanos, a note of dislike in his voice, 'He drills his men too harshly in my opinion.'

'Discipline is crucial,' Diokles pointedly added. 'For all of us. I'm well aware of his methods. He's a first class soldier, and most of all, dedicated to the task ahead. I don't mind admitting it, his hoplites are the best thing we've got this side of Athens. Every one of them was personally chosen by Pericles himself. We'd do well to accept some of his methods,' Diokles added with some seriousness.

'Our men will fight with the best of any he has,' replied Stephanos, defensively. He paused reflectively. 'I think he looks down on the rest of us, Diokles. He regards us Plataeans as some kind of lower class.'

Diokles gave a slight grin. 'I think you're being too judgemental. Give the man time. This is as much a change for him as it is for the rest of us, judging by his aristocratic ways.'

Away to the east the sun had risen higher since they had climbed the steps to the wall-walk and Diokles pulled off his cloak. The late summer heat would soon be beating down on them. Below him, men were dispersing about the city for there was much work to be done on their isolated outpost, and everyone had been assigned his or her own duties. They had stockpiles of grain, sun dried and salted foodstuffs, dried fruits and nuts, and honey from the hives. There were livestock in the form of cattle and goats, while covert hunting parties ventured into the deeply wooded mountain at their backs, supplementing their rations. There was sufficient water from several wells and other natural sources. For the time being, we're self-sufficient, thought Diokles, but the Athenians must come soon. Our provisions won't last forever.

He noticed an axe being carried by one of the men, down near the gate. As he swung it over his shoulder, and it glinted in the sunlight, the garrison commander suddenly thought of Glaucus. He recalled his brief encounter with the big Thessalian and wondered where he was now. Wherever he is, he made a good decision in leaving Plataea, he thought, somberly. Hopefully he's manning a great trireme in the mighty Athenian fleet. In thinking of Glaucus his mind automatically drifted to the man called Clytes, that mysterious figure who seemed to be all things in one. The

Eleusinian, from the land of the mysteries, who proved to be a mystery himself. A mime, a musician, an actor of sorts and most surprisingly, a most useful swordsman. The Plataean wondered if the Eleusian still lived. Did he still carry the gift presented to him by a grateful garrison?

Stephanos interrupted his reverie. 'Is that Alexeis down there?' he asked anxiously. He pointed to a striding figure below. The elder brother of Theomenes, walked with some purpose in the direction of the headquarters building that stood near the Temple of Hera, where the Sacred Shield had recently been placed. At his back followed two soldiers of the garrison. Diokles knew them well. The taller man with a quiver full of arrows on his back and a bow in his fist was Epiktetos, familiar to his friends as 'Hawk-Eye', the young man who played a critical part in the fight at the Athenian temple, and saved Diokles' life. His companion, Iairos by name and 'Strong-Arm' by reputation, carried a pickaxe and spade over his well-built shoulders.

'Your fears are correct, Stephanos,' Diokles said seriously. 'He's been on a task ordered by Eupompides. He wanted the work completed before people were abroad.' He looked with concern at Stephanos, believing this news would enrage him more than the sight of the burnings, and reignite the argument as to why they just had to sit and take it.

Stephanos groaned softly. 'How many this time?' he asked.

'Three. Found a little before sunrise', Diokles said, with sadness in his voice. 'A man, a woman and - the gods be with him - a young lad. The usual thing. Their heads mounted on staves, not far from the East Gate.' He paused and Stephanos saw the pain in his commander's eyes. 'From the descriptions given to me it must be old Pharpates and his wife, and their grandson. He would not have known what was happening. The boy's mind was never right. The family of Pharpates have farmed here since long before the Persian invasion.'

'But they lived less than half-a-mile from us!' exclaimed Stephanos.

'That's why they died,' Diokles said flatly. 'They thought, like the others, that being so close to the city, they'd be safe.'

'How many is that now?' asked Stephanos.

'Since it began a couple of weeks ago - eleven,' Diokles replied.

'It seems the Thebans are doing this to mock us, to expose our helplessness.' Stephanos spoke frustratedly, his knuckles turning white as he gripped hard on the shaft of his spear.

'Alexeis is finding his orders hard to take,' said Diokles, with some compassion.

Stephanos shrugged. 'It's hard luck being a junior officer. They get all the shit. We've all been through it.'

Inside the headquarters office of Eupompides, the general was poised over a spread-out plan of Plataea and its environs, the corners held down with lighted oil-lamps. He looked up as Alexeis entered, motioned him to a stool, and indicated a half-filled wine jug and a recently emptied cup. The young officer helped himself and drank thirstily before making his report.

Eupompides listened, outwardly unmoved. This was the third report that Alexeis had made about the gruesome discoveries over the past few weeks. The reports did not differ, except for the present one, for jammed into the unprotesting mouth of the young boy, were his own genitalia. This is something new, by Zeus, thought the general! Obviously done to increase provocation, to get us to come out from behind our walls. All the severed heads had been stuck on wooden posts, and placed so that they faced directly at the East Gate.

'They come in the night like phantoms,' Alexeis went on. 'Nobody sees or hears anything. It's unnerving the sentries, sir.'

Eupompides, a man of calm demeanor and seemingly endless patience, pursed his lips as the young man finally completed his hasty findings. 'We always have guards on the gates, don't we? he asked. Day and night, correct?' Although the outer wall of Plataea's defences was now largely deserted, the tall towers at the gates on the plateau were still manned at all hours.

Alexeis nodded. 'Yes sir, but they report nothing untoward.'

Eupompides sat back wearily into his sheepskin covered chair. To Alexeis, the general's face was strained and he looked thinner than the last time they'd met. It was several minutes before the commander finally spoke. 'Send Diokles to me,' he said, finally.

The men on watch at the East Gate were doubled, and braziers were lit at sundown. Patrols walked the walls at irregular intervals, night and day. Eupompides wanted these unsettling incidents stopped before they undermined morale even further. Diokles had informed him that the men were already disgruntled at not being able to leave the confines of the plateau, to attack the Theban patrols burning their lands. These latest atrocities had only added to their frustration, but the general was unmoved. 'We don't have the cavalry for that, Diokles. The handful of horses we do have, are for emergencies only. There can't be many people left in the villages now. These atrocities will surely make them move to Athens. We cannot be provoked into leaving the city unguarded.'

On leaving the headquarters building, Alexeis almost collided with the hurrying figure of Imbros. Since his furnaces had been taken over for the forging of weaponry, instead of statuettes and ornaments; swords, shields, arrow and spearheads, were the only orders taken now.

'How are you, Alex?' Imbros asked, looking flustered.

The young man briefly mentioned the discovery of the heads of the farmer and his family.

Imbros shook his head sadly. 'What a world we are forging, eh, Alex?'

'Indeed, Imbros,' he replied. 'How is the lovely Amara? Still disobeying you?' he asked, trying to change the subject.

'I've begged her to take up Diokles' offer, to have her conveyed to the safety of Athens while there is still a chance. All to no avail,' said Imbros.

'You should be grateful to her for such loyalty, Imbros. I wish someone thought about me in that way,' said Alexeis, forcing a grin.

'She is stubborn to the point of stupidity, like that brute of a mule belonging to your brother! How is the young hothead? Have you heard any news?'

'The latest was, he is fully recovered and living at my uncle's house,' replied Alexeis. 'Yes, and that impossible animal, Cyclops, also. He is now part of the Athenian garrison.'

Imbros laughed. 'Who? Theo or the mule?' he joked. He shifted the bag he carried from one shoulder to the other and asked, quietly, 'Is he in there?'

'The general? Yes, he's within, but I don't think I've left him in a very happy mood, so go carefully.'

'Thank you for the advice,' muttered Imbros as he went cautiously into the building. It was not long before he exited again. His plea to Eupompides to save his bronze Zeus fell on deaf ears, and yet another of his exquisite creations was ordered into the furnace to be made into weaponry.

'What about the metal shavings then, from the workshop floor?' Imbros had asked, hopefully. 'Can I use them for my own purpose? I've an idea for a sculpture that I would very much like to work on.'

Exasperated, Eupompides spread out his hands. 'No, Imbros. Every arrow head is vital. You can use all the clay you want, we have more than enough of that. But no metal, that's an order, soldier!'

The commander, in a mood of despondency, made his way up to the protected walkway on top of the fortifications. He nodded in acknowledgement to Diokles and Stephanos, then passed along the ramparts to stand alone, gazing across the wide, empty plains towards Thebes. As he stood there, a shadow blotted out the sun and he shivered. An eagle, flying high on the mountain thermals, was momentarily curious and peered down on the plateau; a tiny island of life in an otherwise desolate landscape. Eupompides, shielding his eyes, watched the giant bird as it soared slowly back over the mountain, and felt his isolation all the keener.

FIFTY-ONE

THE SHAPE THAT SCUTTLED across Clytes' path, emitting sounds of indescribable terror, looked neither human nor animal. The creature vanished into the undergrowth as Clytes, his sword drawn, walked forward cautiously, keeping his eyes strained for any signs of attack. He saw, what had once been a man, crawling in agony on the ground, his low moaning making Clytes shudder. He approached him slowly, speaking calmly, but the man was out of his mind. Blinded and mutilated, he was beyond saving. Mumbling a prayer, Clytes quickly cut the poor man's throat, then staggering to a nearby rock, sat trembling in the sudden silence.

This had been his first killing since following the route of the invasion force, but by no means, the first killing. He had seen similar scenes of atrocity in the villages he had passed through and the image of dead faces staring back at him from a well, where he had stopped, hoping for a cool drink, would haunt him for some time. He forced himself onwards, through the heavily trodden mountain pass. He had to be there when the fighting started. Our army has to face them now, he thought, savagely!

People who'd had time to flee into the nearby forests on the mountain slopes, were gradually creeping back down to check on their homes, only to find destruction and a life suddenly turned to one of destitution. All those that were able, now travelled along dejectedly with Clytes towards Athens. There were more people still living in this area than Clytes thought wise, and he was soon part of a long procession of the suffering and dispossessed. He found it understandable that some had wanted to stay and defend their livelihoods, but without military protection, what chance had they? Indeed, without the army, what chance had he? Many were quite elderly and there were a lot of women and children; men of fighting age having already left the villages to join the army or the navy. Sling-shot or bows and arrows were their weapons of defence. A few had spears or knives, but very few possessed a sword.

Clytes realised he had to stay with these people until they reached safety, and his conscience pricked him. In this group could well be relatives of the man he'd dispatched earlier and he ended up carrying on his back, an exhausted elderly man who had difficulty walking. Also, was the fact that for once, he was relieved to be in the company of others. Images of the mutilated man; blinded, his genitals removed, had for now quenched his desire to find Lykaon. He did not want to be discovered by a Spartan patrol; an isolated individual, carrying a Boetarch's sword, especially a Theban contingent - no chance! To hold onto his balls he could wait a little longer to catch up with the Theban. They arrived at Athens without incident, but to the north of them they looked fearfully at the horizon which was dotted with plumes of black smoke. The fires looked very close.

Terches was remarkably pleased to see Clytes. He'd received the message from Leon that Clytes had sent from Eleusis, and immediate action had been taken. Riders swiftly galloped to the large township of Acharnae to warn any of the inhabitants with lingering doubts as to whether or not to stay, to get out as quickly as possible. By the time Archidamus and his army arrived, it was deserted, and consequently many lives were saved. Terches had received so much praise from Pericles, that he felt obliged to pass on some of the leader's gratitude to the Eleusinian.

'What is Pericles' strategy, Terches?' asked Clytes, pacing the floor, in exasperation. 'When in the name of Zeus is our army going out to fight? The city is so crowded, you can't find a place to piss without splashing someone. The young men are beginning to fight with each other, they're so eager for combat!'

'Pericles believes there is not an army in the whole of Hellas that can breach our walls,' replied Terches, raising his hands, almost apologetically. 'Nothing has been allowed to remain on the plains that can sustain the enemy. It is his thinking that the army of Archidamus will have to leave soon, or starve.'

'But the Acharnians are watching from these very walls as their township goes up in flames!' insisted Clytes. 'Surely by supplying Athens with the largest part of her army, they should be listened to. I've witnessed with my own eyes what the Spartans are doing out there! They're taunting us and we're doing nothing! Nothing!'

'We are sending one-hundred triremes to harass their coastal towns,' explained Terches, by way of counteracting Clytes' accusations. 'Safe havens are being provided for any helots brave enough to escape. The Spartans cannot risk a full helot revolt. Without their slave labour, Spartan society will collapse. This one act alone will make them eager to return home.'

'Too little!' groaned Clytes. 'We are being made to look like cowards! Too afraid to fight them, face to face!'

'Well, we know whose face you are thinking of, Clytes,' said Terches, with some sympathy, but you are right. Pericles does fear the Spartan warriors against our troops. They are bred for war. Near psychopaths! Not for them the study of oratory, philosophy, the workings of the cosmos. How to kill is their only schooling, and Pericles is naturally cautious about taking our army into the field and leaving the city defenceless. We can only trust that Athena is guiding his wisdom.'

'I cannot stay in Athens, Terches, doing nothing, knowing what they are doing to anyone they find outside the city. If the army won't go out and fight,' said Clytes, with disgust, 'then it will have to be the navy. I've two cousins at the Piraeus right now, looking for a ship which will get them into the action. I intend to join them. I wish you and this overcrowded city, well, Terches. I'll get messages to you - if I can.'

FIFTY-TWO

WITH THE PLATAEANS BEING more watchful, no further severed heads appeared at their gates, but in late autumn, with the year's campaigning ended, it was unusual to see a lone armed man, on foot, approaching the city. The man held a spear, and carried the club sign of Thebes on his shield. He was bare headed. Because of the earlier atrocities, the guards were instantly alert.

Stephanos, accompanied by three archers, strode out from the East Gate to intercept. As they drew closer they noticed surprisingly that the man was elderly, his thinning hair and untidy beard were flecked with grey, and he was limping as he walked. Yet there was something distinctly odd about this Theban. For he did not slow his advance and showed no sign of fear. Rather, he increased his pace as Stephanos and the others closed with him. Both parties halted on opposite sides of a dried-up stream, and the solitary Theban hoisted up his shield to cover his chest.

One of the bowmen whispered. 'Take care, captain. He has the look of a madman.'

'Certainly that,' said Stephanos, flatly.

'Shall I fire?' said another.

'No. Just mark him well for the moment,' said Stephanos.

The Theban began to descend to the bed of the rill, but halted at the sound of Stephanos's urgent voice. 'Come no further, whoever you are! Throw down your weapons, and we'll show mercy to you. If you disobey, we'll kill you where you stand.'

The man stopped, his chest visibly heaving from his efforts. 'Murderers!' he croaked. 'My son! Butchered by you damned Plataeans!' With that he pulled himself upright and hurled his spear with more force than could have been expected from such a frail-looking individual. Stephanos and his men ducked their heads instinctively, as the missile flew harmlessly to bury its sharp blade in the earth, startling a yellow lizard basking in the sun.

Then the space between Stephanos's men and the elderly Theban was eaten up swiftly as the latter, with an angry scream of hate, charged forward, sword drawn. Stephanos swore, then nodded briefly to his men. All arrows hit their mark. Two pierced his chest, the third hit him full in the throat. He was dead before he hit the ground.

Stephanos jumped down into the gulley and stared at the corpse. 'Why?' asked one of the younger Plataeans softly. 'What was to be gained by it?'

Stephanos shook his head. 'It doesn't matter a goat's fart, does it? He was a bloody Theban. What were his sufferings compared to ours? What was he rambling on about?' The most senior of the bowmen knelt down for a closer look, then turned to Stephanos as he rose.

'I know this man. His name was Skillias. I saw him at the games once. An athlete of some merit, I remember. He could run as fast as most animals on four legs. Many were the honours he earned for Thebes. His son was one of the prisoners we executed, after their attack.'

Stephanos noticed the mark of respect in the archer's tone. 'May the gods give him haven, then,' he said, reluctantly. 'I think the old man died long before today.'

Bending, he retrieved the weapon from the fist of the dead man and briefly examined it. 'Well, the old sod carried a good blade,' and he shoved it into his belt. 'Spoils of war!' he said, winking at his men.

'Collect the shield and armour,' Stephanos ordered. 'And bury the body,' he said contemptuously. 'We don't want to attract wolves.'

This was the closest any Theban had attacked them since their night raid the previous spring, and the Plataeans believed it was due to the piety of the Spartans. With still no further help from Athens, they were now forced to rely on the religious nature of their enemy. Archidamus still believed that with continued pressure, Athens would stop enlarging her empire, and would be forced to allow present members of her League to leave if they wished. Believing they were on the side of the righteous, what Sparta did not want was for her ally Thebes to involve them in an invasion of Plataea, thereby breaking the oath of Pausanius, to protect the tiny city-state for all time. Athens would readily use such a violation to her advantage. And so the situation at Plataea continued, and they waited for what was to come.

FIFTY-THREE

FOR THE FIRST YEAR of the war, both leaders thought their respective strategies were working according to plan. Archidamus buoyed up his generals with the fact that the Athenians were afraid to come out and fight them, although they had given them all provocation by laying waste their lands - and this they would continue to do until eventual victory, which could not be long. Pericles held his generals in check by reiterating that Athens itself had not been attacked, although their mighty navy had caused major destruction around the Spartan coast, and provided safe havens for fleeing Spartan slaves - and this they would continue to do until eventual victory, which must be soon.

But in the second year of the war, the enemy that entered the gates of Athens was not the Spartan army, but a merciless pestilence from the east. Beginning in Ethiopia, it spread to Egypt and Libya, attacked Persia and eventually arrived in Attica, carried aboard the merchant ships, the first signs showing up in the region of the island of Lemnos in the northern Aegean. When it reached the port of Piraeus, the inhabitants at first suspected members of the Spartan alliance for poisoning their reservoirs. It was the hottest summer anyone could remember and within the walls, the city boiled and festered.

Unfortunately, the situation was exacerbated by the decree issued by Pericles. Well-intentioned as this action seemed at the time, the city of Athens quickly became overcrowded, the population swelling to more than twice its normal size. With people forced to live in such close proximity, the plague swiftly took hold and the disease became more rampant with every passing day. The death toll rose as the city groaned under the demands of this terrible epidemic, the likes of which had never been seen before, not even by the very old. Now, there was more fear of the disease, than of the Spartan threat. This was an adversary that could not be fought. Healthy or weak, young or old, rich or poor. No-one seemed immune. The symptoms began with headaches, then the inflammation of the mouth and eyes, followed by a painful difficulty in breathing. Severe coughing and chest pains came next. After that the infection would attack the stomach of the victim, which led to extreme vomiting and diarrhoea. Outwardly a person's body felt cool, but inside they burned, bringing about a constant demand for water which could not be satisfied.

Most of those unlucky enough to catch this abomination died within ten days.

Those that did survive could end up blind or lose extremities; fingers, toes, genitals. Others were left with memory loss so that they knew not themselves nor recognised loved-ones or others once familiar to them. The plague was all encompassing in its lust for souls. Authority began to break down in this normally well-ordered city, and it became so unmanageable that unburied bodies were left to lie publicly in the open places and streets where they fell. Strangely, these corpses were not fed upon by carrion or scavengers in the expected way. It was as if all living things knew it would be certain death to do so. And while the dead piled up, the dying were seen staggering through the city's byways and squares, or fighting around the municipal fountains in vain attempts to slake an agonising thirst.

There was a further aspect to all this which Athens could well have done without. Lawlessness. The city became rife with robbery, rape and murder, prompting some to say that they would rather take their chances against the invading Spartans than stay imprisoned behind these long walls of death. Citizens who had never before thought to commit a lawless act in their lives, gave way to deeds they would have abhorred before. There was little fear or respect now for the ancient gods or the law. Only the selfish and unbridled pleasures of the hour mattered. Why continue to revere the immortals, when both the good and the bad suffered equal fates? As for the law, no-one expected to live long enough to be brought to justice, so they took the risk.

Much of the blame for this suffering was focused on the strategos and orator, Pericles. It was a terrible error of judgement in many people's reckoning, to leave the fertile plains of Attica unguarded, to be ravaged by the foe, while burying alive, or so it now seemed, its population behind the city walls. Nobody was a winner here. The poor, who before had little, now had nothing, while the better-off watched their estates being looted and burned, all because of Pericles and the scorched-earth policy adopted by the Council of Athens.

So this was the parlous state in which Athens found herself in the second summer of the second year of strife, when Spartan might came down once again into Attica, plundering and slaying with total ruthlessness, anything in its path. Witnessing the funeral burnings, Archidamus avoided the metropolis for fear the epidemic would spread to his own army, and headed further into Attica as far as the silver mines at Lavrion. After just forty days of causing as much destruction as he could by burning crops and orchards, he returned his army to Sparta, where it dispersed to its various states, in time to gather in their own waiting, burgeoning harvests.

Within sweltering Athens, the plague continued unabated.

Theomenes, accompanied by Mydon and two slaves from the household of his uncle Hypatos, urged Cyclops through the stifling, overcrowded streets. The smell of the sick and dying affected the animal badly and he had to be pushed and pulled to make him move the cart forward. Each of the four men wore a cloth tied tightly to cover their nose and mouth, but it made little difference. The stench was so strong they wanted to retch. In the cart were the bodies of newly freed men, old Orchas and the groom from Hysiae, together with two slaves from the Hypatos household. All had succumbed to the pestilence and were being taken to the nearest funeral pyre. There were rarely individual, respectful ceremonies now, such as at the farewell to Chief Magistrate, Eubalos. Pyres now burned ceaselessly and fresh bodies were thrown on top of already burning bodies. This gruesome task had become a regular routine for Theomenes and Mydon, as part of their garrison duties, and the big white ghost of a mule with his single malevolent eye, was hurriedly avoided; healthy people believing that if he were to merely glance at them, they too would end up in his cart. But now the disease had entered their own household. Hypatos himself, was very ill and being nursed by his devoted wife. With her female slaves, she took over his care, all faith in doctors, if any could be found still alive, having ceased. And sacrifices to the gods were a waste of time. It was obvious their once revered deities had deserted them, and their magnificent edifices were now filled with the dying and the dead.

Atheni did not expect her husband to live, such was the strength of the disease which ravaged his body. His inflamed skin, broken with ulcers, was unable to bear even the lightest of fabric and naked, tortured by thirst and pain, he struggled against his nurses, finding no rest day or night. In the city, the unattended sick threw themselves into any available water supply in desperation to cool themselves, but as yet, their own stone-lined well was uncontaminated and Atheni organised a constant supply of clean water to be fed to Hypatos, and also to cool his body. To combat the smell from the bile and diarrhoea, Atheni sprinkled the room with herbs and perfumed oils and also soaked the cloths around their mouths in lavender water.

By the seventh day, the fever broke and Theomenes was finally allowed to see him. Three days later, Atheni herself went down with the pestilence, as well as two of her household women. Everything was carried out as had been done for Hypatos, but eight days after becoming ill, Atheni passed from the world, together with her personal slave, as though still in her service. There were murmurings of, 'I told you so!' when the bodies of Atheni and her servant were brought through the city to their private burning. 'That mule of theirs has the 'evil eye'!' Once again, Theo was left motherless, and he and Hypatos were inconsolable, such was the sense of loss in the household.

It was inevitable that Theomenes and Mydon would eventually contract the disease. Hypatos, having acknowledged Theomenes as his adopted son and heir, was in despair. Still not fully recovered himself from the illness, he sought out anyone who had already endured the plague, but like himself, had fully recovered. He wanted people in attendance who knew what to expect and to understand what the patient required. Money was no object and by luck or design, they both survived. Theomenes came through surprisingly well. Like his uncle, by the eighth day, his fever broke. He was eating normally by the tenth day and able to help in the care of Mydon who was still suffering badly. The course of his disease took longer. Although the slave did not take a ride on the cart of Cyclops, he was left a cripple. The toes of the right foot, having turned black, were removed in case the infection spread further up the leg.

Many Plataeans succumbed. Being forced to live in crowded, often unsanitary conditions, they had little chance of avoiding the worst of the epidemic. Corinna, with the help of her daughter Phoebe and slave Eudora, nursed a large number of their fellow citizens through the trauma, many not surviving, but due to their close proximity to the sickness, the good women in the most squalid of circumstances, finally succumbed themselves. With none of the living Plataeans fit or able to arrange the wood for a pyre, they were hurriedly buried in a mass grave by the Keramikos Cemetery, with the simplest of grave goods. Had Admetus the Plataean historian been well, he would have paid for the funeral arrangements, as he had for other fellow Plataeans without sufficient funds, but it was weeks later that he finally recovered from the pestilence, and when he learned of their fate, it was by then too late.

This nightmare was repeated in almost every household, the scythe of death showing no distinction between high-born or slave as it swept time and again through the city.

FIFTY-FOUR

WHEN WORD REACHED PLATAEA of the plague in Athens, Eupompides ordered that no outsiders be allowed into the city, no matter what the reason. He knew that if it broke out in their confined quarters, very few of them would survive. Heralds from Athens were asked to impart their news from outside the city, and letters from friends and relatives were read out to an eager audience, leaning precariously over the walls to listen.

As time went on, news of Plataeans dying far from home became harder and harder to bear, and the sight of a herald soon filled them with dread. Imbros, aware that he was fortunate to have his wife at his side, felt embarrassed to meet the eyes of his comrades who had lost loved ones, and advised Amara to spend more days with the women for the time being. Diokles bore the news of the death of his son from the pestilence with fortitude, but for some time, no-one except Stephanos, dared approach him to offer condolences.

Months went by when the Plataeans could do nothing but watch as their farmers were brutally killed and their homesteads destroyed, but there came a day when not to act was unthinkable.

It came about because of the desertions. It had happened only once before, when Demetrious, driven half-mad by the demoralising inactivity and anxiety for his wife and daughter in Athens, had gone missing from the plateau, only to turn up two days later after a harrowing chase by Theban infantry. He had been given a lenient sentence of ten lashes and bread and water for a week. He was a good archer, and every man was needed. This time there were two absconders. Terillus and Gellio were their names. Shirkers and tricksters, the pair of them, and no strangers to the lash; who served under Stephanos's command.

The night-watch having reported seeing an indistinct fire on the plains in the area of the sacred burial grounds, suspected that the deserters could be sheltering there, and Alexeis on his gift horse Cerus, accompanied by four armed men, had been ordered to go out and apprehend them. He returned with his harrowing report.

Eupompides, fully armed, rushed from the headquarters building, calling out urgently. 'Diokles! Bring the horses! We are riding out!'

With Eupompides on his stallion, Alexeis on Cerus and Stephanos and Diokles on horses used by men in the garrison, they set off back to the fields of the dead with twenty heavily armed men running quickly alongside as support.

'This is an unnatural hatred!' exclaimed Stephanos, as he witnessed the destruction.

'More like unbridled jealousy!' replied Diokles, as he dismounted.

The tombs of their illustrious ancestors had been broken into. Remnants of smashed stone altars lay on the ground. Bones and crushed pottery urns, once containing the ashes of the deceased, were strewn all around. These were the dead of the heroic defenders of Hellas. Athenians, Spartans, Plataeans and all the other Hellenes who had come to these plains to stand against the mighty Persian army of Xerxes. For over fifty years these fields, with their sacred burial mounds, had been tended and cared for by the Plataeans on behalf of all Hellas. Theban jealousy and hatred had tried to extinguish that glory. For obvious reasons the Thebans had not disturbed the mound containing the Spartan dead, but the Plataeans decided to take these heroes also, back to the safety of the plateau.

As Diokles walked the sullied ground, he fell back in horror. His horse also shied as the smell reached its nostrils from this scene of torture. Nailed to the charred wooden uprights of what had once been a small temple, were the blackened remains of two bodies. Bone protruded through their burned flesh. Empty eye sockets, under blood matted hair, stared blankly, the twisted contorted mouths speaking silently of their last agonies. A dark coagulated mess of slime, stench and palpable fear.

'Terillus and Gellio,' said Diokles, lowering his sight. 'Poor sods!'

A rider was dispatched to the city, and he was quickly back with a wagon, pulled by the garrison's two remaining horses. The land was scoured for anything that could be transported, and the wagon was hurriedly loaded with the remains and relics collected from the desecrated tombs. Also placed on the cart, were the tortured remains of the two deserters. The soldiers, ever watchful for the return of the enemy, were rewarded for their vigilance when a dark swirling cloud was seen in the distance, moving towards them at speed.

'Thebans!' shouted Alexeis, startling Cerus under him.

Diokles urgently shouted to the soldiers to take what they had and to go, quickly. 'We can do no more!' Driving the horses, dragging their precious cargo, the wagon set off with two archers onboard for protection.

Eupompides immediately set about causing as much distraction from the exposed wagon, as he could. 'Kick up as much dust as possible, men. We need to provide a screen for the wagon. If the Thebans see it, they will attack it. Stretch the line as long as possible! Come on, men! Get to it!'

Backwards and forwards the horses and men stirred up the dried earth. Round and round they went until it was almost impossible for them to see one another. Finally, Eupompides called a halt and rode out from the choking gloom. He looked warily in the direction of the Theban advance, but could see nothing ahead of him but an empty landscape and a clear blue sky.

'They've gone!' he shouted, jubilantly, and some of the exhausted Plataeans smiled on hearing him. It was a rare event, these days, to see such confidence in their commander.

On their return to the city, the sorry occupants were finally given some news to cheer about. They had carried out a perilous mission to rescue the remains of their ancestors and had frightened off a Theban patrol.

'I think they believed it was the Athenian army!' laughed Eupompides.

'Who needs them!' Stephanos was heard to remark.

By the shrine to Zeus of Freedom, they created a mass grave, and with everyone present, it was here they reburied the sacred remains of the saviours of Hellas.

FIFTY-FIVE

IN THE THIRD SUMMER of the war, the army of the Peloponnesian League did not march into Attica. There was nothing left to loot or destroy. Archidamus now set his sights on Athens' allies in the north, but to ensure safe passage for his army through Boeotia, he needed first to capture the small fortress in his path.

Encamped on the plain in front of Plataea, was the entire Spartan army! With the decimation of the populace of Athens due to the plague, no further reinforcements had come to the aid of Plataea, and Archidamus expected to take the disillusioned city quickly. But he had not counted on the indomitable spirit of the Plataeans.

With Alexeis and Stephanos flanking him, they sent out their most erudite member, Astymachus, who was well versed in oratory, to talk to the Spartan king.

'Archidamus and Lacedaemonians, in invading the Plataean territory, you do what is wrong in itself, and worthy neither of yourselves nor of the fathers who begot you. Pausanias, your countryman, after freeing Hellas from the Medes with the help of those Hellenes who were willing to undertake the risk of the battle fought near our city, offered sacrifice to Zeus the Liberator in the marketplace of Plataea, and calling all the allies together restored to the Plataeans their city and territory, and declared it independent and inviolate against aggression or conquest. Should any such be attempted, the allies present were to help according to their power. Your fathers rewarded us thus for the courage and patriotism that we displayed at that perilous epoch; but you do just the contrary, coming with our bitterest enemies, the Thebans, to enslave us. We appeal, therefore, to the gods to whom the oaths were then made, to the gods of your ancestors, and lastly to those of our country, and call upon you to refrain from violating our territory or transgressing the oaths, and to let us live independent, as Pausanias decreed.'

Archidamus, not one to suffer long speeches, raised his hand, cutting him short. He was finding it difficult to focus. A brightness was blinding him and it was not the glow of daybreak. Overnight the Plataeans had been busy. Constructing a wooden framework, they had then strapped the golden Marathon Shield to it, and hoisted the structure onto the rooftop of the prominent Temple of Hera. Catching the rays of the sun, they directed the brilliant glare at Archidamus.

The king understood immediately the significance of this action. Marathon - where the Plataeans had stood against the mighty army of Darius, King of Persia. The famous battle where the Spartans turned up - but too late. They were in the middle of a religious festival at the time, which they refused to postpone - whatever the circumstances! He nodded politely towards the light, in acknowledgement of their bravery, and with respect for his adversaries, answered the plea of Astymachus.

'There is justice, Plataeans, in what you say, if you act up to your words. According, to the grant of Pausanias, continue to be independent yourselves, and join in freeing those of your fellow countrymen who, after sharing in the perils of that period, joined in the oaths to you, and are now subject to the Athenians; for it is to free them and the rest that all this provision and war has been made. I could wish that you would share our labours and abide by the oaths yourselves; if this is impossible, do what we have already required of you — remain neutral, enjoying your own; join neither side, but receive both as friends, neither as allies for the war. With this we shall be satisfied.'

The Plataeans discussed these terms, but they had concerns.

Diokles anxiously asked, 'How can we be neutral? We have a treaty with Athens!'

'What about our families in Athens?' said one. 'What chance is there of seeing them again if we break the treaty?'

'They've not sent the help they promised us,' said another. 'They've abandoned us! They must allow us this chance of survival.'

'What if, as soon as the Spartan army withdraws, the Thebans come and take possession?' suggested Alexeis.

Astymachus was sent back to Archidamus with these concerns. 'Because our families are with the Athenians, we must first ask their permission before we can make a decision,' spoke the herald, bravely.

Archidamus could see that the Plataeans were prepared to come to terms and answered, reassuringly.

'You have only to deliver over the city and houses to us Lacedaemonians, to point out the boundaries of your land, the number of your fruit-trees, and whatever else can be numerically stated, and yourselves to withdraw wherever you like as long as the war shall last. When it is over we will restore to you whatever we received, and in the interim hold it in trust and keep it in cultivation, paying you a sufficient allowance.'

Envoys were allowed to go to Athens, and Archidamus agreed to wait for their answer.

But, the response from Athens was firm. No surrender.

'The Athenians say that they never hitherto, since we became their

allies, on any occasion abandoned us to an enemy, nor will they now neglect us, but will help us according to their ability; and they adjure you by the oaths which your fathers swore, to keep the alliance unaltered.'

Such was the message the envoys brought back to Plataea.

The Plataeans resolved not to be unfaithful to the Athenians, and to endure whatever may come. There were no further negotiations between them and the Spartans.

The Spartan King, not wanting to appear the aggressor, prayed to the gods.

'We have made many fair proposals but have not been successful. Graciously accord that those who were the first to offend may be punished for it, and that vengeance may be attained by those who would righteously inflict it.'

He then set his army to blockade the city, and for seventy days and nights, taking turns in shifts, his soldiers worked on building a wall of earth and timber which completely surrounded the town.

FIFTY-SIX

LEON AND PANTHAS WERE overjoyed when Clytes turned up at their lodgings. They were so relieved to see him still alive. But they were fearful. They still had the same room which Clytes had shared with them after the play, but the building now reeked of sickness and there seemed to be no-one responsible for keeping the premises clean or secure. Clytes had witnessed scenes of open debauchery and callousness at every turn, and was not surprised when his friends, at first, were reluctant to open their door to him. It was Panthas who finally let him in, his eyes sunken, his once fleshy cheeks now deeply hollowed, but it was Leon who spoke first, from the bed. Clytes thought there was just a garment thrown across it, but then realised it was a living being.

'Have you had it, Clytes?' he asked, hoarsely, trying to rise.

'The pestilence, Leon? No. I've just returned to the city. The ground still seems to be moving beneath my feet,' he replied, almost gagging at the nauseating smell in the room. 'What in the name of Apollo, is happening, Leon! Did the Spartans cause this?'

'At first we did think our enemies had poisoned the water supply,' said Leon, coughing wretchedly. Clytes was moved to go to him, but Panthas shouted, 'Don't Clytes!'

'People coming from the east say it is there too,' continued Leon, struggling. 'I believe it is worse here because of the overcrowding and the incredible heat. It has been the hottest I can ever remember! People are dying of thirst. Clytes!' he said, trying to raise himself up from the bed, 'Panthas and I have both had it, but are recovering. If we go down with it again, it may not be so severe. But you, dear friend. You are in mortal danger!'

'Get out of the city quickly, Clytes, before you too get sick!' pleaded Panthas, wiping away tears of emotion; completely exhausted.

'Where to, Panthas?' asked Clytes, his hands raised questioningly. 'It seems everywhere is in the grip of it.'

'Don't stay here!' Leon said, with as much emphasis as he had strength for. 'We will manage. We have each other,' and he stretched out a weak hand to Panthas, who grasped it, fervently. 'Clytes! It is so good to see you, but please go! This building is riddled with the pestilence.'

With imploring looks from Leon and Panthas, Clytes was persuaded to leave their fetid room, and the door was closed firmly behind him. He was so shocked at the wretched state his once cheerful and talkative companions were in, that he stood for a moment, wanting to stay and remonstrate with them, but understanding their reasonings, he pulled up his tunic to cover his nose and mouth. Blocking out the stench, he ran quickly down the stairs, ignoring the insistent cries for water emitting from a room somewhere on the ground floor.

His journey through the city to the house of Terches was to walk through a waking nightmare, the stifling air vibrating with the droning sound of swarms of flies. Bodies had been left where they fell, and as he hurried past a swollen corpse, a large black buzzing cloud suddenly rose up, enveloping him. Desperate individuals had drowned in the rainwater tanks in an effort to quench their thirsts, but no-one seemed to notice or care. Constantly, he had to step out of the way, as hand-carts loaded with the dead, drawn by the half-dead, their faces masked by tightly bound cloths, rumbled past him with their grisly cargoes. On one cart, he saw the shattered bodies of a woman and her two blind-folded children. They had jumped from the Gates of the Dead, he was told. Apparently there were many suicides in the city, these days.

Again, he found a changed situation at the once well-run home of the social climber, Terches. The courtyard was overgrown. There were no dogs running to greet him this time. No aromas drifted from the kitchen. He was told he could see neither Terches nor Baras, and he feared the worst. A distinguished looking, well-educated man introduced himself as Methodios, and said he was in the employ of Terches, to handle his affairs in the city. He informed a relieved Clytes that Terches had left the city for his country estate, Baras having become ill with the sickness, and the couple would remain there, despite its ruinous state, until Baras was well again. With the Spartans' attentions focused on besieging Plataea that year, anywhere was preferable to staying within the festering city environs, and they'd taken the risk to venture beyond Athens' walls.

Methodios asked Clytes, politely, if he would follow him and he was led to a heavy wooden door, with a very large iron lock. It was guarded by two handsome but rather menacing, muscular slaves, their arms and chests covered in tattoos of wild exotic animals. They bore a striking resemblance to one another. Methodius informed a sceptical Clytes that the two Thracians were now the most loyal members of the household. Terches had purchased them recently from Paramanos, the slave trader, believing they were far too good looking to end up in the silver mines. Realising their good fortunes, the twin brothers were fiercely devoted to their new master, and little mercy would be shown to any looters that ventured onto Terches' property. Clytes was tall but he had to look up at them when he entered the secured room, which he could see was a small armoury. His eyes grew wide at the sight of the fine weapons and he whistled, involuntarily. Methodios smiled and stepped aside to let Clytes enter the room.

'I can see that you are confused, so I will explain quickly what my duties are in your connection, young sir,' said the assistant. 'I have here a document, signed by Terches which you can read for yourself,' and he handed Clytes a small roll of papyrus.

'I don't quite understand?' said Clytes, amazed, after he had quickly perused the contents. 'Are you saying Terches is letting me choose a set of armour from his own armoury - why?'

'I have to tell you that your benefactor may not return from the country. He has seen many of his friends perish, and knows his chances of surviving are slight. But, he has asked me to tell you that even if he does survive, and he has signed your letter verifying his wishes, he would want you to retain the armour, in payment for keeping your word. Your messages throughout the campaign helped him become much closer to Pericles, and if the sickness hadn't come, he feels sure his career would have risen.'

Of course, Clytes didn't get to choose just what took his fancy. Terches could survive. There were limitations written into the letter, but he was able to equip himself with a serviceable shield, a helmet, a full set of body armour, and a good spear. He had no need of a sword, having already the fine weapon once owned by Pythangelus, which he would never part with. Instead, he selected a good bronze dagger to complete his entitlement. Methodius, satisfied that he had fulfilled his duties, arranged for slaves to help Clytes carry his new possessions to the cramped room he was now sharing with his cousins.

It was soon after this incident, that the trio heard the welcome news circulating the city, of a winter campaign to the Gulf of Corinth under the command of the acclaimed Phormio.

The epidemic in Attica caused the death of so many trireme crews, that at its height during summer's end, in the second year of the war, Corinth and Sparta took full advantage of the fact that Athens' mighty fleet could not now, be everywhere. On the west coast of Hellas, guarding the valuable sea routes to Italy across the Ionian Sea, was the independent state of Acarnania, and with no naval opposition of any worth to stop them, the Corinthians and other Spartan allies began harassing their coastline. An Acarnanian delegation was sent urgently to Athens to ask for their assistance. In particular, the help of the brilliant General Phormio, who was famous in their land for having saved them once before. But after their long journey, they were informed that the general was now in enforced retirement and residing on his farm. Because of the interest the Acarnanians had in the general, and also the fact that Athenian presence was urgently needed around the Peloponnese, Phormio was reinstated and his honour restored. He was given only twenty triremes, which was all Athens could equip with healthy crews, but in compensation he was allowed to take the sacred 'Paralos' as his flagship - the pride of the Athenian navy.

To be under the command of the great Phormio, brought back from obscurity, was an adventure not to be missed and with the Paralos at the head, what could be more glorious!

But foremost on the cousins' minds that winter wasn't the glory, but how to get out of Athens again as quickly as possible. While they'd been at sea, the city had become a cesspit of disease, and it would only be a matter of time before any one of them would fall sick. Since early summer, thousands had died and funeral pyres burned ceaselessly around the city. The once proud capital seemed devoid of hope. The previous winter, following their tours of duty, Clytes and his cousins had returned to their home town of Eleusis, the Spartan army having dispersed in order to gather in their respective harvests, but now Eleusis was also sick with the pestilence. There seemed to be no safe place left to go.

Of the two brothers who had remained in the capital that blistering summer, Alastor the youngest had sadly perished but Audas, mercifully, was found to be still alive, although in a weakened state. Believing he was now immune, having caught the disease and recovered from it, he was returning to Eleusis where he could care for his friends and family now in the grip of the epidemic. Going with him would be the ashes of his brother. His mother, Callidora, would want both sons to return to her.

Clytes shamefully admitted that he had become callous in the face of so much suffering, and instead of offering his help, because of the fear that he too could end up like young Alastor, he'd deliberately avoided anyone with the pestilence. As soon as the three cousins heard that twenty ships were being equipped to sail from the Piraeus, Clytes immediately sought the assistance of Methodios. At his request, Terches sent a letter of recommendation to his friend, Androcles, one of the captains going with Phormio. Thanking their benefactor and any gods still listening, Clytes, Arkadios and Adelphos were able to escape the dying city, being assigned to the crew of the ship 'Ariste', the eleventh ship of the fleet.

With such a small assembly, Phormio needed to carry as many hoplites as were deemed safe for a ship's stability, and twenty marines instead of the usual ten, were carried on each vessel. Although Clytes did not belong to the Athenian middle-class - due to the shortage of the usual manpower, and the fact he had fighting experience and a full set of armour, he was assigned to the Ariste as a combatant. His cousins as skillful rowers, having proved themselves in the summer raids around the Peloponnese, would be in the top bank of oars with the sixty other thranitai. Adelphos being the strongest of the two, would serve as Clytes' military attendant and Arkadios would be responsible for keeping his armour oiled and his blades sharp. They made a formidable team, these cousins from Eleusis, and this would be the cause of some feathers being ruffled among the Athenian fighting men.

Clytes, with shame, would never forget the first words the great Phormio said to him! 'You there! You long streak of piss! What do you think you are doing?' he shouted, red faced with fury. Phormio, with his twenty trierarchs in tow, was walking around the harbour, introducing the new captains and their helmsmen to their triremes, and he took Clytes unawares. Clytes' fellow hoplites, who were standing in small groups on the deck, could easily have given him warning that they'd seen the large party heading in their direction, but they had together decided that Clytes was an upstart, not of their officer class and therefore, smirking in anticipation, left him to be humiliated.

Waiting longer than expected for the inspection, Clytes, on the top deck and his kinsmen below him in their set places at the oars, were recounting tales of their shared experiences, but the actor in Clytes got the better of him. With a trapped audience of one-hundred and seventy rowers and other crew members, he began re-enacting the storming of Astacus, which he and his cousins had taken part in, the previous year. Although out of sight from most of the oarsmen, they could hear his dramatic commentary, and encouraged by their loud cheers from below, Clytes was leaping across the twin decks, sword in hand; the ship rocking beneath his feet.

'You have my permission to drown this idiot, trierarch Androcles, if he does not learn how to behave on deck!' yelled Phormio. He strode over to Clytes, took his blade from him and looked it over carefully. 'How did you acquire such a weapon, soldier?' he asked gruffly.

'It was presented to me by grateful Plataeans, sir!' answered Clytes, trying to muster some semblance of decorum, befitting his new rank.

'Plataea?' said the commander, curiously. Then, almost to himself, 'Unfortunate Plataea.'

Looking questioningly at Androcles, the newly appointed captain of the Ariste, Phormio asked him how was he going to deal with his ill-disciplined crew member.

'He was recommended to me by Terches, an acquaintance of Pericles, commander,' said Androcles, by way of answer. 'All three Eleusinians were with Pericles this summer around the Peloponnese. Terches informs me this man has been on several secret missions on behalf of the state, sir. Apparently the strategos has an interest in him.'

'Hmm,' replied Phormio, scratching his grey beard and looking anew at Clytes. 'Well from what I've just witnessed, I can't understand what the interest could be. Can you?'

'Not at the present moment sir!' answered the trierarch, honestly. 'But I'm confident he'll prove his worth, if what I hear of him is true.'

'I will leave it to you then, captain, to decide his punishment,' said Phormio, dismissively, leaving the ship to continue his inspection of the other triremes.

'Let that be the last time you embarrass me in front of the commander, Clytes!' barked Androcles, 'or I'll have you chained to an oar in the hold for the rest of this venture with the whip on your back! You're not on a bloody stage now! Terches has assured me of your worth. You'd better prove it to me!'

He gave orders to the newly instated helmsman to keep the rowers at their benches because there was going to be a trial run of all twenty triremes, just as soon as conditions were right. With double the number of hoplites on the deck of each ship, discipline would be essential to keep the vessels stable during engagements. 'You heard Phormio's orders!' asserted Androcles to Clytes. 'Any further antics and I will make life very hard for you!' Then he leapt down the ramp to catch up with the commander.

Suitably admonished, but burning with shame and anger, Clytes glared at one group of hoplites gathered at the prow. Some were watching him haughtily and with leering hostility. 'You may have impressed 'the old man' with your 'plucky little Plataea' story, but for all we know,' said Tyrron; one of the group, 'you could have stolen that weapon!'

'There's always one,' muttered Clytes, angrily. 'And I guessed it would be you, Tyrron!' Clytes advanced menacingly towards the trouble maker, who instantly drew his dagger. Looking down at the shorter but well-muscled soldier, he snarled. 'What's your problem, short-arse?'

Tyrron looked around anxiously at his fellow Athenians, then encouraged by their voiced support, asked loudly, 'We are curious? Who is your family, soldier? Just what does your father do?'

Hearing the ensuing uproar, Adelphos, below them, feared the worst and unable to leave his place at the oars without permission, shouted up to Clytes. 'Don't get involved in a fight now, cousin! He's trying to provoke you. Walk away!'

The helmsman, Basileos, seeing there was a fracas about to start, strode over to Clytes and grabbed his sword arm, telling him to calm down or he would be put on a report. The sooner we get going the better, he thought.

So, with the plague still raging through Athens and the Piraeus, Phormio boldly set off that winter, in the hope of keeping his crews free of the pestilence. With his small fleet he sailed round the treacherous waters of Kavomaleas and the Peloponnese, landing at the bay of Naupactus on the northern shore of the Gulf of Corinth. Here they sat out the winter as welcome guests of the Messenians, keeping a look out for enemy ships moving through the gulf towards Acarnania.

Naupactus was home for the Messenian helot slaves who had revolted against their Spartan overlords twenty-five years previously. In return for their surrender, the Spartans had allowed the rebels to leave Sparta, and Athens had provided them with a safe haven at Naupactus. It was not entirely a charitable gesture on Athens' part. Naupactus, protected by Athens, was a constant thorn in the side of the Spartans, becoming a draw for every escaping slave. It was part of Pericles' strategy to give encouragement to the helots to flee Sparta, knowing how much the warrior race relied on its slaves for survival. So when word spread of the Athenian fleet being in the gulf, more and more helots were prepared to take the risk.

There was no action to speak of against the enemy for the entire winter, but for Clytes, these months were not uneventful. Tyrron and his followers took great pleasure in goading him at every opportunity, and of course Clytes' kinsmen were only too eager to offer their assistance when any fights broke out. The foreign archers, who also seemed to offend Tyrron, often threw themselves into these melees, in support of the trio. Trierarch Androcles found it impossible to act fairly in any of these incidents, the Athenians having powerful connections back home, and the three Eleusinians were often on the receiving end of punishments. Authorising the mildest form of disciplinary action allowed - supervising slaves at their lowliest of tasks; the order from Basileos the helmsman became a familiar cry. 'Clytes! Arkadios! Adelphos! Latrines!'

Amongst the heavy papyrus rolls of orders and accounts carried aboard the Paralos from Athens, had been a private letter. It was a short letter, sent to trierarch Androcles by Methodius before the sailing, and on the instructions of Terches it was to be given to Clytes when he reached Naupactus and not before. In it Terches wished Clytes continued good health and plenty of opportunity to use his new weaponry. But it was the final part which made the petty aggravation of Tyrron and his fellow hoplites dwindle in his mind. Lykaon was in Lesbos! Unable to return to Thebes when the campaigning ended for the winter, he had sought the island hospitality of the Mytileneans. With Boeotians sharing a common ancestry with the Mytileneans, Lykaon and his men would find a warm welcome there.

'Why didn't he tell you this before you left Athens?' asked an incredulous Arkadios.

'Because he knew I would go straight to Lesbos,' answered Clytes, with a sigh. 'Terches always thought the odds of thirty to one, was guaranteed suicide on my part!'

'Thirty to three!' added Adelphos, determinedly.

'Thank you, cousin. Thirty to three!' he repeated. Also, it's my guess that because he's deliberately let me know that Lykaon still lives, he believes I'll be sure to guard my own life. Terches, even with death knocking on his door, is still the opportunist. With this message, he's saying nothing has changed. In fact, with so many people dying, he only has to survive in order for his chances of promotion to increase! I only hope The Wolf will still be on Lesbos when this enterprise is over,' said Clytes, deliberately patting the pommel of the sword which had once belonged to the Theban's uncle.

'This is going to seem a long campaign,' said Adelphos, wearily. 'Terches is right, though. You do have something to stay alive for. I know you have your own way of doing things, Clytes, but Tyrron means to do you harm. Can't you try and ignore him?'

'When he insults me - my family, Adelphos? No, I can't!' replied Clytes, hotly.

Whether Clytes actively encouraged Tyrron's antipathy towards him, as an entertaining diversion for his own frustration at not being able to get to Lesbos, the cousins couldn't decide, but throughout the winter, some sort of physical encounter with Tyrron and the other hoplites, became a regular event. The Messenians, grateful to have such formidable protection moored in their small harbour, did their utmost to make the marines comfortable and made their whorehouses available to the Athenians. Clytes' other regular physical contact came in the form of 'Sweetie'. Sweetie could never remember her clients' names, consequently everyone was called Sweetie. Her conversation was limited, but she had other skills with her mouth which Clytes thought more than made up for her lack of discourse, and she also became very adept at taking care of his never-ending cuts and bruises.

Phormio, more comfortable on campaign than in the artificial, pretentious world of the capital, was well used to the company of seamen, and he made sure the men under his command were kept busy during the long winter months while there was no action against the enemy. Athletic games, military competitions and rowing practice - when weather permitted, stopped many a fight breaking out. There was musical entertainment too, and Clytes organised a play. To appeal to his rough-and-ready audience, it was his own more lewd version of 'The House of Wrongdoings'. Phormio's booming laughter reminded Clytes of his old comrade, Glaucus, and it made him want to know the whereabouts of the big redhead. With so many mortalities, he hoped he was still living.

So, winter passed into spring with still no movement from the enemy fleet, while in grief-stricken Athens, the death toll continued to rise.

FIFTY-SEVEN

DURING THE THIRD SUMMER of an inconclusive war, desperate messengers from Acarnania arrived at Naupactus. After months of watching for enemy ships, Phormio was out-witted. The Spartans had slipped through the strait unnoticed, and were again preparing to attack the very people he had been sent to protect. At the same time, news arrived from the east that Corinth had put to sea with her strong fleet, and together with vessels from other Peloponnesian ports, were also on their way through the gulf towards Acarnania. Phormio, in urgent talks with his captains explained that although he owed it to the Acarnanians to go immediately to their aid, to split his forces was not what a good commander ought to do. Having only twenty triremes, he made the decision to keep the fleet intact and told the fearful Acarnanians that they would have to fight alone, for now. His duty was to protect the gulf.

Only a few days later the Athenians watched as ships of the Spartan alliance made their way along the opposite coast, and Phormio immediately set off with his entire force, shadowing them as they pulled their way through the narrows. They counted forty-seven triremes, mainly heavily laden troop carriers, together with support vessels - more than twice their number, but Phormio knew these waters well and he held back from ordering an attack. He waited until they were in the open sea, when the enemy's sea-borne army would be as far from land as possible, and watched with satisfaction at his adversary's first counter-move. Trusting the successful tactics of old, the Peloponnesian triremes formed a wheel formation, ships prows pointing outwards, the troop carriers and support vessels protected in the centre. Phormio had previous experience of this traditional arrangement and knew its weaknesses.

He ordered his captains to sail round and round the enemy ships, encircling the gathered formation, and although he put his own ships at risk by exposing their flanks, he gradually forced the huddled ships closer together. When disorder broke out within the group, as oars became entangled, Androcles, trierarch of the Ariste, and other captains acting under Phormio's precise instructions, gave the order to his crew to swing their ship about and to feign a ramming attack on the enemy ships. With these prodding manoeuvres on all sides, the formation was squeezed even tighter, causing total confusion within the enemy fleet as troops in heavy armour were tipped overboard and crushed between the rocking vessels. Hearing the panic-stricken cries and seeing disorder spreading, Clytes, Tyrron and the other fighting men were eager to make contact, but Phormio had still to give the order.

With intimate knowledge of these waters, he knew that when the sun rose and the sea warmed, a strong breeze blew every morning from the east through the Corinthian gulf. He also knew that his own crews, being far more experienced, would not be unnerved when the subsequent sea squalls hit the ships. Within the wheel formation however, because of the overcrowding and the crashing together caused by the sudden turbulent waters, mayhem ensued, and this was the moment when Phormio finally gave the order to attack. The odds seemed impossible. Twenty triremes against forty-seven. To Clytes however, who together with his fellow hoplites had spent months in training preparing for battle, the situation felt more like a pack of rabid wolves attacking a herd of bleating sheep trapped in a wooden pen. Phormio's triremes rammed ship after ship, crushing and drowning many men in the process, and quickly holed one of the enemy flagships.

High on adrenalin, Clytes used his new weaponry to gruesome effect and with Adelphos at his side, they'd soon taken many prisoners, which could mean rich revenue from potential ransoms. Tyrron sliced off the thumbs of any rowers unlucky enough to be caught by him, ensuring they would never pull oars again, while others afraid to surrender to him, were drowned; pushed under the water by their own oars. Looking for easy pickings, Tyrron and some of his followers made an unprincipled attack on Clytes, in an attempt to relieve him of his prisoners, but they got more than they bargained for. Although Tyrron later boasted his wounds had been the result of fighting a Spartan warrior, the cousins knew differently.

Before midday Phormio had captured twelve enemy ships, including their crews of more than two-thousand men. Some ships managed to escape, but the admiral ordered his eager captains not to give chase. They'd more than enough to cope with. Any more prisoners, and they could turn on his outnumbered crews. Forty-seven against twenty and yet not one Athenian ship was lost. At Cape Rhium, on the northern shore of the narrow strait, they set up their victory trophy. Raising their voices to give thanks to the sea-god Poseidon, whom Phormio believed had intervened on his behalf, they sang their victory songs, loud enough for their chorus to be heard by the enemy encamped on the far side of the narrow waters less than a mile away.

Unfortunately, their triumph was short-lived.

Word soon reached Phormio that the enemy fleet which had failed in its attempt to invade Acarnania, was uniting with further ships arriving from the Peloponnese. His men watched with growing dismay as seventy-seven vessels weighed anchor, opposite the Athenian camp. Phormio, hearing the disgruntled murmurings among the crews, had to use all his skills of motivation in order to quell their fears, and not known for his use of oratory, he spoke plainly.

'I see, my men, that you are frightened by the number of the enemy, and I have accordingly called you together, not liking you to be afraid of what is not really terrible. The Peloponnesians already defeated and not even themselves thinking that they are a match for us, have not ventured to meet us on equal terms, but have equipped this multitude of ships against us. The Spartans use their own supremacy over their allies to promote their own glory. They are most of them being brought into danger against their own will, or they would never, after such a decided defeat, have ventured upon a fresh engagement. Stay at your posts, by your ships and be sharp at catching the word of command. In action think order and silence all-important. Qualities useful in war generally and in naval engagements in particular; and behave before the enemy in a manner worthy of your past exploits. I may once more remind you that you have defeated most of them already and beaten men do not face a danger twice with the same determination.'

This and more Phormio told his men, to instill in them the courage to go out once more against the enemy. This time it was four to one.

With Naupactus further along the coast now unprotected, the admiral was again in a dilemma. He knew that to try and sail through the narrow straits, with such an enormous force opposing him, was risky, but he had no choice. When he saw the enemy fleet in a four deep formation start to sail towards Naupactus, he set sail also, in single file. The supporting Messenian army shadowed his small fleet, marching along the coast to protect their city, while on the opposite coast, the army of the Spartan alliance followed alongside their fleet.

Exactly as Phormio feared, once he was in the narrowest part of the straits, the enemy ships turned to point northwards, directly facing the exposed flanks of his ships. With incredible speed, the wall of ships was upon them. Phormio's fleet split in two, eleven ships escaping towards Naupactus and the open sea, while the others were driven ashore. Even though fully armed, the Messenians dived into the sea and managed to save several of the crew members who had jumped overboard, and even boarded some of the empty Athenian vessels which were being towed away. After some fierce fighting they were able to recover them. But one ship, a fully crewed trireme, was successfully towed away. The seamen who were not saved by the Messenians were either slain or captured.

The Ariste was last in the line of eleven ships to escape the onslaught, and caught in the wake caused by the fleet's fierce rowing ahead of them, they started to fall back. Androcles, seeing a fast trireme break away from the pursuing enemy fleet, ordered the piper to increase the strokes. Then the deck crew, Clytes included, took up the beat, bellowing to the men below to pull harder, pull faster. As they neared Naupactus, the enemy trireme began closing on them with the rest of the fleet not far behind, the crews singing loudly their songs of victory. They were premature. The crews of the Athenian ships that had reached safety, were now roaring encouragement from the decks of their ships, to the rowers of the Ariste, urging them onwards towards the harbour. In deep water, near the entrance to the harbour was an anchored merchant vessel, and Basileos the helmsman, steered the Ariste around this craft, just in time. As the pursuing trireme came upon them, trierarch Androcles, together with Clytes and the others in the deck crew, jumped aboard the merchant ship. Turning her about, they managed to ram the fast approaching enemy ship; sinking her instantly. The Peloponnesian fleet, approaching in disorder due to overconfidence, was now chased by the Athenians who, with loud shouts, took off after them. They captured six enemy ships and recovered their own disabled ships. Later, under a truce, the dead of both sides were exchanged, then the Spartans fled under cover of darkness, fearing the arrival of reinforcements. Not long after they'd left, twenty triremes arrived from Athens. Too late! Phormio had fought his second battle against seventy-seven vessels, with the same twenty triremes he had commanded in the previous battle against forty-seven.

During the battle, Clytes proved himself more than worthy of bearing arms, and he wanted Terches to know how much he appreciated the faith he'd had in him. When word arrived from Methodios that his benefactor had passed from this world, Clytes felt the loss keenly. On his return to Athens, in the spring of the following year, he learned that playwright Baras, having survived the plague, had been cruelly left without his sight. Within days of Terches crossing the river Styx, Baras had their eunuch cook prepare him a draught of hemlock. Then, following the soul of his lover; the ferryman Charon carried the spirit of Baras to the Underworld.

That autumn, the pestilence had returned with a vengeance, making no distinction between the great and the good or the weak and base. Pericles in desperation called for the distinguished physician, Hippocrates, to be brought to the city from his home on the island of Kos. The doctor immediately set in motion several hygienic measures which did in time bring about results. But it was too late for Athens' leader. Following a period of deep mourning for the deaths of his two legitimate sons and his beloved sister, the soul of Pericles of Athens, the great general, statesman and orator, began its journey to the Islands of the Blessed.

The quarantined household of Aspasia, where lived the beloved consort of Pericles and their ten-year-old son, Pericles Junior, was mercifully unaffected, and it was within this sanctuary that the wife and child of Phalinus of Plataea were being cared for. To the great relief of the surviving Plataeans, the lives of Akaterina and little Akylas were spared. These two, together with The Shield being defended in Plataea, kept the hopes of the dejected and homeless Plataeans alive.

On his return to Athens, part of Clytes' duties was the handing over of the exchange prisoners taken during the Battle of Naupactus, but there were no riches awaiting the cousins ``from expected ransoms. Because there were equal numbers of prisoners taken on both sides, the exchange was man for man. But one major advantage in being part of such a small contingent, was the share of the spoils. Phormio was generous with the men who'd so valiantly served under him. The heroes with Phormio at the Battle of Naupactus would tell and retell their stories until their dying days.

Tyrron had been one of those captured, and on his release, Clytes was not surprised to see that the Spartans had removed his thumbs.

FIFTY-EIGHT

PERICLES AND TERCHES WERE dead, and the obligations Clytes once owed to them no longer dominated his life. Being in funds after his return from a successful campaign under the command of Phormio, his thoughts once more turned to seeking out Lykaon. The Theban's last reported sighting being on the island of Lesbos.

Lesbos, just a few miles off the Persian coast, consisted of several towns and cities, all independent from one another, but all under the protection of Athens. Their payment for this protection came in the supply of ships and fighting men in times of war, but for some time not all of Lesbos was happy with this arrangement. Mytilene, the largest of the provinces, was being encouraged by their Boeotian brothers, to revolt. Lykaon and his followers, sharing an ancient lineage with the Mytileneans, had been made welcome in their city after his banishment from Thebes, and since his arrival, Lykaon had encouraged this dissent, which he helped to spread to other towns on the island.

Believing his forceful exhortations that the Spartans and Boeotians would come to their aid against the Athenians, the leaders of the city ordered a strengthening of their fortifications and for new triremes to be built. Lykaon however, was not interested in freeing Lesbos for the Mytileneans - he wanted Lesbos for himself. A wolf in sheep's clothing, he was driven by his desire for power, to unite the towns of Lesbos against the Athenians for his own devious ends.

Mercenaries were needed to bring the Mytileneans plans - or rather, his plans - to fruition. As part of a delegation to Pontus on the Black Sea, he arranged a shipment of additional supplies and men. He resisted the temptation to hire the female archers known as Amazons, who were renowned in those parts for their bravery and spirit. Although greatly intrigued by stories of their promiscuous and free lifestyle, it was their disregard for men's authority he resented. There was only one woman he'd accept dominance from. He'd pondered on whether he should make a diversion on his return journey and visit Larachne in Lydia to tell her of his ultimate objective. He would be ruler of Lesbos, and with her Persian connections, what a formidable pair they would make. Yet there was one more part of his scheme he wanted to see completed first. The Marathon Shield. With that icon in his possession, men would flock to him and once in overall control of Lesbos, Larachne he believed, would see him in a new light.

He had missed her. No-one understood him, as she did. As he'd watched the coastline move by, the rhythm of the rowers cutting easily through the calm waters towards Pontus, he suddenly laughed. The laugh was a bitter one. Plataea was being starved into submission. The weakened garrison could not hold out much longer. He mused on the fact that it was fortunate for him, that the golden treasure had not been taken to Athens, and he began to speculate on just how far his ambition could take him - if he had possession of it. His dreams were indeed limitless.

There was one town on Lesbos which remained loyal to Athens, however, despite the threats from her neighbours. Methymna. From here a message was sent urgently to Athens, to the effect that if they did not send military aid immediately, Lesbos could be lost. Being informed that, if they hurried, the Athenians could arrive when the entire population of Mytilene would be outside their city walls celebrating a festival to Malean Apollo, they quickly diverted forty triremes which had been about to sail around the Peloponnese.

Arkadios and Adelphos were part of the crew of the ninth ship in this fleet of forty and Audas; the brother who had survived the plague, was a rower on the tenth in the line. They'd already said their farewells to Clytes and his new slave, Heliodorus; a young man recently hired to help carry his armour. But, immediately the brothers were informed that their new destination was to be Lesbos, Arkadios and his siblings were not surprised to hear that the pair of them had turned up at Piraeus, asking around the harbour as to their whereabouts. The hired slave Heliodorus was disappointed not to be going with the fleet. If he could be taken on as an oarsman he'd be granted his freedom. But he had to be returned to his master, a man who had several slaves for hire for a variety of purposes, depending on the price - no questions asked.

'Well cousin, I don't know how it has come about, but it seems we are all going to Lesbos,' said Arkadios. 'Maybe this will be the end of the Lykaon saga!'

'When he's dead, then it ends!' said Clytes, forcefully. 'Be witness that I smell out swiftly the tracks of evils that have long been done!' he said theatrically, quoting the tragedian, Aeschylus.

'Or when *you* are dead, cousin,' replied Arkadios, looking at him, concerned.

'I value my life for one reason only, Arkadios. 'I want to be the one who sends that coward to Hades! He'll pay for taking my family from me. Have we been spared by the gods, him and I, for their entertainment? I'm beginning to think so! Who knows?' he said, shrugging his shoulders.

CHAPTER FIFTY-EIGHT

'But if it's a show the gods want, then that's what they'll get!'

When the fleet arrived at Lesbos, they found the festivities had been cancelled. The citizens of Mytilene had received prior warning of the Athenian fleet sailing towards them and they were now secure behind their newly built fortifications. Buoyed up with encouragement from the Boeotians, and with their numbers being increased by a contingent of Black Sea archers, the oligarchs ignored demands to surrender their fleet, and instead ordered their ships to attack the Athenians. They were no match however, and to Lykaon's annoyance they were soundly defeated.

Still convinced that the Spartans were coming to their aid, the Mytileneans agreed, at the insistence of Lykaon, to play for time. They asked the Athenian commander if they could send envoys to Athens to plead their cause, and this was agreed. At the same time, unbeknown to the Athenians, another ship slipped out of Lesbos - heading for Sparta. On board was Lykaon. He intended to seek out general Skopas; to demand of him the promised help. Even if he had to make generous offers to his greedy ex-comrade-in-arms - which he had no intention of keeping - he would not let control of the island slip from his grasp, not now. Only forty ships! Athens was on its knees because of the plague. There could be no reinforcements. They could be taken. If only the Spartans could be motivated to venture out to sea.

In his absence, his old adversary Clytes, was fighting the Mytileneans on the beaches of Lesbos, his eyes ever watchful for that one face which haunted his dreams. But as night came, the islanders retreated behind their walls and the frustrated Athenians returned to their ships.

Lykaon did not find Skopas in Sparta. He was in Boeotia, being one of the commanders laying siege to luckless Plataea, and much to Lykaon's vexation, the decision to send a fleet to Lesbos was delayed until members of the Peloponnesian League met at Olympia later in the year. As usual, the Spartans were slow to react and his plans were floundering. While delayed in Sparta however, he became friendly with a man he thought was much like himself. This man, by the name of Salaethus, became intrigued by the presumptuous young Theban and always made time to talk with him. After learning that only forty Athenian ships were defending the whole of Lesbos, Salaethus was also eager for his fellow countrymen to make a move, and as the Theban became a little over-confident in promoting himself, more information slipped from his lips than was prudent. Details of the valuable, jewel encrusted relic at besieged Plataea, definitely interested the bold Salaethus.

Clytes and his cousins were involved in several skirmishes during that summer, but they had insufficient strength to bring about a surrender, and Clytes was beginning to think that Lykaon was not on the island after all.

Realising that the Spartans were being given the impression that Athens was too weak to defend Lesbos, the Athenians did two things. They called in the help of one-thousand hoplite allies, who were sent to the island under the command of Paches, an Athenian general, who immediately set about building a blockade around Mytilene, while one-hundred ships were equipped to raid the coast of the Peloponnese. The cost was enormous in men and silver, and a new tax had to be enforced; the first of its kind, and the rowers of the one-hundred triremes consisted of wealthy landowners and rich foreigners, so depleted was the population by the pestilence. But it worked. The Peloponnesian League meeting at Olympia, which had already voted in favour of a fleet being sent to Lesbos, and the island being brought within their League, thought they'd been tricked by the Mytileneans into believing the Athenians were finished. They now withdrew their enthusiasm. They'd campaigned enough already that summer, the allies decided. Anyway, harvests needed to be brought in.

With nothing to gain by waiting, and eager to get back to defend 'his' island, Lykaon travelled back to Lesbos, taking his new friend, the bold Spartan with him. It was now winter and the journey was perilous, but Lykaon was afraid that the Mytileneans would surrender in his absence. He needed to convince them to hold out; and that help would come. The two men found that Mytilene was now under blockade, but Lykaon's comrades inside the city managed to smuggle them through the lines of fortifications. It wasn't long however, before Lykaon realised that Salaethus was a little too much like himself. The Spartan soon won the trust of the desperate oligarchs, eager to hear details of the mighty invasion force being prepared to help their cause, and soon Salaethus was put in charge of their defences. It was a major mistake.

By summer, with food running out and still no fleet on the horizon, Salaethus decided the Mytileneans must make a break for it, and he ordered that every man be fitted out in full hoplite armour. Once armed however, the citizens turned on their leaders. They had other priorities. They demanded that the stores be opened up, and all remaining food fairly distributed among the hungry population. They next threatened to surrender, and the leaders were given no option but to negotiate with the Athenians.

Watching as events reeled out of control, Salaethus, together with Lykaon and some of his followers made the decision to vacate the island, and with the assistance of watchers on the ramparts keeping a look-out, a handful managed to sneak past the patrols.

On that dark night, if he had but known it, Clytes was only yards away from The Wolf.

Only the city of Mytilene was under blockade, the rest of the island was as yet, not under Athenian control, so heading north up the coast, away from the guarded harbour, they quickly found a ship to take them the short distance to the Persian coast. Four men managed to sail away to freedom. Lykaon; two of his original followers, one of them being Hippodamus, and an archer from Pontus. A fifth man, Salaethus, Lykaon had forced overboard on the point of his sword.

'Jump, or your dead body will feed the fishes!' ordered, Lykaon.

'What about our plans for Plataea?' asked an alarmed Salaethus. You will need my help!'

'Your help?' exclaimed Lykaon. 'I won't make that mistake again! Jump!' he ordered.

With the Theban's blade pressed dangerously hard against his back, the Spartan climbed onto the rail and dived majestically into the black water. He could be seen swimming strongly back to the shore. Lykaon watching him, spat into the sea.

'Where now?' asked Hippodamus. 'Larachne?'

'Not yet,' answered Lykaon. 'First, Plataea!'

FIFTY-NINE

ON THE DEATH OF the old king and warrior, Archidamus, General Cleomenes became commander of the Spartan army. Agis and Pausanias, heirs to the twin thrones of Sparta, were both deemed too young for such an undertaking, so with the coming of summer it was Cleomenes who took the army into Attica, laying waste once again an undefended landscape. There was little left to destroy, but that did not stop their renewed ruthlessness. Any sign of new growth was trampled or burned. It was a particularly destructive invasion, with the precise intention of keeping the Athenians close to home. The Spartan Admiral, Alcidas, had finally prepared a fleet of forty-two triremes, specifically for the relief of Lesbos.

Without sufficient numbers to face any more resistance than was already guarding the island, Alcidas was fearful of meeting the Athenians at sea, and his progress was delayed. Consequently, before he'd even reached his objective, the news came to him that Mytilene had already fallen. As soon as he heard this, his objective was to return the fleet to Sparta as quickly as possible, without an encounter at sea. But his flight was spotted by the two Athenian messenger ships, Salaminia and Paralus. With Mytilene now secured, general Paches was ordered to set off with his fleet in pursuit of the fleeing Spartans, but Alcidas did not slow down or stop until he was safely back in the Peloponnese, thus avoiding any confrontation.

Returning to Lesbos, the Athenian commander Paches, went on to successfully subdue the rest of the island and captured the Spartan, Salaethus, who was found hiding in one of the island villages. Clytes found himself with a large part of the army being sent back to Athens, together with the ring-leaders of the revolt, including Salaethus. The Spartan made a vigorous plea for his life and in his speech, he referred to the ongoing siege at Plataea, to which he said he could bring about a solution. The Athenians were intrigued, but his fervent talk about the priceless shield held at the fortress city was considered contemptuous by the Athenians, and he was executed without a trial.

Being extremely angry that the Mytilenean revolt had brought a Spartan fleet into their waters, the Athenians demanded a suitable sentence be pronounced against them. Fired up by hardliner Cleon, the same Cleon, Baras had made fun of in his play, the decision was brutal. Such was the intense feeling in the Assembly that day, it was decided that all men involved in the revolt should be sentenced to death, and their women and children enslaved. A trireme was sent to Lesbos carrying orders to Paches to put these punishments into immediate effect.

No sooner had the trireme carrying its dire news left the harbour, than the Athenians began to have doubts about their harsh judgment, and a second gathering of the Assembly was called for the following day. Cleon still argued strongly for the executions; deriding the fact that he had been reluctantly drawn into a rhetorical battle, when the right decision based on their emotions had already been reached.

'Do not be traitors to yourselves, but recalling as nearly as possible how you felt when they made you suffer, and how you would have given anything to crush them. Now pay them back!'

But Diodotus, a moderate, whose father had been close to Pericles, denied Cleon's assertions that anyone standing up for the Mytileneans must have been bribed, and called for a more lenient decision, stating that such harsh treatment would immediately alienate other states in their empire.

'Pass sentence on the Mytileneans whom Paches, deeming them guilty, has sent hither but leave the rest of the inhabitants where they are. This will be good policy for the future, and will strike present terror into your enemies. For wise counsel is really more formidable to an enemy than the severity of unreasoning violence.'

His logic that only the ring-leaders should receive the death sentence, the rest of the citizens being potential future allies, was narrowly accepted.

Members of a delegation from Mytilene who were in Athens to plead their cause, came forward with a desperate offer. They would give a substantial reward to all members of a crew, if they could get to Lesbos in time to stay the executions. This offer was approved by the Athenians, and a suitable vessel and crew were urgently sought out.

Young Iandros, his father still financing the upkeep of the vessel, Thetis, was inspired by this challenge. The ship was ready for such a voyage, having recently been refitted at great expense, following campaigns under his trierarchship. He immediately sought out his father, imploring him to gain the support of his powerful acquaintance, Nicias.

General Nicias, his enormous wealth, like that of Paramanos, also acquired from his family's interests in the silver mines at Lavrion, was the accepted successor to Pericles. An extremely wealthy aristocrat, moderate in his views, he was a strong opponent of Cleon. He needed little persuasion. If the second trireme did not get to Lesbos in time, then Cleon's brutal sentence would be carried out. Being assured by the passionate Iandros that he had a worthy crew, capable of such a task, the Thetis was chosen for the mission.

'I know I'm expecting a lot from you, Glaucus, and the rest of you!' shouted Iandros to his crew members lined up beside their ship. No longer the callow young man of Locris, his dedication to the Thetis and its crew during several successful missions had gained the respect of all who now served on her, and the tough, hardened seamen listened intently. 'We've been through many an adventure together and I know you will all do your best,' he went on. 'But I need more than your best. Your backs will scream with pain. Your hands will bleed. You'll get precious little sleep, Glaucus! But there will be no slowing, no stopping. Is that understood?'

'Let's get going, captain!' shouted Bion, excitedly. 'We're wasting time!'

'He's already spent his prize money, sir!' laughed one of the rowers.

True to their captain's word, they did not stop. They travelled as light as possible, with only essential crew members. All excess baggage was left in port, and only dried food was taken onboard, which had to be eaten at the oars. The rowers slept or rested in shifts as the relentless rhythm from the piper, and from favourite rowing songs, carried on throughout the night. Glaucus was totally unfazed by the darkness. Although rarely at sea in a trireme at night because of the dangers of the unseen, he confidently directed the Thetis ever northwards, guided by the stars and the beacons on island headlands. Using his immense knowledge, his great hands gripping the twin tillers, he steered around known dangers, through strong currents, avoiding submerged rocks. The muscles in his arms bulged and constantly throbbed with pain, until periodically he was relieved by others, sometimes a man on each rudder, while he rested. Hour after hour, Iandros walked the decks, shouting out encouragement. 'Think of the glory, men! Think of the gratitude! So many lives saved! What have you spent your bonus on, Bion?' Some told jokes and stories. All sang songs. The relentless rhythm was maintained.

There was one point when Glaucus became particularly alert, and he sent a message down to the bow watch to be on his guard; to listen out for the sound of warning chimes. Submerged rocks, the result of local volcanic activity, were a menace in these waters, and if they were holed in the dark there would be no rescue. Hollow bronze tubes suspended from chains had been fixed to these hazards, the constant shaking by the winds and waves creating a vital alarm for sailors, but in the darkness it could be difficult to judge the distance.

Suddenly there were exclamations from some of the oarsmen. 'Look!' shouted Iandros, excitedly. Glaucus smiled, indulgently. It was obviously a new experience for this young trierarch. 'Thetis is lighting the way for us!' he shouted to the men below. 'The sea nymph has brought down the stars!' As the oars plunged into the waters, bright blue lights danced all around the boat, illuminating the fearsome visage of the sea goddess. The serpent at the stern, shimmered and glowed eerily. Then something happened which even Glaucus had never witnessed before. The dancing blue lights travelled up the oars, and onto the deck. They danced across to the feet of Flamebeard, moving up his chair and to the very top of the carved canopy overhead, and the forked tail of the serpent. The big man was infused in a moving stream of blue light. His curled red hair and beard looked to be stirring in an icy breeze, as he sat transfixed by the strange phenomenon.

'Captain!' he shouted, with sudden inspiration, as he heard the muffled sound of the chimes drifting towards them. 'Get the men to splash their oars on each stroke! Make as much disturbance of the water as they can!' Iandros, with absolute trust in his helmsman, didn't hesitate to give his rowing master the unusual command.

The men were confused to be ordered to do this, as it was always drilled into them to cause as little drag as possible, but an order was an order. The bow watch, leaning over the side, observed that the rowers were causing waves of blue lights to filter out from the ship. As the ripples of bright stars travelled out into the darkness, they illuminated jagged black rocks, jutting out of the water ahead of them. Urgently, the deck officer called out the danger. Glaucus put all his weight on the right rudder. The rowers quickly drew in their oars, and the vessel glided by the rocky hazard.

'That was the most wondrous thing I have ever seen!' exclaimed Iandros, after the lights were suddenly extinguished, and Glaucus, hearing the clanging sounds fading, assured him they were out of danger. 'Our mission is blessed, men!' Iandros called out to his crew.

The captain of the ship bearing the execution order had been in no hurry to carry out his sad duty, and had delayed his voyage as much as his situation allowed, and it was with great reluctance that he finally handed over the proclamation to general Paches on the island of Lesbos. As the commander began unwillingly to read out the first few lines to the captured Mytilenians, a trireme was seen fast approaching their harbour. Trumpet calls and shouts could be heard from the nearing ship, and some of its crew began jumping into the water, whooping and hollering. Others fell exhausted onto the beach. Their trierarch was seen running towards the fortified town. In his hand was the miraculous stay of execution. Iandros had set sail a full day behind the first trireme, only for them both to arrive simultaneously.

As Diodotus had envisaged, the Lesbians were eventually allowed to re-farm their island, under leasehold from Athens, and only the ring-leaders dispatched to Athens by Paches, were executed.

Unfortunately for Bion, the gratitude of the Mytileneans did not match his wild expectations. Thinking he would receive enough to go into a business venture with his brother-in-law, he'd used all his savings and a large amount of borrowed money, to put down his share of a deposit on a small shop. He was found by Cassa sitting at the latrines with his head in his hands. All Cassa could get out of him was, 'Oh God! I should have waited! What have I done?'

As word spread of the remarkable feat of the Thetis, many of the crew members' names became famous, but in Bion's case, his name became well-known for another reason. Anyone considering borrowing or spending money because of a belief in some future gain, was warned, 'Don't do a Bion!'

An unfitting end to the whole Mytilene affair occurred later, when General Paches was brought to trial to discuss the incident of his failed capture of the fleeing Spartan fleet. Believing he was being accused of cowardice, Paches took his own life.

SIXTY

EUPOMPIDES LOOKED AT THE gaunt, exhausted men seated around him. They were into their fourth winter defending the city, and since the Spartans had cut them off entirely from the outside world, their food stocks had become dangerously low. They'd fought valiantly against the building of the double-walled blockade, withstood bombardments from siege engines, and survived a fire which destroyed most of their city; a fire the like of which no man there had ever seen before, and only brought under control due to a freak storm. The Father of the Gods, had for a second time, come to the aid of the Plataeans.

'Zeus will be our saviour once again, Eupompides!' spoke Theanatus the seer, excitedly. 'This is the third time I've been given the same dream! In a storm, I see a fox being stalked by wolves. In the darkness, the fox evades them and the wolves, believing the fox is returning to its lair, bolt in that direction. The fox however, runs towards the wolves' own territory, the last place the hunters would look for him. Once free from pursuit, the fox, under cover of the storm, doubles back to the safety of the mountain. We could do it, Eupompides! In mid-winter! They would never expect us to make a break for it. At night, and a stormy night at that, some of us might make it!'

'It will need to be planned meticulously, Theanatus,' replied Eupompides, stroking his bearded chin, thoughtfully. 'Zeus may help us by sending down his torrents, but it will still be a risky undertaking.'

'I want to try it,' said Stephanos, firmly. 'Anything is better than slowly starving to death!'

Ammeas, another captain and a brave fighter, stood up. 'I want to be first over the wall, general!' he growled. 'My men are more than ready to slit Theban throats!'

Other voices rose up in agreement, and when Eupompides arranged a vote of the four-hundred Plataeans under his command, it was unanimous. A white stone placed in the jar meant agreement with the plan to escape. A black stone meant, remain and face the consequences. There were no black stones.

Lecadonis, captain of the eighty Athenian contingent, asked his soldiers outright what they wanted to do, full-knowing their response. 'Do we stay or go, men?'

'We go!' they shouted, as one.

The women were not included in the plan. The break-out was thought to be dangerous enough. Mostly slaves, they would have to take their chances. One woman however, was determined to be part of the escape party. Amara, the wife of Imbros. There was no way she would be separated from her husband. For her to remain in the city without Imbros, was unthinkable. Naturally, Eupompides was firmly against the idea of her going with them, and tried to explain to Imbros how difficult an undertaking it would be.

'Amara could jeopardise the whole venture, Imbros! I will personally take on the responsibility of getting her returned to you, should we reach Athens. Once our garrison has gone, the Spartans will quickly take the city. The women will be fed. As a lady of Plataea, Amara will be ransomed. I promise I will take a full part in any negotiations. That's all I can do, Imbros.'

'Do you honestly believe the Spartans or the Thebans will treat the women decently?' exclaimed Imbros, pleadingly. 'Amara will be especially mistreated; held up as an example. She should be allowed the same chance as the rest of us. She's defended the city alongside us both - side by side on the battlements!'

'Imbros!' said Eupompides in exasperation. 'Your position will be up front, where I need your sword arm. You will not be able to protect your wife, without putting us all in danger, man! If this plan is to succeed, we will need all the luck of the gods and then some. Theanatus believes his dreams signify success, but he mentioned no woman in the revelations. We have much to do, Imbros. Let's get to it!' With his hand placed firmly on the sculptor's shoulder, the general guided the desolate Imbros towards the gathered men of the garrison eagerly awaiting instructions outside the Temple of Hera.

Above them shone the symbol of their city. Strapped to a wooden frame and hoisted to the highest point on the roof, its light was reflected in the eyes of all who now gazed upon it. Murmurs grew gradually louder among the men. They knew it would be impossible to escape over the walls with such a weighty object. If they were to succeed, they could not be encumbered in any way. They would have to move quickly and with stealth.

Before Stephanos could stop him, Diokles stepped forward. 'I ask to remain with The Shield, general,' he said, determinedly. 'I'll wait for the reinforcements which you will assuredly bring back from Athens, if your escape is successful.'

Demetrious also stepped forward. 'There is nothing for me in Athens, sire. My family perished in the plague. I also ask to remain with The Shield.'

A few others, believing they would hinder the escape plan, due to injuries sustained during the siege, also decided to wait for the reinforcements. Eupompides accepted the logic of their thinking.

'When we reach Athens,' spoke the general, with passion, 'we will gather a force which will drive the Spartans and the Thebans from our lands! While The Shield is in Plataea, the city still lives!'

Afraid of drawing the attention of the enemy at their gates, there was no cheering, but the men gripped each other's hands in solidarity and hope. Diokles took an emotional Stephanos to one side. 'When you get to Athens, find my wife and daughter,' he told him, earnestly. 'I'm placing them in your care, Stephanos. You know as well as I do,' he said, his voice lowered, 'there is little chance I will ever see them now.'

Theanatus and Diokles worked on the specifics of the escape plan together. Drawings were made of every part of the site fortifications and possible route maps were carefully considered. Adhering to details in his dream, Theanatus insisted that the escapees take the road to Thebes, after the initial break-out, and a risky strategy was eventually arrived at.

'We keep the shrine to Androcrates on our right,' asserted Theanatus. 'It will be a marker in the dark,' he said, pointing at the drawings. 'When we reach the junction we turn back, taking the road directly to Hysiae. Once there, the mountains will cover us. And then - to Athens!'

'You make it sound so easy, Theanatus! May the gods be on your side on the night!' sighed Diokles, as he checked his own facts and figures for the venture. 'I need as accurate a measurement as possible for the wall ladders,' he said, looking at his lists. 'Too short, and men will fail to reach the top. Too long, and we could warn the enemy of the escape.'

'We will count the bricks, Diokles!' said Theanatus, smiling. 'There's always a way!'

To ensure accuracy, Diokles had several men, including himself, to count the layers of exposed brickwork encircling their shrunken city. With all bricks being of a uniform size, he was eventually able to reach a number he was satisfied with.

But these were not the only plans being worked on for the break-out.

Imbros was scheming also. In the company of friends; Alexeis, Stephanos and Epiktetos, he was discussing how best to help Amara escape with them.

'Amara deserves to be with us, Imbros,' said Alexeis, but she cannot go with you. You'll be in the first group. It will be bloody fighting to get through the guards. If they raise the alarm, well, it will be every man for himself. I'll be at the head of the second group, but it will still be no place for a woman. I cannot guarantee that I could protect her, Imbros.'

'Same goes for me, friend,' said Stephanos, apologetically. 'I'll be in the first group with you.'

'She will come with me and my archers,' said Epiktetos, decisively. 'Amara has earned her place with us. We will protect her, Imbros. Have no fear!'

Imbros, relieved and thankful, embraced Hawk-Eye warmly, and went to tell Amara the news. They'd never been separated. All through the long siege Amara had stayed with him, had suffered and fought with the rest of them. They would win freedom together or die together.

As Theanatus had prophesied, it was not long before, on a dark moonless night, a storm swept down from the north. Merciless arrows of freezing sleet rained down from the heavens, driving the enemy guards to take shelter in their wall towers. Visibility was non-existent. Eupompides decided that this was the night, and the men, having gone over the details many times, made ready. Each one looked up in the direction of The Shield, kissed whatever weapon he carried, then quickly turned and headed for the first ditch, keeping a planned distance apart for fear of causing their weapons to clash together, so giving warning to the enemy.

It was brave Ammeas, leading his twelve men, who scaled the inner wall first, quickly killing the sentries sheltering in the adjacent towers which bridged the double fortifications. Eupompides and Theanatus were next up the ladders, guiding their men through the towers, to reach the outer wall. At some point, a roof tile became dislodged, clattering down and giving warning to the besiegers, and the air was suddenly filled with their cries of alarm. The Plataeans who had still to scale the ladders became fearful that their comrades had been captured, and quickly climbed back across the ditch to re-enter the city. Diokles, was already carrying out his instructions, by causing a diversion. He'd ordered beacons to be lit along the Plataean battlements, which caused total confusion to the Thebans who were trying to send fire signals across the plain to Thebes, for help. The returning Plataeans joined Diokles in trying to distract the enemy, realising all-too-well that the biggest threat to the escapees, was the three-hundred strong patrol whose purpose it was to guard the outer perimeter. If they got caught by the patrol, then it was all over. Everyone who was left in the city, the women included, roared and shouted above the storm, to give the impression that the city was still fully occupied, while running around the battlements with lighted torches.

Amara and Epiktetos got caught up in the confusion. They were just about to mount one of the ladders when the news was passed to them from Alexeis and Simonedes that the escape had been aborted. Their comrades had been captured. Shocked and shaking, Amara gripped the ladder, and looked upwards through the rain, towards the freedom she felt was so close. She began to climb.

Epiktetos watched as Amara, her small bow and quiver strapped to her back, clawed her way up the ladder, buffeted by the wind and the rain, her hair and garments clinging to her.

'I'm going to bring her back!' spoke Alexeis, struggling to be heard through the driving rain. 'Imbros is either dead or been taken,' and he started to mount the ladder.

'I'm going with her, Alex,' said Epiktetos, determinedly, securing his weapons on his shoulder. 'I just can't go back!'

Desperately torn as to what to do next, Alexeis made a decision. 'Someone has to stand with Diokles,' he stated, decisively. 'If our men have been killed, no relief will come from Athens. I can't leave him with sole responsibility for The Shield, Hawk-Eye. I'll have to go back.' As they changed places on the ladder, Alexeis gripped his comrade on the shoulder. 'Good luck!' he said, fiercely, then was swallowed up in the darkness.

With his fellow archers behind him, Epiktetos followed Amara to the top of the imposing battlements, pulling up the ladder after them. As they reached the outer wall, and looked down at freedom, they watched in horror as a multitude of torches came into view. 'It's true, then. The patrol has them,' spoke Epiktetos, grimly. 'It's no use going any further.'

Suddenly, they watched in astonishment as the torches, one by one, fell to the ground.

'What's happening?' asked Amara, trying to shield her eyes against the driving rain.

'I believe the patrol's being fired at! Our men must still be at large!' exclaimed Epiktetos, jubilantly. 'But it's too damn dark to see.'

'Strong-Arm must have made it!' said one of the archers. 'Those javelins are finding their mark!'

'They make excellent targets!' shouted Epiktetos, against the wind. 'They are lit up like a bonfire! Let's give our boys a fighting chance!'

Spread out along the enemy fortifications, the Plataean archers, Amara included, poured arrows down onto the heads of the patrol. Covered by the storm and the darkness, the escaped Plataeans' position on the ground was also impossible to judge and they too, continued to pour javelins and arrows at the lit-up column.

Then, in total blackness they melted away northwards, up the road to Thebes, according to the plan of Theanatus. Also, going in accordance with Theanatus' plan, the joint force of Spartans and Thebans sped along the road eastwards, towards the road for Athens, their torches lighting up the way; hunting in vain for the fugitives.

Below them, the archers could see many more soldiers arriving, carrying rushlights, patrolling the outer ditch in the search for any escaped Plataeans. 'We've no chance of getting away now,' cried Amara, despairingly, her hair whipped around her by the storm.

'Look!' Hawk-eye signalled urgently, and peering over the wall, they could just make out the figure of a man being dragged from the icy ditch. Illuminated by the rushlights, his frozen features could clearly be seen. 'Lukas!' gasped Epiktetos. 'He's under Iobates' command.'

'Did he see us, do you think?' asked Amara, concerned.

'Well, if he did, he didn't give us away - and he won't. Let's go!' urged Hawk-eye. 'There's nothing we can do to save him. We did all we could to help the others.'

'Do you think Imbros got away?' asked Amara, her voice faint with anxiety.

'There is every chance they all got away!' replied Epiktetos. Except for poor Lukas. The patrol set off on the wrong road, just as Theanatus predicted! Eupompides will bring back troops, Amara,' he said reassuringly, taking her hand in his. 'Bring the ladder,' he ordered his men. 'We can do no more. We must wait for the return of our general, and the relief force!'

Amara, looking out through the blinding rain, said a silent prayer for Imbros's safety, then dejectedly followed the others back across the ramparts - back to loneliness, fear and hunger.

When their small band returned to the acropolis, they were dismayed to see that Lecadonis had not made it over the wall. He and twenty-four of his Athenians, who were to have been in the rear-guard, were sat around a brazier, trying to warm themselves against the fierce wind. Their mood was sombre.

Diokles hurried over to Amara, reaching out his arms in obvious relief. 'You're a welcome sight for my sad eyes, my dear! I thought you must have perished with the rest. What words can I offer you which will ease your grief, except that I will send a herald to the Spartans to release their bodies to us. Imbros will be given proper burial, as will the others.'

Epiktetos, seeing the shock on Amara's face, rushed to intervene. 'There will be no burials Diokles!' he shouted, loud enough for all to hear. 'Our brave heroes have escaped, just as Theanatus said they would!'

'What?' asked Lecadonis, eagerly, striding over to listen. 'I was told they had been taken! Are you certain of this, archer?'

'As certain as anyone can be, captain,' replied Epiketos, enthusiastically. 'The weather blinded us somewhat, but from what we witnessed, the main group got away, just as Theanatus predicted!'

Lecadonis, looking totally bereft, put his hands to his head. 'We'll pay dearly for letting fear hold us back from this one chance of freedom,' he groaned. 'We will not get another!'

When, the following day, it was confirmed by a herald sent to the Spartans that there were no bodies to be recovered, Diokles ordered a head-count. Eupompides and Theanatus had escaped, together with Imbros, Stephanos and Iairos - two-hundred and twenty in all. Left trapped on the acropolis were Lecadonis and his Athenians, as well as two-hundred Plataeans, including Diokles, Alexeis, Simonedes and Epiktetos; the original one-hundred women who took care of them - and Amara.

Two-hundred and twelve of the escapees eventually reached Athens; a city they soon discovered was severely crushed by the on-going plague. Hardened by grief, and pessimistic about the future, pleas for the relief of Plataea fell on deaf ears, just as Diokles feared.

Iairos, whose strong arm had helped in their escape, didn't go to Athens. Together with two of his comrades, the safety offered by their great ally was spurned, and preferring instead to further test their luck with The Fates, they carried on going north.

SIXTY-ONE

AFTER THE BREAK-OUT, THE siege of Plataea still dragged on for six more desperate months, and the responsibility for monitoring the beleaguered city was now shared between the Thebans who guarded one half, while a reduced contingent of soldiers from the Spartan alliance, under the eyes of Skopas, commanded the rest.

Not welcome in the Theban camp because of their banishment, The Wolf and Hippodamus, together with a few other fellow Thebans, and ten mounted archers hired by Lykaon in Phrygia after his escape from Lesbos, were therefore made welcome in the ranks of the Spartan general. Encamped between the high double banks of fortifications surrounding the city, they were protected against any further break-outs from the Plataeans, or an assault from the Athenians, although neither was now considered a serious threat. Athens was too afraid of bringing about an almighty battle on the plains of Plataea, which they feared they would lose. Consequently their promises of reinforcements had sadly not materialised, and the tiny fortress so cruelly abandoned was being starved into submission. All the besiegers had to do now was wait.

Lykaon made good use of the time. Reunited with Skopas, he falsely contrived with the avaricious general as to how he could get his banishment from Thebes, rescinded. Deceiving the Spartan into believing he wanted to return to his home-city, and promising to pay Skopas handsomely if he'd speak to the present Boetarchs of Thebes on his behalf, the general happily agreed to assist. The Wolf however, had bigger plans in mind than a return to his hometown, and Skopas was just an unwitting dupe, but Lykaon's false pledge of future reward had dulled the Spartan's normally astute thinking, and he greedily accepted the agreement. Lykaon's arrival had livened up the rather dull time he'd been having of late, and he anticipated a long friendship with this daring young Theban, which he felt sure would lead to lucrative times ahead.

Following the escape the previous winter, the Plataeans were reduced to some three-hundred and twenty-five souls, and by the time the scorching heat of summer began to beat down on the plateau, these men and women, weakened by starvation, were unable to defend their city any longer. When the besiegers stormed the walls this time, the inhabitants put up no resistance. Skopas, under instructions from Sparta to get the Plataeans to surrender, voluntarily if possible, offered them a fair trial if they would give up their city to him. By surrendering, Plataea would have to remain part of the Boeotian League, even if a future peace treaty was agreed with Athens. They had no choice other than to trust the Spartan general, and the Plataeans watched helplessly as jubilant soldiers burst through the gap in their walls. Four long years after the Thebans had attacked them during their spring festival, Plataea finally fell.

Under the orders of the Spartan general, their weapons were quickly gathered up and the men and women separated. The victors and the vanquished now faced each other. The thin and haggard survivors of this defiant, long-time stand-off, some of them bearing wounds and too weak to stand, watched balefully as Skopas imperiously strode up and down their ragged line. He bore a self-satisfied look which conveyed that even these, the most resolute of men, could be brought to a degrading end. After some long moments during which he seemed to gloat upon their humiliating condition, he ordered the male prisoners to be taken inside the Temple of Hera. Diokles, Alexeis and the others, with violent blows and curses, were brutally herded into the building, and every last one of them unnecessarily shackled.

Outside, the women were forced together by the temple wall, some crying out in terror. Shouts of encouragement could be heard from the chained Athenian, Lecadonis, despite his exhausted state, in an effort to keep up their morale, but fear was palpable both inside and outside the temple. Diokles, who had acted as protector to Amara since her husband's escape, was frantic about what would now happen to her.

Skopas noticed Amara immediately, of course. Despite her weakened state, she still looked beautiful, her height and bearing making her stand out against the other women. He made a mental note to keep this one for himself.

Lykaon looked up at the shining disc, which had been gazing down on them like a golden eye for so many months. Hanging suspended from the temple roof, it blazed with an unparalleled brilliance in the summer sun. The Spartans, being superstitious and religious people, were cautious about taking the aspis of Agristones back to their own country. They were conscious of the fact that they'd not merited the right to take possession. In their opinion, the respected relic should now be housed at Delphi, where it could be seen by all, and be protected for all time. The Thebans thought otherwise. They *demanded* possession. Plataea was in their territory. As far as they were concerned, this was spoils of war. It now belonged to Thebes, and Thebans would decide its fate.

Skopas ordered for it to be brought down. With grappling hooks, the soldiers soon broke the wooden structure holding it, and the bejeweled trophy slid towards them down the tiled incline, coming to rest on the edge of the roof. Lykaon, who was looking on with intense anticipation, scrambled up a ladder and reaching across, shouted to the men below to provide support. He remembered all too clearly another occasion, at another temple in Plataea, when he had come this close to his desire. But this time, he thought savagely, the Plataeans are most definitely defeated! The memory of Plataea's glorious past will be extinguished forever, he thought with grim satisfaction. It will become a desolate pile of rubble, unacknowledged and forgotten, her citizens scattered to the four winds. This time, he contemplated confidently, his plan could work.

But it wasn't The Shield that fell from the roof. It was Lykaon. Shot in the leg with an arrow, he lost his footing and toppled from the ladder to land on the men below. Aghast, Skopas and the soldiers looked around anxiously, for signs of attack. Mystified, they could see no-one, other than their own men and the Plataean women still huddled in the corner of the temple wall. Believing them to be of no threat, the women had not been chained, and no guard was watching them. Amara, able to reach her small bow, concealed in the folds of her tattered cloak, had managed to fire a single arrow, and was deeply gratified to see it hit its mark. The imprisoned men could hear the ensuing commotion, and believing the women were being attacked, began shouting out in desperation.

Barely recognisable because she'd lost so much weight, the wife of the sculptor, Imbros, stepped proudly forward, still carrying her bow in her delicate hand. Ianthe tried to pull her back, but Amara wanted no violence inflicted on the other innocent women, and was prepared to accept her fate. Her uncombed hair hung limp about her pallid neck and her eyes were sunken, but by all the gods, every man present had to concede, she was a beauty, even in these dire circumstances.

Two Spartan troopers intercepted her, one snatched the slender bow, the other giving her a blow to the head with such brutish force that she fell to the ground. The unlikely heroine of Plataea eyed the injured figure of Lykaon lying next to her, with abject hatred. The Theban glared back with equal venom.

'You'll live to rue the day you did this, bitch!' he muttered through clenched teeth.

'Take her away and tie her up!' Skopas yelled, with unconcealed frustration. 'But don't put the whore with the others. Take her to my tent!' He would make her pay for what she did. He would make sure that this was her last act of defiance. These Plataeans never know when to give up, he thought dismissively, as he watched Amara's limp body being dragged away.

******

THE AGORA WAS NOISY with activity as wagons were being piled high with Plataean weaponry and plunder. The Shield, wrapped in sheepskins, lay on a wooden litter to be loaded onto a covered cart. The victors were stripping Plataea of anything left of value. A small armed guard of Thebans and some hoplites from the Peloponnesian League, under the command of Skopas would travel with the wagons. As there was no enemy for many miles, there was little fear of attack. In separate carts were placed the female slaves. The women were in a poor state, having suffered worse than the men due to the shortage of food, but they might still have some value. The Thebans had taken possession of about thirty women. Sparta, the same. The remaining thirty or so were split up between the different member states of the League.

Amara, now the possession of Skopas, was to be taken back to Sparta together with his share of slaves and plunder. Tied by the reins on one of the pack-horses, her ankles also tied beneath the animal, Amara was slumped forward, showing no outward sign of life. Raped and brutalised by Skopas, her mind had withdrawn. She was as though dead. Anthousa, another beauty who had gained the attention of the Spartan general, was also among the women going to Sparta, and she watched Amara anxiously. Before the attack by the Thebans during their festival, these two women had never met, and it was unlikely that they ever would have. But during their incarceration they'd become like sisters, helping one another through the worst of times and, when they'd been fit enough, both had taken part in the military training.

'Skopas!' shouted Lykaon, as he rode towards him across the agora, followed by some of his men, also mounted. It was obvious his leg was still giving him pain.

'Is everything ready, Skopas? I don't want anything to go wrong.'

'I'm ready to fulfill my promise,' the Spartan replied with emphasis. 'The Boetarchs will hear of the part you played in the fall of Plataea. The fact that you and your men have not taken your entitled share of the spoils, will be appreciated, I'm sure. When they receive The Marathon Shield, Lykaon, they will believe your sincerity. You can count on me to get your banishment reversed.'

'I won't forget you, general,' replied Lykaon, smiling broadly. 'But I do have another favour to ask of you, before you leave.' Then, at his prearranged signal, his men moved their horses closer.

'Another favour?' asked Skopas, looking around, warily.

'I want the woman who fired the arrow!' Lykaon said forcefully, his eyes narrowing.

'That's not possible. You can't have her!' exclaimed Skopas, astonished. 'She's a beauty, despite her condition, otherwise I would have had her killed. No, she's going to Sparta with the others. To my own household, in fact. A rare treasure indeed, to be found in this god-forsaken place!'

'I must have her, Skopas!' reiterated Lykaon. 'You should understand! Look at what she did!' he shouted, pointing at his bandaged leg.

'Then you'll be happy to know that I made her pay for that futile act of defiance,' replied Skopas, gloating. 'Can't understand what she was doing here, though. She was no slave. Anyway, she won't be any trouble now.'

Lykaon moved threateningly closer to the Spartan general, looking down on him from his horse, and Skopas quickly beckoned to his own men to come to his aid.

Suddenly, there was a stand-off in the market-place, between Lykaon's Thebans and Skopas's Spartans. Everyone rushed to see how this battle of wills over the Plataean woman would be resolved. Shouts were exchanged between the two protagonists, and the threatening actions by their followers caused alarm to spread in the agora.

'Name your price then, Skopas,' said Lykaon, waving his hand, to silence his men. 'I can see you mean to force a hard bargain!'

The general, realising that Lykaon was in earnest about wanting Amara, saw a profitable opportunity emerging. His greedy eyes glinted at the thought of how much the Theban would be prepared to pay.

'That was never my intention, dear friend!' replied Skopas, looking around for support from the onlookers, who had now crowded round the scene.

'Nevertheless, you have me in a corner,' said Lykaon, lifting his hands in feigned defeat; playing to the eager faces pressing all round him. 'But I think you'll find this is satisfactory.'

Lykaon threw down a heavy purse to land at the feet of the Spartan general, who slowly picked it up, all the while watching Lykaon, with a sly smile on his lips. He knew how frail the Plataean beauty was, especially after he had taken out his punishment on her, and glancing across at her slumped, motionless figure, he judged that she would never reach Sparta alive. He looked into the purse and then at Lykaon. More than satisfied with the contents, he said, 'She's yours, Theban! I've had my fill!'

As Amara was being roughly untied from the horse, Anthousa's cry of anguish pierced the air. She believed Amara was dead, but when one of the soldiers splashed water on her pale features, her beautiful eyes slowly opened. Her first sight was of Lykaon's burning gaze staring at her with a depraved intensity, which was mercifully beyond her comprehension.

'I'll need one of the women to tend to my wound, Skopas!' he shouted. 'And also to take care of this bitch!' he said angrily, glaring at Amara. 'I want her to live long enough to enjoy my company, since she took it upon herself to emulate our God, Eros! Choose one who will satisfy your own needs also, general. While we're both stuck in this miserable hole, we may as well enjoy some comforts.'

Skopas laughed, harshly. 'You talk sense, Theban. Untie her!' he shouted to his men, pointing at the downcast Anthousa. 'This one attracts me, Theban. Keep her for me, until my return.'

'I will!' called Lykaon, heartily, and then under his breath, muttered, 'I will keep her!'

'My thoughts and my gratitude go with you to Thebes, general,' he said to Skopas, as the loaded wagons trundled out of the city.

'I will return soon with favourable news, Lykaon, replied Skopas, grasping the Theban strongly by the hand. 'Your city will welcome you home, within the week!'

A line of carts, loaded with spoils and slaves, stretched in a long, straggling column from the gates of Plataea on its way towards The City of the Seven Gates. Heavily laden pack horses being taken to Sparta, followed behind. Many of the women were in tears as they glanced back fearfully at the receding view of the temple where, guarded by Theban soldiers, the last of the Plataean menfolk still lay, trapped and shackled, awaiting their fate. When the convoy reached the nearby crossroads, the parties divided and went their separate ways, carrying with them their ill-gotten gains.

In front of the Theban Boetarchs, the plunder from their long-time enemy was revealed by Skopas, in triumph, but when it came to the unwrapping of the sheepskins, it wasn't the coveted golden shield that was uncovered, but several battered bronze ones. In horror, Skopas remembered the prophetic words of Nicander, years ago at Megara. He was right, he thought, with black hatred gnawing at his heart. The Wolf of Thebes was not to be trusted!

During the angry exchange of words in the agora between Skopas and Lykaon, when all eyes were upon them, a switch had been achieved by Hippodamus and another of Lykaon's men, and now strapped to the back of a sturdy pack animal, led by Hippodamus, with The Wolf and his men following close behind, The Shield was being taken quickly away from the city. Guarded by the Phrygian archers, their distinctive red pointed caps flapping as they rode, the group spurred their horses towards the port of Creusis, where a boat was waiting. Travelling with them was Amara, and Anthousa.

Lykaon winked at Hippodamus, as he surveyed the Tanagran. 'Skopas has a good eye! I couldn't have chosen a more delectable nurse myself!'

Lykaon had needed a ruse to divert Skopas's attention, as The Shield was being loaded, and the Plataean beauty had fitted into his plan, perfectly. She'd tried to save her city's memorial, he thought bitterly as his hand touched his wound, but had in the end been responsible for him being able to steal it! He now possessed them both.

Laughing out loud, he thought of Skopas trying to explain the loss of the prized shield to the Thebans. They would obviously suspect that the Spartans had deceived them. 'Oh, poor Skopas!' he chuckled, maliciously. But even if Skopas did succeed in convincing the Thebans that it was The Wolf who was responsible for the theft, he knew by the time a search party could be sent to apprehend him, his hired crew would be pulling hard on their way up the coast. His enemies were many. He would need speed and guile to outwit them.

SIXTY-TWO

JUST AS THE SETTING sun slipped behind the rooftops of Athens, Mydon the slave navigated Cyclops along a now, sadly regular route, which eventually led to The House of Vines - his master's last known port of call. Leaving the mule tethered in the open yard to the rear of the building, Mydon lifted the heavy tarp covering the back entrance, and peered inside. Oil lamps flickered on several benches and a single rushlight held back the gloom as his eyes took in the regrettably familiar scene. He saw perhaps half-a-dozen fashionable young men sat about, being served from a large wine krater. Men of the cavalry corps. There was much raucous laughter, which increased as they recognised the personal man-servant of their companion, Theomenes.

'Oh, it's the lame one leading the blind one!' somebody chortled. What is it, slave?' a voice shouted. 'Come for a crafty poke, have you? Well, you can shag this one,' he said, grabbing at one of the scantily clad women present. 'Tell you what, we'll be your audience. There's coin in it for you!' A dark-skinned girl eyed Mydon, indifferently, from beneath thick black lashes. Neither of their faces showed any emotion. In such circumstances, signs of empathy could lead to a beating.

'I've come for my master Theomenes, my lord Dadilos,' he said evenly.

'Are you sure that's all, slave?' asked Dadilos, winking slyly at his companions.

He has a stupid looking face, thought Mydon, suppressing his annoyance. He'd seen too many of these arrogant, dissolute faces of late. Sons of the Athenian hierarchy. It's a countenance ripe for bruising, he thought, angrily. Over-privileged spawn of his so-called betters, who cruelly flaunted the advantages given them. Since the arrival of the plague, manners and morals seemed to belong to another age, and Mydon believed that his master, in trying to emulate his peers, was becoming increasingly distant and unreachable.

'You've come for your lord?' shouted another loud voice at the table. 'Theomenes of Hysiae?'

There were more sniggers of mirth. Mydon shifted the weight of his body to take the pressure from his crippled foot and said nothing.

'Well, there he lies!' announced Dadilos. 'In all his glory! Arse-up for any tool that wants him.'

Mydon moved to where the Athenian indicated and saw his master stretched out along a bench, slumped face down-wards. He looked despondently at the leaden features then suppressing a curse, tried to raise his master's semi-conscious body.

'Leaving so soon, slave?' spoke Dadilos, turning to his comrades. 'Not at all sociable, is he? Come on you lazy slobs! Let's give old Mydon a hand.'

Mydon, standing protectively over Theo's inert form, turned to face the Athenian. 'I need no help,' he muttered, but Dadilos, now intent on having some fun, pushed Mydon roughly aside and threw the limp Theomenes over his shoulder. 'Right, slave. Show us the way!'

Shouting and jeering, several of the group trooped after the limping Mydon, wearing his specially made boot to compensate for his deformity, to the dimly-lit yard where Cyclops was tethered. Sensing trouble, the mule's ears were pricked, and his one eye blazed, menacingly. Before Mydon could warn them, one of the men by the name of Makron, leapt onto the mule's back.

Cyclops was approached on his blind-side, and panicked by the drunken noise, immediately kicked out, sending Dadilos flying backwards. He and the limp Theomenes fell back inside the inn, while the others ran in panic around the yard trying to avoid Cyclops' lethal hooves. The more they shouted, the more agitated the mule became, and the white beast tore around the yard in a frenzy. Makron, who was quickly thrown from his back, crawled desperately towards the inn entrance. Eventually, Mydon's familiar voice calmed the animal and the mule stood, quivering and sweating, his head down, glaring balefully at the cowering huddle of men.

'May we leave now?' asked Mydon, trying not to smirk.

'Get the fuck out of here!' shouted Dadilos.

Theo, now partly conscious, was helped to his feet by Mydon, and slung onto Cyclops' back.

Looking around at his fellows, who were glowering and silent, Theo asked, 'Did I miss something?'

In response, he heard Mydon whisper, as they left the yard, 'Well done!' but in his befuddled state, it seemed as though Mydon was talking to the mule.

As they travelled back through the darkened city, Mydon wondered what he could do to stop his master's downward spiral. They'd both endured much since the Theban attack on Plataea, and Theomenes, now a rich young man under the protection of his uncle Hypatos, was trying hard to wipe out those bleak memories. With his uncle's influence, he had acquired a position in the city's cavalry corps and now at the age of twenty, thought he was a man of the world. Mydon, however, listened to what the servants of the other cavalrymen reported to him. Apparently, his master was thought of as a country-bumpkin, with a devotion to an ass. He heard stories which enraged him, of how his master had been tricked and cheated by some of his so-called comrades, but he would never repeat them to the unsuspecting, wasted young man behind him.

SIXTY-THREE

SINCE THE HARROWING NIGHT of the break-out, Imbros the sculptor had found his feelings of guilt at having left Amara behind, almost impossible to bear. It was only his work which kept him focused, living in constant hope that, any time soon, he would hear that Plataea was to be relieved.

Each day, he could be found on the Acropolis, wearing only a labourer's cheap exomis, his once stocky physique now sparse and burned almost black by the sun. He worked with a fevered intensity on one particular project that required all his skill; a larger than life-size image of the goddess of victory, Athena-Nike. A creation which would eventually stand alongside other works of art by fellow artisans, in a new temple being built for the goddess, in the hope that she would bring victory over the Spartans. Entrusted by Athens' celebrated city architect, Callicrates, to further enhance the beauty of the Acropolis, it was an honour to have his talents recognised by the great man. Something Amara had always envisaged, his work became a labour of love for her, so all-consuming as to resemble insanity.

Passing strangers thought him a madman in his unkempt state, with hair uncombed and his normally immaculately trimmed beard grown long and matted. For the troubled Imbros, night brought only demons, so throughout the daylight hours he worked diligently and in solitary, well away from the other masons, concentrating on the form which only he could see hidden within the stone. He was trying to hold onto not only a lost wife, but what he sensed was the loss of the golden age of Athens, also. In his fertile, creative mind, he promised himself that this would be his greatest creation, because it was born of love. His shield and sword had been put aside, as well as his pride, for these things had failed to save all that had been dear to him.

At mid-morning, he paused in his task and removing the dirty rag tied around his head, wiped the perspiration from his brow. On the precipice all was activity; the rhythmic tapping of sculptors and masons; the shouts of carpenters and labourers; sounds all very familiar and comforting to Imbros, and standing on the heights with its magnificent vista over the city, the ruinous war seemed far away. He sat on a lump of discarded stone and drank sparingly from a wineskin, while watching below him a group of laughing children, chasing a goat that had strayed from the herd. Its mournful bleat carried on the air, but the sculptor, lost in momentary revery, barely heard it. His thoughts were of how he and Amara had hoped for a family, and suddenly his shoulders started to shake, and tears began to sting his eyes.

A shadow fell over him and a quiet voice inquired, 'Imbros?'

'Admetus!' cried Imbros, immediately rising; relieved and happy to see his old friend. 'You find me in a contemplative mood. I apologise!'

'My dear Imbros,' said Admetus, gently. 'You have no need to apologise to me. We're like family.'

'Have you come to see how my work progresses?' asked Imbros, feeling embarrassed, as he vigorously shook dust from his tangled hair.

'I would very much like to see that Imbros,' replied Admetus, 'but that's not why I am here,' he added, as he sat down next to him. 'Imbros,' he said gently, looking at him concerned, 'you had better prepare yourself. I am the bearer of very sad news. It is the worst of situations, my dear friend,' said the historian. 'Plataea has fallen.'

The face of Imbros drained of colour. 'Amara?' he asked, almost forcing the sound of her name from him.

'We know nothing of the women, Imbros. Only that there is to be a trial,' replied the older man, gravely. 'Five judges are to be brought from Sparta,' he added.

Admetus looked anxiously at his friend, who seemed to have deteriorated even further from when he'd last seen him a few weeks previously, and then, indicating to his elegant manservants waiting nearby, said to Imbros, 'you had better stay with me until we know more. Come! We need to notify the others.'

Onlookers watched with curiosity as the distinguished historian gently guided the dishevelled and down-hearted figure of Imbros from the plateau.

SIXTY-FOUR

MOUNT CITHAERON BLAZED IN a sunlight so brilliant, it seemed as if the mystic world of the gods wanted all mankind to witness the unbridled sacrilege taking place against Plataea and its exhausted defenders, by the combined forces of Sparta and Thebes.

For the first time in an eternity of long days and watchful nights the high wooden gates of the city lay open, now guarded by troops of the enemy. The enslaved women were gone, scattered throughout the lands of Hellas. The men, some two-hundred Plataeans and twenty-five Athenians, awaited the arrival of their judges; five dignitaries from Sparta, and during the delay they decided on how they should best form their defence for the forthcoming trial.

'We will put our trust in the Spartans,' said Diokles to Astymachus, who again had been chosen to speak up for them. 'Make your plea to them. It will be no good appealing to the Thebans.'

"Emphasise how many years you Plataeans protected the sacred burial grounds,' said Lecadonis, the Athenian. 'And how you saved the bones of their ancestors from Theban desecration. With the death of King Archidamus, you have less chance of being listened to, but of all the Hellenes the Spartans are the most religious, and they may be moved to leniency.'

Lecadonis and the other Athenians believed there was no chance of freedom for them. They expected to be executed. But these Plataeans, with whom they had shared years of hardship, had earned their respect. If there was the slightest chance that the Spartans would be merciful with them, then every possible pressure should be brought to bear.

Everyone had a suggestion or a legal point to make and Astymachus, surrounded by his eager audience, worked hard on his oratory skills, in the days of waiting for the legal team to arrive from Sparta. But if any had expected a fair trial, they would be greatly disappointed. There was no charge brought against them, to which they could legally appeal. There was only one question asked by the judges.

'*Have you done any service for Sparta or her allies, during this war?* And only one answer was permitted. '*Yes, or no?*' they were asked, decisively.

The Plataeans, knowing full well it was the Thebans who were behind this mock-trial - not the Spartans; and they were not to get the fair trial that was promised when they surrendered, were incensed. They demanded the chance to give a full account as to how they had come to their present predicament.

'*Spartans, when we surrendered our city we trusted in you, and looked forward to a trial more agreeable to the forms of law than the present, to which we had no idea of being subjected; the judges also in whose hands we consented to place ourselves were you, and you only (from whom we thought we were most likely to obtain justice), and not other persons, as is now the case. As matters stand, we are afraid that we have been doubly deceived.*

Were we unknown to each other we might profit by bringing forward new matter with which you were unacquainted: as it is, we can tell you nothing that you do not know. We fear, not that you have condemned us in your own minds of having failed in our duty towards you, and make this our crime, but that to please a third party we have to submit to a trial the result of which is already decided. Nevertheless, we will place before you what we can justly urge, not only on the question of the quarrel which the Thebans have against us, but also as addressing you and the rest of the Hellenes; and we will remind you of our good services, and endeavour to prevail with you.

During the peace, and against the Persians, we acted well: we have not now been the first to break the peace, and we were the only Boeotians who then joined in defending against the Persians the liberty of Hellas. Although an inland people, we were present at the action at Artemisium; in the battle that took place in our territory we fought by the side of yourselves and Pausanias; and in all the other Hellenic exploits of the time we took a part quite out of proportion to our strength. Besides, you, as Spartans, ought not to forget that at the time of the great panic at Sparta, after the earthquake, caused by the secession of the Helots to Ithome, we sent the third part of our citizens to assist you.

On these great and historical occasions such was the part that we chose, although afterwards we became your enemies. For this you were to blame. When we asked for your alliance against our Theban oppressors, you rejected our petition, and told us to go to the Athenians who were our neighbours, as you lived too far off. In the war we never have done to you, and never should have done to you, anything unreasonable. If we refused to desert the Athenians when you asked us, we did no wrong; they had helped us against the Thebans when you drew back, and we could no longer give them up with honour; especially as we had obtained their alliance and had been admitted to their citizenship at our own request, and after receiving benefits at their hands; but it was plainly our duty loyally to obey their orders. Besides, the faults that either of you may commit in your supremacy must be laid, not upon the followers, but on the chiefs that lead them astray.

With regard to the Thebans, they have wronged us repeatedly, and their last aggression, which has been the means of bringing us into our present position, is within your own knowledge. In seizing our city in time of peace, and what is more at a holy time in the month, they justly encountered our vengeance, in accordance with the universal law which sanctions resistance to an invader; and it cannot now be right that we should suffer on their account.

Consider also that at present the Hellenes generally regard you as a pattern of worth and honour; and if you pass an unjust sentence upon us in this which is no obscure cause, but one in which you, the judges, are as illustrious as we, the prisoners, are blameless, take care that displeasure be not felt at an unworthy decision in the matter of honourable men made by men yet more honourable. Shocking indeed will it seem for Spartans to destroy Plataea, and for the city whose name your fathers inscribed upon the tripod at Delphi for its good service, to be by you blotted out from the map of Hellas, to please the Thebans.

Look at the sepulchres of your fathers, slain by the Persians and buried in our country, whom year by year we honoured with garments and all other dues, and the first-fruits of all that our land produced in their season, as friends from a friendly country and allies to our old companions in arms. Should you not decide aright, your conduct would be the very opposite to ours. Consider only: Pausanias buried them thinking that he was laying them in friendly ground and among men as friendly; but you, if you kill us and make the Plataean territory Theban, will leave your fathers and kinsmen in a hostile soil and among their murderers, deprived of the honours which they now enjoy.

In conclusion we say that we did not surrender our city to the Thebans (to that we would have preferred inglorious starvation), but trusted in and capitulated to you; and it would be just, if we fail to persuade you, to put us back in the same position and let us take the chance that falls to us. And at the same time we adjure you not to give us up — your suppliants, Spartans, out of your hands and faith, Plataeans foremost of the Hellenic patriots, to Thebans, our most hated enemies — but to be our saviours, and not, while you free the rest of the Hellenes, to bring us to destruction.'

The Thebans, annoyed that the Plataeans had been allowed to speak, demanded that they should be able to counter their accusations.

'We should never have asked to make this speech if the Plataeans on their side had contented themselves with shortly answering the question,

and had not turned around and made charges against us. The origin of our quarrel was this. We settled Plataea some time after the rest of Boeotia, together with other places out of which we had driven the mixed population. The Plataeans not choosing to recognize our supremacy, as had been first arranged, but separating themselves from the rest of the Boeotians, and proving traitors to their nationality, we used compulsion; upon which they went over to the Athenians, and with them did as much harm, for which we retaliated.

It was in defence against us, say you, that you became allies and citizens of Athens. If so, you ought only to have called in the Athenians against us, instead of joining them in attacking others: it was open to you to do this if you ever felt that they were leading you where you did not wish to follow, as Sparta was already your ally against the Persians, as you so much insist; and this was surely sufficient to keep us off, and above all to allow you to deliberate in security. Nevertheless, of your own choice and without compulsion you chose to throw your lot in with Athens. And you say that it had been base for you to betray your benefactors; but it was surely far baser and more iniquitous to sacrifice the whole body of the Hellenes, your fellow confederates, who were liberating Hellas, than the Athenians only, who were enslaving it. The return that you made them was therefore neither equal nor honourable, since you called them in, as you say, because you were being oppressed yourselves, and then became their accomplices in oppressing others; although baseness rather consists in not returning like for like than in not returning what is justly due but must be unjustly paid.

It was not for the sake of the Hellenes that you alone then did not join with the Persians, but because the Athenians did not do so either. You wished to side with them and to be against the rest and you now claim the benefit of good deeds done to please your neighbours. This cannot be admitted: you chose the Athenians, and with them you must stand or fall.

Lastly, an invitation was addressed to you before you were blockaded to be neutral and join neither party: this you did not accept. Who then merit the detestation of the Hellenes more justly than you, you who sought their ruin under the mask of honour? The former virtues that you allege you now show not to be proper to your character; the real bent of your nature has been at length damningly proved: when the Athenians *took the path of injustice you followed them.*

The last wrong of which you complain consists in our having, as you say, lawlessly invaded your town in time of peace and festival. Here again we cannot think that we were more in fault than yourselves. If we made an armed attack upon your city and ravaged your territory, we are guilty; but if the first men among you in estate and family, wishing to put an end to the foreign connection and to restore you to the common Boeotian country, of their own free will invited us, wherein is our crime? Citizens like yourselves, and with more at stake than you, they opened their own walls and introduced us into their own city, not as foes but as friends, to prevent the bad among you from becoming worse; to give honest men their due; to reform principles without attacking persons, since you were not to be banished from your city, but brought home to your kindred, nor to be made enemies to any, but friends alike to all.

You made an agreement with us and remained tranquil, until you became aware of the smallness of our numbers. Inducing us to retire by negotiation, you fell upon us in violation of your agreement, and slew some of us in fight, of which we do not so much complain, for in that there was a certain justice; but others who held out their hands and received quarter, and whose lives you subsequently promised us, you lawlessly butchered. If this was not abominable, what is? You still affirm that we are the criminals and yourselves pretend to escape justice. Not so, if these your judges decide aright, but you will be punished for all together.'

This and more did the Plataeans and the Thebans speak in earnest to the judges.

After deliberation and heated arguments between the Spartans and the Thebans, the adjudicators finally decided that the question; whether they had received any service from the Plataeans in the war, was a fair one for them to put. They had always invited them to be neutral, and as their offer had been consistently refused, it was considered that they were now released from the long standing covenant of Pausanius.

They were brought into the courthouse, one at a time. Isolated from their comrades, and surrounded by their enemies, each man was made to stand alone before the five judges and asked to reply to the set question, to which there could only be one answer, and for the Thebans, only one penalty.

It had taken four long years for the Thebans to exact retribution for the slaying of their captured comrades, during the attack which began the war. The prisoners, Plataean and Athenian alike, were executed without exception at Plataea, the tiny city-state they had strived to protect. Two-hundred and twenty-five heroes: Lecadonis and his fellow Athenians together with Diokles and all the remaining brave Plataeans. They'd looked in vain for one last glimpse of Agristones' shield, but seeing the wooden structure broken and empty, knew their talisman was gone and with it, any hope of rescue for Plataea.

The last living creature of the siege was a black, high-stepping stallion. Alexeis' horse, Cerus, had not been slaughtered like the others for meat when the food ran out, because of his extraordinary speed. In the event of a last-minute appeal being sent to the Athenians, Eupompides had saved him, at the expense of his own horse. The stallion, now without his beloved master, charged crazed around the plateau, kicking and rearing. A black terror to anyone who tried to approach him. On the acropolis, thick smoke curled upwards from the funeral pyres.

But they weren't forgotten as Lykaon had wished. Their story of loyalty, steadfastness and ultimate sacrifice, spread far beyond the confines of this small plateau at the base of Mount Cithaeron, to bring inspiration and shame in equal measure.

Following months of unsuccessful pleading with Cleon of Athens to send reinforcements to Plataea, when news reached the capital of the executions, Eupompides placed the point of his sword at his heart and fell on the blade.

SIXTY-FIVE

THE FUNERAL OF EUPOMPIDES was attended by both Plataeans and Athenians, and Admetus at one point, became very concerned at the barely suppressed animosity between the two factions. Only the men from Lecadonis's command, who had been in the escape six months earlier, were not shunned by the mourning Plataeans. Still angry at the lack of support given to their besieged city, the Plataeans almost accused the Athenians of having forced them into defending their city to the last man, the Athenians knowing full well they could send no further help. They held their wives and children, after all. And it was very convenient for Athens to have the entire Spartan army encamped around their fortress for an entire summer, instead of attacking Attica. The Athenians, on the other hand, almost accused the Plataeans for being responsible for all their ills. The war would never have started, it was hinted, if the Plataeans had not killed the Theban prisoners. And if the war hadn't started, Athens would not have become so over-crowded as to cause an epidemic of disease. The Plataeans, who had once been made to feel welcome in Athens, and even given Athenian citizenship, now felt unwanted, and they grieved deeply for the loss of their city-state, their menfolk, and their identity.

The funeral feast was held at the house of Aspasia, where Akaterina and her son, Akylas, still resided. After all the deaths and tribulations, this mother and son were cherished by the surviving Plataeans. Young Akylas, with his fair curls and deep green eyes, being so like his father, Phalinus, reminded them of happier times. Now at the age of seven, Akylas was old enough to be told of the misfortunes which had befallen his home-state, and he listened seriously to his sombre elders as they tried to answer his numerous questions.

Admetus looked around the melancholy room; at the people he knew so well and cared for so profoundly. What was to become of them? What was to become of him? His once interminable 'Histories of Plataea', had come to an abrupt end. He looked at Imbros, now washed, but gaunt and haunted. Theomenes, flushed and talking too loudly. Many old friends, once proud men, now struggling to come to terms with their new situation.

Admetus felt a tug on his sleeve, and he smiled down at young Akylas. 'And what questions do you have for me, young man?' he asked him, kindly.

'Admetus?' asked the boy, in a clear sweet voice, which rang around the room. 'If I am to be Guardian of The Shield of Marathon one day, like my father - where is my father's shield?'

Admetus startled the boy with his sudden fit of coughing, and when he finally regained composure, he noticed the room was filled by an embarrassed sound of silence. This was one question no-one wanted to answer.

SIXTY-SIX

A WEEK AFTER THE FUNERAL of Plataea's general Eupompides, Theomenes decided it was time to present himself before his uncle, Hypatos.

He knew where to find him. He'd be at the Royal Stoa, in the northwest corner of the Agora, discussing details of the new Athenian temple with the King Archon and the city architect, Callicrates. The progressing work of Imbros the sculptor, which Hypatos was funding, was thought sublime by the team involved in the decoration of the temple, and they were considering Imbros for further work on a proposed elaborate frieze.

It was no secret in the Hypatos household that the relationship between uncle and nephew had been strained of late, and they were now barely on speaking terms, so great was Hypatos' disappointment in Theomenes. If Theo was determined to idle his life away, then so be it, he'd accepted, resignedly.

At first Hypatos made excuses for his nephew's behaviour. After all, the boy had suffered the loss of his father, brother and aunt, in terrible circumstances, and had himself cheated death twice. Since joining the cavalry, which Hypatos had thought would make a man of him, he'd watched sadly as Theo squandered money unnecessarily in an effort to impress his fellows. Being of lower birth than his elitist comrades, he'd received only ridicule for his pains, often ending up on the receiving end of their endless practical jokes. To Hypatos, his nephew didn't even seem to care.

But today he saw a markedly different Theomenes arriving at the archon's office, asking for permission to speak with him, urgently. Gone was the unkempt appearance. His face had lost its pallor and his hair had been neatly curled in the latest fashion. Making his apologies, he withdrew from the discussions, and guided Theo to sit with him in an adjoining room, dismissing several slaves pouring over scores of documents set out on the long wooden tables. All around them, shelves were piled high with assorted papyrus scrolls reaching from floor to ceiling.

Hypatos sat silent, waiting for his nephew to speak, and Theomenes, seizing the opportunity, spoke hurriedly.

'I'm here to ask for your forgiveness, uncle. I know only too well the disappointment I've caused 0f late, to you and others. You've fed me, clothed me, and nurtured me back to health,' he carried on quickly, not wanting his uncle to interrupt, 'and I've repaid you badly for all that kindness. I've brought shame to the family.'

'You are my brother's son. I could do nothing less,' answered Hypatos, resignedly. Yet it must be said, Theo,' Hypatos continued sternly, 'I've watched you keenly these past months, not happy with what I've seen. You've squandered a small fortune on trivialities, all to impress your cavalry chums. It was with great reluctance that I fulfilled my duty in making available to you, Alexeis' share of your late father's estate. He died a hero, Theo, never having a chance to spend one single obol! Mydon keeps much to himself,' Hypatos went on, angrily, 'as to what has gone on in the city, and he'd not report on you, his loyalty being commendable. But I have eyes and ears! That incident recently, involving Cyclops and some men in your unit - you're fortunate Dadilos didn't demand the unfortunate animal be destroyed!'

Theomenes remained silent throughout this tirade. 'Everything you say is true, sir,' he managed at last. 'That's why I'm here, now. To make amends. Since the funeral of Eupompides, uncle, I've changed!'

'I'm relieved to hear it,' replied Hypatos.

'When I looked into the eyes of Akylas, uncle, I'm certain I could feel the Shield Guardian's presence!'

'And?' Hypatos prompted.

'I realised what I was fast becoming. A wastrel! It's then I made my decision.'

Hypatos leaned forward. 'Which is?'

Theomenes drew himself up, and taking a deep breath he announced, with determination in his voice, 'I'm going to bring back The Marathon Shield, uncle!'

Hypatos gasped. 'That, my boy, is sheer madness! 'Back from where?' he asked, incredulously. 'The Thebans don't have it. The Spartans don't have it. Nobody knows where the sacred relic is, unless the rumours are true - that The Wolf of Thebes stole it!'

'Uncle, I want to do this in memory of my brother,' Theo responded firmly. 'In memory of Phalinus and Diokles, and all the other fine Plataeans we've lost. I cannot watch any longer as our people suffer slights and insults from the Athenians!' Theo paced the floor angrily, his frustration building, in his effort to win the approval of a shocked Hypatos. 'Some have lost everything and are begging in the streets,' he continued, with passion. 'Imbros is wasting away before my eyes, his mind on Amara. Since the funeral, Admetus has taken to his bed and won't admit visitors. Plataea may be lost to us, uncle, but if I can bring back The Shield, it will give those of us who are left, some hope that one day we can return it to our city. I feel that if this was Alexeis talking, you wouldn't be so reluctant. I want to do this in his memory, uncle! Can't you understand that?'

Hypatos, momentarily taken off guard by his nephew's earnestness, began to argue against the dangerous plan. The thought that this wild scheme could lead to the death of his much-loved heir, made him resist, but he underestimated Theomenes' determination. He was resolvedly unmoved by all the doubts expressed by Hypatos.

'Come and see me this evening, Theo,' he said finally, preparing to return to his meeting, 'and I will listen to all you have to say. I have serious concerns, but I'm relieved to have had this talk with you,' he added. 'I'd begun to have regrets in making you my heir. Now I'm more proud than I can say!'

Becoming excited himself at the prospect of the venture, Hypatos later promised Theomenes all the help he needed, but voiced obvious reservations. 'You are still only twenty, and have no experience of command, Theo, as you will readily agree. You'll need good men around you. This is going to take a lot of planning - and money!'

'Money I have, uncle, and good men I shall find!' said Theo, his eyes bright with anticipation. 'Now I've told you my plans, Mydon will be next to be informed.'

'Well, I don't envy you that!' exclaimed Hypatos. 'No doubt he will have an opinion to voice!'

PART THREE
THE SHIELD

SIXTY-SEVEN

THEY COULD HEAR THE quick stomp of feet coming down the corridor, and Theomenes immediately rose from the table he shared with others in the group, to greet the man he hoped had decided to join them. Stephanos, having sent his slave ahead of him to let them know he was back in town and ready to play his part in their venture, burst through the doorway. Bronzed and fit, he looked every inch the soldier, and glances of approval passed between Theomenes, Imbros and the other men present.

'I've brought someone with me,' he announced, quickly. 'He insisted on being party to this meeting!' Stepping aside he allowed his companion to enter the room, and immediately there were exclamations of surprise.

'What is this?' boomed Glaucus, standing on his own at the other side of the room, unable to take in what he was looking at. 'Is it male or female? And what is that sickly sweet smell?'

'Don't you know me, 'big man'?' asked the flamboyant individual, striding across to greet him, his long silk robes edged in brilliant purple, sweeping the floor.

'Whoa there, friend!' exclaimed Glaucus. 'That's far enough. Your scent is making my eyes water!'

'I remember a punch I gave you, that made your eyes water, Glaucus!' the man said, laughing.

'Clytes!' bellowed Glaucus, in sudden recognition. 'My dear friend! Zeus! What part are you playing now? I didn't recognise you under all that hair.'

Clytes brusquely swept back his braids, grinning broadly. 'It's no part, Glaucus. I've been in Ionia, working for Cleon. I got wind of more trouble being planned in Colophon while on the trail of Lykaon. I've been living under cover there these past months. The Lydian, Pissuthnes has been inciting the locals again to reject their Athenian rulers. I was waiting for Stephanos here, to put down the rebellion!'

'Me and a few others!' added Stephanos, modestly.

'And Stephanos told you about our quest, no doubt,' interrupted Theomenes.

'It's what I've waited ten years for!' explained Clytes. 'On my own I haven't been able to get close enough to kill the bastard. You've got to take me with you!' he insisted.

'But you have no allegiance to Plataea, Clytes,' said Theomenes, surprised.

'I've already told him that, Theo,' spoke up Stephanos. 'You try and explain. The man won't listen to me!'

'I know of your personal vendetta against this enemy of yours, Clytes,' spoke Theomenes, but our quest is to bring back The Shield of Marathon. To restore the pride of the Plataeans. It may no longer be in Lykaon's possession.'

'He's got it all right!' snapped Clytes. 'I know him better than any one of you. He's a cunning bastard and you'll need my help in tracking him down. You don't know who you're up against!'

Glaucus raised his hand for silence, as murmurings were heard from the men sat around the table. 'I can vouch for him, Theomenes,' he asserted.

'I also!' spoke up Imbros, rising from his seat. 'He risked his life during the Theban attack on our city, when he had no need. He's a fighter, a worthy addition to our cause.'

'Despite how he looks!' grimaced Glaucus, good-humouredly. 'Do you still have the sword, Clytes?' he asked, suddenly remembering.

'Of course!' replied Clytes, displaying the weapon slung from his belt. 'Presented to me by Diokles, commander of your own garrison, Theomenes. And, here is something else I received at Plataea!' He exposed the raised scars, stretching from thigh to ankle, the result of a Theban's failed attempt to bring him down.

'Everyone taking part in this endeavour will be required to swear a pledge,' spoke Theomenes, seriously. 'To find The Shield, wherever the search may take us, and no matter how long it takes - whether Lykaon has it or not. If you want to come along, Clytes, you will be expected to do this.'

'I'll do whatever is requested of me, and I'll swear the oath wholeheartedly!' replied Clytes, theatrically.

Theomenes asked for a show of hands from the rest of his companions, as to whether Clytes should join them.

Glaucus grinned as every man seated around the table raised his arm, forcing a hesitant Stephanos to do likewise. 'Welcome aboard, old friend!' he said, warmly, as he gripped Clytes' hand. 'I would embrace you, you mad bugger, but your aroma is a little overpowering!' His booming laughter released some of the pent-up tensions felt by the Plataeans, and in a more relaxed mood they too joined in some good-natured joking with the Eleusinian.

'I take it that you are with us then, Glaucus?' asked Theomenes, relieved.

'I was in two minds whether or not to join this crazy adventure,' replied the big redhead, scratching his beard. 'I don't mind admitting it, you wouldn't find a better helmsman,' and he unconsciously swelled out his huge chest. 'But Clytes here has reminded me of that time in your city, when you Plataeans fought like demons against the Thebans, and I believe you will fight to regain The Shield. Yes, I'm in!'

'I'll get my uncle to speak to Cleon, Glaucus,' said Theomenes, with urgency. 'The rest of the company have been released from military service, for the duration of the quest. He will persuade the general to get you freed from your agreement with Paramanos.'

'I'm the hero of Mytilene, Theo!' bellowed Flamebeard, jokingly. 'I will speak to Cleon. No doubt he has seen an opportunity in this for himself - if the trophy is returned. He needs some good news to please the masses.'

SIXTY-EIGHT

ON THE TWENTY-FIRST DAY of the month of Anthesterion, by the Athenian calendar; five years after the unprovoked Theban attack on Plataea; Theomenes chose Imbros to accompany him by ship to the western port of Cirra, to seek the advice of the Pythia at Delphi on Mount Parnassus. Situated over a hundred miles northwest of Athens, Delphi, the navel of the world, where vaporous gases escaped from a chasm deep in the earth, sending the priestess into an induced trance enabling her to channel the words of the sun god, Apollo. The sculptor had enthusiastically thrown himself into the venture of seeking The Shield, since he'd learned that Amara had also been taken by Lykaon, and he was now, never far from Theo's side. His hair and beard had seen a barber of late, and encouraged by Theomenes, he was now dressed as a respectable citizen of Athens.

The God Apollo only visited his temple once a month, consequently a queue of people waited for admission. It had been agreed that Theomenes would pose the one question allowed. He was funding the venture, after all. Between sunrise and sunset, the priestess would be in attendance, but once the sun went down, there would be no more audiences until the following month. They couldn't wait that long.

To try and ensure a place early in the day, Theomenes and Imbros bathed in the sacred springs just as dawn broke, ensuring their purity before entering the temple. One of the fattest and most expensive sacrificial goats was chosen from the hundreds corralled at Delphi, and Theomenes also paid handsomely into the temple coffers. The lavish outlay he hoped would avoid him having to draw lots for a place in the queue. The line being long, could result in not having an audience at all that day. It worked. A male attendant separated him from Imbros and ushered him into an anteroom, where his question was discussed and suggestions made as to its wording. He was then taken to a heavily adorned waiting area, where many others were seated, anxiously anticipating sight of the Oracle. All around the walls were shields taken in battle and now dedicated to the God Apollo. Theomenes looked at the weaponry taken from the Persians at the Battles of Marathon and Plataea, and he lifted his head up proudly. One day, he swore silently, I will bring The Shield of Marathon to join them, until it can be returned to its rightful home!

Finally, it was his turn to enter the inner sanctum and a strong scent of burning laurel leaves, the sacred tree of the sun god, filled the air. On entering he could vaguely see the Pythia in the centre of the room. The priestess, wearing a headdress of laurel leaves, was seated on a golden tripod, the breath of Apollo billowing from the chasm beneath her. The sweet smell of ether assailed Theomenes' nostrils. Feeling heady and intoxicated, he watched expectantly, as the priestess, with vapours swirling around her, reached out her arms towards him.

'Well, what did she say?' asked Imbros, impatiently, when Theomenes returned blinking into the sunlight.

'I have it here, Imbros!' replied Theo, his voice shaking. 'An attendant wrote it down for me,' and he spread out the small parchment roll, on a stone bench situated just outside the temple.

Brave Theomenes; the sharp eyes of Athena's owl will guide and protect you, but beware of snakes in the walls. There is in Delos what you seek.

They were both stunned. 'Delos? Do you really think The Shield is there? And perhaps, Amara? I didn't think it would be that easy!' said Imbros, amazed.

CHAPTER SIXTY-NINE

'Nor did I!' said Theomenes, unable to restrain his exhilaration.

'Snakes in the walls?' said Imbros, questioningly. 'What's that all about?'

'Cleon, probably,' replied Theo, knowingly. 'He was suspiciously eager to give permission for this endeavour. No doubt he has his own reasons. Well, at least I've been warned!'

Encouraged by the Pythia's message, Theomenes arranged a meeting with the independent Delphic Council. He needed their permission to bring The Shield to the Temple of Apollo, for safety, and he was a little uncertain as to how they would react. At the beginning of the war, the Spartan king, Archidamus, had also sought the advice of the Pythia at Delphi, fearing repercussions if he broke the peace treaty by making the first move. The Pythia's answer implied that if the Spartans fought with all their might, victory would be theirs, and Apollo would be on their side, whether they invoked him or not! With such support for Sparta from the Oracle at Delphi, the Athenians had since felt unwelcome, preferring to go instead to Apollo's island home on Delos, which was under their control. But Theomenes left with firm assurances from the Council that this was certainly not the case. He was given guarantees that The Shield of Marathon, and anyone wishing to attend its presentation, would be gladly received, and special permission would be granted for travel. The council elders, knowing the treasury coffers were in a dire state due to the war and the plague, thought this grand event, should it ever happen, would rectify that.

SIXTY-NINE

THE QUEST FOR THE Shield entered into history under a pale dawn light, as the dark mass of Mount Kynthos on the sacred island of Delos emerged slowly from the long night. Lycimachas, High Priest of the Apollonian temple, who's fetid breath Clytes the Eleusinian decided, smelt far too strongly of garlic for so early in the day, was about to complete the sacrificial ritual which it was hoped would ease the passage of fortune for the sworn members of The Sacred Band.

After more than a week on the island, there was still no word of the stolen shield ever having been on or near Delos. No sighting had been reported of Lykaon. Theomenes and Imbros had been certain that the Oracle's cryptic message at Delphi had referred to their quest, and the pair were now confused as to its real meaning. At Apollo's temple on Delos, they hoped to unravel the god's confusing message.

Lycimachas had white hair as long as any maid's. It fell lankly over stooped shoulders to his waist, a thick hirsute waterfall of frayed ends and greased plaits from which various coloured ribbons hung loosely. An elaborate wreath of laurel encircled his frail head, seeming to bow him forward with its weight. As he turned away from the altar to face the small assembly, he raised his hand that gripped the curved sacrificial knife saying; his voice a cracked whisper, 'Beware of your words!'

'What words?' Glaucus muttered irritably to no-one in particular. 'When did we speak?'

'Clown!' Clytes answered beside him, giving him a sharp nudge. 'It's probably customary here.'

'Probably,' groaned Glaucus, 'Customary, but pointless.'

The five were attired in quality light armour, presented to them by Hypatos before their journey east from Athens. Their leather breastplates were embossed with the simple emblem of a hoplon which would not draw undue attention, but significant to The Shield Company. Their bare heads, like that of the priest Lycimachas, had been crowned with wreaths, and they stood, heads bowed and feeling rather foolish, as beads of brown water dripped from their brows; the result of a laurel branch taken by the priest from the brazier, being cooled in a scented bowl, then sprinkled over their heads and shoulders.

It had been a good sacrifice. The lamb hadn't struggled; in itself a good omen. When barley grains were placed upon its head, and it bowed to the god, the beast's throat was cut swiftly and the blood shot into the flames with seeming willingness. The priest's assistants then set about the skinning and other preparations with practiced hands, while the prayers were intoned. The chine and thigh bones were placed with care, over the spitting fire so their aromas would ascend to the gods on Olympus, while the remains of the carcass, save that hived off for the participating members of the order, would go to The Sacred Band and their accompanying slaves, when the rites were completed.

As far as Glaucus was concerned, it was only this final part of the proceedings that gained his interest. While they patiently eyed the roasting spit and savoured the aromas wafting into the open air, where they all sat at the feet of the enormous statue of Apollo, Lycimachas, sifting through the entrails of the lamb like a beggar looking for a lost coin, suddenly glanced up, smiling with toothless satisfaction. Wiping bony fingers on a piece of cloth, he allowed the silence to prevail for a few moments, thinking the drama of quiet would somehow give greater meaning to his findings.

Stephanos, however, scratching his short beard, was getting impatient. He said, his harsh voice splitting the sacred air like a spear in flight, 'Priest! If you have ought to tell us, please do so, otherwise we will have to conclude that our time here has been wasted.'

'Tell him we'll take back his fee and tie him to a pillar the wrong way up if that damn food isn't on the way soon!' Glaucus bawled.

'And some wine wouldn't go amiss either,' added Clytes, dryly.

'Wasted!' exclaimed Lycimachas, a hurt look on his skeletal face. 'Wasted it has not been. What we have here,' and he lifted a piece of the bloody entrails aloft with a theatrical flourish, 'is an encouraging sign from the God Apollo, no less.'

'You speak of Agristones' shield?' spoke Theomenes eagerly, rising.

Said Imbros, already on his feet. 'Amara? Was that name spoken?'

Stephanos eyed the priest with a cold stare. 'You'd better be sure of what you are about to say, or it could go badly for you.'

Lycimachas looked uncomfortable for a moment. 'Amara? Where is that?'

The colour drained from the face of Imbros as he grasped tightly the scrawny arm of the priest, his grip so tight that Lycimachas visibly winced. 'It is no place,' the sculptor said quietly and menacingly. 'Amara is the fairest woman in all Attica. She's my wife!'

Lycimachas, shaking his arm free, rubbed it vigorously. 'No, this name was not given to me. I am sorry. But a vision was granted.'

Glaucus smiled at this. 'Yes? A vision of The Marathon Shield, was it?'

Lycimachas glanced at the helmsman with undisguised annoyance at being interrupted, and carried on. 'Yes, this was shown ....'

'And.......?' prompted Theomenes.

Said Clytes, exasperated. 'This is like pulling teeth!'

'Where should one search for it?' prompted Stephanos. 'Where Lykaon the Wolf is surely?'

The dark eyes of Imbros narrowed at the now familiar name. 'Yes, priest. Where is this viper? Has your oracle spoken?'

'The Wolf of Thebes is where The Shield lies,' said Clytes flatly. 'We all know that. He most likely sleeps with it.'

'As you lie with that Theban sword, Clytes!' joked Glaucus.

'Don't link this man with Thebes,' said Lycimachas, shaking his head. 'He does not dwell there.'

'Tell us something we don't know, priest,' Glaucus remarked disparagingly. 'Or must we report to Cleon in Athens that all this was in vain?'

Lycimachas eyed the helmsman as he would an annoying child. 'A sacrifice to Apollo is always acknowledged,' admonished the priest, throwing the blood-stained cloth to one of his acolytes. 'Lykaon and his followers are at this moment, the guests of the Phocians. They sailed from an Illyrian port more than a month since and disembarked at the port of Cirra.'

'Cirra?' exclaimed Stephanos. Then he has gone to Delphi. He seeks the advice of the Pythia!'

'For a high fee, the oligarchs have granted them a pass of safe conduct to cross their lands,' continued, Lycimachas, knowingly. 'It has been shown to me that they will travel south from there.'

'You can tell all that from a beast's innards?' Theomenes asked, incredulously.

'Phocis is an ally of Sparta and therefore of Thebes,' said Stephanos, deliberating. 'Why would they risk Thebes' displeasure for the sake of a man who stands disgraced? A man who has been banished from his own city?'

Lycimachas smiled, smugly. 'As to why these things came about, I cannot say. I can only tell you what I see.'

'I wonder that the gods show you anything, priest,' said Stephanos, testily. 'We came here on the advice of the god Apollo, given at his temple home in Delphi, but others in our group have more faith in the messages of the god of truth and light, than I do. It appears to me that you have been receiving reports which we are not party to. No doubt you could inform us of what Lykaon had for dinner?'

'I see you mock me, young man,' replied the priest, his smile fading. 'Perhaps I should remind you that it wasn't I who asked for this ceremony. I am merely the herald of Apollo in this business.' With that, Lysimachas turned from them, bringing their speculations to an end. 'You may eat now,' he said, finally.

When the priests had retired to within the precincts of the temple, and food had at last appeared, Theo sat down on the steps beside Stephanos. 'Do you believe him?' he asked his wiser companion.

Stephanos was cynical of the intervention of the god Apollo, but not of the information given to them. 'I could dismiss every word he uttered like I would spurn poor wine, but on this occasion I'm drawn to believe what he has told us. He's getting news from someone - somewhere!'

'Lycimachas would be delighted to see The Marathon Shield claimed by Athens, Stephanos,' remarked Clytes, interrupting. 'It would enhance his position enormously in the eyes of crowd-pleaser, Cleon, if it was known he assisted in its recovery. Our priest is distantly related to him, I understand.'

'How would you know something like that?' asked Stephanos, incredulously.

'Ah! Just one of many bits of information I've picked up on my travels,' replied Clytes, knowingly.

'Well, that explains it,' remarked Stephanos. 'Cleon's spies are passing him this information.'

'I don't trust him,' Imbros uttered, jerking his head in the direction of the temple doors, now shut fast. 'He knows a lot more than he's telling us.'

'A part of what he told us, is convincing, though,' said Stephanos, considering the implications.

'But why travel into Phocian territory?' Glaucus ventured.

'For protection,' explained Stephanos. 'Phocis, although part of the Spartan confederacy, was never a friend of Thebes. Accepting Lykaon and his band of followers, is an unlooked for opportunity to get back at Thebes for invasions into their territory, and the harassment of their citizens. Phocians have long memories and enjoy their resentments. For whatever reason, I believe the old fox is telling us the truth.' A jug of watered wine provided by Lycimachas sat on the steps. Stephanos picked up a cup and poured, then passed on the jar.

'Doesn't help us though, does it?' Imbros remarked with unconcealed bitterness. 'Amara may well be with that lowlife in Phocis. My Amara, there, with him, while we are sat here talking. Damn his carcass! How can we get to him in Phocis?' Frustrated, he threw the bowl of half eaten food towards a group of doves pecking nearby, and moving a short distance away, stood staring dejectedly across the blue waters, in the direction of the mainland. The rest of the group stayed silent for a few moments, lost in their own thoughts, the morning sun encroaching upon them swiftly now, lighting up the statue of Apollo and the terrace, where snarling stone lions guarded the way to his temple.

It was Glaucus who finally spoke. 'Listen to me, all of you!' he exclaimed. 'When we have our ship, Phocis will not be a problem. I know of a place. The tiny island of Atalante, just off the coast of Locris. A few years back, I helped take men and supplies there to build a new garrison. If he leaves from the Phocis port of Daphnus, and is heading south, we can keep watch from that fortified island and catch him when he makes a move through the Gulf of Euboea.'

Clytes shook his head wearily. 'Listen to the man. We have few men, no ship as yet, and here he is talking as though the murdering scum is caught! I could get into Phocis and find him myself, before he has time to put to sea again!'

'No, Clytes!' shouted Imbros. 'That is crazy talk. How could you rescue The Shield and Amara, on your own? We stick together, as Theomenes planned.'

'Fine!' came his retort. 'But where exactly is Atalante? And how are we going to get there? We still haven't found a bloody ship! If they've not been commissioned for the war, they're as rotten as the old priest's teeth!'

'Delos and her surrounding islands are some of the richest in the Aegean, Clytes,' remarked Glaucus. 'Bankers, wealthy merchants, you name it, have made their homes here and their ships are among the best. Give me a little more time, and with Theomenes' money, I will find us a vessel. If it's not The Shield we find here at Delos, then it will be our ship!'

And a ship he did find. A thirty oared triaconter. Not the latest in vessel design. In fact she had some age, but according to Glaucus, built of the finest materials and extremely well maintained by her rich merchant owner. 'He used her for his own personal travel throughout the Aegean,' explained Glaucus. 'But now he wants something bigger. For a triaconter, she is remarkably well fitted out. She's built for speed and she's robust. I'd recommend buying this one,' said Glaucus to Theomenes, confidently.

The ship, 'Delias', was drawn up on rollers, lying alongside the seller's private jetty, and the five companions slowly inspected every inch of her, from the heavily carved stern, to the curved oak projection at the prow, giving a good impression of knowing what they were looking for. 'Well, 'Maid of Delos', or rather 'old maid', laughed Clytes, as he read the name painted along the highly polished bow of the ship. 'I guess you do look in good shape, for your age!'

'She's a classic!' declared Glaucus. 'Look at her lines, Clytes! She's quality, been made by craftsmen! There's a good few years left in her yet!'

'I like her,' said Imbros. 'Those carvings at the stern are very fine!'

'Bugger the carvings!' said Stephanos, exasperated. 'We're not buying a bloody ornament! How does she go?'

'What would you, a Plataean know about ships, Stephanos?' Imbros answered back, testily. 'I suspect you've never held an oar in your life!'

Stephanos glared back, but said nothing.

'Arrange a trial run, Glaucus, to see how she handles,' said Theomenes, authoritatively. 'As a Plataean also, I know nothing of these vessels. If your confidence remains intact, Helmsman, then the Delias is our ship!'

Then turning to Imbros and Stephanos, he said, calmly, 'We're going to be in each other's close company for some time. There'll be no space for clashes of personality. Store your energies for the task ahead!'

The older men looked around at each other, surprised at the logic coming from the mouth of their youngest member. Slowly, Imbros and Stephanos nodded in agreement.

SEVENTY

WORD HAD SPREAD QUICKLY around the island about the quest, and the fact that their own 'Delias' was to carry the adventurous band, made a quiet exit from Delos impossible. For such an early hour, the harbour was crowded with boats of all sizes, all wanting to accompany the ship on the first moments of her voyage, and the harbour walls were lined with cheering crowds. The Delias, her new sail emblazoned with Imbros's design of the owl of Athena, as foretold to him by the Pythia at Delphi, cracked against the breeze, the spread wings eager to take flight. Over the deck, at the stern, curved the newly painted carving of Oeno, the wine-producing daughter of Anius, the mythical king of Delos. According to the legend, all three of his productive daughters were changed into doves by Dionysus, to avoid being captured by King Agamemnon on his way to Troy, and doves were consequently protected on the island. Something the five adventurers were well aware of at the temple, the mess of bird droppings being seen everywhere.

Mydon, hampered by his lameness, had some difficulty in chasing away several noisy and excited children who'd been clambering nimbly about the craft all morning, as nineteen seasoned Athenians, including Bion, generously released from war duty by Cleon, and eleven not-so-experienced Plataeans, began strapping their circular hoplons along each side of the ship, taking their allotted places at the rowing benches.

'So much for a quiet getaway!' remarked Stephanos to Theomenes, listening to the deafening shouts of well-wishers. 'The world and his wife will know of our ship, and her intent. Lykaon will know our every move!'

'The interest could work in our favour also,' replied Theomenes, trying not to notice that a young woman on the jetty was waving at him eagerly. 'Hopefully, we will also be passed information of Lykaon's comings and goings.'

'Who is that?' asked Stephanos, smirking, unable to keep his curiosity under control any longer.

The younger man was embarrassed that the lovely Dorothea had come to see him depart, and was making herself so noticeable to the rest of the crew. He could hear their whistles and calls from the ship, but deliberately ignored them. He'd expressly told the girl not to come, but here she was, bearing a myrtle wreath which she insisted on placing on his head, for good-luck. Approaching him eagerly, she embraced him tightly, her quick kisses stirring memories of the previous night and the experiences which had been entirely new for him. The amenable girls in the brothels of Delos could not have given him the delirious delights that he'd enjoyed on one long passionate night, with this spirited shop-keeper's daughter.

He faced the men, mercifully without blushing, as he stepped on board, listening good-humouredly as they drummed their feet on the deck boards, shouting out their lewd advice on how to handle beautiful women.

Glaucus and Clytes were last aboard and the hero of Mytilene was a little worse-for-wear. Drinking too many toasts to the maid Oeno, whose virginal image would protect his back while seated on his helmsman 'throne', he had recklessly downed his wine Scythian style: undiluted, and his consequent hang-over was the result. The thud of his axe hitting the deck, as he stowed it beneath his chair, made him clutch at his forehead, much to the amusement of Clytes.

To the sounds of horns and shrill whistles, and a cheering crowd, the Delias pulled away from the coast, quickly leaving the multitude of bobbing ships behind, and was soon sailing steadily northwards, island hopping along the coasts of the Cyclades islands towards the Euboean Straits. Athena's owl, with its crying beak and its wings spread wide, was a proud sight for those on board, and with Clytes taking the lead they soon fell to singing lustily, as the sense of adventure took hold. Glaucus, his head throbbing, had to grin and bear it, as he focused on the task ahead. He'd not helmed such a small vessel for a long time, and the swell was making him feel sick.

He remembered the last time he'd been in these waters; as helmsman of the Thetis, with the young trierarch, Iandros, at his side. The last news he'd heard of the eager adventure seeker was not good. Iandros had pressed his father Paramanos to be allowed to go on the quest with Glaucus, and the subsequent falling out had been so severe, that Paramanos had sent his son to oversee their business interests at the silver mines, until he came to his senses. After the glory of Mytilene, Glaucus knew just how cruel this punishment would seem to Iandros, but with a father like Paramanos, the Thessalian wasn't surprised. He'd had to release Glaucus on the orders of Cleon, for what he considered a fool-hardy venture. 'Just what does my best helmsman owe to the Plataeans?' he'd asked, angrily.

Being such a small vessel, Glaucus could not risk taking the Delias against the variable currents of the Chalcis Strait, so the ship was taken ashore and carried overland by the crew until it could be safely relaunched in calmer waters. While in the town, they stocked up on supplies, believing there would not be much to spare on Atalante, for if Delos was a small island, then Atalante was tiny. An uninhabited lump of rock, until the Athenian garrison took it over nearly five years previously. A self-made prison for the men stationed there.

Clytes and Glaucus took the opportunity to make a visit to a portside tavern, and seated outside in the sunshine, filling their bellies with fish stew, they watched as ships were loaded and unloaded. Clytes, his long legs stretched out in front of him, was taking particular interest in a tall youth, loading a struggling pair of young colts. He looked familiar, and as he took a gulp of wine, he suddenly remembered the young lad he'd handed over to a horse-breeder, years before.

'I think I know that young man, Glaucus,' said Clytes, pointing. 'He's from Plataea. I was there when his farm was attacked.'

Clytes called out loudly, 'Angelos!' and as the gangly young man spun around, Clytes exclaimed, 'I thought so!'

'You have to take me with you!' pleaded Angelos, when he was told the reason why Clytes was passing through Chalcis. 'I'm Plataean born! Do you remember my grand-mother, Clytes? Do you remember her dying words? Never forget The Shield! You have to let me be part of this!'

'It's not up to us,' Glaucus interrupted. 'It's up to Theomenes of Hysiae. He's the one funding this venture.'

'Theomenes? Son of Eubalos?' asked Angelos, excitedly. 'We supplied the estate of Eubalos with our olives. Theomenes might remember my father, Sebastos!'

'It will have to be decided quickly, then,' spoke Clytes, rising. 'We're leaving immediately!'

'I remember your family very well, Angelos,' said Theomenes, sadly, on hearing of their fate. 'My father always had high praise for your father's knowledge of his olive groves. Our trees were never touched until he'd first checked with Sebastos! He would have been grieved to hear of the death of your grand-mother.'

'Will you take me with you then, Theomenes? I've learned a lot about horses, while on Euboea,' said Angelos, hopefully.

'He can shoot hares also,' remarked Clytes, smiling.

'You remembered?' said Angelos, chuckling. 'It seems like such a long time ago.'

'Five years - and not good ones,' remarked Clytes.

'All skills will prove useful Angelos, but more important, is that you have the heart of a Plataean,' said Theomenes, warmly. 'For the sake of all we have lost, you are welcome to join us!'

When they reached Atalante, the Delias was pulled up the beach to lie alongside one of the two triremes assigned to the garrison. The other, they knew, was out on patrol doing its daily sweep of the straits. Despite word being sent ahead to notify the garrison of their coming, they'd still been stopped and boarded earlier, by armed marines who'd searched their unknown vessel for anything suspicious. The need to keep the straits free for the flow of essential grain and foodstuffs coming from Euboea was vital to the survival of Athens, and privateering was now severely punished.

On speaking with the garrison commander, a discontented individual by the name of Menon, the five were assured that Lykaon had not passed through the straits, unless their man had the means of travelling under water, he'd laughed gruffly. Every strange ship was inspected by his soldiers, he told them, assuredly.

Theomenes handed him a papyrus scroll. It was from Cleon, and it was to be used in any place on their quest, where Athens had control. The instructions were brief. 'Give all necessary assistance to the bearer of this message, in retrieving Plataea's stolen Shield of Marathon, and in the capture or killing of the Theban known as Lykaon, Wolf of Thebes, son of Pelonus.' Menon scrutinised the signature and also the clay seal attached, impressed with Cleon's own emblem of a screeching eagle.

'Can we count on your support?' asked Stephanos, impatiently. 'With the assistance of one of your triremes, we can apprehend this murdering lowlife before he gets to the open sea.'

The surly features of the commander were suddenly transformed by a broad smile, accompanied by a hearty laugh. 'By all means!' he responded, enthusiastically. 'On one condition.'

'Oh?' asked Theomenes, warily.

'That I get off this damn rock and accompany you!' he growled. 'I'd welcome some action. I'll send him to the bottom of the ocean, to keep company with Poseidon!' he added, forcefully.

'No, commander!' responded Theomenes, anxiously. 'The Shield may be on board. I need your help to capture his vessel, not ram it. I want the Theban captured alive, if possible.'

For over two weeks they waited, frustratedly, for news of the Theban's approach, and just when all hope was fading that he would choose this route, the signal was seen by the look-out; three flaming arrows fired at short intervals from a watching craft, as Lykaon's ship, a fifty-oared penteconter, was finally spotted coming around the headland to the north of them. Atalante's second trireme, crewed by men from the garrison, together with Theomenes' contingent of rowers, was launched immediately. On deck were the five trophy seekers; sunlight glancing off their helmets and shields, also the rest of the Plataeans, and Menon with his own command of a dozen fully armed hoplites.

Lykaon, travelling south, saw the warnings in the sky and becoming wary, he prepared his men for potential trouble ahead. Blocking his passage, the towering trireme drew close, and Menon shouted out his orders for the penteconter to surrender. But it was soon obvious that it intended to carry on through the straits, as a bombardment of fire arrows and javelins was directed at the trireme. The javelins had little effect as they flew over the heads of Theomenes and his men, but the fires took hold and sand buckets were soon in use.

Grappling hooks were thrown from the larger ship, catching the rails of the penteconter, and as oars were drawn back, the two ships were gradually pulled closer together, as boarding ramps from the trireme's rowing decks were made ready.

On board the penteconter, Lykaon ordered his vastly outnumbered men to prepare for action, and commanded Hippodamus to tie the women to the rails at the stern of the fighting deck. Amara, Anthousa and the other slave women were dragged to the rear of the ship, while arrows and javelins began to rain down around them. Lykaon's archers, in reply, aimed volley after volley of fire arrows at the oarports on the lower level of the trireme, some finding their mark despite the waterproof coverings, while others fell hissing into the water. Menon's rowers, wedged into their places, were being struck down.

Onto the first ramp leapt Stephanos, with Theomenes and Imbros following. A second ramp bore Glaucus, carrying aloft his great axe, with Clytes close behind. The rest of the Plataeans together with Menon and his men, with shields held ready and javelins poised, lined the top deck waiting for Theomenes' orders.

Amara and Anthousa stared in terror as the ship was about to be boarded, then Amara gave a choked cry. 'Imbros! It's Imbros! Look, Anthousa!'

'And Clytes!' Anthousa cried out, before she could stop herself.

Suddenly, they were gripped by their hair and with hands already tied behind their backs, dragged brutally by Hippodamus along the deck. 'I think these attackers are known to the women, sire!' he shouted urgently above the din, to Lykaon. 'They seem to recognise them!'

'Get them on the rails!' ordered Lykaon, stridently. 'Quickly, man!'

Amara and Anthousa were made to climb onto the deck rail and look toward the looming trireme, her decks filled with armed warriors prepared to do battle.

'Are these women known to you?' Lykaon shouted, loudly, to the men assembled on the trireme. 'They seem to know you!'

'Oh God, it's Amara!' groaned Imbros. 'He's going to kill her!'

'That's Anthousa from Plataea!' Clytes, called out. 'How did she get here?'

Slowly, Lykaon drew his knife under Amara's chin, letting a thin line of blood trickle down her beautiful throat. 'Does anyone care about this woman?' Lykaon screamed, cruelly, as he made to push Amara from the rail.

There was silence from Menon and his men as they struggled to understand what was going on, and they looked anxiously towards Theomenes for orders.

'Well? What's your answer? Imbros, is it? shouted Lykaon, mockingly. 'The woman dies here and now, or you leave me free passage! Such a waste, Imbros!' he called out tauntingly, as he ran his hand up Amara's exposed body. 'What's it to be?' Curiously, he looked at each man in turn, searching for the face he would recognise. Was it the name Clytes, the slave Anthousa had called out? Could it be the Eleusinian?

'Theo!' gasped Imbros. 'It's Amara! Don't let him kill her!' he pleaded.

Theomenes stood horrified on the ramp, torn between his head and his heart. The Shield could be on the vessel. They had the men to take it. But what if it wasn't? He stared at the terrified figure on the rail, her life in his hands.

Menon, eager to board, shouted down to Theomenes, forcing him to make a decision. 'We have him! What are your orders?' he asked, testily.

Imbros gripped his friend hard by the arm. 'He'll kill her, Theo!' he said, forcefully. Looking once more at Amara, Theomenes commanded loudly, 'Lower your weapons!'

A wild yell split the air. Clytes, incensed that Lykaon was being allowed to escape, tried to push aside Glaucus on the ramp in an attempt to board the penteconter. 'Don't let him pass!' shouted Theomenes, frantically, as he witnessed the scuffle taking place. Flamebeard's bulk easily blocked the way, and Clytes in frustration, leapt back up to the deck of the trireme. Grabbing a spear from one of Menon's marines, he jumped over the still smouldering fires, shoving men aside as he headed toward the prow.

'He's going for Lykaon, Imbros!' yelled Theomenes to his startled comrade behind him.

Looking up, Imbros could see Clytes running in his direction, and he scrambled up to stop him. 'Don't do it!' he cried out, as Clytes collided with him.

'Out of my way, man!' he roared, his eyes wild with anger.

Imbros made a grab for the spear, but seeing the crazed look on the Eleusinian's face, feared for his own life, as Clytes reached for his dagger.

As they fought, they heard a loud shout from behind them, and Glaucus, moving with remarkable agility for a man of his build, threw himself on Clytes, pinning him heavily to the deck.

'Get off me, you fat bastard!' Clytes groaned, struggling. 'Let me get him!'

''Can't do that, friend!' said Glaucus, seriously. 'Sorry to have to do this.....!' And he delivered him such a blow, he knocked him unconscious.

'Let the ship pass, Menon!' Theomenes was heard to shout.

Hurriedly, Lykaon's men began detaching the grappling hooks from their vessel, and using their oars, pushed the penteconter back into the current of the Euboean Sea. This manouvre was accompanied by a brazen, farewell hail of arrows, directed at the deck of the trireme.

'Bastards!' someone in Menon's crew shouted after them.

Silhouetted against the sky, Imbros gazed across the water at the ship carrying his wife away, and placed his hand on his heart. Amara saw his gesture, but was too shaken and full of grief, to respond. Taken down from the rail, she and Anthousa were again bound by ropes to the other women, and while the oarsmen took up their rhythm, they watched tearfully as their chance of rescue and safety faded from view.

From the deck of the penteconter, Lykaon stood at the rail, staring murderously towards the disengaged trireme. His body felt a sudden cold shiver and he drew his cloak around him. Well, he is of no concern now, he thought, shrugging, as he turned away. The Eleusinian can't follow where I'm going.

'Steer a course for Crete!' he ordered his helmsman.

Back on Atalante, and now fully conscious, Clytes was filled with remorse as reality dawned about his skirmish with Imbros, and what might have happened to Amara if Glaucus hadn't hit him.

While he'd been restrained, much had happened. The Athenian rowers had talked of giving up on the quest. The Delias, they thought unworthy of them, and the episode at Atalante was thought to be a farce. Stephanos also was questioning events. He was convinced that neither Theomenes nor Imbros was serious about finding The Shield; only Amara. Clytes was thought by the Plataeans to be unreliable and unfit for the task ahead, and they'd all voted for him to be left behind.

'I need your reassurance that you are dedicated to the quest!' Stephanos had demanded of Theo, angry that he also had not boarded the enemy ship. 'We've only just begun this venture, and already there are divisions within the company. We all need to know just what, or who we're risking our lives for, Theo!'

Theomenes was still shaken by the recent events. To have at his disposal a fully manned trireme, all to come to nothing. He was not surprised at his captain's criticism.

'I value your experience and sense of leadership,' Theomenes told him, with sincerity, but I couldn't risk the life of Amara!' he responded, defensively.

The older man placed his hand on Theomenes' shoulder.

'It must not happen again, Theo!' he told him firmly.

It was Glaucus from Thessaly who finally brought some calm to the situation. 'If we'd boarded, it would have been certain death for the wife of our friend, Imbros. We're not even sure that Lykaon still has The Shield. Theomenes is funding this venture, and it was his call. A difficult decision, in my opinion. As for Clytes being left behind, I think that would be a very bad decision. If you believe, as he does, that Lykaon is going to Asia Minor, then Clytes knows the territory; understands their dialects, and most of all, he knows the Theban. Without him in the company, I tell you all now, I'd have to reconsider my own position.'

After apologies from Clytes, to all concerned, and assurances given as to his future conduct, Glaucus encouraged the members of The Shield Company to vote again, reminding them of the Eleusinian's courage during the attack on their city at the beginning of the war. With some reservations voiced by Stephanos, he was reinstated into their group.

When the Delias left Atalante in pursuit of Lykaon's more powerful penteconter, there was no singing. It wasn't the thought of glorious deeds and heroics which united them now. The Shield Company had seen the man they were up against, and Clytes was no longer alone in his hatred of The Wolf of Thebes.

On its way to Cleon, however, and unbeknown to Theomenes and his men, was a detailed account of the debacle at Atalante. This was not the result the populist leader had expected, and the Athenian rowers wondered just what they'd signed up for.

SEVENTY-ONE

ON THE ISLAND OF CRETE; neutral territory during the differences between Athens and Sparta, was one of the largest slave markets in the Aegean. There were so many slaves brought through this island on a regular basis, that separate auctions were allocated just for the sale of women. But Lykaon was in a hurry. He couldn't afford to wait in the hope of getting a higher price for his female slaves in a few days' time, so he instructed Hippodamus to quickly negotiate the best deal he could, with a local trader.

The Wolf was hearing repeated rumours that a Sacred Band of Plataeans, with Cleon of Athens' blessing, had set sail in search of the stolen Marathon Shield. Everyone was talking about the venture and wondering where the treasured aspis could be. Realising that the episode at Atalante was not the work of the garrison on their normal patrol, and that Clytes of Eleusis could well be part of this venture, he decided it was too dangerous to waste any time, and immediately a fresh ship was hired to take him and his increasing band of followers, past the island of Cyprus to the port of Issus and the great landmass of Persia. From there, The Shield would be taken on the long journey overland to King Artaxerxes in Ecbatana, where the royal household stayed during the summer months. Amara and Anthousa, as well as some of the women taken from Phocis, were now expendable. In fact, they'd become a hindrance. There would be willing women enough, without having to worry about a blade being plunged into his back.

'Don't bother being choosy about who buys them!' he told Hippodamus, as he glowered in the direction of Amara. 'In fact the more questionable the individual is, the better I shall like it!'

He walked over to the frightened women, grouped together on the jetty and glared, menacingly at Amara. 'I will be thinking of you, my angel!' he said hatefully. 'We've had some enjoyable times together, have we not?' he gloated.

Amara, roped to the other women, struggled to strike out at him. 'My curses will follow you every day that I live - and beyond!' she cried out, bitterly.

'Your future life will become so wretched,' said Lykaon, laughing; his face menacingly close, 'that memories of our time together will seem sweet to you!'

Amara, her face twisted in disgust, spat into his face. 'They're coming after you, Lykaon!' she said, her eyes blazing with hatred. 'Think of that, when you try to sleep at nights! The Plataeans won't rest until they've killed you! That thought alone will make my life sweet!'

Lykaon slowly wiped the spittle from his face.

'And I'll be waiting!' he answered, coldly. 'Especially for - what did you call him? Imbros, was it? Yes, Imbros!' he emphasised cruelly, as his hand moved to touch the sword at his side, and he watched with satisfaction at the look of fear in Amara's eyes.

'Well, what are you waiting for?' he shouted at Hippodamus. 'Rid me of these bitches!'

Huddled together in the darkness, unable to see the other women imprisoned with them, Amara and Anthousa clung to one another for comfort. Thirty women, of all ages and from different ethnic groups, had all been bought by a single dealer from Syria. For three days and nights they were kept in a squalid, windowless room, beaten like animals if they protested, and barely fed. At all times during the day and night, buyers came to inspect the wares on sale, and one by one their group diminished, but unable to obtain the high price the trader wanted for Amara and also for Anthousa, they were still unsold when the day of the auction arrived.

Supervising the efficient running of these miserable transactions was Actullus, a Cretan, a hard businessman devoid of compassion. The women for sale, were split into groups of six, stripped of their clothing and pushed, naked onto the platform, to be ogled at by male, prospective buyers. Amara, tall and statuesque, now shorn of her beautiful long hair, stepped onto the platform as though a queen surveying her subjects. Seemingly undeterred, she fixed her unwavering gaze on a statue. The beautiful carving was of the goddess Artemis and she was holding her bow, ready for firing an arrow. Anthousa saw what Amara was looking at, and it gave her courage also. They stayed like this, unflinching, as they were poked and prodded, had their teeth inspected and all manner of humiliations inflicted, as Actullus called out to the eager bidders, their attributes and details of their known pedigree. Finally, they were led away by their new owner. Relief overwhelmed them. They were still together.

After the degrading experiences at the slave market, they were taken immediately to an ornately decorated ship lying in wait in the harbour. The two women were surprised that they had been purchased together and also that there were no other women bought with them. The tall Persian who had outbid all others at the auction, spoke little, but they were mercifully unmolested while on the sea journey which took them to the mainland of Asia Minor. Here, they were transferred to a mode of transport totally strange to them. Single humped, long legged animals with large lips and small ears. Closely watched by their exotic looking bodyguards, who were also on these superior looking animals, each of the women had their hands tied to the front pommel of an elaborately caparisoned wooden seat, and the camel train set off across a foreign land, all Amara's questions being totally ignored. To the women, their destination was unknown.

SEVENTY-TWO

PROGRESS ON THE DROMEDARIES was slow but not unduly uncomfortable for the women, as they were taken ever northwards, zig-zagging through the mountain passes of a land they'd previously only heard about in the strange and wondrous tales told by travelling storytellers. Amara thought of the personal effects she had once owned in Plataea, her mirror and comb especially - decorated with what she'd thought were scandalous images of women wearing loose fitting trousers. Here, she saw such women everywhere and she noticed also - they did not appear to need male escorts. Both men and women were dressed in elaborate flowing robes, consisting of several colourful layers, the outer garments adorned with more gold and silver than anything she could have imagined. Men wore more jewellery than the women. Amulets, armbands and signet rings were commonplace, and many had pierced ears to hold heavy gold rings.

The previous night they had stopped at a small village, and on the outskirts, their guards erected several small tents around an open fire. With a lot of grumbling, the dromedaries collapsed to their knees and lay down heavily beside them, while under the stars, a tasty meal of local goat meat and roasted vegetables was prepared, skewered onto long daggers and cooked over hot timbers. The women were becoming less and less nervous as time went on. Anthousa had overheard some of the men talking, and although it was in some form of Aramaic, one word was distinguishable. Plataea. The two women convinced themselves that this was promising. They'd been treated moderately well so far, and their hopes began to rise that someone from their home city had rescued them. They'd been constantly guarded throughout their journey, but they assumed that because of the lack of communication, this was for their own safety, in case they tried to escape. And so the journey passed without serious incident until they reached 'the city'.

Magnificent in its situation on the great acropolis, overlooking a vast fertile plain, it shone like gold in the evening sun, like a brilliant jewel within its glowing limestone walls. Sardis; the capital city of the Persian province of Lydia, governed on behalf of King Artaxerxes by his satrap, Pissuthnes. The same Pissuthnes whom Clytes had discovered was encouraging the city of Colophon to the west in Ionia, to revolt against its Athenian rulers. It was a city famed for its alluvial gold, the dust flowing through the city in a stream at the base of the acropolis. Their long dead king Croesus was thought to be, during his reign, the richest person in the world.

The party passed slowly through the bustling city overspill of workshops, noisy marketplaces and crowded corrals of camels and horses, until they entered through the immense gates of the walled lower city, where most of the people lived in a maze of mudbrick houses. Amara glanced at the tall Persian riding at her side, and noticed a slight smile cross his lips. As he slowly turned to look at her the smile became a cruel smirk and immediately she became alarmed. Glancing back at the receding gates, she felt the great walls close in about her.

They proceeded towards the citadel, finally arriving at another impressive fortification and gateway, and here the party dismounted. A steep busy thoroughfare with steps cut into the rock, wound upwards and as Amara and Anthousa were untied, it was evident from indications that they were meant to walk from here. Passing magnificent terraces on either side occupied by impressive civic buildings, private houses and gardens, they climbed up the side of the great acropolis, eventually stopping at the entrance of a high-walled residence guarded by a pair of opulently attired attendants. The Persian pushed Amara and Anthousa ahead of him, up through terraces of immaculately landscaped gardens leading to a shining white limestone villa. Peacocks strutted imperiously, displaying their brilliant plumage; screeching as the humans passed by. On the lawns in front of the villa, sat two black-skinned male servants. In their charge, exotic large cats with spotted golden fur. Expensive gold collars encircled the necks of both the men and the animals. One cat bared its teeth and snarled, making the women leap back in terror, but the chained leopards did not move; only stared at them coldly, with seeming disinterest.

They passed through a colourful portico tiled with lapis lazuli and white marble, where a fountain splashed pleasantly, and entered the interior of the building cooled by vast rose marble floors. In the large inner chamber, gossamer silk drapes moved gently in the warm breeze and the scent of intoxicating sweet incense, burning in ornate bronze burners suspended from the roof, wafted on the air. All was calm and serene, but the women felt uneasy and were on their guard.

'Mirhab!' called a voice, and a beautiful woman, extravagantly bedecked in gold jewelry of the most exquisite workmanship, glided into the room. A group of six female attendants, their heads bowed, hurried shuffling at her side.

'From Plataea, Mirhab?' she asked, harshly, and for the cruel benefit of the two frightened women, she asked him to reply in their own tongue.

'From Plataea!' confirmed Mirhab, triumphantly to Larachne. 'Bought at the Cretan auction, from a Syrian slave-trader. This one cost you the most,' said Mirhab, pulling Amara forward, roughly. 'She has some grace, by Athenian standards. This one was also more expensive than others you've acquired, but I knew you would approve!' he said, looking lasciviously at Anthousa.

Amara had been looking at the women in attendance and thought that one of them kept glancing up at her, as though trying to tell her something. She couldn't help but think that she recognised her from somewhere, and then in a shock, it came to her. It's my Ianthe! The girl, dressed from head to foot in Persian robes, was cowed, and obviously terrified. Glancing quickly at the others, Amara suddenly realised they had all served with the garrison at Plataea, and each one of them looked frightened. Amara, trembling, now understood why she and Anthousa were there. This was not the rescue she'd hoped for. Before she could speak out, Larachne, imperiously ordered Mirhab to take her and Anthousa to a man by the name of Cynares. Amara noticed the look of alarm which crossed Ianthe's face.

If Ianthe could have spoken, she would have warned them of the dire situation the women were now in. As it was, she'd risked the wrath of her mistress in just looking up from the ground without permission. Larachne, vengeful to the point of derangement since being forced to leave Thebes, took pleasure in buying any of the Plataean women who'd been dispersed after the end of the siege. It was Mirhab's job to seek out any that came to the Cretan market, and purchase them. Made to work in fearful conditions, either attending to Larachne's personal needs or on her large estate, it was a life of utter misery. Neither Amara nor Anthousa had any notion of who the woman was who now owned them, or of her connection with Lykaon, but they soon would.

As they were led away, Amara looked back and caught sight of Larachne, her embroidered emerald green robes floating about her, as leading her pet leopards she swept through her perfumed gardens of roses and oleander like a queen, her women trailing closely after her. A golden diadem set with precious stones, sparkled in the sun, and colours of the rainbow radiated in her lustrous black hair. Amara thought it resembled a vision from the ancient and sometimes disturbing stories told to her as a child.

She was just about to look away, when she heard raised voices and saw Ianthe being dragged away from the other women by the black male attendants. Terrified, the young woman looked frantically towards Amara and Anthousa for help, and started to run across the lawn. Horrified, the two women watched as the leopards were deliberately released by Larachne. Tearing across the grass they brought Ianthe down in one pounce. As her screams rent the air, Anthousa turned on Mirhab, violently lashing out at him to get away. Amara, able to free herself, ran towards the fallen woman. Before she got near, she halted in horror. Between them, the big cats had ferociously torn the body apart.

Larachne called out the names of her pet killers and the cats immediately stopped their feeding, returning to lie meekly at her feet. Ianthe's dismembered remains were quickly removed from the lawn while Amara and Anthousa, beaten by Mirhab with the flat of his curved sword, were forced from the villa.

'There is no escape,' said Mirhab, coldly, as the sobbing and shaking women were taken back through the city gates and led towards a village on the plain. 'If you try - or you displease your mistress in any way, you will bear the consequences, as you have just witnessed. My mistress's passion is for the hunt. She keeps many hounds for just that purpose, and they are in constant need of exercise!' he added, menacingly.

SEVENTY-THREE

'THERE'S NOT A HORSE in all Persia that could hold your weight, Glaucus!' spoke Theomenes, with some frustration, looking seriously at Flamebeard, seated frowning at the stern of the Delias. 'And we will need to ride fast if what Clytes believes is true - that The Shield is most likely on its way to the Persian king!'

'I'm sure of it!' shouted Clytes from the central mast, as he helped other crew members struggling against the prevailing wind, to control the large sail. 'Where else would he feel safe, now all Hellas knows of its theft. The Persian king will pay him handsomely for the shield that defeated his grandfather, the great Darius. Plataea must be etched into his soul! Remember, the battle at Plataea defeated his father also. Xerxes, King of Kings. The Wolf will be making his way to Persia, believe me!'

'I did not sign up to be left behind, nursemaiding half a crew, while the rest of you have all the fun,' growled Glaucus. 'You'll need my strength. I'm like two men!'

'Exactly!' spoke up Stephanos. 'That's why you can't come!'

One week after the episode at Atalante, at the end of Spring, they disembarked on the shores of Anatolia.

After losing sight of Lykaon's fleeing penteconter, the band now put their faith in Clytes' belief that The Wolf was on his way to Persia, and after pouring over maps, a plan was finally agreed. The group chosen to go overland would use The Royal Road when they could, which led from the Aegean Sea to the Persian city of Susa; one of the main administrative cities of the king's vast empire. Already an ancient route of over 1,500 miles; extended and improved by Persian kings for fast communication and trade, the road was a well organised means of traversing a huge territory. Fresh horses would be bought or hired at the various staging posts along the route, which hopefully would give them an advantage; if Lykaon was travelling with what they suspected - a small army. How they would recover their precious relic before it reached the king, was a matter too early to be discussed.

'Glaucus,' said Theomenes, persuasively, when The Five were out of ear-shot of the Athenian crew. 'If we do recover The Shield, we shall need a safe place to take it. We have to decide where that place will be. We won't be able to entrust it to anyone but our sworn band. Zeus, we've not just Lykaon to worry about! Cleon is obviously intent on having the trophy taken to Athens for his own purposes. Why else would he release his rowers for the quest? He'll stop at nothing to acquire it, and I can't let that happen. Not after they failed to save Plataea!'

Theomenes looked directly at the Thessalian. 'I need you to tell us which port we must head for, Glaucus, and for you to arrange it, so that you and the Delias will be there to pick us up! I can't entrust this to anyone else, Helmsman. It could be vital to the success of the mission, that we have a sound ship, equipped with a trusted crew, ready to leave immediately with any survivors. The gods willing, with The Shield!'

'And Amara!' spoke up Imbros.

'I haven't forgotten Amara,' said Theomenes, sincerely.

Believing that if they were successful, it would be unwise to return the same way, the group decided on a northern escape route, and Glaucus knew just the place to pick them up. Inhabited almost entirely by Hellenic tribes for many generations, Pontus, on the Black Sea.

'Just give me time to get there!' boomed Glaucus.

'Oh, we'll have this done before you've reached the Hellespont!' laughed Clytes.

'Give us five full moons from now, Glaucus,' said Theomenes, seriously. 'If you've not had any word of us by then, do whatever you wish with the Delias, but leave Anatolia before the bad weather hinders your journey back to Athens. We will be making many sacrifices to the gods to ensure safe passage for us all!'

It was another parting for the friends. 'See you get there, 'big man',' said Clytes. 'I want to see you and the 'old maid' waiting for us, when we arrive at Pontus.'

'I'll be there, landsman,' replied Glaucus, slapping him on the back. 'Just make sure you bloody well are!' and adding a curse, said, 'I hope you get the swine.'

They made sacrifices and the omens were good, which made the parting easier.

The group travelling overland consisted of twenty horsemen. Theomenes was accompanied by Mydon; Stephanos with his cousin Echus; Imbros with Telios, the son of a Plataean who had served him well in his workshops, and Clytes was supported by Angelos. Backed up by twelve hardened Plataeans, who'd escaped the siege with Stephanos and Imbros. All free men. Chosen for their loyalty and dedication to the cause. Mydon and Telios had been given their freedom and asked to swear the oath, just as their masters had done. There were some misgivings expressed by Stephanos as to Mydon's suitability for the arduous job ahead, but Theomenes was adamant that Mydon's disability would not be a hindrance, and as he was funding the venture, there were no more arguments.

Cassa, Bion and the deckhands went with Glaucus, together with the eighteen seasoned Athenian rowers on loan from Cleon. Theomenes had left his helmsman with sufficient funds to replenish or even replace the entire crew if he thought their loyalties were suspect. The Plataeans were determined. The Shield, if recovered, was not going to be taken to Athens.

'And have the Delias completely refitted Glaucus, before your journey to the Black Sea,' said Theomenes, as they were getting ready to depart. 'She'll need to be in excellent shape for the task ahead!'

SEVENTY-FOUR

'THINK GOOD THOUGHTS! SPEAK good words! Do good deeds!' spoke the priest, loudly to his small congregation as they sat around a fire burning fiercely in a large iron brazier. 'Do what is right and true!' the Zoroastrian continued. He was disturbed when a group of determined looking horsemen, urging their mounts up the rise towards them, called out for assistance. The priest halted his sermon and asked the men in a gentle manner, what they wanted.

Hippodamus, pushing his horse forward from the sweating group, speaking in broken Aramaic, asked, 'Where are we, priest? What is this place?'

'You are nearing Mari in West-of-the-River province, replied the preacher.

'We've been in West-of-the-River province for weeks,' remarked Hippodamus to Lykaon. 'When will we get east of the river?' he asked, in frustration.

'Which direction for the land of the Armenians?' shouted Lykaon, who had some understanding of the language.

'You have two great rivers to cross before you reach their mountains!' shouted a man seated in the congregation. 'The first river, the Euphrates, is not far from here.'

'At last!' exclaimed Lykaon. 'Can anyone point us the way, and find us a ford where we can cross?' he asked impatiently. 'We're in a hurry.'

'I can, gladly!' called out a young lad brightly, and he was hoisted up quickly to sit behind one of the riders.

'May you find the path to true happiness!' shouted the priest after them, as he watched the grim faced travellers and their intimidating entourage, mercifully, move on.

'Oh we will, old man!' shouted Lykaon, laughing harshly, and he spurred his horse down the other side of the hill, onwards towards the great Euphrates.

They soon reached the wide river and immediately checked with their spears as to the depth. They did not touch the bottom. 'It's flowing too fast for the camels, sire, especially with the loads they are carrying,' said Hippodamus. 'It's just as we were informed. We need a local guide to show us where to ford.'

'And that's exactly what we have here!' said Lykaon, smiling at the young lad. 'You know where the ford is, don't you?'

'I do, lord!' he replied, proudly. 'The Euphrates is low this year but you would still never find it without help. We need to travel north,' he said pointing. 'For about a mile.' At the crossing point, they couldn't see anything which indicated it was safe to enter the water, except when they dipped their spears into the current this time, they hit solid ground. Hippodamus looked at the myriad sailing boats navigating the wide blue river. 'They're too small for our purposes,' remarked Lykaon, dismissively. 'We can't risk splitting our force!' The youth walked confidently into the water, beckoning to the men to follow him closely. The water only reached to his chest, but the current was strong and he needed the use of the soldiers' javelins to hold him upright. Roped together in small groups, he eventually led the entire contingent safely to the eastern bank, without any losses.

'The most direct route to Armenia is that way,' he said, indicating a line of low hills to the north. 'Do you still want me to guide you? I can direct you to a route suitable for the animals,' he added, enthusiastically.

'You've done your work,' said Lykaon impatiently, and then indicating to one of the soldiers, said, 'Get on with it! Leave no marks. Make it look like a drowning.'

As the armed men approached him, the boy sensed danger and started to run, but he was too slow. Hippodamus grabbed him and with the help of another, held the boy under the water until he stopped struggling. His body was then thrown out into the river to be carried away by the powerful waters. The horsemen, turning away from the hills pointed out by their young guide, headed in another direction, following the river bank of the Euphrates; as for some miles, the great watercourse flowed east.

'Do you think the Plataeans can be following us, sire?' Hippodamus asked Lykaon, as the troupe guided their horses through the green landscape of Mesopotamia, watered by the two great waterways of the Euphrates and the Tigris. 'We've been laying a false trail since we left the coast!'

'With all the sacrifices we've made to the gods, they should be going around in circles by now!' replied Lykaon, in exasperation. 'We continue as we have done. We leave no-one alive who could report our actual route - not until we've safely reached Ecbatana and the king.'

The followers of Lykaon were driven on by promises of plunder and power. Besides Hippodamus and his mounted Thebans, his force included twelve highly skilled archers hired on the island of Crete. There were also an equal number of slingers, the best in the region, taken on at Rhodes, and thirty lightly armed peltasts who'd joined them along the route. Together with six camel handlers, who also took care of the horses, and the cooks and attendants who cared for them all, their group now amounted to more than a hundred, and was increasing almost daily.

The horses became excitable as their nostrils were filled by the smell of sweet grass growing along the water's edge, and to stop them eating too much too quickly, the riders pushed them onwards, before the sun rose high. In single file they trotted along the bank of the Euphrates, the forgotten body of their young guide floating unseen, as it was carried on the flowing current alongside them.

The baggage animals at the rear; dromedaries purchased for the purpose, carried on their backs, spare armaments, tents, bedding and food, also metalware which was scarce in these parts, to trade along the route. Safely guarded in the centre of the line was a strong mule bearing The Shield, the means by which their fortunes would be assured somewhere in this vast, rich kingdom, which stretched they were told, to the ends of the world.

When they turned a bend, their progress halted abruptly. Smoke from village fires could be seen directly ahead of them. Being in similar situations many times before on their long journey, the men cautiously looked around for any signs of attack. They were vulnerable with their line strung out against the water's edge. The irrigation canals cut deeply into the landscape could be hiding a hundred attackers. Lykaon ordered some of his mounted Thebans to go back and protect the rear, then moved ahead slowly, keeping their weapons hidden but within reach. As they drew closer to the riverside village, children ran alongside them, shouting excitedly. Lykaon bent down from his horse and pulled up a young boy, to sit in front of him. Hippodamus did likewise. The other children ran on quickly ahead of them, and by the time the troupe reached the unwalled township, the inhabitants had armed themselves and were blocking their path.

'Let me do the talking!' shouted Lykaon. 'We don't want any trouble, so no show of arms!' He walked his horse confidently over to the one who seemed to be the head man, all the while his arm encircling the young child.

'We mean no harm to you or your village!' spoke Lykaon in a strong voice. 'Babylon!' he said, by way of explanation. 'We are heading for Babylon!' he lied. The head man spoke animatedly to the men gathered around him, and there appeared to be some agreement among them as heads nodded and relief was seen on their faces. The elder came forward and held up his arms to retrieve the boy seated with Lykaon, but the Theban joked with the child and encouraged him to remain where he was.

'We want no trouble,' Lykaon reiterated and the head man, looking concerned, backed away. 'Allow us free passage through your village and we will deposit the children unharmed as soon as we are out of range of your arrows.'

'We agree,' spoke the head man, gruffly, after a second of deliberation. 'You give us no choice!'

Warily, the line of camels, horses, men and women moved through the main street of the village of clay-brick houses, all the while being watched by the tense and cautious inhabitants. At any moment the group expected to be attacked, and their hands were never far from their weapons. Once they were well clear of the village, and Lykaon was sure they'd not been followed, he halted the column.

'What's to happen with the children?' asked Hippodamus.

'Children are not to my taste!' said Lykaon, as he dropped the small boy to the ground. 'Let them go. We don't want to give any reason for the townspeople to attack us. They could send for reinforcements. Our progress is getting slower and slower, the more people who join us.'

'We need the strength of numbers to protect the treasure, but at the same time, they are holding us back,' remarked Hippodamus.

'Once we've crossed the Tigris, we can breathe more easily,' said Lykaon, decidedly. 'We'll be in the king's own territory. We can travel faster by going ahead with just the horses. The others can arrive later.'

The following night they were encamped near a natural spring, ready to press on the next day towards the river Tigris, and as soon as the cooking fires were dampened the usual guards were posted. At some time during the early hours, the camels suddenly got to their feet, grumbling noisily, their small ears on the alert. The tethered horses also started to move about, whinnying nervously. Before the guards could warn the camp, shouts could be heard all around them, as armed men rushed towards the tented enclosure. They were surrounded.

'You are in the territory of Lord Khorvash!' shouted their captain. 'In his glorious name, I command you to put down your weapons!'

Lykaon emerged from his tent, hastily covering himself in a cloak, as he pushed in front of him, shielding him, a terrified young woman. He screamed out at Hippodamus who was already hurrying towards him. 'Didn't I tell you those idiots would bring trouble upon us!' he yelled, as he pushed the girl roughly aside. The heads of the' idiots' referred to, were stuck on javelin spikes near his tent - as a warning to others. Returning to the river village to do a little looting, two of Lykaon's peltasts had stayed on to rape a woman and her daughter. Not satisfied with that, when they were challenged by the menfolk, they'd turned on them, killing at least one of their pursuers. Normally these events would not have been condemned so harshly by The Wolf, but his express orders not to cause trouble which could bring undue attention before they'd reached the king, had been ignored, and that he would not tolerate.

'Is it concealed?' asked Hippodamus, in an urgent whisper.

'They won't find it,' answered Lykaon, quickly, his voice low.

The Persian captain quickly ascertained who was in charge. Leaving his troops to guard the camp, he took Lykaon, Hippodamus and the other Thebans away with him as prisoners.

SEVENTY-FIVE

FOR KHORVASH, 'THE SHINING ONE', Governor of Babylonia, life was good and he intended it should remain so. Distantly related to King Artaxerxes, he was one of that select group permitted to wear the royal purple and a narrow blue and white sash around his head, which represented the heavenly power bestowed upon the king. Dressed as brilliantly as any peacock in his elaborate headgear adorned with jewels, and a sumptuously embroidered long blue coat which was worn over layers of richly coloured silk robes, he sat being preened and fussed over by his female attendants. Around his neck the women carefully placed a heavy gold chain from which hung a bejeweled winged griffin of solid gold. Young girls fitted blood red, golden threaded slippers on his feet, while others tended to his curled and perfumed long black hair and beard. Many were his daughters, but he had so many he could not remember their names or even which of his many wives or concubines had given birth to them.

Seated on a gilded chair, elaborately carved with lions and eagles, he gazed lazily down the avenue of evenly planted trees to a rectangular, sparkling goldfish pond; his favourite part of the palace gardens. Just one of several such magnificent gardens situated within his many fortified residences. He casually picked up a hand mirror from a side table on which were silver bowls filled with dried fruits and nuts, and inspected himself carefully. Satisfied, he clapped his hands. 'Leave me!' he said, waving the women away, his many rings flashing in the sunlight. 'Bring them in!' he called to his guards.

Bloodied and angry, Lykaon and his bound fellow Thebans were pushed, staggering, into his presence. Their arms were tied painfully to slats of wood placed behind their backs which made it difficult for them to stand upright.

Lykaon glanced with dismay at the Persian noble, seated above him on the marble dais. Thirty-one years old, handsome, rich and powerful, this astute Persian's attention was precisely what he had wanted to avoid.

'Who are you and what are you doing in my province!' demanded Khorvash.

'I am Lykaon, son of Pelonus of Thebes! This is Hippodamus, my second-in-command together with other fellow Thebans, also under my command!' replied Lykaon hotly. We are on our way to your king Artaxerxes to offer him our services.'

'There is a war in your country, Lykaon of Thebes,' said Khorvash, coldly. 'Why are you offering your services to our king?'

'I am no longer welcome in my own country,' replied Lykaon, trying to look the Persian directly in the eyes.

'We are receiving many of you Hellenes seeking their fortunes in our lands, having fallen foul of their Hellene masters,' said Khorvash, fingering his beard, thoughtfully. 'Your sense of loyalty is weak. How can our king trust your supposed loyalty to him?'

'That can only be proven over time,' answered Lykaon, carefully. 'I have brought with me some of the best cavalry, archers, slingers and peltasts at my own expense, to be put at his disposal. With these men, and the others who will surely follow, I will prove myself more than useful.'

'And what do you expect in return, Theban?' asked Khorvash, suspiciously.

'Only what the great king thinks I am worthy of,' said Lykaon. 'Opportunities to improve my prospects lie in his hands only.'

'Not necessarily,' said the Persian noble, suddenly rising. 'Remove his bonds!' he ordered. 'Bring him out to the garden.'

'I will speak plainly,' said the Persian, once he and Lykaon were some distance from the guards and hovering attendants. 'I have an enterprise in mind which I think you and your men could help me with.'

He moved onwards, following a geometric pattern of walkways, towards a high wall built of clay beehives. For several moments he stood watching the constant coming and going of the bees, seemingly impervious to the threatening sounds coming from within. As their voices were obscured by the continuous droning sound of the honey makers, Khorvash continued. 'Spies are everywhere!' he said, with emphasis, looking back towards the palace. 'As you can see, I trust no-one. That is how I have kept my power!'

'I have already sent a messenger on the Royal Road to Artaxerxes, informing him of our progress,' lied Lykaon, trying to keep control of his situation and feeling decidedly uncomfortable as the bees settled on his skin. He wanted desperately to rub his numbed arms but the drone from the thousands of bees unnerved him. It seemed to have no effect on the Persian, he noticed. 'If we are hindered in any way, the king will be displeased!' he continued, boldly.

'And how will you get to the king?' asked Khorvash, shrewdly. 'Do you have ships to cross the Tigris? The spring thaw has melted the mountain snows. The fords will now be impassable.'

Lykaon realised angrily that Khorvash was right. He was trapped. The longer it took to reach the king, the more chances there would be for the coveted prize to be discovered. Khorvash, or someone like him would be only too happy to relieve him of the treasure and accept the gratitude of the king. 'I will consider your proposition,' he replied, diplomatically. 'What is it you have in mind?'

'My half-brother, Varakasa, is stirring up trouble in the north of my province. He is gathering men to come against me, so my spies inform me. If there is one thing I cannot tolerate, Theban, it is ingratitude. Anyone who crosses me, can expect no mercy! The sooner the deceitful, ungrateful wretch is dealt with the better! I would like to make a surprise attack before he has had time to increase his force. You and your men would be well rewarded for services rendered. Once I have his head, I will personally arrange for ships to take you and your men across the Tigris. What do you say, Lykaon of Thebes?'

Knowing he had little choice but to accept the Persian's offer, and eager to move away from the bees, Lykaon replied quickly, 'Let's get to it! My men will welcome a little action, in return for some plunder!'

'The city of Assur will be reduced to rubble, and anyone supporting Varakasa there, will be destroyed!' Khorvash muttered, almost to himself. 'Plunder? You may have all you can carry, Theban, if you help rid me of the traitor!' he added sharply.

As they returned through the gardens, Lykaon noticed a group of men in chains, being dragged towards the beehives.

SEVENTY-SIX

'WELL, I'M GOING WITH Beranus!' Imbros said finally, after a fruitless argument with the others. 'I'll take Telios with me.'

'How many false leads have you followed now, Imbros?' asked Stephanos, tossing the dregs of his cup into the fire. 'Who is this Beranus? He appears out of nowhere, with dubious information, and you're falling for it - again!'

'I have to trust him,' muttered Imbros, seriously. 'How else could he have got this?' and he looked tenderly at the lock of curled dark hair, lying in the palm of his hand.

Clytes shook his head, sadly. 'What proof have you that this was taken from your wife, Imbros? It could be anybody's, man!'

'It's hers!' replied Imbros fiercely, standing away from the fire and buckling on his sword. 'Even if it's not and this news again proves to be false, I must find out. His eyes challenged them all. 'I will find her!'

'Well, you're not going without me, damn it!' spoke up Theomenes. 'Her husband you may be Imbros, but Amara has been dear to me for more years than you've known her.'

'We will give you and Theo until midday,' said Stephanos, exchanging angry glances with a silent Clytes. 'If we're going to make it to the river before nightfall, we cannot wait any longer!'

A silent Beranus led the way on foot, closely followed on horseback by Theomenes and Mydon, and an impatient Imbros accompanied by Telios. All were lightly protected by their leather cuirasses, and for weapons, Imbros and Theo had armed themselves with sword, dagger and hoplon; Mydon and Telios, with bows and arrows. When they arrived at a poor village, women came out of their doorways to watch silently as the riders moved down the main street.

'Have you noticed anything?' remarked Imbros quietly.

'The lack of men?' Theomenes suggested warily, unnerved by the foreboding silence. 'Probably away hunting.' But what was there to hunt, he thought? He hadn't seen anything except a few lizards since they'd started out. Near the end of the village, Beranus beckoned frantically with flailing arms for them to stop, and once dismounted, he ushered them fussily through the open door of a dilapidated small building. The interior was gloomy after the brightness outside and they struggled to adjust to the change. It seemed that only two others occupied the room. A burly man, seemingly unarmed, and a slim veiled figure, lying stretched out on a narrow bed.

At their camp, Clytes and Stephanos quickly gathered their weapons, and together with some of their comrades, lightly armed with bows and arrows, mounted their horses and set off after Theomenes and Imbros. Whilst they all felt his pain, the intensity with which Imbros greeted any glimmer of hope - no matter how unlikely - had caused several wasted days on their journey so far, and Stephanos had found it difficult to hold his tongue, especially when Theomenes all too readily took Imbros's side. Stephanos felt their lives were being put at risk, unnecessarily, and he suspected something was amiss with this character, Beranus. If the Persian was genuine or merely mistaken, then his apprehensions were unfounded, but when Clytes also voiced his concerns, that was enough for him to take action.

The well-built man beside the bed, stepped forward. 'Money!' he demanded in a harsh voice.

'Not so fast, friend,' Imbros answered, shaking his head. First the proof, then you'll be paid in full,' and he pointed at the prostrate form, indicating that he wanted the veil lifted. When there was no movement, Imbros started forward, but Theomenes gripped the anxious sculptor by the arm. 'Let me look, Imbros,' he said firmly, fearing the worst on seeing no movement from the body on the bed, and he moved quickly into the shadows, ripping the veil aside.

'Is it Amara?' asked Imbros, desperately.

'If it is, she's grown a beard!' shouted Theomenes, as the man on the bed leapt up. 'It's a trap, Imbros!' Theomenes drew his dagger swiftly and its point found the fat man's exposed throat. Blood spurted like a fountain. The veiled figure fled out into the street, calling for help.

With a cry, Beranus blocked the exit and drawing a curved knife from beneath his long cloak, lunged towards Imbros who, nimbly stepping aside, thrust his sword into his attacker's belly. 'That's for wasting my time!' he yelled, frustratedly. Outside the hut, Mydon and Telios could be heard calling to them to get out quickly. With their shouts of anger permeating the air, hiding villagers now emerged from their houses, running down the street towards them, clearly bent upon their destruction. Imbros's sword quickly found another victim and the attacker crumpled, while the shield of Theomenes smashed with a sickening thud against an unprotected skull, as the four men fought their way through the throng. For some moments the melee continued fiercely as their weapons struck again and again, but when a fresh group of angry villagers appeared at the top of the village, bearing cudgels and carrying rocks, it seemed that they were trapped.

Then, galloping towards the village were seen the Plataean horsemen. Summing up the situation, they drove their horses straight into the group at the top of the village, mowing down some of the men and scattering the others. With arrows drawn, ready for firing, they plowed on down the village street. Stephanos, sword in hand, charged towards Imbros and Theomenes. Clytes, his blade held high, galloped whooping and yelling, through the crowd of now terrified villagers. Mydon and Telios quickly brought the horses, and while their comrades continued to cause havoc, managed to rescue Theomenes and Imbros from the clutches of their attackers. Rocks flew dangerously close. One struck Imbros savagely on the side of the head. Although he was wearing his helmet, blood poured down his face and he slumped forward across his horse's neck, appearing unconscious. Telios pushed his horse forward and grabbed the reins of Imbros's horse, and together with the rest of the Plataeans, took off after Theomenes and Mydon.

'No Amara?' shouted Clytes to Theomenes as they galloped across the barren terrain.

'No Amara,' echoed Theomenes, dejectedly. 'You were right.'

'I really did hope I wasn't,' said Clytes, sympathetically, when they halted their horses to check on Imbros. 'But all these false leads are wasting our time, Theo. Find The Wolf! That's where you'll find Amara.'

'You would say that!' said Theomenes, turning on him angrily. 'You've insisted on following every unreliable lead on Lykaon for weeks now, wasting time. You went missing for ten days, believing that story about a band of Thebans taking the road north into Armenia. So much for your promised loyalty! We thought you weren't coming back!'

'But I did come back! And so much for bloody gratitude!' responded Clytes, looking incredulously at Stephanos.

But, Stephanos was more frustrated than either of them, and as soon as the party had returned to their camp, he could hold his peace no longer. He drew Theomenes to one side, out of earshot of the others. 'Not for the first time, Theo, you have put the lives of our men at risk!' he muttered, furiously. 'And not in order to recover The Shield, which is why we're all on this quest! I know this was your idea, and it's your money funding the venture, but if things don't change - I'll not be held responsible for any loss of lives.'

Theo tried to interrupt, but Stephanos wasn't finished. 'Imbros has been injured. Others could have been killed. And for what? This is not your own private mission, Theo!'

Theomenes stressed how much he valued the strength and experience of his fellow Plataean, and admitted to his own inexperience. 'What do you think we should do now?' he asked, suitably chastened.

'We should stop running around like headless chickens, Theo. The men are getting disheartened at the lack of any realistic information regarding Lykaon. Imbros needs rest. We should use the time to review our situation, and plan carefully our next move.'

With a renewed and mutual understanding as to how the quest should now proceed, they set about finding help for Imbros.

SEVENTY-SEVEN

SITUATED BY THE RELAY-STATION, the people of the village were used to strangers, and they helped to carry Imbros still unconscious to a local house, where female help was available. Theomenes carefully removed his friend's helmet as soon as they laid him on the bed, and mercifully found no skull damage, but there was dried blood from his left ear.

'Imbros! Can you hear me?' asked Theomenes, anxiously. There was no response. 'We need a physician,' he said, looking around the room at the other anxious faces. 'We'll also need an interpreter.' When a translator was found by Mydon, and he was told that money was no object, they were informed that the best doctor in the area could be found in Assur, a nearby city on the Tigris. The following morning, when there were still no signs of improvement, Imbros was gently placed in a cart, and the entire party headed for Assur.

Once the pride of the Assyrians, but brought to ruins by their Persian overlords, Assur still preserved the remains of her greatness. The remnants of her once gigantic walls and temples could still be seen, as was the ziggurat, the man-made mountain home of their god Marduk, reaching to the sky. Entering through the west gate, their interpreter and guide quickly found temporary accommodation for Imbros and his closest companions, while the rest were taken to a hostelry with stabling facilities for the horses.

'It is advisable to make yourself known to the local governor, Varakasa, as quickly as possible,' urged their guide. 'There is unrest in the territory. He will want to know your business and reasons for travel.'

After making enquiries, it was discovered that the notable physician recommended by the interpreter, was at the old palace, where the governor and his family were in residence. Theomenes and Stephanos hurried with their guide to announce their presence and also to request the urgent services of the doctor.

Varakasa, half-brother to Khorvash, the overlord of Babylonia, lived in modest circumstances compared with his powerful relative in the south. Residing in just a small rebuilt part of the once enormous palace of the mighty kings of Assyria, he carried out his brother's increasingly harsh orders with growing reluctance. Varakasa was aware of the rumours that the king, Artaxerxes, was not a well man and therefore not surprised when his messages, warning of unrest, went unanswered. Just so long as Khorvash paid the required tribute in silver and young eunuchs, the king left his satrap to manage his own affairs. Constantly petitioned by a fearful, desperate populace, both rich and poor, the sub-governor at Assur was awake to the fact that the removal of Khorvash and his brutal regime was crucial, before peace could come to the region.

Once he was made aware of the group of Hellenes making their way through his territory, he was immediately interested. Having visited Athens in the glorious days of Pericles, he had an abiding appreciation of her art and poetry. The company of these travellers would, he hoped, be a welcome distraction. Imbros was immediately brought to his household and the family physician directed to give him a full examination. In his opinion the blood in the ear was local and not from the brain. The nursing women were instructed to raise his head with pillows and to keep the forehead cool with light compresses, and all the while they were to talk to him, as though he could hear them. Immediately Imbros stirred as though understanding what was happening, but he did not regain full consciousness.

He was, instead, at that moment, enjoying the Daedala festival at Plataea, with his wife, Amara. They were part of the lively crowds walking to the sacred oak groves to choose the tree for the festival. Dressed in their finest clothes, Amara looked so beautiful and so happy. Cooked meats were thrown up into the branches of the young oaks, and they waited for the crows to choose the tree which would be chopped down to become the wooden effigy used in the celebrations. The ancient festival related to the estrangement of the god Zeus from his wife, Hera. In an effort to bring her back to him, Zeus arranged a mock marriage to Plataia, daughter of the river god Asopus. When Hera heard the news, in a fit of jealousy she flew to Plataea to confront her husband, but when she tore away the veil from the bride, she realised it was just a wooden carving. Seeing it had all been a trick, she was amused and quickly became reconciled with Zeus.

The bullock-drawn cart, accompanied by cheering Plataeans, was taking its beautiful 'bride' to be bathed in the Asopus, and the people ran alongside, eager to be there for the ceremony. Suddenly Imbros could not find Amara. His heart beat faster as he searched for her in the crowds. He heard her urgently call out his name, and when he looked towards the sound he saw her on the bullock cart, dressed as the bride. Her arms were stretched out towards him as the cart sped towards the river. 'Imbros!'

He woke with a start to find strangers sitting by the side of his bed. 'She's alive!' was all he murmured, before dropping back into a restful sleep.

While he recovered, he was surprised to find he was in the household of an admirer of Phidias, the talented sculptor of Athens, and when Varakasa learned that Imbros had been a pupil of the great man, he was shown all there was to be seen in the city of architectural or artistic merit. Clytes also was encouraged to do recitations and act out scenes from plays, remembered by Varakasa during his visit to the land of the Hellenes, and a pleasant interlude was spent in the city by the Tigris. As before throughout their journey, with no mention of The Marathon Shield, Theomenes and his comrades were able to convince their host that they were on a mission of honour to apprehend a murderer, thief and wife kidnapper, and had no other intentions while travelling through the state. Varakasa, as had others they'd encountered, was astonished at their determination, but he said he also admired their unity, and agreed, without demanding tribute or hostages, to allow them to continue their quest.

This respite was soon interrupted, however, when messengers arrived telling of a large army being assembled by Khorvash. Its purpose; the death of his brother, his family and all his followers. What Khorvash underestimated however, was just how many followers his half-brother had, or rather the vast number of enemies his own cruelty and greed had created. Over the following days, upon hearing of the threat from the south, gallopers were sent across the land to a number of tribes Varakasa hoped would come to his aid. Consequently, the population of Assur very quickly grew in size as the warriors arrived - intent on finally dealing with the tyrant, Khorvash.

At a hastily called War Council, to which a surprised and flattered Stephanos was invited to attend, Varakasa discussed with the various commanders and their interpreters, his proposed strategy. To the Plataean's dismay, rebuilding the immense city walls and blockading the city, was thought by many to be their only option. An all-out, face-to-face confrontation against Khorvash, was thought by the council, too hazardous.

For obvious reasons, Stephanos, recalling Plataea and the horrors of undergoing a drawn-out siege, argued forcefully against such a proposal, pointing out the brutal conclusions of them all stagnating within the confines of Assur. Instead he encouraged Varakasa and the generals to put their faith in the number of men arriving daily; and when they'd gathered sufficient strength; to march out boldly and fight their battle in the open.

SEVENTY-EIGHT

FROM THE SOUTH, A dust cloud which stretched along the horizon moved slowly across the dry plain towards them, but this was no approaching storm. It was the army of Khorvash.

Two weeks previously, Varakasa's men had apprehended a group of scouts, sent out from the camp of Khorvash, and under extreme torture they'd divulged that their army was gathering, preparing for an attack on Assur. The Hellenes had been asked if they wanted to watch as the men were broken, but they'd all declined. Imbros was disappointed to learn that a man so well-versed as Varakasa; a man with such an appreciation for the arts, could stand by and watch men being deliberately burned and mutilated. 'If he is the moderate brother, what's the other one like?' Clytes had ventured, sardonically. But there was one piece of information brutally extracted, before the men finally expired, that interested them greatly. It was Theomenes who brought the news.

'A band of Theban horsemen has recently joined Khorvash's cavalry!' he told his comrades, barely able to contain his elation.

'Let it be him!' prayed Clytes fervently, as he looked towards the gods in their heavenly realm.

'We've found the scum at last!' said Imbros, relieved.

' Well, not before time!' exclaimed a frustrated Stephanos. 'We've been following too many false trails on this quest of ours,' he added, glancing at Imbros and Clytes in turn. 'Just two more full moons, and Glaucus will leave these shores for Athens!'

'But what's he up to?' asked Theomenes, anxiously. 'If Lykaon is in this bunch of Thebans, does he still have The Shield, or does Khorvash now have it? I fear our Theban has thrown in his lot with this local satrap.'

'Yes, if this is him, why isn't he taking his prize to Artaxerxes?' asked Stephanos. 'This goes against your theory, Clytes, that his destination was the king.'

Looking around at his men, Theomenes spoke again. 'We're not here to lose our lives in some local war. Don't take any risks. If it is Lykaon, we need to find him, and we need him alive; until he has told us what we need to know.'

'Do not kill him, Clytes, even if the opportunity arises!' ordered Stephanos.

'If it is him,' murmured Imbros with deliberation. 'I'll get the truth from him!'

From their differences in clothing and armaments, it was evident that warriors were arriving from many regions to join with Varakasa, all ready to seize this opportunity to avenge their years of tyranny. Rumours of vast prisons beneath Khorvash's many palaces, could be holding the hundreds of prisoners who'd been taken from their various lands as hostages; held in order to subjugate his unhappy subjects. They were eager to have the tyrant's underground realms of horror opened up.

From the walls of the city, Stephanos watched out over the growing encampment. With its myriad tents and colourful pavilions, another city had sprung up outside Assur's walls, and as the sun went down and campfires were lit, they began to resemble a host of stars flickering into life, mirroring the skies above. On the air, he heard melodic sounds of pipes and rhythmic drumming. They are in a jubilant mood, thought Stephanos. He smiled grimly, thinking of Clytes, and how he hadn't seen him so buoyant in months. But tomorrow? After all the false trails and disappointments, were they really this close? He wrapped his cloak about him and headed towards his quarters and sleep. They would be on the move at daybreak. The musicians would play on throughout the night.

A strong wind came with the dawn, making their myriad, waving banners flap and crack as to the sound of drums, with the great Tigris on their left, ranks of determined men marched south, urged on by shouts from the charioteers and the wild ululating cries of the camel riders on their flanks. Even though they covered their faces, blown dust found a way into their eyes and mouths, making vision and speech difficult, and the journey wasn't made any easier by the constant riding up and down the line, of the high-spirited Scythian cavalry, showing off their acrobatic riding skills.

Imbros, fully recovered, shouted to Clytes that it reminded him of herdsmen hurrying on a flock of goats.

Briefly removing his dust-covered mask, Clytes shouted back, 'Hopefully, not to their slaughter, Imbros!'

Some of the commanders began to grumble and raised doubts about leaving the protection of the city, but Stephanos riding with them at the front of the column, was adamant. 'Had you remained sat on your backsides in Assur, the consequence would have been inevitable! A slow death by starvation, or a surrender ending in drawn-out torture. Believe me, I've been there! Where's the glory in that?'

Two weeks after leaving Assur, at a barely discernible incline in the landscape, close to the deteriorating riverside fortress of Tikrit, Varakasa halted his army and, under his waving banner, declared decisively that this was where they would make their stand.

Not since King Xerxes and his formidable army had marched by, half-a-century earlier - on its way to be defeated by the Hellenes at Plataea - had the fortress witnessed such a force of arms.

Satrap Khorvash, moving his force unhurriedly north, was surprised but not unduly perturbed on seeing the line of fluttering, colourful pennants in the distance. It came as a tedious change of plan to see that his half-brother had mustered something resembling an army and was prepared to do battle against him, but he anticipated making short work of this leaderless rabble. His previous plan had been simple enough. To entrap his brother at Assur. Instead, he rather relished bringing him down on this exposed plain, where the open arena would best show off the skills of his charioteers. He'd expected his disloyal relative to be in chains within the month. Now it would only be a few hours!

On a flat stretch of ground between rock-strewn high banks, close to the once important stronghold, he set up his standard and assembled his impressive force. He considered the site to be to his advantage, as the steep terrain on either side would make it difficult for his traitorous brother to outflank him.

There was no parley or exchange of any kind. Khorvash confidently set out his battle order in full view as though sure of success, and Varakasa, in the accepted practice, organised his own force to mirror it. Standing proudly beside his chariot driver, Varakasa drove along his front line, to the reverberating sound of cheers and the beating of drums, partly for the benefit of his half-brother, who he knew would be watching intently. His matching pair of black stallions, gaudily caparisoned in gold with red tassels; their elaborately plumed headdresses nodding majestically with each stride, drew the chariot with ease as it sped wildly across the open terrain.

As prayers in many dialects were intoned, and rituals of various kinds were performed, Clytes, in a clear voice, struck up the paean to the god Apollo; his fellow comrades following his lead. In full voice, in a strange land, the Hellenes directed their hymn westwards, to their homeland; to Mount Olympus and their own sun god. 'May he protect us all and bring success to our venture!' spoke Theomenes, earnestly. 'Whatever happens today, my friends and comrades, it has been an honour to have been in your company these past months. If I don't survive,' he announced solemnly, 'I want you all to swear that whoever does endure, will continue the quest, and take The Shield home!'

'We swear!' all cried in unison.

The harsh cry of a warhorn carried on the air, and a booming drumbeat like rolling thunder drove Varakasa's men forward. Hoarse defiant shouts went up as his infantry, pushing their long wicker shields before them, slowly advanced towards Khorvash's army, as a salvo of arrows from the advancing enemy ranks rained down on them from a darkening sky. As men fell, others stepped forward to take their places while Stephanos and his men waited impatiently for the order to advance. Surviving in surprisingly good order, with Varakasa giving encouragement from the front ranks, his longbowmen continued their march towards Khorvash's lines.

Theomenes, in full armour, sitting restlessly astride his horse, wondered what the historian, Admetus, would make of all this. He doubted if this battle would ever figure in the old man's histories, but he personally had to admit, the sight and sound of these warring Persians was a great spectacle to witness.

Stephanos had strategically placed himself and the rest of The Shield Company to the left of Varakasa's ranks of foot-archers, directly opposite Khorvash's right flank. Due to the practice of holding the shield on the left arm, and therefore giving protection to the man standing to the left, the extreme right flank, without that protection, was a vulnerable position in any army line-up and this was where it was expected Lykaon and his men would be; together with other Hellene mercenaries already in the pay of the Persian satrap.

Varakasa's infantry, archers, slingers and peltasts, was many rows deep - a formidable if disorderly force, but he presented a weak front to his adversary by deliberately stretching the leading lines thinly. The plan was to keep his true numbers hidden behind a rise in the ground, until the appropriate time.

The sound of the drums increased and the two forces of archers moved ever closer together, as from either side the shield bearers once again stepped forward, setting their long wicker and leather shields into the earth. Protected by these tall barriers, the long-bowmen let loose a continuous volley of arrows, which arched upwards into the sky before noisily smashing into their enemies shields. The rushing sound unnerved men and horses alike.

'Can you distinguish the Thebans yet?' shouted Theomenes, anxiously, above the din. 'I can't see anything from here!'

We're still too far off!' Stephanos yelled back. 'We'll have to wait until the cavalry is ordered out!'

'He's got guts, I'll give him that!' shouted Clytes, as he tried to calm his restless mount against the onslaught of sound, with a firm stroke of the hand. He nodded in the direction of the thin lines of infantry, indicating the bravery of Varakasa, who was now marching boldly in front of his men. 'But what in Hades is he doing?' called out Imbros. 'He'll be cut down, the idiot!'

Suddenly, there was movement from the other camp as a richly adorned Khorvash in his fine chariot drawn by a pair of prized Nissian horses, the colour of pale gold, began to charge towards Varakasa's line, followed by his mounted archers and javelin throwers. On the flanks, moving at speed, were his camel riders emitting their high-pitched warbling war-cries from their high vantage points; their bows drawn ready for firing. Scorning his brother and the meagre force being sent against him, Khorvash, in his impatience, wanted the battle won quickly and the ground shuddered as his generals in their chariots and their accompanying heavily armed lancers, thundered across the dry earth. In their wake came his highly trained personal guard, who were running, screaming, with sabres raised in order to be there for the kill.

Then, across the battlefield in front of the watching, anxious Plataeans, a small cloud of dust was seen moving quickly. Varakasa's war chariot was being driven at speed, and they looked on incredulously as he athletically leapt aboard to stand beside his driver. Racing back towards them, with his shield-bearers and archers running swiftly behind him, it was thought the battle was already lost, and Stephanos and the others watched aghast at Khorvash's fast approaching army. But Varakasa, knowing his mixed assortment of combatants would be no match against Khorvash's highly trained warriors, hoped that guile and surprise would win the day. His driver handled the black stallions with consummate skill, halting at intervals to allow Varakasa to harangue the men in his main force, hidden from his brother, just over the rim. He spoke of the years of oppression under the rule of Khorvash, and called on gods and men to now destroy the tyrant.

Yelling and screaming they rushed fearlessly over the rise, to bombard the oncoming horses and camels with javelins and heavy projectiles. Line after line stepped forward to hurl their weapons, and animals fell or reared in pain as the javelins struck, throwing their riders to the ground, to be trampled to death. There was brutal mayhem as those following; slowed down by the already fallen, plowed into Varakasa's front ranks of foot soldiers. But the lines held firm. The din became deafening; the clash of arms; the animal-like cries and screams of men engaged in the bloody business of killing one-another. On either flank, Varakasa's camel corps and the Scythian cavalry grew restless, their eager mounts barely controllable, but still they waited for Varakasa's signal.

Lured on by the sight of his brother fleeing before him, but totally underestimating the strength of numbers under Varakasa's command, Khorvash now watched enraged from his chariot as his men were dragged to their deaths. He urgently ordered his driver to turn about, as a trumpeteer sounded the strident signal for the personal guard to make an immediate retreat. It was then that Varakasa called on his cavalry to give chase. Into clouds of swirling dust, camel riders and Scythians, together with Theomenes and his fellow Hellenes, charged after the retreating enemy, bringing down every man in their path. With Theomenes warning, not to take risks, totally forgotten, The Shield Company roared across the plain, blood-lust driving them onwards as they cut a bloody swaithe through Khorvash's men. The mounted archers were deadly, and Angelos hit many a target with his preferred weaponry. Using skills taught him by Anatolios of Leuctra, he weaved his tightly controlled horse through the fighting, firing arrows forwards and behind him, as his long legs strongly gripped the mount under him. Avoiding slashing blades, he ducked, but continued firing arrows, gaining an appreciative yell from a Scythian horseman riding close by. Stephanos, his sword arm already dripping in gore, used such force as to cleave a rider's head clean from his shoulders, while Imbros, galloping alongside him, sliced a man's head from crown to neck.

The ground previously thought by Khorvash as being impregnable, now proved to be an impediment to his fleeing forces as they became confined between the banks on either side, and grisly slaughter ensued. The Shield Company kept as close to Varakasa as possible. Due to the diversity of armour and weaponry on both sides, they were totally confused as to who was the enemy, and took their lead from Varakasa's men. Urgent shouts in different languages and dialects from the various tribal commanders only added to the chaos and it was difficult to know which side was winning.

Suddenly, through the bloody hand-to-hand fighting, Clytes saw what his eyes had been searching for. The glinting of domed helmets. This had to be them! The unmistakable knot of riders, their bouncing crested helms setting them apart from the rest of Khorvash's men, seemed to be urging their horses away from the battle. Believing he'd seen The Wolf himself amongst them, he dug his heels into the sweating flanks of his horse, and with a wild yell, charged off alone through the carnage. Imbros, watching him go, urged his horse past those of Theomenes and Stephanos, and sped after him. Calls for them to stop were lost in the din.

'You stupid idiots!' roared Stephanos, wild-eyed. Then turning towards Theomenes, he shouted, incredulously. 'They're leaving the field! They must have seen something!'

'If Clytes has seen Lykaon, he could well kill him, despite your orders!' yelled Theomenes, frantically.

'Imbros has gone after him!' Stephanos shouted. 'He'll stop him!'

'We all go, Stephanos!' answered Theomenes, decisively. 'We stick together!' and with signals to the others to join them, the entire Shield Company, grim-faced and blood-splattered, was ordered to give chase. A Persian foot-soldier, rushing towards a distracted Theomenes, with sabre raised, received a vicious kick to the head from the ever watchful Mydon. With his strengthened leather boot, he sent the man falling backwards to be trampled under the hooves of the swiftly moving horses. As he went down he slashed wildly at Mydon's horse causing it to rear up and Mydon was thrown heavily to the ground, dropping his shield. His cry was heard by Philon, the last in the group of fleeing Plataeans, and he wheeled his mount around, quickly grabbing the reins of Mydon's panicking animal. On the ground, Mydon's lameness was causing him difficulties as he struggled to gain his balance. Unhorsed, he was suddenly defenceless in a quagmire of blood, vomit and excrement; the deafening screams and groans of fighting men all around him. He swore in relief as he saw Philon, digging spurs into the flanks of his mount, drive both their animals at two Persian soldiers bearing down on him.

'Grab your shield, Mydon!' yelled Philon, as he used the bulk of the wheeling horses to guard his comrade from attacking blades. Terrified, the animals used teeth and slashing hooves to good effect and Mydon, shaken but rearmed, was quickly pulled to safety by the strong arms of Philon.

'I'm in your debt, Philon!' shouted Mydon.

'You'd do the same for me!' the Plataean answered, as they spurred their mounts in pursuit of their comrades.

SEVENTY-NINE

THE GROUP OF RIDERS AHEAD of him was clearly leaving the fighting, and certain that he had identified Lykaon, Clytes urged his horse onwards, with Imbros closing in swift pursuit. The fleeing Thebans spurred on their horses unmercifully, and the noise and the dust of the battle was soon left behind, until, on reaching a shallow dry ravine; just as Imbros caught up with him, Clytes realised he'd lost them.

'They've gone this way!' shouted Imbros, pointing out hoof prints in the dry earth.

'No, they went this way!' called out Clytes, excitedly, also seeing signs of disturbance, but going in the opposite direction.

Theomenes and the rest of the company, having waited for Mydon and Philon to catch them up, were relieved to see Clytes and Imbros ahead of them. They were dismounted, searching along the dried-up river-bed.

'It was him!' Clytes called out to the approaching company. 'I saw Lykaon!'

'Did you see him, Imbros?' asked Stephanos, suspiciously.

'No, but I thought.....'

'Your obsession with finding this man is making you see things, Clytes!' yelled Stephanos. If this is another waste of time......!'

'It was Lykaon. I'm sure of it,' asserted Clytes, remounting and eager to continue the pursuit. 'We can't lose him now!' Looking towards

Theomenes for support, he said firmly, 'we'll have to split our numbers. I counted twelve riders. We are twenty. It was him, Theo!'

'I believe you,' replied Theomenes, calmly; to the surprise of Stephanos. 'If he has The Shield, we can't let him get away!'

Splitting their force, the two groups headed in opposite directions. Theomenes and Imbros went north-west and Clytes went with Stephanos riding south-east, each party following a dusty trail to wherever it would lead them.

After a couple of miles, Clytes and Stephanos arrived at a small village where women were drawing up water from a well, and they ran for cover when the men rode in. They saw several baggage animals; camels and mules, together with their elderly handlers who were seated cross-legged on the ground. 'Where are they?' shouted Clytes, angrily. 'Where's the Theban who calls himself Lykaon?' There was no response, but one old man looked nervously in the direction of a small encampment, seen at the end of the village. Nudging their horses slowly towards it, they realised they could be ambushed, and Stephanos silently signalled for the men to separate. He went up a side street with Echus and a few others, while Clytes and the rest rode straight on. Encircling the camp, consisting of a large pavilion surrounded by smaller tents, they saw some horses being watered at a murky stream. Some of the Plataeans drew their swords, others fitted arrows to their bows, as they watched keenly for any sign of movement from the tents.

Lykaon uttered a curse when he'd caught sight of the Hellenes in Varakasa's force. Twenty mounted warriors, wearing highest quality armour, with their shining crested helmets and expensive bronze hoplons. This was no coincidence. It had to be the Plataeans! Well, what of it, he thought? They'll soon be eating dirt! It was only when Khorvash's cavalry was set upon, that his thoughts shifted from killing anyone within reach, to worrying about the coveted relic. Leaving most of the men he had brought with him to their fate, he summoned the mounted Thebans to him, and deserting the field, they set off at a gallop back to their camp and the men he'd left on guard there. One ship would get him across the Tigris. He didn't need Khorvash's help. He wouldn't have the force of arms he'd planned to impress the king with, and that was unfortunate after all the expense he'd gone to, but he would have The Marathon Shield.

'We're being followed, sire!' called out Hippodamus, as they'd sped towards their camp, their cloaks flying out behind them.

'Once we get The Shield, head for the river!' shouted Lykaon.

'What about the others and the camp followers?' asked Hippodamus, who had a woman waiting for him back at the village.

'They'll have to take their chances,' replied Lykaon, coldly.

Hippodamus knew that meant no chance at all, knowing how cruelly Khorvash would extract his revenge for The Wolf's desertion.

Clytes and Stephanos, with Angelos and Echus, drove their horses directly into the tents, causing the hiding Thebans and their women to rush out, where the rest of the Plataeans were waiting. With weapons raised, Lykaon's men fiercely stood their ground. Clytes slashed heavily at one of the soldiers with his sword, spilling brains from the stricken man's skull, splattering Clytes' sword arm. Stephanos trampled another under the slashing hooves of his spirited horse. Pushing their mounts into the billowing extravagant pavilion, acquired by Lykaon from Khorvash, they found four more of Lykaon's Thebans. These men had obviously not taken part in the battle, and they fought back strongly. From horseback, Clytes finally brought down one of these warriors with a lucky thrust at the man's exposed neck. The sword of their deceased Boetarch, was indeed a fine weapon, he thought. Echus, with his strong hands, managed to throttle one man with the reins of his horse, and after a life or death struggle on the floor of the tent, Stephanos succeeded in getting his dagger into the groin of his opponent, severing a main artery. As the fourth man backed his way out of the tent, Angelos was waiting, and his arrow found its mark. Two more of Lykaon's deserted band put up a final brave defence, but being outnumbered by the Plataeans, the outcome was inevitable. The Thebans and Plataeans had fought each other fiercely - their shared animosity enduring, even in these foreign lands.

They found Lykaon's camp bed thrown aside, as were the exotic animal skins and brightly covered Persian rugs, now heavily blood-splattered. The men stared at the circular pit, dug into the earth. It was empty!

Stephanos bending down, scooped up a handful of the recently disturbed soil. 'Pearls, Clytes!' he exclaimed, holding out his open palm. 'Known by all Plataeans as 'Akaterina's teardrops'. I remember when they were added to The Shield, after the death of her first child with Phalinus.

Damn him, he did take it!' he muttered angrily. 'You were right, Clytes,' he admitted. 'But where, by all the gods, has he gone with it? To Khorvash?'

'That's not likely,' replied Clytes. 'Lykaon will know that Khorvash is not the kind of man to share anything. I doubt the Persian even knows of its existence, or else it would already be in his possession. My guess is the same as before. Lykaon is on his way to the king.'

'Once he crosses the Tigris, Clytes, it's all over,' said Stephanos, seriously. 'We'll have The Immortals to contend with. Artaxerxes has ten-thousand elite warriors at his command - so the stories say!'

'Then we'll have to catch him before he can get a ship,' young Angelos spoke up, eagerly.

'What about Theomenes and Imbros?' asked Echus. 'Do we wait for them?'

'We haven't time,' responded Stephanos. 'Let's go, before he can get far. The weight of The Shield will be slowing him down.'

In the other party, Theomenes and Imbros, following the trail westwards, finally caught sight of the second group of Thebans. They'd changed direction and were now heading east, back towards the Tigris. Taking turns to ride ahead, so as not to lose sight of them, Theomenes' team kept on their tail.

Lykaon had also ridden furiously to the river. Since deserting the battlefield, he knew Khorvash would be after his head, but due to all able-bodied men being called upon to carry arms in the ongoing confrontation, he found the great waterway unusually quiet of ships. He sent Hippodamus along the river bank to find a vessel. He'd split his small force in the hope of throwing off his pursuers, and sacrificed the lives of his fellow Theban warriors, who'd been ordered to remain at the camp to hold back the Plataeans. But, it couldn't be helped - he needed the precious time it would gain him - but unless the other group made it to the river, he was now left with only Hippodamus and four of his Anatolian peltasts. It was vital he found a ship, any ship, before his enemies found him! Before long, a small vessel was seen approaching. Onboard was Hippodamus, holding a knife to the throat of its owner, while the man's young sons and nephews - too young to go to war - plied the oars.

'We can't get the horses onboard that!' said Lykaon, angrily. They'll have to swim across. Unfasten The Shield!' he ordered. Before they could do so, however, he cried out, 'No, damn it! They're here!' as in the distance he saw riders heading towards him.

'They could be Thebans!' said one of the peltasts.

'No, you idiot! Are you blind? It's the Plataeans!' exclaimed Lykaon. 'Can't you see the colours on their crests?' Looking out into the river, he could see the small trading vessel getting closer, and he roared to Hippodamus to pull faster, but he knew it would not reach him in time. He was so close! Desperate, he leapt onto his horse, then pulling on the reins of the animal bearing the heavy trophy, drove them both into the river. The weight was a burden too much as the horse struggled to keep its head above water, but Lykaon dragged it onwards. If he could only reach the boat, the priceless relic could be lifted onboard. Sounds of fighting came from the riverbank behind him, as Clytes, Stephanos and the others were taking care of Lykaon's stranded followers, but he carried on regardless.

Clytes, after quickly despatching his adversary, untied his cuirass, to dive recklessly into the water, swimming strongly towards the floundering horses. The Shield horse was struggling to stay afloat. Clytes had to make a decision. Lykaon, or the Plataean treasure.

Lykaon glared at the Eleusinian as he swam up to him. 'What's it to be then?' he spluttered. 'If I let go, the horse will go under, and The Shield with it!' The horse bearing the heavy disc, was willing to struggle until its last breath for its master, but without encouragement the animal would quickly succumb, and Clytes knew that. Without hesitation, he made his decision. This was not the time to take on Lykaon.

'Go, you miserable, bastard!' said Clytes, snorting water, realising the horse could drown at any moment, and as Lykaon swam off, he turned to drag the weakening animal back to the riverbank, just as Imbros, Theomenes and the others rode up, leading a group of riderless horses. Having successfully dealt with the rest of Lykaon's Thebans, they'd brought with them their precious Thessalian mounts.

As Clytes and the spent animal collapsed exhausted onto the embankment, Theomenes, Stephanos, Imbros and others gathered around to stare exultantly at their revered trophy. The rest watched as Lykaon, helped by Hippodamus, clambered aboard the waiting boat. He'd lost the prize, but nothing was more precious than his own life - and anyway, he thought, the Plataeans had still to get it home. His dream was not over yet.

He climbed onto the low rail at the prow of the vessel, and stared balefully towards the land passing swiftly by, as the rowers, threatened by Hippodamus, pulled with all their young might.

'You haven't seen the last of The Wolf of Thebes!' he yelled, balancing defiantly on the rail. 'The Shield is mine! You'll never get out of here alive! You're all dead men!' Holding onto the curved prow, he laughed insanely. He'd lived to fight another day!

Clytes grabbed one of the javelins, throwing it with all his might towards the receding boat, but it fell harmlessly short into the water. He heard Lykaon's harsh laughter and watched helplessly as the Theban waved, taunting him.

'Leave him, Clytes!' ordered Theomenes, mounted and ready to move out. 'We waste no more weapons or time on that bastard!'

'We have The Shield!' shouted Stephanos. That's all that matters!'

Ignoring him, Clytes placed his hand encouragingly on Angelos' shoulder. 'You always boasted you could shoot a fast moving hare, Angelos,' he said, looking menacingly towards Lykaon. 'Can you shoot a wolf?' he asked softly.

Angelos, calmly fitted an arrow to his bow and taking careful aim, fired. The arrow whistled through the air. With held breath, Clytes watched and waited for what seemed an age, and then whooped with joy, as he saw Lykaon topple from the rail into the water, vanishing from sight. Hippodamus peered over the side for a moment, and then to everyone's surprise, he turned his attention to berating the rowers, and the vessel quickly pulled away from them.

'The Persians could be upon us at any moment, Clytes!' yelled Stephanos again. 'Be satisfied! He's done for!'

Still ignoring him, Clytes cried out, 'He could still be alive!' Then he dived back into the current. He was seen a short while later, dragging through the water, a wounded but struggling and still very much alive, Lykaon. As he hauled the wet, bleeding figure onto the riverbank, Angelos' arrow protruding from his shoulder, Imbros ran to stand over him as he lay violently coughing up water.

'Where's my wife?' he shouted, angrily.

Lykaon groaned, his hand feeling for the arrow shaft.

'Where is she?' Imbros insisted, the sword in his hand wavering menacingly.

CHAPTER SEVENTY-NINE

'She's dead!' snarled Lykaon, maliciously.

'You're lying!' snapped the Athenian, kicking hard at the Theban's wound. 'I know you're lying!' he shouted, remembering how vividly he'd seen Amara in his dreams, and he pressed the point of his sword at Lykaon's chest.

'Imbros!' shouted Theomenes, furiously. 'You can't believe anything the bastard tells you!'

'Kill him, Imbros!' yelled Clytes, struggling to get near.

'I'm giving you both an order!' shouted Theomenes, again. 'Kill him, or leave him for Khorvash to deal with. Get mounted! We're leaving!'

'I want him alive until he's told me where she is!' answered Imbros, ignoring Theomenes pleas while trying to keep an angry Clytes at bay.

'You're not Plataean!' screeched Lykaon, looking towards Clytes, as he frantically sought a way out. 'Join me! Artaxerxes will give us all we want - if we bring him The Marathon Shield. There are riches here - for the taking!'

'You killed my family, you sadistic bastard!' yelled Clytes, trying to get near.

'That was a long time ago,' answered Lykaon groaning, as he tried to push himself away. 'You're a fool to have wasted so much time seeking revenge. You're a good fighter. We would make a fine team, you and I!'

'You're a mad dog, Lykaon, and mad dogs need to be exterminated!' spat Clytes.

'What about the rest of you?' Lykaon asked the others, desperately. 'What is there for you in Plataea now? Here you could all be rich! Use The Shield to further your own fortunes. This is your opportunity!'

'It's because of you and your kind, you maniac, that we have no city!' snarled Stephanos, from his horse. 'If you kill him Clytes, you'll give him a better death than he deserves. Why give him a hero's end? Leave him - for the Persians! They'll know how to deal with him.'

'And let him escape, Stephanos! I'm not risking that!' argued Clytes. 'I've carried this sword since the Theban attack on Plataea, in the hope that one day I would kill him with it!'

'Then hamstring him, Clytes!' shouted Theomenes. 'But be quick about it!'

Lykaon, in terror, began pushing his body backwards, trying to get away from Clytes' raised sword.

Looking frantically at Imbros, Lykaon pleaded. 'Don't let him cut me! I can take you to where your wife is!'

The Shield was now safely strapped to a fresh horse and members of the company were mounted and shouting urgently.

''He's playing with you!' shouted Theomenes, in exasperation. 'I don't care what the pair of you do with him, hamstring him or kill him, but just do it!'

Imbros looked up at Theomenes and Stephanos, and held up his hand as though to ward off their advice, then looking down on Lykaon, he spat on him. Stepping to one side, he said grimly, 'he's all yours, Clytes!'

Lykaon, looking up at Clytes standing over him, suddenly gave a bitter laugh. 'You can't do it can you?' he smirked. 'You're like a man I knew once. His name was Phalinus!' he grimaced, with cruel satisfaction. 'He also had a virtuous streak - just like your brother!'

'You mother-fucking, son of a bitch!' snarled Clytes, as with both hands he raised his sword high. Lykaon glared back at him, his eyes defiant. He whispered urgently, one word. 'Larachne!' The sharp blade of his uncle's sword went cleanly through his heart, and he died with a mocking sneer still on his face.

'He goaded you into killing him, Clytes. Better to have left him for Khorvash!' said Stephanos, dismissively.

Standing mesmerised over the body, Clytes answered quietly, 'I can't believe he is dead. Some dark force protects him!'

'Well, I'll make sure the monster's dead, Clytes!' said Imbros, and he viciously drove his sword into Lykaon. 'That's for Amara!'

Theomenes, on hearing Lykaon speak the name Phalinus, had become incensed. All thought of escaping with The Shield momentarily forgotten, he leapt to the ground and swinging his sword in both hands, brought it down heavily on Lykaon's neck. Blood seeped into the earth, as the head severed from the body, rolled in the dust. 'He's definitely on his way to Hades now!' he shouted, his eyes wild with anger. 'But without his head!' and with a final kick, he sent it flying into the fast flowing river.

A vision momentarily flashed through Theomenes' mind. He was standing in the Temple of Athena at Plataea, facing the shield carried by the goddess, and in the reflection of the golden image of Medusa, he saw his own stern features. There was no scream. Somehow he knew that the recurring terror which had haunted his dreams for so many years, would be no more.

Khorvash's troops rallied after the shock of their cavalry's humiliating retreat. This was mainly due to the fact that Varakasa's army later fell into confusion and disorder, due partly to the varied tongues of their generals, and also because of the brutal whippings carried out by Khorvash's personal guard on any man seen running away. In spite of the early setbacks, Khorvash finally claimed the day to be his. When the satrap realised that Lykaon and his mounted hoplites had quit the field, he had the Theban's abandoned force rounded up and transported to his nearest palace, where he cruelly took his revenge. He had the Cretan archers covered in honey and placed in wicker cages to die of shock, as thousands of bees were poured into the confined space. The Rhodian slingers were forced to drink goat's milk and honey, to such an extent that it caused their bowels to open. Trapped inside a pair of hollowed out tree trunks, they were slowly eaten by myriad small creatures. And, as a warning to anyone else thinking of taking sides with Hellenic mercenaries, the Anatolian peltasts were flayed alive; the tyrant having their mutilated bodies strung on staves lining the route to his military pavilion.

Before they died, the few that had knowledge of its existence, revealed everything they knew about The Shield of Marathon. Upon hearing the startling news that the famous relic had been right under his nose, caused Khorvash to go into such a rage that not one of his counsellors was brave enough to approach him, despite being threatened with incarceration in one of his notorious prisons.

His victory however, was short lived. The tribes opposed to his harsh rule continued to flow to Varakasa's aid and after their final battle, it was the head of Khorvash and not Varakasa, that finally ended up on a spike.

The wild Scythians returned triumphant to their hunting grounds, taking with them their war trophies. Not plunder or weaponry, but heads, scalps and flayed skins, which were considered tokens of bravery by their nomadic tribes.

EIGHTY

THE KING SENT SCOUTING parties in all directions in the hunt for the Plataeans, after his spies had brought him the news that the object which had contributed to his grand-father's defeat, had been only a few miles from his palace! Patrols searched along routes to his principal cities of Babylon, Ecbatana, Persepolis and Susa, believing their objective could be the enormous reward the king would give for securing The Marathon Shield. Another headed west along The Royal Road, being the fastest route back to Attica. These misjudgements gave Theomenes and his company a vital lead. Skirting widely around the area of confrontation between the half-brothers, and keeping the river Tigris to their right, they took the least expected route - north over the mountains towards their rendezvous with Glaucus; the fittest of the Thebans' captured horses going with them.

Although they'd suffered no losses in the struggle to recover the shield of Agristones, they had the wounded to worry about. On their flight, Chares, a respected Plataean and Olympic champion, succumbed to a mortal wound, the agony of which he'd kept hidden from the others. He was buried with as much ceremony as their fleeing circumstances allowed. One thing the wounded were certain of; they did not want to be left behind, and after the death of their comrade, all now brutally realised that time did not allow for encumbrances.

Camped one night, after several days and nights of hard riding, as they sat huddled over their small fire, Clytes looked around at his companions. Their faces in the firelight looked tired and drawn, but these weary-looking Plataeans impressed the Eleusinian, with their mutual strength of character. They punch above their weight, he mused. He was the only one in the group with no family connection to Plataea, and it suddenly occurred to him that he felt very privileged to be part of their quest. He listened quietly to their steady banter, as what little food they had was shared out between them. He became aware that Stephanos was bemoaning the fact that he'd not actually killed Lykaon, himself. He spoke of his regret at not having avenged the deaths of Diokles and his comrades in the garrison.

'But you have The Marathon Shield, Stephanos,' said Clytes. 'Be grateful for that.'

'Yes, thanks to you!' interrupted Theomenes. 'You were the one to recognise him on the battlefield.'

Imbros then spoke up, and praising Clytes' bravery at the river, shook him by the hand. Others around the campfire noisily agreed with him, and one-by-one, they all did likewise. Stephanos, grudgingly forced to accept the large part this non-Plataean had played in rescuing his city's relic, gruffly conceded.

Clytes slowly drew his sword from its scabbard, looking for a moment at the dried blood still on the blade. Seated with his companions he experienced a sudden, unexpected feeling of release. Going to a nearby stream, he washed away Lykaon's blood. As he kneeled by the riverbank, he said a prayer for his sister. The memory of her young body floating in the river Cephissus would never be forgotten. But, he could do no more. It was finally over.

Having with them an excellent change of horses, they were able to make good progress and were soon free of the hot open plains. Using the sun and stars for guidance, and following the Tigris towards its source, they continued their journey northwards until they reached the foothills of the range of mountains and rivers which lay between them and the sea. They were heading for the satrapy of Armenia, and again dangerous territory, being still in the far-reaching kingdom of Artaxerxes. Theomenes and Stephanos discussed their plan of action.

'We are a small force,' said Stephanos, earnestly. 'Strong enough to defend ourselves against a few villagers, but not a fortified town. We avoid all towns. There's plenty of game to hunt, to sustain us. We only stop to acquire guides and necessary provisions. If need be, we trade the Thebans' horses. We've ten good Thessalian horses with us. Some, still full stallions and a few mares. To acquire such a horse to improve their weak stock, it will be too good an offer for them to refuse.'

The idea was accepted and the company, their plan working for a time, gradually made progress through the difficult terrain. They passed through territory where people made their homes under the ground; crossed the upper Euphrates, shallow enough to wade across, and saw all kinds of animals unfamiliar to them. Enormous flightless birds looked like easy prey, but with their powerful long legs, they easily out-ran all attempts to catch them. They did not linger. Theomenes, forever glancing backwards, urged them constantly onwards.

At a prominent riverside village, at the foot of a seemingly endless range of hills gouged by mountain streams, they were forced to stop and seek directions, and here their luck ran out. They were discovered by one of Artaxerxes' patrols. The villagers fled in terror as the Persian warriors charged through their narrow streets, loosing flights of arrows at the fleeing Plataeans. Theomenes and his company forced their horses down a bank and into a fast flowing torrent, pulling the spare horses behind them. Fending off arrows with their shields, most managed to reach the opposite side unscathed, but some were hit. Two of their men fell wounded into the water. One of them was Echus; first cousin of Stephanos. The other was Philon.

'Shit!' yelled Stephanos, momentarily shocked, and he pulled on his horse to go back, only for Clytes to grab his reins. 'Think of The Shield, man! Keep going!' he urged. For a second, Clytes thought he would have to use force, as Stephanos looked at him threateningly, but reluctantly the Plataean followed the other horses scrambling up the wooded hillside; the men pushing with their shields at the impeding branches until they reached the summit. They immediately took cover and prepared their small force for an attack. The Persian horses were powerful and seemed to have little difficulty in climbing the steep incline, but the Plataeans, having the advantage of the heights, were able to bring down several of them with a barrage of javelins, arrows and slingshot. 'Aim for the horses!' yelled Stephanos. 'They can't follow us on wounded horses!' A few of the king's men pushed their way up on foot and a fierce hand to hand struggle was fought among the trees, leaving some of Theomenes' men injured, but due to their superior weapons; the pursuers suffered many more casualties.

'Let's go!' shouted a grim-faced Stephanos, grabbing the reins of his horse, and the company, once remounted, fled down the side of the mountain, slithering and sliding until they reached the plains below. Galloping as fast as their injuries allowed, they soon left the depleted Persian patrol far behind them.

'Echus and Philon!' groaned Mydon, when they stopped to rest the horses. 'We should never have left them!' Other members of the company muttered angrily in agreement, and Theomenes looked anxiously towards Stephanos.

'They're soldiers! They knew this could happen,' said Stephanos, trying hard to remain composed. 'I know my cousin,' he added, glancing quickly at Clytes. 'He would not want us to go back, and risk The Shield being taken.'

'There's a way to go, yet,' said Theomenes, his voice shaking; his face looking deeply anguished. 'The Persians now know where we are heading, and will be on our trail as soon as they acquire fresh horses. I'm sorry for your loss,' he said, looking concernedly at Stephanos. 'Echus was a good Plataean and a good friend.' Then, shaking his head in disbelief, his voice finally breaking, added, 'Philon's strength too, will also be sorely missed.'

'His wrestling skills were admired throughout all Hellas!' spoke up Mydon, his voice hoarse with emotion, feeling especially hard, the loss of his comrade.

'The gods will welcome them as heroes!' asserted Imbros, attempting to be reassuring. 'Eternal glory will be theirs!'

A sombre moment followed, as Stephanos placed his hand in comradeship on Theomenes' shoulder, saying supportively, 'It could have been any one of us, Theo.' Turning to the others, he said brusquely, 'You know why we all swore the oath! We have in our possession, that which will restore pride to our displaced citizens. Hope too, that one day Agristones' shield will hang once again in Plataea. Chares, Echus and Philon would not want us to fail in our mission, and we owe it to them not to. Now, let us attend to our wounds and move on.'

Pushing their horses ever northwards, they crossed numerous rivers and streams, climbing many hills to avoid places of heavy population. Fighting when it was unavoidable, and bribing whenever possible, they kept to their plan of stopping only at isolated villages, thereby avoiding any serious confrontations. But travelling through a narrow gorge, they suffered the loss of another valued Plataean. Set upon by a wild band of mountain men, their only weapons, slingshot and dislodged rocks, the crashing boulders terrified the animals and some of the riderless horses bolted. Androdamos, a relative of the noble Phalinus, was one of the men who galloped after them. When he didn't return, they went to find him, but it was too late. His horse had stumbled over a tree root, and Androdamos had been thrown awkwardly from its back. Realising his injuries were severe enough to halt their progress, the stoic Plataean did what he thought best. He severed the veins in his wrists. Unable to do anything to help him, his grieving comrades, knowing his time would not be long, stayed with him until the end came.

His final words were for Theomenes. 'Phalinus is with you, Theo. I can feel his presence very close,' he said, weakly. Theomenes grasped the dying man's hand. 'I've believed this since the day of Eupompides' funeral,' he answered him, his eyes bright with tears. The strong features of Androdamos relaxed a little, then he struggled once more to speak. 'My kinsman is waiting, Theo,' he murmured. Then he was gone.

A simple wreath of laurel was his only grave marker, in recognition of the many honours he'd won for Plataea, and once again, young Theomenes was called upon to rally the remaining members of the company, as low in spirits, the group pressed relentlessly onwards.

Their guide was now a young shepherd, who seemed to indicate to them that he'd been born in Pontus. Drawing a map in the earth, he showed the bleary-eyed Plataeans, the route to the sea. After a long climb, and over a month since they'd fled Khorvash, the young lad ran forward, then started shouting, excitedly. The men hurried to the ridge, to see what he was looking at, then they also started to cheer loudly. 'I can smell it!' one of them yelled. In the distance was a thin blue line. At last - the sea! There was just one more range of mountains in front of them, before they reached freedom, and they hurried down onto the plain between the two ranges to camp for the night by a river, the wounded being unable to go any further. Here, they sacrificed a wild goat to the gods, when prayers were said for their lost comrades, and pleas made for guidance and deliverance. Unbeknown to them, they'd drawn the attention of a band of roaming warriors.

Attracted by the fine looking horses they'd seen traversing their land and now being watered along the riverbank, wild rough-riders galloped towards them across the plain. With the river at their backs, The Shield Company tried to protect themselves from the arrows which started to rain down around them. Theomenes rushed to conceal the treasure, then quickly joined the others as they lined up, javelins at the ready. As the riders streaked by them, the men realised the warriors were women! These were legendary Amazons! Whooping and yelling, the tattooed women made a fearsome sight as they twisted and turned their small mounts, firing arrows from all angles, avoiding the javelins thrown at them with ease.

At a signal from one of the riders, their horses came to a sudden stop and the women regrouped. Outnumbering The Shield Company four to one, they faced Theomenes and his men. Holding hand-axes aloft, they looked as though they were about to charge. Their obvious leader indicated to the men to put down their arms.

'We might take out a few, but we can't kill all of them!' said Stephanos, bitterly.

'We call a truce,' said Theomenes. 'Then we can negotiate. Clytes, you understand their language better than the rest of us. Talk to them. Tell them we want no trouble!'

Mounted but unarmed, Clytes slowly rode toward the line of Amazons, nudging his horse forward with his knees and keeping his hands in the air to show he held no weapons.

As he reached their line, he carefully removed his helmet and nodded an acknowledgement to their leader.

From along the line, came an excited cry. 'Clytes!'

He recognised her voice immediately and stared, uncomprehendingly. Seated on a perfectly formed small horse, dressed as an Amazon warrior in a spotted leather tunic and striped trousers, was Anthousa! Tattoos of wild animals covered her arms, and the hair on her head which had grown thick and unruly, was strikingly decorated with an eagle's feather.

Clytes laughed joyfully. 'What are you doing here? Last time I saw you, you were in the Euboean Straits with that mad dog, Lykaon!'

'What are you doing here?' Anthousa answered back. She spoke urgently with her leader, and after a short conversation, said to Clytes. 'We will talk. Tell your men we are coming over. No trouble!'

'You fired on us!' replied Clytes.

'We missed you deliberately,' answered Anthousa, 'or you'd be dead by now! We just wanted you to put down your weapons.'

'We don't want any trouble either,' said Clytes. We just want to get to the sea. Tell your leader that!' Then he swung his horse around and galloped back to tell the men the unexpected news.

To be reunited with Anthousa was a surprising and welcome event. The women appeared to be very skilled in the use of herbs, and taking several small bags of different blends from pouches carried with them, immediately set to work in treating the wounds of the injured men. These Amazons were not at all like the women the men were used to back home. Strong, independent and fiercely proud, they appeared a match for any man. When they understood that the company was on its way to the Black Sea, they agreed to accompany them part of the way, but first their wounds had to heal and that would take time - time to get to know one another.

With their horses safely hobbled, and after a cooked meal shared between them as equals, one of the women scattered an aromatic herb onto the fire. As the smoke began to rise and the circle of men and women breathed in the fumes, they began to feel light-headed, and some of the women began to dance. With no inhibitions, they moved freely and rapturously around the men, who were also feeling blissfully relaxed. Sexually permissive, the women took no time in choosing their partners. If two or three women liked the same man, what of it? There'd be no jealousy. They would share him! One by one, the women took the men to their tents. Several didn't bother with modesty and made love out in the open, under the stars.

Anthousa quickly rekindled her relationship with Clytes, but no-one would be sharing her man! Pushing him down on his back, she straddled him as she would her horse, and made love with such passion, that Clytes thought she would cause him some injury. The snarling tigers on her upper arms seemed to be alive, ready to pounce, as he felt her teeth bite sharply into his shoulder. 'Let me get on top, woman!' he urged, grabbing her by the buttocks, but when he did so, she wrapped him so tightly between her strong thighs, he could hardly breathe. 'Ouch!' he cried out, as she bit him again, this time on the lip. 'Whatever happened to my gentle, sweet Anthousa?' he said, licking blood from his lips.

'She's still here, Clytes,' she whispered softly, then with feeling, told him, 'I've missed you!'

'Well, my beautiful savage, miss me a little less and love me a little more!' he answered her, laughing.

They made love for most of the night, interspersed with the telling of their stories, as to what had happened to them since their last sighting of each other near Atalante. Anthousa was so happy to hear what had happened to Lykaon.

CHAPTER EIGHTY-ONE

'He treated Amara so badly, Clytes. Worse than any slave,' she said sadly.

'Were you there when she died?' he asked gently.

'Is she dead?' asked Anthousa, tears immediately filling her eyes.

'Lykaon said she was dead. I assume he killed her,' answered Clytes. 'I thought you knew.'

'He didn't kill her, Clytes. He sold us both together in Crete. We were at the same estate in Lydia, until I was lucky enough to escape, but Amara didn't have the strength to climb the wall. Once we understood the connection between Larachne and Plataea, Amara lived in constant fear that the monster would turn up in Sardis. Mercifully, he never did! She was alive when I saw her last!'

'I've got to tell Imbros!' yelled Clytes, excitedly, and he ran off without bothering to put on any garment, to his tent, throwing aside the door flap. Imbros, the light from the campfire flooding into his small enclosure was sandwiched between two lithe, tattooed women, looking more content than he'd done for a long time. 'Imbros, wake up man! Amara's alive!' he shouted.

EIGHTY-ONE

THE AMAZON WARRIORS ESCORTED Theomenes' company as far as they could, after having scared off what remained of the pursuing patrol, seen from a distance on a nearby ridge. The Persians stayed for a while, watching, then turned and were gone. 'Probably gone to get reinforcements,' said Stephanos. 'We must keep moving!'

The women were eager to return to their hunting grounds, but one of their number wanted to travel on with the men. 'I'm coming with you!' said Anthousa, determinedly. 'You'll never find her without me. I can fight, ride, shoot as well as any of you!' she added fiercely. 'I owe it to Amara, Imbros. I could never have survived without her.'

'I want Amara back more than anybody, but first I have my duty to guard The Shield, Anthousa,' said Imbros. 'I'm bound by my oath to see it gets safely back to Attica. Then I'll be free to look for Amara.'

'Without Anthousa's intervention,' remarked Clytes, pointedly to Theomenes who was standing by listening, 'you might not have The

Shield. In fact, we could all have been killed, either by the Amazons or the king's men. That patrol could have finished us. The horses and the wounded were exhausted.'

'Hmm,' responded Theo, thoughtfully, looking at the tattooed wild-rider. 'Well, if she joins us Clytes, you are responsible for her.'

'I'll try and keep her out of trouble!' he said, wholeheartedly, grinning at Anthousa.

The last of the Thessalian horses were taken by the female warriors, leaving the men with just enough healthy mounts to complete their journey to the sea. They were also travelling with a heavy wagon. Believing the Persians would be on the lookout for a group of horsemen, The Shield was concealed in a mode of transport which would not draw undue attention. Driving the cart was Clytes, disguised as a grimy hunter in a wolfskin cap and a fur jerkin, together with Angelos, equally scruffy, and the young shepherd Leukos, who'd refused to go back to his village.

Two days later, they rode into the city of Trabezus, the main port of Pontus on the Black Sea; occupied by Hellenes for many generations, but still under the auspices of the Persian king. They immediately headed for the harbour, where they'd arranged to meet up with Glaucus. Some of the men ran into the water, shouting for sheer joy! Relieved, they saw their ship Delias, drawn up on the beach, but could see straight away that all was not right with the worthy triaconter. Her owl sail was patched. Burning could be seen along her sides. On closer inspection, they could also see that her deck was splintered and holed in places.

'The old girl's been in action!' said Clytes, amazed, and then asked anxiously, 'Where's Glaucus?'

A search party was immediately organised to look in every tavern, whorehouse and hostelry, for the whereabouts of the crew of their ship. Theomenes was starting to panic. The Shield was still in danger. Artaxerxes knew their destination. Persian troopers could arrive at any time. Two of the first to be found were Cassa and Bion, at a boarding-house near the harbour.

'Are we glad to see you, Mydon!' yelled Cassa, rushing forward to grip him by the shoulders. Bion also ran towards him, slapping him enthusiastically on the back, in his excitement.

'How was it, Mydon?' asked Bion, cautiously, eyeing Mydon's wounds, some old, some still raw. 'Were you successful?' he asked, hesitantly.

'We have The Shield!' Mydon answered with relief and pride, 'but sadly the gods demanded a price. We lost some good men. What happened to the ship, Cassa?' he asked, seriously.

'The Delias is sea-worthy,' Cassa explained quickly, almost apologetically. 'She just doesn't look her best. I'll leave it to Glaucus to tell you what happened.'

'Cassa!' said Mydon, with great urgency. 'There's a Persian patrol chasing us! We must sail as soon as possible. Where is Glaucus?'

'Follow us!' said Bion, and with Mydon limping excitedly between them, the trio set off towards the harbour.

'You wouldn't believe half the stories I could tell you,' chattered Mydon, as they hurried through the streets, 'but they'll have to wait.'

When they arrived at the harbour, they immediately saw the Persian patrol. The king's men were searching all the ships, even the battered Delias, and every wagon and cart was being stopped, their cargoes roughly unloaded and inspected thoroughly. Soldiers could be seen entering houses, and with threats to the inhabitants, their possessions were being thrown into the streets. Mydon and his companions were relieved of their weapons, and made to stand in line with other men who'd been rounded up. In the line-up of both residents and travellers, Mydon could see the glowering visage of Glaucus. Theomenes and Imbros were forcibly pushed into the harbour area, where, suitably disguised by Clytes using his make-up skills, they did their best to blend in with the locals. Stephanos and the other Plataeans had split up to avoid detection. Some were found by the patrol, but due to the hatred of the king's men and their brutality, locals gave them protection and no suspicion fell upon them. As word of the violation spread, the merchants of the town began to arrive in force, protesting loudly at their trade being disrupted, but they were roughly jostled aside and threatened with violence if they interfered. Turmoil continued unabated.

Clytes was ordered to bring his lumbering cart forward, and the soldiers ripped aside the covering. 'Get down! All of you!' shouted one of the Persians.

'What have you got here, old man?' one of them asked.

Leukos made a sign that the 'old man' couldn't hear. 'Deaf as a statue!' he said, convincingly.

'Take everything out!' he was ordered, and onto the ground were thrown the wolf and deer skins given to them by the Amazons in exchange for the horses. Savagely stabbing at them with swords, the pelts were strewn about on the ground, while others in the patrol climbed onto the wagon, prying up the rough wooden flooring.

'Alright! Move on!' a soldier shouted, as nothing was found. Then he ordered another wagon to be brought forward to be searched.

As the hours wore on and the protests against the disruption became more violent, the patrol was finally forced to leave Trabezus and ride onto the next town.

One by one, The Shield Company became joyfully reunited on the Delias.

'I'm not impressed with the refurbishment, Glaucus', stated Theomenes, looking aghast at the obviously hurried repairs. 'What's the story?'

Glaucus was recovering from burns, but otherwise he was just as he always was. Loud! 'This old bird has a past, Theomenes!' roared Flamebeard, patting the scorched arms of his great chair. 'And her past caught up with her. I'll tell you all about it.'

'But what about the crew?' asked Theomenes, urgently. 'Where are the Athenians?'

'Gone back to Athens!' boomed the helmsman. 'And good riddance! But don't worry, I have a crew. They're a mixed bunch, but steady men. They'll get us home, Theo, I promise you!'

******

AFTER GLAUCUS HAD SEPARATED from his friends and headed up the coast of Asia Minor to be ready for their hoped-for meeting at Pontus, there was a long journey ahead of him and a disgruntled and depleted crew to keep in order. The professional Athenian rowers, used to their mighty triremes, thought the humble Delias a death trap, and after the Atalante incident wondered what had possessed them to get involved in what they now thought a hopeless venture. With threats and coercements, Glaucus had managed to keep the crew together until - not without some difficulty - they'd sailed through the Hellespont and reached 'the inland sea'.

The result of stopping at one of the islands however, where Glaucus had intended to stay long enough to have the ship completely refurbished, according to Theomenes' last instructions, was the final grievance for the Athenians. The decorative triaconter was recognised by pirates who menaced the area. Her previous owner, on the island of Delos, wanting to extend his trade once more beyond The Hellespont, had made no mention of the vessel's colourful past, and the real reason he needed to buy a new ship. When Glaucus recommended to Theomenes that he purchase the Delias, he was unaware that the little ship was already well known in these waters. Some years before, she'd been involved in the kidnapping of a local beauty by the name of Anastia, wife of Bassim, a well-known privateer, and a powerful man at that time. One summer night, sailing with a favourable wind and carried by the strong current of the Hellespont, the Delias took Anastia and her Delian lover away from 'the inland sea', forever. The role played by the distinctive little ship had long stayed in the memory of the family of Bassim - who sought revenge.

The Delias suffered some damage in the ensuing fight with the pirates, but the crew, with the help of Glaucus' knowledge of the winds and currents, managed to free themselves and sail on to Byzantium, where Glaucus failed to persuade the Athenians, some of them wounded, to travel any further. When word reached Cleon, he lost all faith in the venture, and ordered his rowers back to war duty.

Using funds left with him by Theomenes, he was eventually able to hire enough crew to assist Bion, Cassa and the few Plataeans who were left, and somehow they managed to limp the ship through the narrow channel to the Black Sea; and gradually the battered Delias progressed along the coast to Trabezus.

*****

HAVING SUCCESSFULLY OUTWITTED THE king's men, Theomenes and The Shield Company made a sacrifice of a great ox on the beach by the Black Sea, giving grateful thanks to the gods for their deliverance, before eventually leaving the harbour, heading homeward along Anatolia's northern coast. Left behind on the strand was a heavy, crudely made wagon, with one wheel missing. The large wooden disc was aboard the Delias, safely concealing The Marathon Shield.

The mixed crew of rowers made good progress westward towards

Sinope, another Hellene coastal city, and it was here that Theomenes made a decision. Desperately torn between his duty to return his city's relic, and his desire to have Amara found, he released Imbros and Telios from their pledges. From the port of Sinope, a good road ran directly to join The Royal Road, which went straight to Sardis - and Amara.

'This is your best chance, Imbros,' said Theomenes. 'They would not be suspicious of a man and his woman, coming from the east. By all the gods, I hope you find her Imbros!'

Clytes watched, fidgeting, as Imbros and Anthousa prepared to leave. 'I'm also releasing you Clytes, and Angelos if he wishes,' spoke Theomenes, gravely. 'You've done more than anyone could expect, as an Eleusinian, to help Plataea. And I know you want to go too.'

'You're going into the den of the lioness!' groaned Glaucus to Clytes, sorry to be losing his friend again, so soon. 'Be careful!' he said, concerned.

'I'm not the one who's covered in bandages!' Clytes pointed out, shaking his head at Glaucus. Turning to gather up his weapons, he added, 'I'll see you at Delphi!'

'Why Delphi?' asked Glaucus.

'For the ceremony! Theo is taking The Shield there for safe-keeping - until it can be returned to Plataea.'

'Cleon won't like that!' growled Glaucus. 'He won't have given up on it going to Athens, so he can take all the glory.'

'Well, I'm sure Theo will let him share the glory - but only at Delphi!' replied Clytes.

'Your luck will run out one day, friend,' said Glaucus, looking seriously at Clytes as he prepared to leave.

'You're not home yourself yet, Helmsman,' he replied. 'Don't worry about me! Just don't get into any more scrapes, yourself! The Persian patrols will still be out searching. By the way, you never did tell me what happened to the Delias.'

'It can wait, Clytes,' replied Glaucus, gripping his old friend a little too firmly by the hand.

Surprisingly for Clytes, it was Stephanos who came last to wish him well. 'Just in case the gods don't allow us to meet again,' he said, drawing him to one side, 'I'm indebted to you Clytes, for your loyalty and fellowship throughout this venture. It pains me to say this,' he added smiling, 'but without you I believe we could have failed.'

'You're a proud man, Stephanos,' replied Clytes,' grateful for his words. 'I know what it took for you to say such things - to a non-Plataean!'

'I hope to see you at Delphi, Clytes,' added Stephanos, with emphasis.

'At Delphi, Stephanos!' Clytes replied, as they clasped hands in farewell.

EIGHTY-TWO

ANGELOS WOULD NOT BE parted from Clytes and it was therefore, a party of five that set off on newly acquired horses, back to the wide expanse of Anatolia. Imbros was colourfully attired, as would befit a wealthy merchant travelling with his wife and manservant, while Clytes, wearing the purple edged robes he'd acquired in Colophon; and brought with him for just such a clandestine undertaking, had disguised himself outlandishly as a minor nobleman, with Angelos playing the part of his fawning attendant. On the crowded trade route known as The Royal Road, busy with travellers from all parts of the known world, they merged easily, and with Clytes maintaining a confident performance, he gave courage to the others, and progress towards Sardis was swift.

Anthousa led them to the vast sacred burial site, six miles north of Sardis, known as The Thousand Hills. The enormous tombs of the Kings of Lydia rivalled the pyramids of Egypt, and their group mingled with visitors who'd come from far and wide to view these wonders. It was to this area of gigantic tumuli, seen from a distance, that Anthousa had fled after her escape. And it was in these hills where she had fashioned her crude bows and arrows, using skills acquired during the long siege at Plataea, when they'd run out of bronze arrow heads. Chipping away at the hard rocks found around her, she fashioned implements sharp enough to kill her prey. In this way she survived living wild, until finally being discovered by the Amazons.

Between the cemetery and the city lay the wide, fertile valley of the river Hermus, where Larachne's estate was situated, and where they expected to find Amara.

Once across the river, the road towards the city was busy with traffic. Choked with camels and horses, as well as mule and ox drawn carts, it made the going slow, but it gave them time to look at the lie of the land and to seek out any means of avoiding detection after the rescue. 'We'll have to do it at night,' said Imbros, seeing nothing which could hide them, but they noticed there was a good road heading west towards the sea. 'There's no chance of getting away in daylight!' he affirmed.

'First you'll have to silence the dogs, Imbros,' said Anthousa. 'They run loose, and they've been trained to kill!'

'Let's pray your herbs work on dogs also, Anthousa,' replied Imbros. 'They gave me the best night's rest I've ever had!'

Anthousa tried to suppress a smile. That's not what the women of her tribe had told her!

'If it hadn't been for the dogs, I wouldn't have got away,' she added, seriously. 'They were chasing one of the workers who'd broken loose from his bonds. He was in a group of men being taken to the rock quarries. Just as the gates opened, he made a run for it! Amara and I had been ordered to clean up in the abattoir. Some old horses due for slaughter had just been delivered, but the men were distracted by the commotion. Before I could stop myself, I'd jumped onto the back of the tallest horse and managed to climb onto the roof. Amara was too weak and couldn't make it. I reached the top of a building backing onto the wall. She begged me to go, Imbros!' said Anthousa, tears stinging her eyes, 'but I should never have left her!'

'If you hadn't got away, Anthousa,' said Clytes, gently, 'Imbros wouldn't know where to find her.'

The farm estate of Larachne covered a large area. Enclosed by dried brick walls in some parts, high banks of earth and wattle fencing in others. On the east and west sides, were immense, double-gated entrances, the high pillars and walls of which were of brilliant white limestone, ornately carved with animals, birds and sinuous reptiles. There was no way in without attracting attention.

'Was Amara ever taken from the estate?' asked Imbros, hopefully.

'Sometimes, we were both taken to Larachne's terrible villa!' answered Anthousa, shuddering. 'We saw things there we'll never forget! But Amara became sickly and Larachne lost interest in tormenting her, and Mirhab got bored with me, so we were left in the hands of Cynares, her estate manager - an evil man!'

'Then we have no other choice. We drug the dogs and cut our way in through the fence. Draw us a plan so we know where the women sleep,' he said to Anthousa. 'We need to know exactly where we're going.'

That night a bright moon shone, and the dogs were howling constantly. Carrying sacks filled with lumps of fresh meat wrapped around large portions of Anthousa's herbs, the five quietly spread out, encircling the perimeter of Larachne's estate. At regular intervals, they threw the drugged meat over the fence, finally joining up again an hour or so later, when they waited as the moon moved slowly across the sky, to be finally hidden behind a cloud. In the air was the faint smell of sulphur.

Clytes climbed up the bank and gently rattled the fencing. Nothing. He walked further and did it again. Still nothing. The horses which were fidgeting nervously, they left fettered and tied to trees as near to the perimeter fence as possible, then equipped with all they could safely carry, they cut their way through. 'Are we ready?' Imbros asked the others, quietly. They all nodded.

In near darkness, they headed towards the faint light coming from the night fire, mapped out by Anthousa as the location of the jumble of farm dwellings where the women were kept. Clytes and Imbros carried swords and daggers. Anthousa, Angelos and Telios carried bows and arrows and slingshots. As they crossed the open ground, a loud rumbling sound was heard and they immediately froze, looking around anxiously for attacking dogs. The rumbling came again, but it was coming from beneath their feet. The ground started to move. ''Wait!,' Imbros whispered urgently. Suddenly, all went still. 'Let's go!' he urged. They reached the building indicated by Anthousa as being the women's quarters, but discovered a large padlock on the door. As quietly as possible, Clytes, Angelos and Telios, made a pyramid of their bodies which Imbros quickly climbed to reach the thatched roof. With urgency he cut an aperture through the reeds, squeezed through the hole, then dropped to the ground. The smell of unwashed bodies and human waste made him gag. Unable to focus, he called out Amara's name. At first there was silence, then terrified sobs came from several women. 'I'm not here to hurt you!' whispered Imbros. 'I'm a friend. My name is Imbros. I'm searching for my wife, Amara.' He instantly felt hands on his body, then thin arms clung around his neck. 'Imbros?' he heard weakly. The voice was Amara's. 'Thank the gods!' he said, embracing her emaciated yet familiar body, kissing her passionately.

'Can you walk? Can you get up through the roof if I hold you? Are you there, Clytes?' he called upwards.

'I'm here,' replied Clytes. 'Pass her up!'

Clytes athletically swung his body down to reach for Amara as she was handed up by Imbros. Angelos, now also on the roof, pulled with all his strength to help her through the narrow aperture. One by one Imbros passed the women up to waiting arms, until he also was hauled to safety.

As they all reached the ground, the rumbling began again but louder this time. Amara and Anthousa, clinging to each other in mutual relief, staggered as the surface all around them began to ripple and crack alarmingly. 'Get to the horses! Quickly!' called out Angelos, agitated. 'Before they bolt!'

'But what about the women?' pleaded Amara. 'We can't leave them, Imbros!'

'We don't have enough horses, Amara. We have to leave, my dearest, or we will all be lost!' he said urgently.

Men began to emerge from the farm buildings, unnerved by the rattling and crashing of the roof tiles. They called out loudly for the dogs, but were too concerned about their own safety to notice in the darkness, the fleeing group of men and women.

Running past the guard dogs, some stretched out dead or unconscious on the ground, others staggering aimlessly, the group found their way back to their frightened horses. Angelos immediately set about calming them, talking quietly and gently moving his hands along their flanks until they stopped quivering. Anthousa shared her horse with Amara, being the lightest of the riders, and they sped, guided by the outer estate wall, towards the west gate, knowing there was a hard-packed road from there towards the Aegean.

As they rode, cracks began to appear in the walls as the quaking grew worse. Mud-brick houses in a poor settlement near the carved stone gateway to the estate, started to tumble into the streets, and people were seen running in all directions as flames spread from house to house, when the thatched roofs collapsed onto smouldering household fires.

'Anthousa! Amara!' they heard someone shouting. In the light from the burning buildings they saw two haggard, barely clad women running towards them, desperately trying to reach the horses.

It's Elpida and Kori!' said Amara. 'We've got to help them, Imbros! They were with us during the siege!'

Imbros, remembering the Plataean slave women very well, immediately wheeled his horse about and rode towards them, with Clytes following. Leaning down, he shouted to them to come to him, just as a sudden loud crack rent the air. The ground churned like the sea beneath them and his horse, in terror, reared up. Both mount and rider fell heavily. Amara let out a loud scream. 'Imbros!' Swaying violently was one of the tall limestone pillars supporting the gates, and she watched in horror as it twisted crazily then crashed to the ground. Lying buried beneath the large slabs was Imbros. He groaned, and Telios instantly jumped down and rushed over to help him. Clytes, trying to control his horse, shouted out a warning. 'Watch out!' The matching stone pillar had become detached from its foundations, and before Telios could get out of the way, it also fell, crushing him and Imbros. While Angelos and Anthousa desperately tried to hold onto the horses, Clytes and Amara clawed frantically to lift the stones from Imbros, while Elpida and Kori went to help Telios. They realised immediately, both men were dead. Imbros's skull had been crushed, and only the lifeless arm of Telios could be seen protruding from the heap of rubble. Leaping flames lit up a stone fragment which Clytes held in his hands. He stared at the broken slab in shock, as his fingers ran over the carving of the writhing serpents. He remembered suddenly the words from the Pythia's warning. Beware of snakes in the walls! And we all thought she meant Cleon, he thought, grievously.

Without Imbros, the lives of those left in the group were suddenly Clytes' responsibility, and his immediate concern was Larachne. Sardis was at the end of the long Royal Road which led to Susa. With a regular change of horses, riders could relay messages from the king within ten days. Larachne may already know of the death of her ex-lover, Lykaon, and of the hunt for the coveted shield. The huge stone slabs being too heavy to move, meant the bodies of Imbros and Telios could not be recovered and their identifiable weaponry would have to stay buried with them. If they had any chance of getting out of Lydia alive, they must travel quickly before the she-wolf became aware of their existence.

In desperation to leave immediately, he and Angelos dragged a weeping Amara from the body of her dead husband, hardening themselves against her anguished cries of, 'No, Clytes! Leave me! Oh Imbros!' and forcing the suffering woman, broken in body and spirit, back onto the horse with Anthousa. Elpida and Kori rode Telios's horse. The mount of Imbros had been severely injured by the falling masonry, and Clytes quickly despatched the suffering animal.

Although not a major quake, the city of Sardis suffered little damage, but the continuing tremors sent Larachne's pet leopards into a terrified frenzy. They broke loose from their enclosure, severely mauled their handlers, and ran crazed around the terraces of the villa, desperately seeking a way out. Larachne and Mirhab, together with the rest of her household, awakened by the shaking, rushed from their various quarters to assemble on the lawns. Roof tiles crashed down and statues toppled as Larachne, emerging from the villa, stridently shouted out her orders. At her side, followed the large hunting hounds which shared her bedroom. They snarled, then barked madly as a scream from one of the women, rent the air. Larachne turned quickly to see her leopards creeping slowly across the lawns, their pale green eyes staring intently at the dogs. Larachne yelled in terror for their handlers to come, but none appeared.

'Mirhab! Stop them!' she called out urgently, but Mirhab, fresh from Larachne's bed, was unclothed and unarmed. Time seemed to stand still as Larachne stared, frozen to the spot. Then in an instant, the big cats leapt on the dogs. The fight was ferocious and gruesome and people ran from the scene. Armed guards, hearing the fracas, hurried from their posts at the gate, but as they saw Larachne had become trapped between the fighting animals, they held back from firing their weapons. No-one attempted to save Larachne, not even her loyal Mirhab, who seemed reluctant to intervene. One of the dogs escaped and ran off, terrified. The rest were torn to pieces. Badly injured, the cats stood their ground, and with shoulders hunched, they snarled and hissed as blood dripped from their jaws, ready to pounce. Seeing Larachne's body had been mutilated beyond any help, a rain of arrows and javelins finally put an end to her pet killers.

Mirhab turned towards the guards and imperially ordered them to remove the body of their mistress. Nobody moved. Defenceless, he watched the grim faced armed men move menacingly towards him. After years of torture and ill-treatment meted out by both Larachne and

Mirhab, the guards now took their revenge. Overwhelming him, they cut out his tongue so that he could not report what he'd witnessed, forcing him to run for his life. Mirhab knowing he was fortunate not to have been killed, fled in agony, blood pouring from his mouth. The guards then set about rampaging through the rooms, taking anything of value. Magnificent embroideries, exquisite jewellery, beautiful ornaments and personal effects, were all thrown in heaps onto Larachne's colourful silk rugs. The Plataean women at first looked on in horror, then encouraged by the guards and the rest of Larachne's household, they also joined in ransacking the evil residence. With all they could safely carry, they fled into the night. The confusion caused by Poseidon the ground-shaker, gained them precious time. Some would make it to the coast, free at last from the horrors of Larachne's villa.

EIGHTY-THREE

TWENTY-FOUR HOURS LATER, TWO men and four women mounted on four horses, rode into the Persian ruled city of Smyrna on the Aegean coast, just fifty miles from the port of Erythrae on the Athenian ruled peninsula. Clytes wanted them all to push on to Erythrae, but Anthousa insisted she could go no further.

'What is there for me in Attica, Clytes?' she asked him, truthfully. 'I can't go back to how I lived before! It would be a torment to me now. My life is with my warrior family. That's where I now belong.'

'Will I ever see you again?' asked a heavyhearted Clytes.

'I may be with child,' replied Anthousa, glancing quickly at Clytes. 'If I am, I don't intend to take any herbs to miscarry,' she added defiantly. 'If it's a girl, I will rear her myself, according to our way of life. If it's a boy, then it is usual for the father to take responsibility,' she said pointedly, looking keenly at Clytes for his reaction.

Anthousa was relieved to see him smile broadly. 'Expect to see me in a year's time, then!' he said readily, 'and you can show me what we have!' Then he moved his horse closer and kissed Anthousa, lovingly.

Amara clung to her friend, unable seemingly to let her go. 'I'll never forget you, Anthousa,' she said through her tears, and her fingers moved to touch the livid brand on her own upper arm, inflicted by Cynares, Larachne's estate manager.

'You will always be in my heart, Amara!' cried Anthousa, exposing her similar brand, now obscured by the head of a leopard. 'May the gods protect you and one day, give you peace!' Then she wheeled her horse, kicking up the dust, galloping at high speed away from them, calling out the wild cries of her tribe as she did so, until she was gone from their sight.

'You will ride with me now,' said Clytes, gently to Amara, then turning to Angelos and the women, he added, 'Our next destination is the port of Erythrae. From there we will take a ship to Piraeus and then - to Athens!'

Amara knew what was expected of her in Athens. She would have to break the news of their son's death to Imbros's parents. Elpida and Kori being innocent but constant reminders of how Imbros was killed, Clytes found places for, with a family with no connection to Plataea.

EIGHTY-FOUR

CLEON MADE MUCH OF the fact that by releasing some of Athens' best rowers for the start of the quest, he had shown his utmost confidence in Theomenes and his company of Plataeans, not like the many doubters he could name. His anger had cooled since discovering The Marathon Shield was not being brought to Athens, and unable to discover its whereabouts in the months since its rescue, he now took what small credit he could from his early involvement. He had it put about that The Shield being brought to Delphi was his idea! Standing uncomfortably, elbow to elbow with his political rival, Nicias, and accompanied by several high-ranking personages from Athens, he watched as the glowing shield was carried along the processional way towards the Temple of Apollo.

Those individuals who had never made the journey to Plataea, and stood in the city's Temple of Athena, were awestruck at the magnificence of the embellished aspis from the Battle of Marathon. Following its arduous and damaging journey throughout Asia Minor, the famous relic had been restored to its former glory, and beams of spring sunlight flashed and radiated from the gold and dazzling gemstones of its decoration.

The gilded frame bearing The Shield, was carried proudly on the strong shoulders of Theomenes and Stephanos who were leading, and Clytes and Glaucus at the rear. Directly behind the magnificently attired foursome, walked Mydon, trying hard not to limp. In his hands he carried solemnly, the helmet of Imbros. Gifts to Apollo donated by the families of Androdamos, Chares, Echus and Philon were carried with dignity, by the surviving Plataeans from The Shield Company including Angelos. Last, but insisted upon by Cleon, marched the Athenian rowers holding their upright oars. As they stepped solemnly along the route to the Temple of Apollo, acknowledging the delighted people lining the way, flutes and trumpets were played loudly and the singing of priests in celebration filled the air.

Arriving at the temple, they were greeted by a smiling Cleon. Holding in front of him, his large hands resting on the boy's shoulders, was fair haired Akylas, the nine-year old son of Phalinus. An overly emotional Admetus, stood with other people of note from their ruined city, while behind them crowded many of the displaced Plataeans who'd come from far and wide to witness the return of their sacred relic. As it drew closer to them, sounds of released emotion could be heard. Amidst all the suffering of the continuing war, this was a rare and joyous occasion.

The burnished gold shield was carried into the great marble hall, already adorned with other trophies taken in famous battles. There it was placed in a niche which had been created specially to hold it. Akylas was asked to draw aside a small curtain to reveal a marble plaque. It was inscribed:

The Shield of Agristones, Plataean: Saviour of Miltiades, Victorious General against the Medes at Marathon.

Everyone then pushed and jostled their way into the room to take a long proud look, seeking also a glimpse of young Akylas, the expected future Shield Guardian of Plataea.

'The success of this venture will bring good fortune to our cause!' said Cleon, boastfully, so all could hear, and he placed his arm around Theomenes' shoulders, as the man of the moment. 'Boldness and imagination! It is just the inspiration we need, right now!' he said pointedly, looking sourly in the direction of the undisputed, over-cautious politician, Nicias. 'Things will change in Athens from now on. I'll see to that! Come and see me in Athens, when you return to your duties with the cavalry, Theomenes.'

Theomenes was not paying Cleon the attention he thought he deserved. The demagogue noticed the young man kept looking around the room as though searching for someone.

Amara was supposed to have travelled up from Athens with Admetus, in the company of a group of Plataean dignitaries. Since Clytes had deposited her with Imbros's family some months before, Theomenes had not set eyes on her. In fact, apart from the terrified vision he'd had of her on the rail of Lykaon's penteconter, it was six long years since he'd seen her. He wished to speak with Admetus about Amara, but he searched without success to find the old man in the throng.

His uncle Hypatos, hurriedly approached them, and after exchanging the usual pleasantries with Cleon, drew his nephew aside, grabbing him fervently by the hand. 'This is such a special occasion, Theo!' he gushed. 'I wish Eubalos could have lived to see you now. Your father would have been so proud!'

'Without your help and support, uncle, it may never have happened,' replied Theo, with sincerity. 'I'll be forever in your debt!'

During the sixth winter of the ongoing war, Theomenes had stayed at his uncle's villa on the island of Mesembria in the Black Sea. Being close to the mainland, Hypatos used this tiny island as a base to keep an eye on his investments in the Thracian gold mines. Recently brought into the Delian League, Theomenes thought Mesembria, being so far from Athens, a safe destination to take his city's treasured icon, until it could be brought to Delphi. So it was to this little fortified outcrop that Glaucus had sailed the battered Delias from Pontus.

'Have you seen Admetus, uncle?' Theomenes added, casually.

'Ha!' exclaimed Hypatos. 'You cannot fool me, nephew! You will find her much changed, Theo. Admetus has gone to seek the advice of the Pythia. He's been struggling to start his new work on the fall of Plataea.'

'I shall go and wait for him, uncle,' answered Theomenes. 'Make my excuses to Cleon. I can suffer no more of his boasting. You would think he had recovered The Shield!'

'Akaterina and the rest of the women will have their day of celebration tomorrow, Theo. You may not be able to see her until the following day,' Hypatos suggested.

'Then I shall have to see her tonight!' replied Theomenes, eagerly, wanting so much to share with Amara his mixed feelings of elation and loss. For all the joy and sense of celebration, the serious, noble figure of Imbros was grievously missed by all the company.

EIGHTY-FIVE

ADMETUS THOUGHT AT FIRST he ought to be discrete in describing Amara's current situation, but he was so disturbed by her precarious state of mind, that he talked freely with Theo, knowing he, of all people, would understand. 'She is still beautiful, despite the hardships she has suffered, Theo, but her eyes bear such a haunted look, it is sad to behold. When she learned that her parents had been taken by the pestilence, I thought we would lose her also! Imbros's parents are sympathetic, of course, but the rest of their family have made it fairly obvious that they think of her as an expensive, decorative ornament. Without children, and the belief that she is unable to carry a child full term, her situation is not a happy one. They say that no man would want a used, emotionally damaged woman, unable to bear him an heir. I am afraid for her, Theo!'

Theomenes, even after his talk with Admetus, was not prepared for what he saw when Amara entered the room. Dressed plainly as her new circumstances dictated; her eyes downcast, she seemed to be sleep-walking. Now, at the age of twenty-five, Theomenes thought her more lovely than ever, but when she raised her eyes to look at him, a cold shiver suddenly attacked his body. Those gentle, sparkling eyes that had so bewitched him when he was just a blushing youth, were now devoid of emotion.

'My dear friend!' he said, gently. 'I am so relieved to see you! It has been too long!'

'It is good to see you too, Theo,' Amara replied, with seeming indifference.

'Amara!' said Theo, impetuously, moving to take her hands into his. 'I want you to come and live with me at my uncle's house.'

'Dear Theo,' said Amara, quietly, trying to turn away. 'I am not good company these days. If I can talk truthfully to you, as an old friend, I just want to follow Imbros. There is nothing left for me now.'

'I won't have you talking that way!' exclaimed Theo, frantically. Having saved The Shield, he seemed to believe he could save anything. 'You will stay with us in Athens. I insist! And when my military duties end, we will go to my uncle's villa in Mesembria this winter, where you can recover your health.'

'It would not be right, Theo,' answered Amara, flatly. 'Hypatos is a widower, and you are not married. What would people think?'

'I don't care what people think,' replied Theo, honestly, 'if you don't. Will you consider it, my dear?' pleaded Theo. 'You will not be judged by Hypatos in any way, and certainly not by me!'

'Thank you, Theo. I will consider it,' Amara replied. By her demeanor, however, Theo could not be sure she would.

EIGHTY-SIX

'IF IT'S A BOY, Ortronus, I don't think I could bear it!' confessed Marissa. 'If the baby is weak, they will kill it, and if it is strong, he will be brutalised in the agoge!' She had known for some weeks that she was pregnant again, and her situation had unfortunately not changed since her last child was born two years previously. The baby girl, just like the one born in her first year in Sparta, had been taken from her as soon as the umbilical cord was severed, and handed over to a wet-nurse. She was told that her second child had not survived, but knowing the strict criteria in Sparta, that only strong babies were allowed to live, Marissa had always believed that the baby had been deliberately killed. Her surviving daughter, now aged five, was being brought up by the family of Nicander; by his wife Kora in fact, just as Marissa had feared before she'd set foot in Sparta. Marissa saw her daughter as often as Nicander could arrange it, from a distance, and it broke her heart to know that the little girl was unaware of her. It was Nicander's reasoning that his daughter, in order to have a secure future, should be brought up as a full Spartan, and that Marissa was not sufficiently conversant in their ways. She might be too gentle with the child, in other words.

Nicander, when he wasn't campaigning or with his men in their barracks, had his time taken up by family needs. Also his cousin, Pleistoanax, was king again, his years in exile finally ended. This meant that Nicander was constantly called to his side as an advisor. Marissa, although safe and unmolested, had no family of her own in Sparta, and had become closer to her helot slaves than Nicander thought wise. Ortronus had mellowed, and over time they had become co-conspirators in their joint need to survive in the enforced environment which was their 'home'. Whenever merchant ships arrived at Githium, they both eagerly awaited any news of how the war was progressing, and although it was dangerous, they would discuss the implications far into the night. Marissa, first fretted on the long-running siege at Plataea. Then the quest to bring back the stolen Marathon Shield, fired her imagination - giving her hope. Ortronus listened for news of the city-state of Naupactus, a place he dreamed of escaping to one day, since he hoped some of his own family line would be there. The Spartans had broken a helot revolt thirty years earlier, and Athens had re-homed some of the Messenian rebels at Naupactus, something these grateful and courageous people never forgot.

But the woman concerned for her unborn child was not the unworldly Marissa that was brought to Sparta six years previously. She was now a strong-limbed competent rider and a skilled archer. Working with Erasmos and Dorias in their business had been a successful collaboration. With Marissa demonstrating the beauty and quality of the musical instruments to potential buyers, the business was thriving, and she had acquired some wealth of her own. Something she could never have achieved in Plataea. Ortronus too, was prospering. An unusual situation for a helot, and entirely due to being under the aegis of Nicander. On the vast slopes of Mount Taygetos, he sought out the fine woods required for the instrument inlays, the patterns for which were exquisitely designed by Marissa. He was allowed to keep some of the profits and because of this working relationship with his mistress, his dream of getting to Naupactus grew more and more real. He took great care of her. He loved her, with his whole being.

But despite Nicander's high status, Marissa was still considered an outsider. She was not Spartan and was at the whim of Nicander with regard to her own life and the lives of any children she bore him. She'd asked him once, why he'd not married her off to one of the merchants who lived in Amyklai.

He had looked hurt and replied, 'I don't understand why you ask me that. Is there someone?'

'Of course not, Nicander!' she had responded. Seeing the look in her eyes, he knew she was telling him the truth.

'I've told you, my dearest, I will always care for you and any children you bear me. I know it is not the life you envisaged, but the whole world seems to be at war, right now. Only the gods know when it will end. The army will be leaving again soon. I want you to come to the city, Marissa. I want you and our daughter to be there, to see me depart.'

For reasons she could not quite understand, Marissa decided not to tell Nicander of her pregnancy.

EIGHTY-SEVEN

MARISSA STOOD ON THE BALCONY of the house she shared with Erasmos and his family, looking towards what she thought were fires to the north of their township. Sounds of screams had disturbed her sleep, and when she called out for the housemaids for reassurance, they were nowhere to be found. The house seemed deserted. Not even Ortronus answered her shouts. She urgently woke the instrument maker and his wife, and together with their daughter, they all watched incredulously at the red glow in the distance.

'What is it?' Marissa asked Erasmos. 'Is it an attack?'

'Our army is still away!' cried out Arlea, fearfully. 'We are undefended!'

'This is not the work of the Athenians!' declared Erasmos, harshly. 'It's the damned helots! They've taken advantage of the fact that the army has not yet returned. I must get to our neighbours and warn them!' He was relieved to see that their locked supply of weaponry was still intact, and he quickly equipped himself with all he could carry. Their slaves appeared to have deserted them, but at least they hadn't armed themselves or attacked the family.

'You must see to the animals, Dorias, and barricade the house. Quickly, now! You may not have much time!' And he sped off into the night, up the darkened street to raise the alarm.

The three women immediately set about securing the main dwelling. All livestock close to their dwelling was brought into the courtyard and a barricade of carts and household equipment was piled against the gates. Anything that could be used in defending themselves was taken into the house. They closed all the shutters, and the furniture was stacked high against all the doors and windows. Only the balcony remained unencumbered, and here the women gathered all the weapons available to them, mainly slingshot, bows and arrows.

Erasmos was right. The Messenian helots, incensed at their brutal subjugation had been waiting for just such an opportunity to revolt, and as soon as the army had set off to invade Attica that summer, plans had started to form. The fittest of their kind, both men and women, had been taken to fight and serve alongside their masters, but even though those left behind were mainly the old and the very young, they still outnumbered the remaining Spartan population, ten to one. News constantly filtered through from the lands outside Sparta of how the war was progressing, and rumours abounded that the Athenians were in support of their plight. If any were brave enough to escape, it was said that safe havens had been provided for them.

Ortronus had been excused from military duty, purely because Nicander had a conscience. He felt responsible for Marissa being without family support, and Ortronus had been left behind to take care of her in his absence. But just when she needed him most, the helot was nowhere to be found.

The revolt spread throughout the land, and the fires seen from the balcony grew in number and magnitude. Word came to the house, intermittently. They were in no danger, just so long as they did not venture abroad. The repercussions against the slaves were being carried out without mercy, but there was unrestrained slaughter on both sides and cries of fighting were heard all around them. Sleeping in shifts, the women were able to keep a constant watch for intruders so when figures were seen scaling the outer walls, they were ready. The blood-curdling screams from these ragged individuals, terrified the women. Mountain folk, clothed in animal skins, it was impossible to tell whether they were men or women, or even if they were human. Sending volley after volley of arrows and slingshot, their feeble assailants were soon beaten off.

Finally, news reached them that the army had returned and the rebellion was under control, but relief was soon followed by grief. Erasmos brought the dreadful news. Lord Nicander had been killed. Reports were that he had fought bravely, after becoming unseated from his horse, but being severely outnumbered, he'd been hacked to pieces by a frenzied mob. His comrades had borne his mutilated body back to the city, carried on his shield; the entire route lined by grieving mourners. To spare Marissa, Erasmos omitted for the time being, details of how the mother, wife and small daughter of the noble Nicander had followed behind his body, and were much admired by the populace for their dignified, silent grieving.

There was no such silence from Marissa! The news was like a knife piercing her heart. All she could do was to cry out, 'Nicander! Nicander!' as she tore around her room, beating her breasts - begging him to return to her. Dorias, worried that she would do herself harm, brought her a cup of diluted wine mixed with a sleeping draught and she and Arlea together, encouraged her to drink the entire contents, before leaving her to rest. It was dark when she woke abruptly, and as a wave of grief hit her anew, sobs broke from her uncontrollably. Someone touched her on the shoulder. 'Mistress!' she heard, urgently whispered into her ear. She gasped, realising it was Ortronus. Before she could scream, he put his hand across her mouth.

'Listen to me, now!' he said softly. 'I did not have to return here. I could have got away, but when I heard about the death of lord Nicander, I knew how life would change for you here without his protection.' Marissa was suddenly afraid. Ortronus could feel her body shaking. 'I came back to take you and the baby you are carrying, to safety,' said Ortronus, quietly. 'I know a safe route over the mountains, but I have to go now. The soldiers could discover it. Do you want to stay - or leave?' he added hopefully, and he gently released his hand from her mouth.

'Murderer! You killed my Nicander!' screamed Marissa, turning on him viciously. 'He warned me about you helots! I trusted you!' she hissed at him.

'I would never have harmed him,' said Ortronus, sincerely. 'For a Spartan, I respected him. But the comfortable life we both had under his shield is over!' he insisted, urgently. 'The family here will not be able to protect you or your child. You will quickly learn what it is like to be an outsider in Sparta.'

With all they could carry between them, and with the kithara strapped to Ortronus' back, the pair silently left the instrument maker's house. Did the family hear them depart and allow them to escape? The fugitives would never know. There could be no farewells. The night was moonless. Mercifully so for Marissa. Bodies of dead helots still had to be cleared from the streets, and rats were starting to feed. Not all the bodies were helots. Hanging from the gnarled olive tree at the end of the street, obscured by the night, was the lifeless form of an old man. At his feet lay his walking cane. Ortronus glanced dispassionately in his direction, then removing his helot leather cap, threw it contemptuously towards him. They hurried on, Ortronus guiding a sorrowful Marissa through narrow back streets, along foul gullies only a slave would know, until they left the town behind and headed towards the looming Taygetos mountains.

Ortronus knew this route very well indeed. During the years he had searched the slopes for specimen trees, he'd delved further and further into the mountain, seeking out hidden caves and trackways, avoiding any signs of habitation. He'd stalked the deer, following their trails high up the slopes and tracked wild boar to secluded watercourses. Sure-footed ibex had led him to areas inaccessible to wolf or bear, where he'd found uninhabited caves. This was to be his escape route, but he could not part himself from Marissa. Now she had chosen to put her life in his hands, he could not fail her. Rumours of an Athenian garrison at Pylos, on the other side of the mountains would be their goal. From there, maybe a ship to Naupactus and freedom!

The helots of Sparta paid a heavy price for their rebellious actions. Individual commanders asked of their slave attendants, the names of any men who had acted bravely while the army was in action against the Athenians, promising reward and recognition for their loyalty. Believing freedom was being offered, the names of two-thousand courageous helots were put forward. Once identified, they were rounded up and executed.

EIGHTY-EIGHT

IN THE SEVENTH SUMMER of the war, up to which time neither side had gained supremacy, Athens won an important victory over Sparta. Demosthenes, who was not yet a general, was with the Athenian fleet sailing for Sicily when a storm drove them ashore on the Pylos peninsula of Messenia, which was under Spartan rule. Always believing that this south-western promontory could be fortified, he successfully argued with the two generals of the fleet, to secure this strategic point of land for a garrison. The Spartans, alarmed that Athenians had built a base on their territory, abandoned their ravaging of Attica that summer, and headed back to defend their homeland, at the same time sending the Spartan fleet to Pylos. Failing to block the harbour however, they became trapped when fifty Athenian triremes arrived, causing hundreds of Spartan hoplites to be stranded on an island in the bay. One-hundred and twenty of these belonged to the spartiate class, and in panic the Spartans surrendered their fleet and sued for a permanent peace, expecting the return of their Spartan elite. Cleon, having personally taken part in the enterprise, now basked in the glory at having defeated the Spartans, and refused to negotiate. The prisoners were taken to Athens to be paraded before the people as exotic exhibits, as many had never seen a Spartan warrior at close quarters before. It had been strongly believed that Spartans never surrendered but would fight to the last man, and their surrender shook their world.

Once Pylos was secured, and Messenian reinforcements arrived from Naupactus, helots escaping the tyranny of slavery in Sparta, fled to this tiny part of their home country. It was to this outpost that Ortronus and many other helots fled, eventually becoming a serious problem to the Spartans as they made a series of bold attacks into territory well known to them.

Ortronus became instrumental in the building up of a well organised escape route for the helots, using the skills and knowledge he had acquired in his own flight. His life was now full of purpose, but for Marissa, life was no more secure than if she had stayed in Sparta. She was now living among the very people who had murdered Nicander, and even the fondness she'd once held for Ortronus, was tainted by this constant memory.

In mid-winter, she gave birth to a son, and her thoughts were now for the future of her new-born child.

EIGHTY-NINE

ONE LATE-WINTER MORNING, AS a pale sun rose over Villa Atheni on the tiny island of Mesembria, just off the coast of Thrace, the usual pattern of daily life was just beginning. The young slave, Erica, chosen by Mydon and purchased specifically to serve Admetus, was carrying out her required tasks. Every day for a week now she'd helped Hesiodos, Admetus' personal assistant, to carry the historian's table and high-backed chair to a particularly sheltered position on the terrace, carefully preparing his writing equipment ready for him to begin work. Because of the cool breeze, she used the heavy bronze statuette of Athena, which Admetus always had standing on his desk, as a weight to hold down his papers. Curiously, she ran her fingers over the incised letters on the base - IMBROS - unable to understand their meaning, just as she'd seen the sad lady Amara do, several times when she thought no-one was watching her. Erica had been instructed by Mydon, that in no uncertain terms, this statuette must come to no harm. Looking around quickly, she carefully set down the figurine.

From this vantage point, the view was of a bay dotted with small fishing boats, beneath a wide, cool blue sky reflected in the sparkling waters lapping at the fortified walls of the island. Admetus had tried every room in the house, with Hesiodos and Erica patiently moving his desk and accoutrements from place to place. None proved satisfactory to the historian. The inspiration simply would not come. Wrapped in blankets, he sat for hours on the terrace, insisting that this was now the right place, but the girl could not help but notice that the papyrus sheets remained conspicuously pristine. It was a part of Mydon's instructions, that she should be helpful to Admetus in his every waking hour, and Erica, who would do anything to please the handsome, estimable Mydon, who was in complete charge of running the household of Theomenes, was disappointed that all she'd been required to do so far, was to make sure the old man's wine jug was regularly replenished.

The fact that the curmudgeonly historian was acting a little more oddly than usual, had not gone unnoticed, and Theomenes put it down to the rumour that a second rival, Hellanicus of Lesbos, was now writing his own version of events covering the seven-year war. Wealthy Athenian statesman, Thucydides, who also considered himself a worthy historian, was already pestering Admetus for his notes on the fall of Plataea, but as far as Admetus was concerned, he was the only one capable of writing down the plain, unvarnished truth of the terrible happenings at Plataea, part of which he'd experienced at first-hand. But where to begin?

Villa Atheni, named in memory of Hypatos' late wife, was on a modest scale compared to some of its grander neighbours. Built on two levels, on a rugged promontory, it looked towards the wooded shoreline of Thrace, while to the right there was the vast open sea. It suited Theomenes' purpose, which was why he had rented it from his uncle for the winter months. It was here that he hoped Amara would recover from her melancholy. He watched her now from the balustrade; at her slim figure as she walked alone, along the narrow strip of sand beneath the cliff, the winter sun glinting on the gold armlet encircling her upper arm. It was his gift to her, made especially to hide her disfigurement. The scars of the mind were proving harder to deal with.

Recently returned from a campaign to the Corinthian isthmus, where Theomenes and his cavalry unit were instrumental in bringing about a successful outcome, he also welcomed the peace of the island. The war was becoming increasingly brutal, and what was once considered barbaric, was now becoming accepted practice. Eighty ships led by strategos Nicias, had sailed from Piraeus, one of them helmed by Glaucus of Thessaly under the command of trierarch, Iandros. It had been good to meet up with the big redhead again. Also Clytes and his cousins from Eleusis, who all mercifully survived the daring undertaking.

Glaucus, now the proud owner of the Delias, was a regular and most welcome visitor to the island. The vessel being completely refurbished since her unlooked-for adventure, was used by the veteran sea-dog in his new and modest enterprise as an importer of sweet Thracian wine, having come to a mutually advantageous agreement with the pirates of the inland sea of Marmara!

Earlier in the winter Clytes had made a fleeting visit, accompanied by the ever faithful Angelos, before the pair travelled on to Pontus to seek out Anthousa. The actor was eager to know if he was now indeed, a father! He was due to call again soon, on his return journey to Athens, where he had a new act to perform with Leon and Panthas, at the Great Dionysia.

He'd left them hissing with indignation at the news that a new comedy play, 'The Knights', by the playwright Aristophanes, openly mocking demagogue Cleon, had been accepted for the forthcoming early Spring Lenaia festival.

'Well, we were first!' Panthas had spat with some satisfaction, and when Leon responded with, 'it can't possibly be as comical as 'The House of Wrongdoings'!' they'd all laughed - remembering the free-for-all during their own efforts.

Brave Stephanos, recovering from wounds received at the Battle of Pylos that summer, after which bold enterprise Cleon had been hailed a hero of the state, had also spent some weeks recuperating at the villa, accompanied by his pregnant wife, Micca - daughter of Diokles. Theomenes encouraged these visits, believing they would help Amara in her recovery, but they had the opposite effect. Whenever his friends came to stay, Amara mostly kept to her room in solitude.

His attention to the woman on the beach was broken by Mydon calling for him. There was another visitor to the villa. 'Who is it, Mydon?' asked Theomenes, distractedly.

'He says his name is Ortronus, and he wishes to know if Amara, niece of Limaois of Plataea, is here?' Mydon replied, unable to conceal his curiosity. 'He has a woman and a child with him!' he added, hastily.

'I'll come down,' answered Theomenes, and he jumped from the balustrade, taking one last look to see that Amara was still alright on the beach below. He was always wary when she went alone to the water's edge.

The man waiting to see him was a powerful, confident individual, toned and well-dressed. Accompanying him was a woman carrying a baby.

'It was Marissa's dying request,' said Ortronus to Theomenes, as he explained who he was and why he had come to the villa, 'that the child should not live with my people. She begged me to seek out her cousin Amara, if she still lived, and that is why I have been searching these past months to find her. It's been a difficult journey, but I wanted to keep my promise to her,' said Ortronus, looking directly at Theomenes. 'She meant a lot to me.'

'How did she die?' asked Theomenes, sympathetically.

'It was a difficult birth, and her health deteriorated very quickly. Fearing that she might not have long to live, she named the child Agapetos. By that name, Marissa wanted him to know always, how much she loved him,' explained Ortronus. Reaching for a leather bag, he handed it to Theomenes. 'I have Marissa's kithara with me,' he said. 'It was a much-loved gift to her from Nicander. She would wish it to be given to her son, when he is old enough to understand.'

'I remember her playing,' spoke Theomenes, thoughtfully, as he ran his fingers over the exquisite instrument, thinking back to musical evenings at Plataea, which at the time he'd not paid enough attention to. 'She was very talented,' he added, sadly.

'I hired a good Messenian wet-nurse,' continued Ortronus. 'Her own child is weaned now and being cared for by her family. She will stay with you for as long as you wish, Theomenes. I am relieved to find Marissa's cousin still alive,' he added. 'There have been so many deaths!'

'I am also much relieved!' answered Theomenes, with feeling.

He had no idea how Amara would react to being told of her cousin's demise. After all her suffering, he worried that this latest tragedy would be too much for her to bear. Yet she listened quietly to all Ortronus had to tell her of Marissa's life in Sparta with Nicander. The good times and the bad times. Sometimes, during the telling, she wept, at other times she wanted to know more, especially of Marissa's daughter now being reared as a Spartan by Nicander's family. When she thought Ortronus had told her all he could, she went to find the wet-nurse.

The baby, now three months old, was a fine strong boy, and he gripped Amara's finger firmly, taking it straight to his mouth to suck on, fiercely. For the first time in a very long time, Amara laughed. The next few days were a flurry of activity as a crib and other baby essentials were quickly acquired. Satisfied that he had fulfilled his promise to the woman he'd cared about so deeply, Ortronus began the journey back to Pylos, to continue his role as liberator of his people.

The following morning when Theomenes looked over the balustrade to check on Amara's wanderings, she was not alone. Plodding along the beach, more cautiously than usual, was Cyclops, slowly being led by Mydon, and seated on the white mule's back was Amara, holding tightly to Agapetos who was wrapped securely against the cool sea-breeze. Walking alongside was the boy's nurse. Amara began pointing out the boats to the baby, then she slowly turned and looked up at the villa. Seeing Theomenes watching her, as she knew he would be, she waved.

Theo glanced across at Admetus who, like Agapetos, was bundled up against the chill. He was bent forward, writing. Erica was hovering expectantly nearby. The old man seemed totally oblivious to her presence. She could see marks on the papyrus.

There was a shortage of oar blades in the busy shipyards of Athens.................

******

EPILOGUE

THE SECOND PELOPONNESIAN WAR covered a period of twenty-seven destructive years, both sides ignoring several opportunities to bring about an honourable settlement. After the Battle of Amphipolis in the ninth year of the war, and the death of war-monger Cleon, both sides were exhausted, and a year later a peace treaty was signed between Nicias of Athens and King Pleistoanax of Sparta. It lasted shakily for just seven years, after which time hostilities recommenced unrestrainedly. At their end Athens was in ruins, its Golden Age consigned to history, and Sparta having no interest in maintaining an empire, allowed other factions to come to the fore.

******

IT WAS NINETY YEARS after the fall of Plataea, before the city was finally rebuilt, and the descendants of its displaced people were able to regain permanent possession.

Begun by Philip of Macedonia in 338 BC and completed by his son, Alexander the Great in 331 BC, the small fortress was eventually restored to its former glory.

The city of Thebes, Alexander razed to the ground.

www.ingramcontent.com/pod-product-compliance
Lightning Source LLC
Chambersburg PA
CBHW020725210626
46807CB00016B/42